Zettourrrrr!!!
Damn you,
u despicable,
vil swine!!!

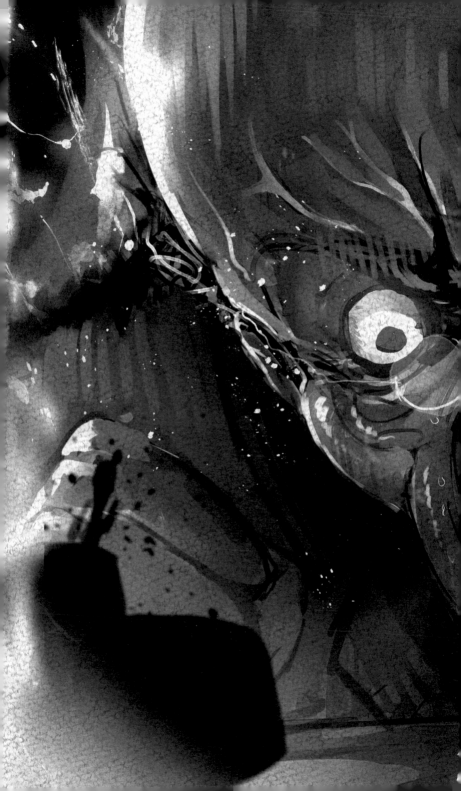

the world's
blic enemy."

THE SAGA OF TANYA THE EVIL

Mundus Vult Decipi, Ergo Decipiatur

[12]

Carlo Zen

Illustration by Shinobu Shinotsuki

New York

The Saga of Tanya the Evil, Vol. 12

Carlo Zen

Translation by Richard Tobin
Cover art by Shinobu Shinotsuki

This book is a work of fiction. Names, characters, places, and incidents are the product of the author's imagination or are used fictitiously. Any resemblance to actual events, locales, or persons, living or dead, is coincidental.

Yen On
150 West 30th Street, 19th Floor
New York, NY 10001

Visit us at yenpress.com
facebook.com/yenpress
twitter.com/yenpress
yenpress.tumblr.com
instagram.com/yenpress

First Yen On Edition: September 2023
Edited by Yen On Editorial: Ivan Liang
Designed by Yen Press Design: Wendy Chan

Yen On is an imprint of Yen Press, LLC.
The Yen On name and logo are trademarks of Yen Press, LLC.

The publisher is not responsible for websites (or their content) that are not owned by the publisher.

Library of Congress Cataloging-in-Publication Data
Names: Zen, Carlo, author. | Shinotsuki, Shinobu, illustrator. | Balistrieri, Emily, translator. | Steinbach, Kevin, translator. | Tobin, Richard, translator.
Title: Saga of Tanya the evil / Carlo Zen ; illustration by Shinobu Shinotsuki ; translation by Emily Balistrieri, Kevin Steinbach.
Other titles: Yōjo Senki. English
Description: First Yen On edition. | New York : Yen ON, 2017–
Identifiers: LCCN 2017044721 | ISBN 9780316512442 (v. 1 : pbk.) |
ISBN 9780316512466 (v. 2 : pbk.) | ISBN 9780316512480 (v. 3 : pbk.) |
ISBN 9780316560627 (v. 4 : pbk.) | ISBN 9780316560696 (v. 5 : pbk.) |
ISBN 9780316560719 (v. 6 : pbk.) | ISBN 9780316560740 (v. 7 : pbk.) |
ISBN 9781975310493 (v. 8 : pbk.) | ISBN 9781975310868 (v. 9 : pbk.) |
ISBN 9781975310523 (v. 10 : pbk.) | ISBN 9781975310547 (v. 11 : pbk.) |
ISBN 9781975323523 (v. 12 : pbk.)
Classification: LCC PL878.E6 Y6513 2017 | DDC 895.63/6—dc23
LC record available at https://lccn.loc.gov/2017044721

ISBNs: 978-1-9753-2352-3 (paperback)
978-1-9753-2353-0 (ebook)

10 9 8 7 6 5 4 3 2 1

LSC-C

Printed in the United States of America

THE
SAGA OF TANYA
THE EVIL

Mundus Vult Decipi, Ergo Decipiatur

contents

Prepared by the Commissariat for Internal Affairs

Federation

General Secretary (very respectful person)

Loria (very respectful person)

【Multinational Unit】

Colonel Mikel
(Federation, commander) ———— First Lieutenant Tanechka
(political officer)

Colonel Drake
(Commonwealth, commander) ———— First Lieutenant Sue

Kingdom of Ildoa

General Gassman
(army administration) ———————————— Colonel Calandro
(intelligence)

The Free Republic

Commander de Lugo **(head of the Free Republic)**

Relationship Chart

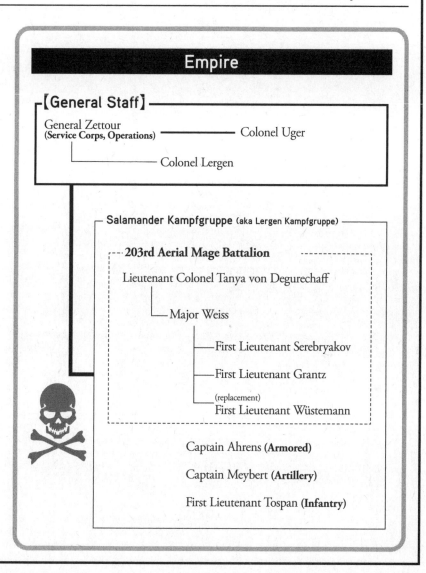

Empire

【General Staff】

General Zettour
(Service Corps, Operations) ———————— Colonel Uger

——— Colonel Lergen

Salamander Kampfgruppe (aka Lergen Kampfgruppe) ———

203rd Aerial Mage Battalion

Lieutenant Colonel Tanya von Degurechaff

— Major Weiss

— First Lieutenant Serebryakov

— First Lieutenant Grantz

(replacement)
First Lieutenant Wüstemann

Captain Ahrens **(Armored)**

Captain Meybert **(Artillery)**

First Lieutenant Tospan **(Infantry)**

[chapter]

Prologue

Loria was furious.

"Zeeettooouuurrr."

He was determined to erase that con artist turned wicked tyrant from the face of the planet.

"You...you dirty!!! Rotten!!! Bastard!!! You filthy fraud!!!"

Loria knew nothing of honor and justice. He was a hunter who embraced the insatiable emotions that drove him.

Exploiting his position as the head of the Federation's secret police, he picked his prey at their ripest and lived his life as he pleased.

This changed, however, the moment he discovered true love. Now, Loria was filled with nothing but a singular thought.

"Aaaah! My purest feelings! My swelling love! How dare that disgusting man ruin *our* happiness!"

Naturally, the beloved he spoke of was a certain fairy. And the villain who had the gall to steal Loria's joy in picking his precious flower was an absolute bastard who had no problem ruining the perfect love story.

Loria was well aware of the identity of the towering pile of shit that stood in his way—Zettour. That bastard was an unforgivable being of pure evil.

"Huff, phoo, haaagh..."

His breaths came hard and fast.

Although the hunter's rage was fueled by a true and noble love, he knew he couldn't allow his mental fortitude to lose ground to his burning passion. He slowly let the air fill his lungs before whispering his newfound resolution.

"I'll kill you. I swear I'll butcher you. You...you scoundrel..."

Loria clenched his fist until it was angry red. He had slammed it against the wall before coming to the realization that his rage was growing borderline illogical.

"I must accept it…"

I, too, have been had.

The Unified States boasted the world's largest industrialized economy and was currently waiting on the edge of its seat for an opportunity to enter the Old World's war. The opportunity finally presented itself when the Empire attacked Ildoa. This was the perfect justification for a preemptive, preventative attack.

From the outside, it looked like the Empire had made a mistake—shall we say, screwing the proverbial pooch—and it was true. The entire world watched in shock.

Despite being bogged down by their war with the Federation, the Imperial Army executed their attack with lightning speed, which was a spectacle in and of itself. However, what should've been very obvious to the Empire was that its invasion of Ildoa came at what seemed like mere days after the forming an alliance of armed neutrality with the Unified States.

Thus, it was only natural for the Unified States to rush in and aid their new ally. This outcome was as plain as day to all observers. The Imperial leadership would've had to be sick in the head if they assumed the Unified States would sit by and idly watch the blitzkrieg play out from the sidelines. That was why the world was shocked by what had transpired. Everyone was in awe of the war maniacs known as the Imperial Army.

Now, it should be made clear that even Loria couldn't figure out what the goal was at first.

The Empire had achieved nothing more than a tactical victory, or perhaps a series of Pyrrhic victories.

But nevertheless! Even so!

Whether it be plotting, scheming, conspiring, or whatever one may fancy—Loria had a bit more experience in the trickery department compared to the general populace.

With the unwavering compass that was love guiding him, he would not be outdone.

It was his pure, unclouded eyes that allowed Loria to quickly deduce the truth, and this was why he was furious…at that piece of shit, Zettour!

What a terrible, vile scoundrel!

"How could I have missed this?!"

There certainly had been a sign, though only one, and it had come in the form of an ominous turn of events. This fact was what annoyed Loria to no end.

It happened just the other day. At the time, Loria was processing a ludicrously thorough report he'd received from a certain gentleman mole he had planted in the Commonwealth Intelligence Agency.

He remembered the exact moment he received the report from one of his subordinates, and the exact words he said in response.

"So the Albion chaps pulled off their assassination? And you're sure about this?"

"We have five separate sources confirming this information. Apparently they've eliminated a group of real troublemakers."

Loria let his numbskull subordinate's tactless "congratulations" slide because he was giddy at the fact it was a group assassination.

"A group, you say. Splendid news."

"Yes, Rudersdorf will no longer pose a threat to our great nation."

Wait. Loria's brow heavily furrowed.

"Comrade, were both threats dealt with? Or only one?"

"What?"

"Rudersdorf and Zettour. That pair of devils. Both of them are dead, yes?"

"No...only the deputy director, according to our intel. However, he was killed with his entire entourage of General Staff officers."

Loria was openly disappointed by that answer.

"What a pity. Those boys from the Commonwealth should've made the con artist their target."

He still remembered the long sigh he gave before treating the news like any other and giving the usual orders to his subordinates to send along thanks to their mole in the Commonwealth...

That was it. He'd already lost interest in the entire ordeal.

This was only natural. For Loria, the death of a random strategist meant nothing if it wasn't the vile con artist who so trampled all over his love. This apathy, however, was a massive failure on his part.

It was actually in the same room he had received the news of Rudersdorf's assassination where Loria finally grasped the entire picture.

"That...that *filthy* con artist! Zettour! He returned home the minute his friend died! How did we let such important information slip through our fingers... And now...you...!"

Zettour now had full control over the Imperial Army, and he was the one who had spearheaded the full-scale attack on Ildoa after the announcement of an alliance with the Unified States.

"You attacked Ildoa! Zettour, you insufferable piece of shit! You went and attacked Ildoa?!"

At this specific stage of the war. At this specific timing.

For Loria, who was preoccupied with both his love and the war, the cunning and underhanded motivation of the attack was as clear as day.

"You've raised yet another obstacle on my path to love!"

Loria was a simple man. He lived for his passion. He wanted to do one thing and one thing only: to taste the fruits of his love with a certain fairy before the passage of time ruined her.

"Why must you and the world reject my purest of feelings?!"

Loria cursed the wicked and evil embodiment of humanity that was General Zettour.

"What a tragedy. We... I don't have much time left."

Loria was left with a looming feeling of unease. His heart was plagued with anxiety as he wondered just how much time he had left.

"Time is my enemy. This is always the case."

It was a race against the clock to pick his fruit and consume it before it was *too ripe*. He certainly wasn't one for rotten apples.

Oh, how few things compare to plucking a flower in full bloom!

There was a specific flower Loria had in mind, one that could only wait so long before it was too late. She was a cheeky little flower, who loved playing tricks on him—his thorny little angel. *Degurechaff* was her name, and she was ripe for the plucking. God forbid she grew too much and her petals fell before he got his chance.

"I'm running out of time!"

Loria was literally shaking at the thought of his ideal prey vanishing off the face of the earth.

From everyone else's perspective, it would be much better if his love never saw fruition. Loria himself was a stain on the world, objectively speaking. The perverted predator cried out in agony because his bottomless lack of self-awareness painted him a picture in which he was somehow the victim in all of this.

"If such a thing came to pass, it would be nothing less than a tragedy."

Should he miss his chance, the regret would surely be the end of him. At the very least, he was losing hair over it, mostly because he kept pulling more out due to stress.

"Ah, damn it, I need more time."

It is without restraint that I wish to share
with the world that our Imperial strategists
are among the best throughout history.
A single division of ours is capable of
defeating three of the enemy's.

However, this comes with a significant price.
For while it may be true...it is also true that the
Empire's undeniable power begins and
ends with its brilliant strategists.

General Hans von Zettour sharing intel on the state of
affairs/deleted off inspection record

In the innermost room of the General Staff Office, General Zettour sat quietly. He was using the Army's bastion of tranquility and intelligence as a spot for a quick breather.

Though hardly comparable to the eastern front, the capital was growing increasingly colder. Winter was upon the Empire. Before the war, those with wealth and standing would often go abroad, seeking warmer climes elsewhere.

Unfortunately, the war raged on. With the current state of things, not even the nobility could hope to take their annual trip down south for the winter months.

It was so bad that there was even concern as to whether or not there would be enough fuel for civilian use this year.

The General Staff Office was already feeling the cold.

"I suppose I'm lucky."

General Zettour muttered to himself with a wry smile.

Luck had nothing to do with it. Thanks to the war, he would be one of the few who got to head south this year for the Ildoan campaign.

Under different circumstances, it probably would've been an enjoyable trip.

"That's it for the paperwork. All that's left is my luggage."

He scanned the room until he spotted a wicker trunk. One of his orderlies had prepared it for him.

"I told him to make it light."

Zettour grimaced at the trunk.

His orderly likely thought that a trunk was the limit. In fact, a ranking general of the Empire traveling so lightly would've been unheard of prior to the war.

Chapter I

Were those still the times they lived in, Zettour would've complimented the packing job. Alas, there was no room for praise.

"Well this just won't do. There's no room for an entire trunk on a fighter."

He rubbed his chin and let out a sigh before reaching for the tightly packed trunk. He was satisfied to find his orderly had at least done a good job organizing its contents. It didn't take more than a few minutes to repack what he needed into a single rucksack.

"That should do it."

With his preparations now finished, the general had a little free time until his next and final appointment before his departure. It wasn't much time, but he could afford to take a smoke break. It would be his last breather before he crammed himself into a fighter headed for Ildoa. The flight would be a stark difference from the luxurious train ride that once connected the two friendly nations. He would no doubt be as tightly packed into the plane as his belongings were in his rucksack. The fighter in question was an instrument of war, after all. They weren't built with roomy interiors in mind. It was pretty much the most uncomfortable means of transportation that could be found. But...the discomfort was a small price to pay if it meant he could get to his destination in one piece.

That being said, this would be his last cigar for a while, seeing as smoking was absolutely not allowed on board.

"I'd better smoke while I still can."

He took out a well-maintained case of cigars from his desk. The attention to humidity control was a sign that even the idiot Rudersdorf was capable of paying attention to finer details when it came to things he liked. Zettour recalled his old friend's face as he blew out his first plume of dark gray smoke with an unpleasant expression on his face. Then Zettour watched the smoke dissipate as it reached the ceiling of the General Staff Deputy Director's office.

Given the time of year, the fact that the only visible wisps came from his own cold, white breath made for a sad sight. Zettour yearned for the sound of a crackling fire in the hearth. When the cigar smoke disappeared, all it revealed was the same old lifeless roof he sat under.

"I really wanted to decorate the ceiling with a nice painting, but it doesn't look like I'll get the chance."

He had no time to be picky about his office's appearance.

"Things are bound to get busy soon enough."

Time, time, time. Time was the law that ruled over all. Zettour effectively spent his days running away from time as it relentlessly chased him down. The Empire was like a train about to leave the station, and it was his job to make sure the horribly sluggish train that finally began running its course did so on time.

Would it make its trip on time, or would it suffer delays? Could he even keep it on the tracks? The point of departure was now, and the destination was tomorrow, but where would it go next? The answer to that was as painfully clear as it was terrifying should he fail in his role as conductor.

The weight of his duty made him want to tremble, so much so that he even began to grow antsy during his brief smoke break.

His train's final destination was the Heimat's future. Derailment meant the end of the Reich.

It was a heavy burden for him to bear. His shoulder gave a quick spasm that was unrelated to the cold office temperature. He continued to fill his lungs with cigar smoke.

"My word. This really hits the spot."

Another sigh left his mouth as he glanced at his watch.

It is funny how time seems to move so slow only when you're feeling impatient.

There was still a bit of time before he had to go see Counselor Conrad, the person waiting for him at his next meeting.

He was set to meet him before departing, but as their appointment was scheduled immediately before the flight, this idle moment felt annoyingly long.

Everything seemed to be like that as of late. The general was overcome with an unshakable restlessness whenever he found himself at a standstill.

"I'm starting to understand why that idiot Rudersdorf was always so uncharacteristically in a rush."

Zettour would carry this burden on his own. He had the weight of the entire Imperial Army pressing down on his shoulders.

"In the end, we've made mistakes at every turn up until here. We started a war we shouldn't have. Then we failed to end it when we needed to. And had the wool pulled over our eyes by the prospects of victory only to be forsaken by the Lord."

And yet, the war marched on. He couldn't even muster up a chuckle at the hubris of a country that refused to end a war it couldn't win and cry about how unfair the world was. He knew he couldn't deceive himself. The Empire was alone in the world.

General Zettour shook his head and gave the frigid room a good look before flashing an intrepid grin. He was ready to shoulder any burden he needed to. He was receiving direct orders from necessity, and orders were orders for an Imperial soldier.

Goodness. The grin on Zettour's face widened.

"This, too, is war. But *what* is a war?"

Zettour unconsciously began rubbing his chin as he launched into a monologue.

"War is the use of force to bend an opponent to your will."

This was the textbook definition that all officers learned. Back in the good old days, a young, pure Zettour once blindly believed in these very words when he studied them with earnest aspirations to one day become a good little Imperial soldier. Now, however, he was beginning to question whether he believed in them at all. He recognized that he had only ever taken the words at face value.

It was something he reflected on whenever he was alone with his thoughts. When there was only winning in his mind, he believed that through power and victory, he could create desirable results.

"That is why I always sought after victory...why I always saw victory as a *panacea.*"

He had been wrong. In the worst way possible. And as a result, he could no longer save his patient, the Empire, be it with a panacea or not.

"If only I'd realized this a few years sooner. I've been saying that a lot lately..."

Ironically, Zettour had his suspicions about the prescription after using the every last bit of his will, his ability, and his talent on the eastern front.

He was challenging the value system that he had originally placed so much faith in. Accepting the discomforting reality made it painfully clear that decisive victory was no longer possible.

Zettour could only shake his head.

"The Empire is no longer salvageable. The majority of our nation, even our military, is still chasing after an ultimate victory."

It felt as if the scale that balanced their objectives against their capability was completely broken. Some might even argue that the Imperial citizenry were quietly *allowing* their ability to face reality to fall apart.

The Empire defied reality for nothing more than a possibility. A heroic yet sad fight where the military didn't know when to throw in the towel. Of all the people they could've fought, they chose to fight against the entire world.

General Zettour stared at the ceiling of his office. Looking at its bland colors almost made him nauseous. He lamented once more to himself.

"A ceiling really isn't complete without a good painting."

It could be a depiction of their fleeting, glorious past, or something that sparked hope. It didn't matter; he wanted something. Something with color. Staring at the stains on the monotonous ceiling was beginning to take its toll on him. It made him feel like he was staring at the future of the fatherland.

The general sighed, then shook his head once more.

It was the hour of twilight in the fatherland. He had no idea twilight could get this cold.

He could accept his role as the general of the losing side. It would all be for naught, however, should he fail to minimize losses. If he allowed the Heimat to lose its youth at the current rate, his final days would be spent pitifully. It shouldn't need to be stated that the general hoped for victory as much as anyone else.

It was something he wanted—were it attainable. But he knew it would come with a price.

"When you buy land, it comes with rocks. And meat with bones. Now, what price will my countrymen set for our victory, and what by-products are they willing to accept in the exchange?"

Would the goddess of destiny sell it to them at an affordable price?

"Even the worst victory we're willing to sell isn't something the world will agree to buy."

A frontal assault was out of the question. They needed to sign a deal with the devil, then scrap the paper their deal was written on just to make it even.

Zettour knowingly asked himself a somewhat childish question.

"Can I outsmart the devil?"

The general planned on doing everything within his power. He was far from omnipotent, but he was confident in his ability to keep himself a step or two ahead of his enemies. There was also no lack of sheer determination. Honor meant nothing to him. He was willing to give up his soul if that was what it took.

But he knew the truth. A praying mantis with an ax didn't stand a chance against *the world*.

"I doubt it… I don't have enough cards to dine with the devil, never mind deceiving the world. I'd better find a long spoon."

A spoon made of silver, if at all possible.

"Enough with this nonsense. It all means nothing."

Entertaining aimless thoughts like these was nothing more than a way to soothe his mind. The Empire was shrouded in a stifling, cruel reality…and navigating out of this quagmire fell to none other than Zettour.

"A soldier… A mere soldier for an entire country."

When he thought about how ill-suited he was for the position, an incredible sense of emptiness filled him. It was like admitting he wasn't smart enough to win. He thought this as he sat with a cigar in his office.

Nevertheless, he couldn't allow himself to lose. In order to cheer himself up…he repeated his words from only a moment ago.

"War is the use of force to bend an opponent to your will."

The Empire didn't possess the power to force anyone to do anything. The foundation for the strength required for that no longer existed.

Any chance of achieving this was long gone. Zettour folded his arms and blew out some more smoke as he sat in contemplation.

"I suppose there was a time when victory had been within reach… Then again, there's no point wallowing in the past."

It was time to do away with this self-pity and embrace harsh reality. Zettour could accept his defeat…his strategic failure.

"This isn't about victory or defeat anymore, but a third path—an acceptable outcome for the Empire. I need to maximize whatever small gains the Empire can eke out of this war."

What concessions could the Empire, in its weakened state, compel from the superpowers it was fighting? Those hostile superpowers would be the true victors while the fatherland would be…the vanquished. There was no changing this. Praying wouldn't amount to anything because even divine intervention wouldn't be enough to save them.

That being said, the fact that the fatherland was on the brink of bankruptcy had yet to be made public information. This small detail afforded Zettour just enough wiggle room for one last desperate act of resistance.

"This may be our final breath, but it also presents an opportunity— however small it may be."

The pride of the Empire, its instrument of violence, still had its fangs. Its soldiers still had the will to fight. And Zettour was ready to accept whatever was to come. *So why not fight tooth and nail until my very last breath?*

"If we can't win, then we will force our will on the world…without winning. So long as I understand the rules I must abide by, I can think of a way or two to make that happen."

There were prospects for success. Even if the odds of success were incredibly slim and the road ahead would be brutal.

General Zettour knew that on the other side of that seemingly insurmountable challenge, there was a slightly better future awaiting the Empire. It was a hellish future nevertheless—a far cry from paradise, but anything would be better than hurtling straight into the deepest pits of hell. It would be the most minor of improvements, but that meant the world when it came to the future of the Heimat.

"That is why I reject fate. I refuse to let the worst come to pass."

His own words reminded him of something.

"I really did believe…"

That I was always making the best choices.

Zettour missed the good old days. They were like a fleeting dream now—a dream where he could wholeheartedly believe in the Empire's victory. These days felt more like a haze, but he remembered being utterly shocked by the mere thought of defeat when he first heard mention of it from a small girl who approached him in the corner of the General Staff library.

"Even now I can remember how caught off guard I was by the notion that avoiding defeat was true victory…"

He wondered if she somehow foresaw this moment back then, considering how she placed so much emphasis on what true victory meant. Or had she been operating under a different logic back then?

"I suppose I'll never know."

It doesn't matter, he thought as he continued to stroke his chin.

"Accepting the notion that there are relative levels of victory makes everything so much easier."

There was a big map plastered on the wall next to him. It showed the latest developments along the front, and the fact that the front lines were beyond the Empire's borders told a story. Every expansion outward was a *victory* for the Empire. These occupied territories, however, were nothing more than tactical victories—tactical victories that would have no impact on the ultimate outcome of the war... Empty victories.

The Empire had won every battle it fought, but this string of victories would eventually lead them straight to their own demise.

"We paid dearly for this land, for all this dirt and rock. So why not put it to good use?"

This space was Zettour's trump card. He needed to use every last resource the land had to offer if he was going to have any chance of achieving an acceptable outcome.

"I am a soldier of the Reich. There is something I must do for the children of the Heimat. Even if it contradicts my duty as a soldier..."

There were words waiting to come out of his mouth as he murmured this to himself. Hans von Zettour could tell himself whatever he wanted, but bold words meant nothing... He simply had two options before him: accept defeat, or refuse it.

His heart wanted to reject defeat with every fiber of his being. His pride shook and his sense of honor wavered... The mountain of bodies behind him made it nearly impossible to do anything besides cry out in denial, but no matter how much his heart desired victory, the only force that could move the world was cold, hard facts.

For him personally, there was a way around this. Zettour could flatly reject his impending defeat until he found himself dead on some battlefield. That way, he would never need to see whatever fate awaited the Heimat. Doing so, however, would be an absurd dereliction of duty.

For a soldier with great responsibility and stature to escape the war by dying…would be nothing less than desertion. Throwing away his life to satisfy his personal desires was a luxury he could ill afford. Zettour was a leader, and he needed to act like one.

"It's at times like these when I start to envy the field officers."

Zettour knew that these were words an officer in the rear should never say out loud, especially after considering all the special privileges they received. Nevertheless, it was something he thought on occasion.

He remembered fondly what it was like to be a commander in the field whose only worry was completing the task at hand.

"Lieutenant Colonel Degurechaff once jested about missing desk work in the rear… I imagine she was just trying to be considerate in her own way."

How tactful of her. Or perhaps it was just the clumsiness of a career soldier who didn't know how else to think.

In any case, General Zettour was pulled away from memory lane by a ringing clock. He looked at the time and saw the second hand hovering over the twelve mark. The general chuckled wryly when he heard a knock on his door. Impeccable timing. He wondered what lengths his visitor had gone to in the name of perfect punctuality.

This was indeed the man Zettour had been waiting for.

Right. General Zettour cleared his mind and prepared for his next task.

"Hello there, Mr. Conrad. Or should I say, Counselor Conrad. You're just in time. You have my thanks."

"How could anyone possibly be late when personally meeting with the general himself?"

The man replied in all seriousness after showing up for their meeting on the dot.

Zettour nodded in amusement because that made it sound like the head of the General Staff was capable of controlling time itself. Even if he did have access to such incredible power, it wouldn't change the fate of his nation. That was the miserable truth. And for better or worse—probably worse—the general had grown so accustomed to absurdity that it barely fazed him anymore. He flashed the gentlest of smiles.

"I've been looking forward to speaking with you for a while now. I have high hopes that we can come up with some good schemes together."

"No, sir. The honor is mine to finally make your acquaintance."

He was a true gentleman. Such pleasantries were refreshing, given the strange times they lived in. The two men shook hands firmly before Zettour showed the counselor to his seat and, as a sign of good will, offered a cigar to his guest. Counselor Conrad graciously accepted. The odor of the cigars left behind by General Rudersdorf permeated his old office. They were good-sized cigars. The two men savored them as they exhaled trails of smoke.

If an outsider had seen them, they probably would've chastised the pair for being too easygoing.

General Zettour took his cigar out of his mouth and gave Counselor Conrad a big smile.

"To think a quiet smoke break like this would come to be seen as such a luxury."

"War takes away whatever room we have for leisure, I suppose."

There was a clear detachment in the way Counselor Conrad spoke. To suggest *this is just how war is* felt blunt. This was simply because he only pointed out the obvious. The days when the Reich was lauded as the strongest nation in the world were no longer.

"It's what happens when war drags on for far too long."

Necessity, necessity, necessity.

The cold, logical principle offered no room for play, and its rules had to be obeyed until the end of time.

Imperial citizens had become synonymous with the word *necessity* in the most extreme of ways. There was no longer room for play even in their minds. The Empire had often been considered a nation of strait-laced people even before the war. Now? The Empire was a completely different place. The war had changed it from top to bottom.

"A superpower with no time to enjoy a cigar is a lonely place."

"For a man in your position, there isn't a soul who would dare reprimand you for merely smoking a cigar. If there was, they'd be going out of their way to see you in a bad light."

General Zettour laughed grimly at Counselor Conrad's directness.

"Bullets on the front lines don't discriminate between officer and soldier. Though, I suppose the Federation's snipers do, if we're being pedantic. I have no doubt they would do their best to pick me out in a crowd."

Zettour demonstratively puffed out his chest, which was decorated with medals.

"I take pride in how much Federation snipers obsess about me."

"That's an awful joke. Should I be laughing? Or would you rather me tell you that all the attention they give you makes me a bit jealous?"

"You can do or say whatever you wish. It's not as if it matters anyway."

The general's curt response caught Counselor Conrad by surprise.

Though it was nearly undetectable, he allowed a somewhat troubled expression to show while thinking about how to respond.

The middle-aged diplomat was used to a little verbal sparring, but this seemed a bit much... By the time the counselor had started pondering the meaning of the general's remark, Zettour simply shook his head and grabbed another cigar before continuing.

"Shoot a man, kill a man—it's all the same because they're destined to die from the day they were born. It doesn't matter how they go."

His words left his mouth accompanied by cigar smoke. It was merely small talk—an icebreaker to get their conversation started.

"Have you ever thought about death before, Counselor?"

"These are the times we live in. It's a reality I'm forced to consider, on occasion."

"That is mighty noble of you. I, for one, find myself only worried about the deaths of my friends."

He shot Counselor Conrad a glance before flashing another vague grin.

The general could tell by the tense expression on the counselor's face that he was trying his best to find a good response. Diplomats were tough in ways soldiers weren't. *This is good*, Zettour thought as he smiled on the inside.

"I probably don't need to say this, but I only ended up here because my predecessor met an unfortunate end, so it's hard not to think about death when you're in my position."

With sadness in his tone, Zettour showed his anguish when he mentioned a fallen friend.

"To think he would meet his end in such a way. Fate can be so ironic."

The general glanced at Conrad once more to see a knowing look. *These diplomats sure are clever.* The counselor wore a grave expression, as if he were compelled by a preestablished harmony.

"It is a tragedy that General Rudersdorf is no longer with us. I never imagined we would lose a man of his standing."

The counselor gave his earnest condolences as a representative of the Foreign Office, and it occurred to Zettour that a diplomat could probably cry on command over something they didn't care about in the slightest. It was part of their job, after all.

Just look at his face!

At a glance, it really did seem as if the counselor felt a deep sense of loss for the deceased general. It almost made Zettour want to clap.

"He died an honorable death on the battlefield, the greatest sacrifice any soldier can make. I want you to know that we mourn every day for the devastating loss."

Even his timing for lowering his head as he spoke was impeccable. It was the slight quavering in his voice that really sold it for Zettour. As every vestige of tension drained away, Zettour couldn't help but clap his hands. He gave the counselor a small ovation. That was the natural reaction to seeing such a spectacular performance.

"That was an excellent show of diplomacy, my friend. You are quite the actor."

"My apologies, but come again?"

A tight expression came over the counselor's face, making it clear he took offense at the remark, but Zettour pressed on with a laugh.

"You see, I've heard about you from Colonel Lergen. I simply decided to be straight with you instead of entertaining this masquerade ball."

A friend he could scheme with. Someone to commit treason with. Or, at the very least, a person who he could grieve with. It didn't matter to Zettour what historians would go on to call them, so long as they made sure to mark them both down as patriots who acted according to the times and endured as best they could.

There was only one important detail.

"I see you as a friend, Counselor Conrad. Let me answer the question currently on your mind before you need to ask it."

He grinned as he enjoyed his cigar before loosening his shoulders and speaking softly.

"It wasn't me."

It truly wasn't. Well, that was true in a certain sense.

Zettour couldn't stop his grin before he spoke up.

"The goddess of fate is so cruel. She is a benevolent witch."

Zettour had the intent. He had been more than willing to do the deed. He even had his orders ready. Everything had been ready, but alas.

The goddess was a devil. Despite refusing to save this nation from its future, the whimsical little witch relieved Zettour from the need to bear the guilt of having murdered his own friend.

"I almost wish I could feel responsible for his death. Fortunately, or unfortunately, I have no right to."

He was certainly ready to commit the act. To quietly bear his guilt under the guise of duty, grit his teeth, and do what needed to be done for the Empire. And yet, it was unclear as to whether or not he was in a place to feel any guilt. He didn't need to shoulder it in the first place. This had to be some form of salvation. But now that he didn't have this burden to shoulder, he only felt emptiness. What kind of salvation was this supposed to be?

"I'm certain of one thing: This world has gone to shit. I almost want to become an atheist."

"General Zettour, does God not stand with the Army?"

"Unfortunately for us, if there even is a God, he is rotten to his core. As someone who only wishes to make the world a better place, I believe the only objects worthy of faith are our nation's guns."

Zettour closed his eyes and shook his head as he jested. This much he always understood—that there was a higher power, something more significant than artillery, that ruled the world. Figuring out whether said higher power was pure chance, a god, or some sort of universal natural order was the work of the pious. Zettour only needed to understand how the world worked as a soldier. And he knew well that the God they knew was an incarnation of supernatural evil, not unlike the devil.

It was repulsive to even think about. Whether it be fate or chance, it brought a fearsome cruelty with it.

"I want you to listen to me, Counselor. I'm under the impression that… something a bit more presumptuous than a deity is controlling our fate. I'm not quite sure how to best describe this something, but…as it is less a god and more a vague existence, I suppose we could call it *Entity X*."

24

Chapter I

"My apologies, General. Are we discussing theology?"

Zettour looked up at Counselor Conrad, who had fixed him a dubious stare, and shook his head.

"I don't need you to understand. I'm simply talking to myself. You can write it off as aimless grumbling."

"I'm sorry, but I don't quite follow… What exactly are we talking about right now?"

"I'm merely trying to open myself up to you to gain your trust. If I must add something to convince you, then let me acknowledge that I considered doing what you suspect me of."

"You *what…?*"

Still standing at attention, Counselor Conrad asked this with profound interest. Zettour responded with a firm, almost self-deprecating nod.

"Your suspicions aren't so misguided. Everything was in order for me to dirty my own hands. But before I could do the deed, our kind friends assumed the role of executioner for me."

It was all too convenient for the general. *God, you truly are despicable.* Zettour quietly cursed the heavens within the confines of his mind.

"I only wish our creator would save the Empire instead of using such boundless power to bring about miracles as unpleasant as this. I cursed our God and praised the Empire. Quite a few firsts in my life. How much better it would've been if the opposite were true."

"Are you serious…?"

Counselor Conrad's gaze told the general that he didn't believe him.

"It is the truth. I swear on my mother and friends."

"Then that means…?"

The answer that would dispel the doubt and anxiety in the counselor's gaze was simple. For this all to have turned out so well was an act of pure deus ex machina. It was almost as if everything had been scripted.

If this were a play, this would be where the audience laughs. As this was reality, though, the general sneered instead. After all was said and done, this much was well known throughout the office.

"They are decrypting our messages. The entire world likely knows our secrets. Thinking back on it, we lagged behind the world in one of the most important ways."

Chapter I

Zettour had his suspicions that their messages were being cracked. Their internal communications were essentially being broadcast to the world.

"I shouldn't have shrugged my doubt off, thinking it was impossible. I don't know if it was a sign, but when our war hound Degurechaff caught the scent that something was off, I should've paid more attention. Oh, there I go again. Regretting what's already been settled."

He accepted this unpleasant reality with a dry chuckle.

Everything discussed in the Imperial Army could no longer be kept a secret from the Commonwealth. The General Staff had access to the strongest ciphers available in the Empire.

Would their enemies pry open the nation's toughest lock with their thieving hands only to ignore the others? Especially when the information inside those vaults was worth its weight in gold?

The logical conclusion to this question was obvious.

"They've even seen our secret telegrams. It's safe to assume that they know the Foreign Office's ciphers as well."

He glanced at the counselor and saw the distress of a man who intimately knew the way things worked.

"You think they know about every message we've dispatched...?"

There was what sounded like a hint of resignation in his tone as he voiced his thoughts. Either way, Counselor Conrad fully grasped the gravity of what Zettour was trying to say. He emitted a sigh before continuing.

"Did you see the documents detailing the transfer of power?"

"Ah, yes. Of course I did. They contained a secret telegram meant for a foreign embassy. Something about subversive actions abroad?"

In response, Conrad offered a dry grin and nodded. Of course, that was no reason for Zettour to let the topic pass without comment.

With an expression that was both solemn and dry in the same way the counselor's was, Zettour gave his frank assessment.

"It's quite the achievement, really. I wouldn't be surprised if the nations of the world send that embassy a special thank-you and some flowers. You really gave them the best fuel they could ask for to ignite anti-Imperial sentiment in their respective countries."

Conrad let his shoulders fall, offering no rebuttal. He was likely already aware of this mistake before he came here. There was no attempt to defend his organization. Feeling a strange sense of satisfaction in this, Zettour extended his hand.

"It seems we're a good match for each other, as two friends who made the same error."

"Can I consider you a friend?"

"Why yes, of course you can. We can even think of clever nicknames for each other if you'd like."

Zettour had offered a hand and a big smile but was politely rejected.

"Let's stop. I'd prefer not to discuss this."

"Oh? And here I was thinking we could become companions who could trust each other."

"I plan on living long enough to go to my grandchildren's weddings. I'd rather not make friends with someone who will bring me closer to a random encounter with Commonwealth forces. Please, understand."

Zettour, who was caught off guard by this response, started shaking. Without putting too much thought into it, he unconsciously began laughing loudly and heartily, like he was having the time of his life. The counselor was simply being logical. Considering what had happened to Zettour's last friend, this was the natural reaction.

Not only that, but the diplomat sitting before him intended on living a long and full life!

This civilian was being quite brazen about living a carefree life in front of a soldier destined to die.

One could only laugh in the face of such glaring absurdity. No matter how warped the notion, anything that could replace the immense pressure Zettour felt daily for even a moment was more than welcome.

That was why Zettour chuckled to himself, alone.

"A spectacular answer. I appreciate it. As thanks…when I'm forced to end the Foreign Office, I'll make sure you die last."

"How terrifying. Are you going to murder us?"

"Not at all! I need you to live as long a life as possible to serve the Heimat. You need to be worked to the bone."

Zettour whispered this to the counselor with a devilish grin. There was a strange cadence to his speech. It must have been because he was enjoying himself. Unable to resist his urge any longer, he took up his cigar once more and took a nice, long pull. It was exquisite. A good cigar was enough to make even the toughest of times enjoyable. What a wonderful thing.

With some reluctance, Zettour placed the cigar back onto the tray. After letting go of that last bit of smoke, he looked again at the man he considered his accomplice.

He could tell Counselor Conrad had guts. At the very least, it was clear to Zettour that he had a good sense of humor. There was nothing more for him to say.

All he needed from the counselor—his would-be accomplice as a fellow public enemy—was for him to return the handshake.

"I think we understand each other."

"Likewise. I believe we've gotten to know each other well enough."

Counselor Conrad gave an unexpectedly firm handshake before showing a somewhat surprised expression.

"A General Staff officer is quite the force to be reckoned with. This may go without saying for yourself…but you all seem out of your minds."

He really emphasized that there had to be something wrong with the institution known as the General Staff while also expressing his awe for them.

"You may be the Empire's best and worst invention."

"You think too highly of us. Though I must admit I'd like to ask why you think that way."

"I once met a Lieutenant Colonel named Degurechaff."

"Ah, her."

That was all Zettour needed to hear.

"Between you and her, it's clear this institution is off the rails. It brings into question what they're teaching you over at the military academy."

"The two of us like to stick to the basics."

"Oh? The basics?"

Zettour knew the perfect response to the question Counselor Conrad asked.

"It's much easier than you'd expect, really."

"Because it's the basics we're talking about?"

It was embarrassing to say out loud something that everyone already knew. Zettour hesitated to answer but he could see Counselor Conrad was patiently watching and waiting. If he wanted Zettour to say it out loud, then he would.

"Precisely. You've probably heard them at a Sunday mass."

"Well then, it seems I may not be devout enough because I'm having the hardest time figuring out exactly what you're referring to. Please do share any useful passages from the scripture."

"Of course," General Zettour said as his expression became solemn. Then, like a preacher speaking from atop a podium, he intoned, "Take the initiative to do what people hate the most."

"Come again…?"

"Simple, isn't it? At every opportunity, you must do whatever your enemy fears most. It is a virtue drilled into us at church from a young age."

Counselor Conrad blinked twice with his mouth agape before the general's words finally sank in.

"How moving… It is almost twisted how much neighborly love I can feel you exuding."

"Precisely. I consider myself a fundamentally good person, after all."

"Are you one to turn and offer your other cheek after being slapped?"

"But of course. Which is why we're spreading the bodies of our fallen youth around the continent. I actually regret the amount of unbridled neighborly love I've spread so far."

He answered the counselor's joke with a joke of his own, offering a semblance of pleasant banter. Perhaps such a jest was the manifestation of their new friendship. Their lighthearted conversation was all laughs and smiles. Were they not at war, Zettour would surely be enjoying this moment with a glass of wine or champagne. It would've been the perfect winter night for a nice dinner. He would much rather use firewood to light his fireplace instead of throwing so many of his nation's youth onto the fire as kindling.

The reality was that all he could do was bark and howl at the setting sun. Still, people found ways to enjoy themselves, no matter what times they lived in.

"Counselor Conrad, I've enjoyed our conversation."

The diplomat nodded in full agreement.

"It's been a long while since I've had to use my wit in such an entertaining way. A conversation with raison d'état is always as bittersweet as it is fresh. How very bracing."

"Yes, Counselor. It is likely a grave misunderstanding."

General Zettour showed the smile of an innocent child.

"For you see, it's not our wits but egos that we used here today."

General Zettour bumped his fist against his own chest before continuing.

"We're not thinking with our minds, but our hearts. I know I'm no longer an officer who operates solely on logic."

Counselor Conrad took a moment to think about what Zettour had said before responding.

"Then what do you devote yourself to?"

"My gut. My feelings. Or maybe it should be called an attachment to a nostalgic illusion."

"Well, I must admit I wasn't expecting an answer like that."

"I love the Heimat."

Cigar in hand, Zettour shared his innermost feelings with the counselor.

"I love my life here, the people of this nation, and our livelihoods. That is why I'm a soldier of the Reich. A loyal citizen of the Heimat, if you may."

There was so much love in his words. It was a common sentiment throughout the Empire. All who worked in the Empire also lived there. And yet, strangely enough, Counselor Conrad found himself straightening his posture as he listened.

Where exactly was Zettour going with this? Whether or not Zettour knew the counselor was listening intently, the general paused to take up his cigar once more and wedge it between his lips.

His next words would leave his mouth behind a thick veil of smoke.

"The Reich's soldiers should crumble into dust along with the Reich."

The general spoke without any hesitation. The passing comment almost made it seem like he was casually commenting on the weather. Ignoring how much his words shocked Counselor Conrad, General Zettour picked up his coffee and continued.

"But can the same be said about the Heimat?"

It was clear what he was trying to say. Despite the general's crescendo into a question mark, his remark made it clear that he would never allow the Heimat to end. It was intense how clear his intent was even though he never touched on it directly.

"Old men are here to protect the future of the babies still being held by their mothers. Which is why it's our job to change their diapers."

"Is that...something the enemy will allow us to do?"

"Counselor, the true nature of war is quite simple, really. Tell me, what do you think war is?"

Zettour coldly answered his own question with his usual answer.

"War is the act of using power to force an opponent into submission. It could be considered a continuation of politics by other means. If this is the case, then let us secure the best loss we can win from the world. That is how we will ensure a future for the Empire that is better than a living hell."

"That's quite the defeatist's ambition. I suppose reality justifies it, though."

"I suppose we'll see about that. Whatever the case may be, there's a next best plan. If we lose our place in the Heimat, then we shall walk another road."

"May I ask which, if you don't mind?"

General Zettour gave a light nod as if to say, *Of course.*

"If we won't make it beyond the war... If we're unable to acquire a future for the Heimat, then we won't die alone. We'll take them all with us. The entire continent will burn."

The lone soldier, Zettour, stated his intentions plainly.

Any patriot would wish for this. For the fatherland's future. To give the fatherland a future.

And if this was unattainable... If, in the future, there was no place for the fatherland, then it was his prerogative, as a patriot, to reject the future entirely. Such a world was unthinkable for a true patriot like Zettour.

"We'll threaten the entire world. Either let us live, or fall with us."

"Are you serious...?"

"You be the judge of that."

General Zettour stood up, then placed his hand on Counselor Conrad's shoulder.

He then brought his face close, so that they could stare deep within each other's eyes.

"I want you to take a good look. Do these look like the eyes of a man who's joking?"

"General…"

"I am a patriot. And a good person to boot."

Counselor Conrad nodded, showing that he understood the general's resolution while also expressing his admiration for the man.

"General, I understand this is a decision forced upon you by necessity. Allow me to show my respect."

For Zettour, who had a bloodcurdling look in his eyes, any mention of *necessity* was the last thing he wanted to hear in that moment.

"Necessity… I'm getting so tired of the notion."

"General?"

"I'm tired of being forced into my decisions."

He slowly brought his cigar to his lips and fiddled around with the lighter as he lit the cigar. Then he continued with a clear note of annoyance in his voice.

"I've done everything in my power for the goddess of necessity. This is different. It's high time for that wretched hag to do her part for the future of the Empire. I'll grab her by her hair and drag her out of the sky if I need to."

"How ungentlemanly of you."

"This is the opinion of a man who's undergone one trial by fire too many at the hands of this so-called goddess of necessity."

All but scorched by the flames of total war, the con artist's voice had become hoarse. And for this, Counselor Conrad had no words.

》》》 NOVEMBER 22, UNIFIED YEAR 1927, THE ILDOAN FRONT 《《《

Colonel Calandro, who led the Ildoan army's last stand against the Empire, had been able to achieve all of his tactical objectives by fighting a delaying action.

He had succeeded in buying as much precious time as possible.

That wasn't all, though. Through fierce resistance and scorched earth tactics, he'd managed to push back the Empire, even if only temporarily. His performance was worthy of being studied in future military textbooks as a prime example of how to use time and space on the battlefield.

At the same time, he would most certainly go down in the history books in a very different manner. He would no doubt be remembered as the commander who turned the land he was supposed to protect into mountains of ash. Setting aside the prior, Colonel Calandro knew the latter would become his legacy in the annals of history.

How could one who loved his nation so much go on like this?

The colonel simply had to set aside his personal feelings while he labored to parlay his tactical victories into political victories. The fact that he maneuvered on the political side of the war even as he fought on the battlefield was what made him a balanced, and arguably ideal, officer.

He had repelled the initial Imperial offensive, creating a brief pause in their advance as they quickly reorganized their forces.

Not letting this chance pass him by, Colonel Calandro brought a limited armistice proposal to an old acquaintance who just so happened to be leading the Imperial forces. Using his personal connections and the law, he tried to acquire a resource more valuable than diamonds for Ildoa: time.

Being the good Imperial citizen he was, Colonel Lergen was more than happy to cooperate. With his assistance, a provisional twenty-four-hour cease-fire was scheduled to come into effect the next day as they began negotiations for an armistice.

While tensions were high on both sides, the two armies scrambled to collect their dead and tend to their wounded while avoiding one another. The attempt by Colonel Calandro to buy as much time as he could during this lull by initiating negotiations with the enemy commanders was the perfect strategy from a tactical standpoint.

Thus, in order to acquire more time, the colonel made his way to the Imperial Army base.

His efforts would turn out to be quite a success. An incredible coup that achieved much more than anyone had expected. Despite bringing about these utterly shocking results, Calandro himself quivered as he rushed to send a telegram back to the capital.

"The Record of the Armistice Negotiations with Colonel Lergen"

As the title of the report suggested, the forces on the ground agreed to a temporary armistice.

- Agreement to evacuate the citizens in the north.
- The establishment of a seven-day cease-fire period.

- A continuation of the current cease-fire.

- The allowance for temporary surveillance to be performed by both sides.

- Military operations to recommence after the seven-day period.

- More detailed report upon return to the capital.

It was a sweet and simple report that left out far too many details.

The man who received everything he could've hoped for from the negotiations found himself looking up at the ceiling and sighing.

"That monster..."

He questioned who came up with his moniker.

"*The Great*... What a crock. More like the Terrible."

The colonel recalled what he had witnessed only moments earlier and shuddered as a chill ran down his spine. He took out the cigars he'd received from the enemy during the talks and began smoking in an attempt to quell his trembling. He could taste the high quality of the cigar as its smoke filled his lungs. It was a provoking feeling.

As he blew out a stream of smoke, he thought:

Ah, the people of the Empire truly are the masters of surprise attacks.

He should have picked up that something was off when he encountered an old mage officer acquaintance of his, standing at attention and awaiting his arrival.

Lieutenant Colonel Tanya von Degurechaff.

He could still clearly remember the days when he was placed under her care as a military observer visiting the eastern front.

He'd let his guard down. Regularly bathing in the blood of her enemies, Degurechaff was the Imperial Army's most highly prized warmongering mage to ever exist. She was a grizzled veteran known better by the name Rusted Silver as opposed to her official title, White Silver.

Why was she attending a commanding officer? Calandro should've realized then and there what he was walking into.

And yet, because this was his one and only chance to make some much-needed gains on the war front, he happily danced in the palm of his enemy's hands.

"Allow me to show you the way, Colonel."

"Thank you, Lieutenant Colonel."

Her working directly with the General Staff must've meant that she had a close relationship with Colonel Lergen.

That was the extent of the suspicion he felt as he made his way to the house where Lergen was supposed to be waiting for him. Except, when he arrived, the man he found waiting for him was much older than he had expected.

"What's this?"

Calandro was met by the gaze of an older general who was smoking a cigar, which seemed to be his posture for the coming negotiations.

Then he saw him grin.

"You must be Colonel Calandro. My apologies, but Colonel Lergen is busy in the field. I hope you'll accept me as the Imperial Army's representative for these negotiations."

Before him sat a man he'd read about over and over again in the reports. General Zettour, the Deputy Director of the Imperial Army General Staff who had ordered the Empire's offensive on Ildoa.

It was shocking to see the very man who was the root of all of Ildoa's problems just sitting in a chair and smoking a cigar at his leisure. This was the enemy commander who had forced Ildoa to burn its own countryside.

He was sitting right there, out in the open. Right as that thought crossed Calandro's mind, so did another. He quickly realized the significance of a mage officer being present for the negotiations. Lieutenant Colonel Degurechaff was this man's guard dog. With a guard dog like her at his side, General Zettour had nothing to fear from a lone middle-aged Ildoan. It was sad, but this was reality.

Calandro definitely wasn't suicidal enough to throw his own life away in exchange for the enemy leader's. He knew the instant he reached for his sidearm, Lieutenant Colonel Degurechaff would turn him into minced meat. He'd seen it happen enough times on the eastern front.

He also knew full well what would become of the negotiations should he point a gun at the other party.

His rational mind was all that kept him within the bounds of the law after coming face-to-face with his sworn enemy.

But still…as an Ildoan, Colonel Calandro needed to ask one question.

Why?

He didn't expect an answer, but he still wanted to ask nevertheless.

"Why did you do this?"

So he did, and the man, sitting with his cigar, sneered at him.

"Why? You're asking that now?"

The disappointment and astonishment in the general's tone was visceral.

He wore a bitter grimace, something he barely made an effort to show.

What struck Calandro the most was the general's eyes. How they ridiculed him with their gaze. Despite his astonishment at Calandro's question, the monster known as General Zettour bared his fangs.

"That's a silly question. It's so ridiculous that I can't even bring myself to laugh. There's a proper time and place for jokes, Colonel."

"What do you mean it's a silly question?! I want to know what you were thinking, General Zettour, when you started…"

"When *I* started what? Hmm, I suppose that's a further testament of your stupidity." Calandro was at a loss for words as the general continued holding his cigar out in one hand. "It was your nation who squeezed the trigger. Armed neutrality, my foot. I can swear to you in good faith that, from a purely militaristic standpoint, we never wanted to invade Ildoa."

"The armed neutrality alliance was meant to keep the Unified States neutral! It was meant to keep countries outside of the continent from meddling—"

"—Listen."

General Zettour was grinning. With a polite tone, he had cut Calandro off mid-sentence.

It was the exact same way a teacher would treat a rambling student. There was a kindness in his tone and gaze reserved only for a mentor trying to help a delinquent student.

"Colonel Calandro… You, and your country, are the victims of a grave misunderstanding."

Calandro fidgeted in his chair as he watched the intellectual representative of the Empire nod to himself and take out a box of cigars.

"Here. Have a cigar."

"With all due respect, General, I don't think we're in a position to enjoy pleasantries right now."

He rejected the offer, bearing in mind that the two nations were at war, but all this did was make the old man sigh once more.

"How remarkably un-Ildoan of you. The call for diplomacy is at its highest during open conflict. You should know this. I won't demand you pay your respects to an Imperial general, but I probably should ask you to do so for an elder."

"I shall graciously accept…"

Calandro let his head hang low, which drew a response from General Zettour that was neither comforting nor self-deprecating despite the words he laid out in his hoarse voice.

"It's strange for a failed citizen of the Empire to have to talk down to a successful Ildoan. Now, I suppose I should think of a proper answer to your question."

"Then…why did these hostilities come about?"

"It's simple."

Smoke blew across the table. In contrast to the veil of light smoke he blew out, General Zettour shared the all too grim truth with the colonel.

"You pulled the trigger. This much is simply fact. From my standpoint, your country started all of this. You really went and did something entirely unnecessary."

Maintaining the same tone from the very beginning, General Zettour held his cigar between his lips. Slowly, he took another pull. There was something grand and magnificent about his bearing.

The monster that dominated the meeting was the essence of a true general. Without even taking a bite of the prey that presented itself before him, the devil known as Zettour continued to flaunt his own thoughts on the matter.

"And so we simply reacted. You forced our hand. The most one such as I can do after you've set the stage is play my humble part."

"General?"

"We are on a tight timetable and you tried to delay our plans. If you mess around on the tracks, you get hit by trains. Do you understand yet?"

He looked at Calandro with the same disappointed eyes meant only for a delinquent student. Without even attempting to his hide his astonishment at this point, General Zettour furrowed his brow.

Chapter I

"You're quite narrow-minded, aren't you, Colonel Calandro...? You would've never made it through the Imperial Army General Staff curriculum. Do they just hire anyone around here?"

As if thinking of something on the spot, General Zettour turned his attention to Degurechaff to his side.

"What do you think, Lieutenant Colonel? I know you have a strong opinion when it comes to education. Do you have any advice for your Ildoan friend?"

"Each country has its own education system and standards. It isn't my place to comment."

He glanced back at Calandro once more, turning away from Lieutenant Colonel Degurechaff, whose firmly attentive posture never wavered.

"Yes, I see. It appears things are peaceful enough in Ildoa...for this to suffice. I must say, I'm jealous."

The general was laying on the sarcasm thick. On a surface level, it was nothing more than a snide remark. And yet, Colonel Calandro could detect hints of actual jealousy in the man's voice.

"Should I take this as a compliment? Though your words are quite cutting... For some reason, it feels like your jealousy is genuine."

"That's because I do envy you, from the bottom of my heart."

"Come again?"

"For you are still a person. You still have your humanity. I'm sure of it."

The friendly old man flashed a pleasant smile before offering the cigars again.

"Now, allow me to explain why your nation's actions incurred our wrath."

Calandro sat on the edge of his seat, watching the smoke leave General Zettour's mouth as he touched upon the truth that was far too bitter to accept at face value.

"It's quite troublesome, really, for the Federation to get so bigheaded."

"The...Federation...?"

Calandro blurted out his question but stopped immediately when he saw the general's intense gaze that screamed, *Silence.* It was clear he wouldn't allow any interruption. Calandro quickly piped down, and the great general nodded in satisfaction before continuing his story.

"This was why I was against General Rudersdorf's plans to invade

Ildoa. Why on earth would we even consider kicking our only channel for diplomacy out the window?"

This was the rational reading of the situation. A simple conclusion anyone could make. Even a child could see that attacking a friendly neighboring country despite being on the brink of collapse was a terrible idea.

"The Empire will be closing up shop no matter how this turns out."

General Zettour said this like it was a joke, but it was exactly as he said.

The most the world's enemy could do was fight back. But, as they wouldn't be able to win in the end, all that awaited them was their eventual defeat.

Calandro saw this.

So did all the experts of the world.

And even the Empire, if only it could take a step back to look at the bigger picture, would've seen this as well.

So how had this come to pass?

"Let me tell you something. To greedily devour our flesh is no small task. If the world seeks to consume us, then we won't go down before giving the world a dose or three of poison."

They wouldn't die without a fight.

Did this mean they would embroil the world into a quagmire, dragging whoever they could down with them? General Zettour could tell Colonel Calandro was a bit confused by the very notion.

"The world is my enemy."

Those strange words left his mouth not in a frenzy or deliriously, but with complete presence of mind. There was something strange about all of this, but the colonel couldn't quite put his finger on it.

"I refuse to let the pathetic Federation beat me. Let me promise you this. I would rather die the world's enemy."

These were grand words. Practically absurd if they had been said under almost any other circumstances. Colonel Calandro's instincts were screaming out at him.

General Zettour must be a broken man. How could any sane person speak like this?

Despite what his instincts were telling him, Calandro could see that the general was rational and lucid.

There was a visible intellect that could be observed in his gaze alone.

As terrible a monster as he may have been, this general of the Empire was nevertheless a monster defined by his great mind. General Zettour was sober as could be. An intelligence officer as trained as Colonel Calandro— one of Ildoa's foremost agents—couldn't deduce anything more than the fact that General Zettour's mental state was incredibly stable. His fanatical words and ruinous argument came from a man with the eyes of an enlightened saint who spoke from a place of absolute purity.

If there was anything ever to fear in the world, it was this gaze. Realizing he was being overwhelmed, Colonel Calandro silently smoked his cigar, puffing out smoke as he attempted to collect his thoughts.

The small diversion helped him switch gears. Gathering his emotions in an instant, Calandro made a heroic effort to glean the true intent of the monster before him.

"I won't let the Heimat perish, no matter what happens, what I must do, and what stands in my way. I refuse to let anyone or anything stop me."

The colonel was beginning to understand. He could almost sympathize with the general's plea. The frightening planning that went on in this man's mind was born from the purest of hopes.

"Whether he be God or the devil, I will show no mercy to him if he defies the Heimat. Remember this, Ildoan. This is the true nature of a con artist born from the depths of total war."

He was serious.

General Zettour's words made this abundantly clear.

"I will be borrowing the northern part of Ildoa as my playground. I'd really like to fight a clean battle there, if I can."

It was clear what he was getting at when he mentioned "clean." Of course, it was difficult to accept his promise at face value.

"Do you…honestly expect us to just believe you…?"

"I only told you this much to make up for all the trouble I've caused so far. If you wish to ignore me, I'm not so narrow-minded that I'd try to force your hand. Though I am quite livid at the way you tried to use the Federation against us."

"When exactly did we ever affiliate with the Federation, General?"

"Don't play coy with me. The moment you tied yourselves to the Unified States through armed neutrality. The Federation will get far too bigheaded…if the Unified States delays their entry into the war any longer."

The way he said this was so nonchalant.

By the time Calandro processed what this meant, his mind had frozen. The colonel knew what each of the words the general said meant. He understood what they meant as a sentence, what their context was.

And yet, the conclusion he needed to reach was all but lost on him.

"But… General! You don't mean to say…?!"

"Mean to say what?"

"That this is all just to get the Unified States to join the war?!"

General von Zettour responded to this with nothing but a smile.

His expression alone made the answer clear even if he didn't say anything in response. *The eyes communicate just as much as the mouth.* The answer was undoubtedly *yes.*

"I'm a man willing to burn his own Heimat down to the ground. Strange. I figured you of all people would understand considering what you've done to your nation."

An urge born from sheer panic to put an end to the monster sitting before him flashed through Colonel Calandro's mind once more as he watched the general smile again.

And without missing a beat, the guard dog sitting behind the colonel chimed in, as if to reassert her presence.

"I'm surprised, General. I didn't expect you to speak this much with the colonel."

"I'm sorry for keeping you here so long for such a tedious assignment, Colonel Degurechaff."

General Zettour playfully shrugged his shoulders as he spoke.

"That being said, I wish to maintain a good relationship with Ildoa. I hope that we can find a mutual point of understanding and eventually cooperate to build a better future."

There was the thinnest veil of sarcasm in their exchange.

It served as a terrible reminder for Colonel Calandro that this was the man who had shaped and molded the infamous Devil of the Rhine.

"Please excuse my subordinate, Colonel Calandro."

The colonel looked behind him to find a small aerial mage bowing her head in apology. At a glance, she appeared to be nothing more than an amiable young girl with a small frame, but Calandro knew that she was a hellhound more than capable of ending his life at any moment.

"What do you say? Do you think we can build a future together? The Empire won't ask for everything Ildoa has. If we can guarantee our safety, we will limit the damage as much as possible."

"Y-you want me to trust you?"

"You're free to feel however you want. But bear in mind that I am public enemy number one. Try and picture what will happen if you choose to refuse our hand."

His eyes were so gentle as he spoke. With the same soberness visible in his gaze, the general continued to warn Calandro.

"You don't honestly believe I'll go down without taking an Ildoan peninsula or two with me, do you?"

He could probably do it—no...he definitely could, if deemed necessary. Likely without any regard for morality, justice, or military law.

"I don't need your trust. You're free to believe that I'm just some hopeless villain who will set the world aflame. A heartless monster that can't be reasoned with."

He *was* a monster. The monster who had brought the flames of war to Ildoa.

"Or you can believe that this is all a frantic bluff made by an old man asking you to fight against the world alongside him. Either way, you're free to try and fight us the good old-fashioned way as well."

The general had likely seen right through Calandro's desperate attempt to appear calm. The monster stood up with a suave bravado, carrying a small box as he approached the colonel.

"I'll tell you what, my Ildoan friend who was once our ally and now our enemy. You're free to do whatever you wish. The Empire will respect whatever decision Ildoa makes. As such, we will accept the terms of your cease-fire."

"What? You'll accept all the terms...?"

"But of course. We're here to fight war the right way. I must say, it was quite the successful negotiation. Good work, my friend. Whether as an ally or an enemy, I appreciate your desire to fight this war like a true gentleman."

As he said this, the general placed a box of cigars on the table before Calandro.

"I see you must go. I'll lead you out."

This was Colonel Degurechaff's way of telling the colonel to *get the hell out.*

The pure oxygen that entered his lungs as soon as he exited the camp tasted so utterly sweet. Calandro quickly made arrangements for his report to be sent via telegram. As soon as he finished writing, he whispered out loud, "That monster…"

The only thing human about him was his appearance.

His logic, his cunning, and his forked tongue had to be signs of the devil.

"The Empire…"

Chills kept shooting down his spine.

"Did the war…create that monster…?"

Tanya is here to attend her boss's meeting with an important business partner. A person in a position of power would only ever assign a task like this to somebody they highly trust, for the most part. This means Tanya being present for the negotiations with Colonel Calandro is likely a good indicator of her boss's evaluation of her. Nevertheless, this isn't necessarily cause for celebration. You see, being called in to perform such a task means that Tanya is deeply entrenched in this organization.

For someone who's currently considering a job transfer, it's a complicated position to be in.

"Thank you for your vigilance during our meeting with Colonel Calandro."

That being said, it's a great opportunity for Tanya to learn how her boss truly feels.

Which means this is a perfect moment to take advantage of the opportunity by showing appreciation and sharing in a bit of lighthearted banter.

"It was my pleasure. By the way, what did you think of the colonel's health? He seemed awfully pale during the negotiations. I only hope it isn't flu season here."

It's not uncommon to catch a flu during the winter months.

My superior responds with a knowing nod.

"I believe he may have a case of *common sense*. Fortunately for us, we're fully immune to it, so there's nothing to worry about."

"Do you suppose you may have gone a bit overboard with your threat...?"

"I merely stated the obvious."

Tanya nods in agreement while keeping her incredulous remarks to herself like the good subordinate she is. There was no way to avoid being caught off guard by her superior's train of thought. To think anyone could look this far into what would become of the country after the war.

His is a perspective that already took into account nearly all the events leading up to this moment. It would be a bit more understandable if he was also from another dimension. Just like the Cold War, the Federation and the Unified States will likely be at odds with each other after the conclusion of this war. The power that plays the largest role in bringing this war to an end will have immense political influence when it comes to deciding the new world order.

The fact that my boss has the foresight to understand the imperative of keeping Communism from being the sole victor of this war is nothing short of incredible. I'm truly impressed.

Even as a person from another world, I feel a profound respect for General Zettour's vision of the future. He really is an amazing boss.

If I could get a letter of recommendation from a man like him, it would be a real asset in jumpstarting my second career.

If only we lived in a regular society.

I'm sure you'd be the magnanimous type to send your subordinates off in comfort.

"Is there something wrong, Colonel?"

"It's nothing, sir. I was just reminding myself how incredible you are."

"Look at me, Colonel. Do you see a tail anywhere? I'm but a man. There's no fork in my tongue now, is there? I'm just a normal, honest man."

"You are also a Zettour, sir."

Seeming to have taken a liking to my retort, General Zettour smiled.

"Hopefully it will take on the meaning of *devil* in the future. I'll pray that it does."

He seems very pleased with himself.

A quick, clever response always stimulates an intelligent mind.

If the name Zettour becomes a common noun, then there must be a lot to look forward to.

"Our future prospects seem quite exhilarating, don't they? You shouldn't compliment an old man too much, Colonel. I'm satisfied with leaving my mark on history as the world's greatest enemy."

"I think that much is a given for you, sir."

Tanya says this from a place of exasperation. But for General Zettour, who has fully committed to his chosen path, it's apparently the highest praise he could hope for.

I'm sure it came off as me giving my blessing.

Which would explain why General Zettour wants to share his exuberance with Tanya.

"Ha-ha-ha-ha-ha, one can only hope! Look forward to it, Colonel. The same goes for you, too. You could leave your mark on history in the grandest way. Let us carve our names in history, together."

Unfortunately for my elated superior, I have little desire to join him in this particular endeavor.

"I have no intention of leaving my mark on history."

"It's too late for that… Any books worth reading are bound to have scathing comments regarding us."

Does he want us to be eternalized as symbols of hate for good people to fear for the rest of time?

He must be joking.

That may be acceptable for a patriot such as General Zettour, but for an individualist like Tanya, this sentiment is incomprehensible.

"That's a dreadful future to look forward to."

If my name ever shows up in a book, I want it to be as a famous author.

This is the moment where I reminisce about a past promise I once made. It wasn't meant to be anything more than just playful words.

But compared to General Zettour, General Rudersdorf was such a thoughtful man. There aren't many superiors out there who would recommend their employees live off royalties!

"Speaking of books, General Rudersdorf was supposed to sponsor a picture book I was going to write after the war. That is sadly something that will never come to fruition now."

"A picture book?"

Tanya nods to her boss, who was surprised by the sudden remark.

"It will be a story about a poor girl, me, who is afraid of the war. The General Staff was going to fund it. He made a promise in jest to publish a book about poor little Tanya. I was hoping to target a home with children who wish for peace."

"Rudersdorf? He agreed to such an entertaining business endeavor?"

Tanya nods with a grave expression.

"I was hoping to one day live purely off the royalties from my bestselling books."

"Life doesn't always go as planned now, does it?"

It sure doesn't, I think in agreement while giving the deepest of sighs.

"I'm always asking myself how things got to be this way."

"I feel the same way, Colonel." General Zettour shows a somewhat lonely expression before continuing. "But that is why I've chosen to forge my own destiny. I will solemnly see my duty through like any good person would."

"What is your plan?"

"We'll concentrate our divisions. Secure local superiority. Employ mobile warfare. You can expect good results, Colonel. We have twenty-two divisions operating in Ildoa."

That's top secret information he's nonchalantly sharing… Though I guess regular information pales in comparison to General Zettour's true intentions.

The soldier in Tanya thinks deeply about the plan Zettour has calmly spelled out for her.

"You could also say we only have twenty-two divisions. Though I suppose twenty-two is an impressive number considering the state of the war."

General Zettour smiles at Tanya as she shares her expert opinion.

"Should Ildoa manage to mobilize its entire army… They would have somewhere in the region of one hundred forty divisions if we're looking purely at numbers."

"That is a ratio of seven to one in terms of our manpower difference. The General Staff sure is unreasonable to pit the Imperial Army up against an enemy seven times larger."

"You're one to talk, Colonel. Need I remind you who was responsible for Dacia?"

"I was quite the rascal in my youth. Not only that, but fighting with the Grand Duchy's forces was more like target practice as opposed to an actual battle."

"That is correct. It wasn't the quantity of their soldiers, but their quality. The same will ring true for Ildoa."

I wouldn't be so sure... And I share those suspicions with General Zettour.

"Allow me to detail my experience in engaging them thus far, sir. The Ildoan forces are far superior to what we faced in Dacia."

"That will be true for forces arrayed on their border, and perhaps along their coast as well."

General Zettour rubs his chin in a pleasant manner before shrugging his shoulders.

"But mobilizing reserves isn't something that can be done overnight. Tell me, has our army been sticking to schedule?"

This, of course, reminds me that our army has in fact not been able to maintain their schedule. As usual.

Even perfect mobilization plans always find a way to go off the rails.

That goes for the Empire, which had its train schedule in order thanks to plans for a civil war. It's a convincing argument, but with Ildoa being nowhere near as worn down as the Empire currently is...

"You believe there will be holes in Ildoa's mobilization plan as there were in ours?"

"My guess is their military is in dire straits right now. Their equipment is state of the art. Should they manage to get the people they need mobilized, they may be able to get fifty-five divisions' worth of functional soldiers. According to what can be gathered from Colonel Lergen's reports, the forces they have available on the front lines are quite limited."

Supposedly, more than half of Ildoa's one hundred forty divisions are just for show.

Compared to that, all twenty-two of the Empire's divisions are battle-ready.

Which makes the power ratio two to seven.

The Empire has a clear advantage when it comes to actual combat experience. On top of that, we do enjoy what is admittedly limited aerial superiority, and we've already penetrated several key points in their defensive line thanks to our surprise attack. All things considered, victory isn't impossible.

And while it's technically doable, this is a moment where Tanya should push back against her superior.

"Even if their forces are just for show, they should be able to promptly establish and maintain a rudimentary defensive line. Look no further than the eastern front for a real-world example. We're all too familiar with their ability to scrape together a ragtag defensive line even in defeat."

The soldiers the enemy can call upon are far from ideal—they can barely move in tandem with one another.

But what if the ragtag band we're about to fight is fully committed to defending their country? I can tell the answer just by looking at First Lieutenant Tospan. Should he receive the orders to defend his post, a serious officer like him would stand and fight until new orders demanded he retreat.

As difficult as it is for me to understand, the man possesses the spirit of a true patriot.

"A human is an animal that is willing to die for its country. As long as they can fire a gun, they can pose a threat."

"For the remaining seventy divisions, it'd be praiseworthy if they can even hold their ground with their guns. The lion's share are nothing more than conscripts forced to serve."

General Zettour brushes Tanya's remark to the side, which makes her come up with a new, wholehearted concern.

"Those seventy divisions, however, are still a part of a larger organization. Their patriotism and love for their homeland may bring about a reckless tenacity."

"Colonel, you're assuming the seventy divisions will command any real stopping power."

That's right, I think with a nod.

"Should they have the personnel necessary to command the divisions, it will be possible to mobilize quickly. While actual mobile warfare may not be possible, they will certainly be able to hold a line. With their standing army as the core, they may even pull off counteroffensives."

They are, in a sense, similar to the Salamander Kampfgruppe. With the aerial mages at its core, their unit could accomplish missions on a provisional basis. It's true that Ildoa's front line is disorganized…but this is only because their line collapsed under our first assault.

"What makes you think they have the capability?"

"So long as the enemy has the framework to bring a division together, they can hold the line. All they have to do is put guns in the reserve soldiers' hands and position them in bases and villages."

Tanya's advice, coming from a place of experience, draws a light-hearted chuckle from General Zettour.

"Ha-ha-ha, so you wager that's what the Ildoan Army will do with its divisions?"

"What else can they do? I believe they have their numerous division command centers set up for a reason, and what other reason could there be besides domestic defense?"

"They're posts."

"I'm sorry, sir?"

A possibility beyond my wildest imagination catches me by surprise.

"So their divisions, instead of representing combat-ready units...they're just a posting?"

"It may be difficult for a soldier as decorated as yourself to process this, but you'd be surprised how much trouble can come from high-ranking officers who wish to remain in the army."

For someone like Tanya, who's desperately trying to make a career change, there's absolutely nothing attractive about such a post when she's doing her best to leave the company. In fact, now that I think about it, the army is kind of like a baseball team that doesn't allow free contracts.

Does a player who wants to become a free agent have the same perspective as a player who wants to renew their contract no matter what? Of course not.

"There are a large number of officers in Ildoa. Now, to have enough spots for all of them...they would need, what...seventy? A hundred forty divisions? But what if all they needed was the command post?"

"I'm astonished. They have no soldiers or weapons, but still have the gall to call themselves commanding officers?"

I've seen managers without direct reports before, but to think there would ever be a command with no troops!

General Zettour flashes Tanya a comforting smile.

"Let us begin bullying the weak, Colonel."

"Just give the orders, sir."

The war in Ildoa is a strange one,
like some kind of show. You'd think it was
a showcase war if it weren't for all the
soldiers dying down there.

Comment made over the phone by a military journalist/
deleted off inspection record

Winter was cold in the Federation, but was it the reason for the chills running down Drake's spine? He knew it wasn't—the temperature wasn't all to blame for this chill in the air. Whenever Mr. Johnson made the trip from their home country, he always came bearing bad news.

The moment the agent caught sight of Drake, he offered a pleasant smile and cheerfully waved his hand. On the surface, he was as gentlemanly as could be. Seeing that alone was enough to convince Lieutenant Colonel Drake he should brace himself for the worst. And yet...or perhaps, as expected...Colonel Drake couldn't keep himself from questioning what Mr. Johnson had to say.

"What? We're going to retreat from the Federation and deploy to Ildoa...?"

"It isn't a retreat, Colonel. You're being strategically repositioned at a new location. I understand how important your mission here is, but the Empire's attack on Ildoa has changed everything."

Mr. Johnson wore a small grin.

"Just take a seat. You'd do yourself a favor to make yourself comfortable. We're going to have a small chat."

Drake picked up on something interesting when he sat in the offered chair. This was the most inviting seat there was, the one closest to the warm, cozy fire.

"And here I thought that this was our command center, and you're the guest."

Kicking back and relaxing, the old gentlemen had taken out a cigarette and began smoking as if he owned the damn place. He nonchalantly shot a glance at the samovar, as if to ask for some tea. Drake ignored this, which seemed to make it clear to Mr. Johnson that his presence wasn't welcome. The man offered a slight frown, only to shrug his shoulders as if he'd remembered something more important. He had really made himself at home. It was quite the show of bravado.

"Let's talk about work."

Drake could hardly believe it. Mr. Johnson had up and decided on his own that now was the time to talk business!

"The sun must set just as surely as it must rise. This is a law of nature. Our country abides by the laws of nature as well; changes in political circumstances always translate to problems in the field."

The old man looked tired when he mentioned the word *problems*. Colonel Drake, however, wasn't so wet behind the ears or pure of heart to be swayed by his pantomime. He knew that whenever a fellow countryman made the far trip to visit Colonel Drake out in the east...they always brought immense burdens with them.

"I know I shouldn't compare myself to someone who fights on the ground such as yourself, but I've been worked to the bone as well. They've sent me all over this continent to deliver absurd messages like the one I'm about to give you."

Mr. Johnson let out a clear sigh as he sat in his chair, grumbling.

"It's so troublesome to be a loyal subject to His Royal Majesty. Truly, we both have our trials and tribulations to endure. Don't you agree?"

He kindly offered a cigarette to Drake as he said this, making a sentimental gesture. At a glance, his words and gesture were convincing enough that Drake instinctively wanted to share his complaints with the man. It was clear, though, that this intelligence agent's gestures were purely superficial. Drake knew that he and he alone was the only one who deserved any sympathy between the two men sitting here. He was sure of this from the bottom of his heart.

"And somehow, all of the trouble seems to fall on us out here."

"That's your ego speaking, Mr. Drake."

"I'm sorry, but it really isn't. Neither you nor the rest back home get shot at regularly on the battlefield. We were deployed here to fight a war. Do you have any idea how long it took to prepare ourselves? And you want us to just drop everything?"

Drake's face was grim as he made his retort, but the easygoing intelligence officer simply shrugged it off.

"I'm not the one who makes these decisions."

"I know that, but it doesn't make this order any less unpleasant."

Drake glared at Mr. Johnson, who maintained his usual calm and tactful persona. The man was a talented intelligence agent who never showed what he was truly thinking.

"Though I'm merely a messenger, I sympathize deeply with your mental and physical anguish. I'm beside myself by the mere thought of the harsh missions you endure."

Elderly Mr. Johnson shared his superficial sympathy as his gentle smile slowly morphed into a more dastardly grin.

"After all…the Ildoan theater will be the ultimate stage for the multinational unit."

Am I wrong? he asked the colonel with his eyes, alerting Drake to exactly what his country's aims were.

The multinational unit was like a mascot for the Commonwealth. Nothing more than a pawn that the politicians back home would happily send to dance in the spotlight at center stage. The feelings of the actors, who had to actually fight on the battlefield, were a lower priority. That said…the Commonwealth soldiers out in the field ate out of the same pot with Federation troops as they went up against the formidable Imperial Army. They may have been Communists, but they were still comrades in arms. Colonel Drake's obligation to the people who fought on the same battlefield compelled him to argue against relocation.

"Mr. Johnson. Please take into consideration the fact that we've finally started to form a strong mutual trust with the Federation soldiers."

Drake didn't want to leave his friends here. He appealed to a bond that could be considered the starting point for all soldiers and warriors—becoming brothers in arms—but all he got in response was a warm smile.

"I understand."

Nodding in agreement as if this were a well-known fact, the intelligence agent patted Drake on the shoulder to let him know his plea had been heard. It was an unsettling reaction that set off alarms in Drake's mind.

"Are you willing to respect the bond we've created here?"

"Of course we will. That's been our intention this entire time. It's why we're making arrangements for you to strengthen your bond further. We wouldn't want you to abandon those who you fight alongside."

Drake questioned Mr. Johnson's words.

"You believe we'll be able to maintain our bond even after relocation?"

How, exactly? It was a small miracle that Drake didn't flatly ask this outright. His eyes made his doubt and distrust clear, but Mr. Johnson simply smiled and nodded.

"We would never separate you from your new friends. You're all going to Ildoa, together. The same goes for Colonel Mikel, too. Everyone will be kept in the same group. You're all headed for Ildoa, where it's much warmer."

"I'm sorry, Mr. Johnson, but it sounds like you're suggesting we move the entire multinational volunteer unit to Ildoa?"

"That is precisely right, Colonel."

It was too convenient. Their entire unit was going to Ildoa, together? To say there was doubt in Drake's eyes as he questioned the gentleman would be an understatement.

"And the Communists are okay with this…?"

"That's right, Colonel."

"I have a very hard time believing that."

There was a time when Communists fully rejected training mages. They were only using them because of the dire needs of war, but it was well known that their mages were under heavy surveillance. Perhaps the idiots who made these decisions weren't aware of this.

"Do you mean to tell me they'll allow their mage troops to go abroad where the government can't keep an eye on them? I'm sure the Communists would be happy to get rid of us Commonwealth mages, but I doubt they'll allow their own to go."

"What a narrow-minded disposition you've got there, Colonel."

"I beg your pardon, but what did you say?"

Mr. Johnson stared at Drake with the surprised eyes of a math teacher who caught a student making an elementary mistake.

"The multinational volunteer unit was a political creation from its very inception. I thought you knew this… Perhaps you forgot during the war."

"How could anyone forget! I understand that fact to my very core. I couldn't forget even if I wanted to."

Mr. Johnson offered a look of bewilderment as Drake blurted out his response.

"It seems your core is overlooking something. And that something is the Imperial invasion of Ildoa. I'd recommend an officer such as yourself to maintain a higher level of awareness when it comes to worldly affairs."

"You must be joking," Drake scoffed. "Is that meant to be an insult? Not a day goes by where we don't pay attention to the Empire's movements."

"So what you're saying, Colonel, is that you have been observing the Empire?"

"Of course we have," Drake said with a nod. "The Empire is only fighting with Ildoa to protect its flank. The true battle is here, in the Federation."

"And?"

"This is where this war will end. And you want us to take our mages out of here and send them to Ildoa? Can't you see how that would be a massive mistake in priorities?"

Drake was brimming with confidence as he spoke but was met with a shrug from the old intelligence agent.

"You're correct from a military standpoint, but fail on the political end of things."

"I'm sorry?"

"It is as you say, militarily speaking. The Empire will die in this land. But this isn't the stage. Now that center stage has shifted to Ildoa, this is where you belong. This is just how politics work."

Mr. Johnson was curt with his retort. Colonel Drake was left blinking to himself at the unexpected remark.

"And your reasoning for this is…?"

"It's simple, you see. We, the world, must help each other to defeat a powerful common enemy."

The intelligence agent sat back in his chair as he casually hit Drake with something beyond his wildest imagination.

"Wait, what? Help each other? Has our raison d'état evolved into something that looks out for countries other than our own?"

Chapter II

"You must throw any illusions you have about your country into the rubbish bin."

Drake was dumbfounded by the remark. It was easy to tell as he leaned back and shot his blank stare up at the ceiling. Seeing this, Mr. Johnson used a bit of a preaching tone to give the man a small warning.

"Both we and the Federation, with our honest egos, will send the multinational forces to Ildoa. Nothing more, nothing less."

Mr. Johnson held out a paper cigarette and sighed.

"The Federation already agreed to this without hesitation."

He thrust the cigarette into an ashtray before taking out a lighter while he stared straight at Drake and continued to speak.

"It's a shame, you see. That good Commonwealth subjects are politically inferior to our evil Communist counterparts. They have a sense of immediate and complete agreement on their side that we lack."

"Excuse me, but…I need to ask. Have you really gotten them to agree to this?"

"They have indeed. I had a wonderful friend of mine help me convince them."

"A friend? I didn't realize you had any friends in the Federation?"

Drake's entire body made his doubt clear to Mr. Johnson, who responded with a knowing look as he explained their country's latest decision.

"The world will be our friend when this is all over."

"You must be joking."

"It's true. The fact of the matter is that our interests align this time. If there is one consistent thing about the devil, it's that he always obeys the terms of his deal."

"The devil?"

"Yes, the loved and respected Commissariat for Internal Affairs. Their soon-to-be chief made this deal possible. Thanks to their efforts, preparations to leave this country are as smooth as can be."

Smooth departures were something Drake was all too familiar with. And yet, he found himself standing up in shock.

"Hold on now, Mr. Johnson. You think the Commissariat will support us in any way?"

"Rest assured, they absolutely will. With a smile on their face. They might even see you off with a nice cup of tea."

For those familiar with the Federation, it was hard to believe anything positive about the Commissariat for Internal Affairs. The world's most terrifying secret police, smiling?

"I'm having a difficult time believing that, Mr. Johnson."

"Quite the skeptic, eh?"

"I've worked with them enough to know," Drake answered, but little did he know, Mr. Johnson was about to surprise him by opening Pandora's box.

"I have a letter of endorsement that will get the bureaucrats moving."

"A letter?"

"Show it to anyone who gives you any trouble. As long as they're not suicidal, they'll let you go with a smile. Take good care of these," the old man said as he tossed the documents onto the table.

Mouth agape, Colonel Drake picked up the bundle of papers and scanned them.

In perfectly legible Federation and Commonwealth writing, he could see that it read: *Highest Travel Priority Authorization*. With this, the multinational unit could even requisition any boat or vehicle they needed. To top it all off, it clearly stated that any entity unwilling to comply would be subject to investigation by the Commissariat for Internal Affairs.

"What the hell kind of orders are these...?"

"It's written out for you to read, Mr. Drake. The entire Federation Army has agreed to allow the multinational unit to leave the country and is willing to support them in every way possible. It has been signed off by both the Commissariat and Army Command."

"So this is real...?"

"That's what I've been telling you this entire time. The same orders should have reached Colonel Mikel by now as well."

He grinned. It was an ominous grin, the sort that made it clear a colonel had no say in the matter. Mr. Johnson had told him that he would be departing for his new post. All Drake could do was comply with these new orders.

That said, there was one thing he still wanted to ask.

Chapter II

"May I ask what circumstances made this all possible…?"

He stared right at Mr. Johnson as he asked this, but the only thing he saw was a grave look. It was the sort of expression that suggested the man wanted him to think for himself. Drake considered this for a short moment before shaking his head. He was a colonel, a marine mage by trade. His country didn't pay him enough to concern himself with the backroom deals and conspiracies that drove these sorts of decisions.

It's not my job to figure these things out. And so, Drake opted for a more direct approach.

"Mr. Johnson. I'm not a canny man. I may very well mess up the departure process due to my inability to pick up on the more subtle side of things. I'd like a decent explanation for all this. I do believe I deserve one."

He knew he wouldn't get a quick answer. Plenty would be kept from him. The principle of doling out information on a need-to-know basis was what oftentimes kept him and the others on the battlefield in the dark.

So what do you have to say? Drake watched the old man…who answered his request with a big smile.

"That's a fair demand, Mr. Drake."

"So you'll tell me why, then?"

"Of course! You wish to know why the Federation is willing to go this far, yes? It's quite simple. We believe it's because rather than be on the receiving end of aid, the Federation wishes to be the providers of it."

The Federation had been widely supported by the nations of the world throughout their long conflict with the Empire. The Unified States was a notable example because of the widely publicized lend-lease program. It was the Commonwealth, in fact, that was in charge of escorting the shipments of lend-lease war materiel. Not only that, but a small number of military advisors, including Drake himself, were stationed in the nation as reinforcements. While it was easy enough for Drake to understand what being on the receiving end of all this aid meant in a political sense…he still had questions.

"So it's a matter of saving face? Why would the Federation need to concern themselves with that? They currently bear the brunt of this war with the Empire. I fail to see why receiving aid is so galling."

From Drake's perspective, the Federation was playing a much more central role in the war compared to the Commonwealth. Sharing the continent with the Empire was what made the two nations such sworn, natural enemies.

"Politics, my friend, aren't as rational as you are."

Mr. Johnson gave a wry chuckle as he pointed this out.

"The Unified States has dispatched their forces now that Ildoa has been attacked. We, too, of course, and the François Republic will send what we can to the new war zone."

"That is reassuring."

"It is indeed." And then Mr. Johnson got in close and whispered to Drake, "With the number of resources the capitalist nations of the world are pouring into this war, the Communists, who are proposing a rich, abundant society for all, can't be seen as begging for aid this entire time now, can they? It goes against their very ideology."

Though confused for but a moment, Drake quickly picked up on what Mr. Johnson was getting at. Of course, he found the sentiment of it all repulsive as someone who was being sent into the fray purely because of this superficial posturing.

"So you're telling me that any reinforcements sent are all for show?"

"Precisely. That said, due to the eastern front encroaching so far into their border, symbolic reinforcements are the most the Federation can afford to send at the moment."

Symbolic. Colonel Drake died a bit on the inside when he heard the disparaging term. The multinational volunteer unit was symbolic in its essence.

"A small number of elite mages such as you and the forces under your command are quite easy to use in this regard. You will be welcomed as a powerful asset on the battlefield while serving as powerful symbols."

Drake didn't hide his disappointment when he heard exactly what he expected.

"If these are my orders…then I will do everything in my power to see them through. This is a nightmare, though."

"A nightmare?"

"We're commanded by the Federation, despite being a multinational unit made up of Federation and Commonwealth soldiers. On top of that, we'll have to keep pace with the Unified States and Ildoan troops in Ildoa…"

It was easy to throw the word *support* around in the political sphere. But what would this look like on an actual battlefield?

In what sense were they expected to fulfill the role of essential reinforcements? As organic firepower?

Such an intricate collaboration wouldn't be possible without significant training, and rushing in without preparing properly would only result in catastrophe. The colonel could see it already. No amount of bluntness was enough to push this serious concern of his. Colonel Drake also sought to curb the optimism he felt coming from his superiors as much as he could.

In a rare turn of events, however, the intelligence officer showed a willingness to listen to Drake's plea.

"Ah, yes. You needn't worry about that."

"I'd much rather not hear more empty promises."

"Let me assure you. The new command will be established in name only. You will maintain total command authority over your own troops. The Ildoans are quite brilliant in this regard."

$\ggg$　　　NOVEMBER 27, UNIFIED YEAR 1927, THE ILDOA FRONT　　

It's those on the front line who must make the impossible possible. This is just as true for the Federation, the Commonwealth, and Ildoa…as it is for the Empire. Without a moment's relief after escorting General Zettour to the rear, Tanya received new orders to support Colonel Lergen's 8th Panzer Division.[1] The plan is for the division to charge down the peninsula at full speed the moment the temporary cease-fire ends. Agreeing to the enemy's proposed weeklong cease-fire was presented as a gesture of goodwill, when in actuality it's simply a facade for the grueling work that the Imperial Army's logistics network needs to do to

---

[1] Why is it usually called an armored division instead of a tank division in English? I supposed that technically, an armored division is made up of more than just tanks, including mechanized infantry and other stuff…but I think the real reason is that languages are hard…

provision the Empire's soldiers and bring resources to the front lines in preparation for the renewed offensive.

This goes for the aerial mages as well, who are being used like pack mules. It's a brutal task. The mages, who can fly on calories instead of fuel, hand-carry the fuel liter by liter so they can power the division primarily made up of tanks and mechanized soldiers. In terms of exploiting subordinates, nothing Tanya has done can even come close to her superiors.

After transporting enough fuel for the upcoming offensive, a meeting is called to discuss Tanya's real job—combat.

It's more or less a kind of discretionary labor system, but Tanya doesn't have a death wish. Living is the highest priority, and Tanya has no plans to watch her subordinates pointlessly lose their lives. Once all the fuel has been delivered, the Kampfgruppe rendezvous with the 8th Panzer Division. The first order of business is meeting the division's commanding officer.

Lergen and Tanya thoroughly examine every little thing that can be discussed in advance. It's not as if they've been estranged to the point where it's difficult to coordinate. The two quickly go over what their respective units' roles will be and how much firepower they each possess, and they finish by sharing intel on the expected battlefield.

All that's left is to guess what their actual orders will be. Both Tanya and Lergen know full well that General Zettour places great trust in them and are more than familiar with his disposition as a commander.

"The general is so full of energy now that he's left the doom and gloom of the east for greener pastures here under the sun in Ildoa."

Tanya shares an idle complaint, earning a deep nod from Colonel Lergen.

"Yes, but...I can't help but feel that he was just as lively back east as well."

"That's fair," Tanya agrees before pointing to a spot on the map laid out on a fold-out table normally used during a field battle.

"It's as you can see, Colonel."

It is clear that, following General Zettour's orders, the Imperial Army was deploying slowly along the map. The cease-fire started on the Ildoan campaign's tenth day and continued for a week of fleeting peace, where the army primarily helped escort citizens out of the war zone. The truth behind this image, however, was much gloomier.

"Our forces have lost combat strength. The line is stretched thin. You can tell from our positions that we're in disarray."

Upon closer examination, there are divisions that have halted in odd places. On the other hand, there are divisions that are actively pulling back. At the same time, there seem to be vanguard units that were tasked with launching decisive attacks and have pushed forward.

Allowing a cease-fire while the army is in such disarray is a bit surprising. If a cadet at the military academy made such an obvious blunder, they would be kicked out of the school.

"At this rate, we'll lose the upper hand. It's also highly likely that the enemy is using this respite to reinforce their line."

The enemy has been given one week. This is an unusually long period of time in the world of military strategy. It's certainly more than enough to prevent the Imperial Army units that advanced recklessly from suffering a devastating counterattack and has also created an opportunity to adjust supply lines...but it also gives the enemy a chance to reorganize. Colonel Lergen agrees wholeheartedly with Tanya's remarks. The reluctance in his nod practically says out loud, *I know, but what can we do?* which communicates all too clearly the dire situation of the Imperial Army.

"We can't ignore the fact that the Unified States has joined the war as Ildoa's ally. We've confirmed what seems to be their advance units at a few different locations."

He lets out a frustrated sigh.

"Time is on their side..."

"So it seems." In annoyance, Tanya touches her watch before she speaks up again. "The front has become a mess because time is against us. If I may be frank, this display of confusion and disarray could be described as an unforeseen disgrace for our Imperial Army."

At the very least, this never would've happened in the early days of this war. If it weren't for the obvious toll the war has had on the Empire, its enemies would've suspected something was obviously wrong. The Imperial Army's formation is messy. Almost too messy.

"This is precisely why I expect General Zettour to play another one of his tricks."

"His tricks, you say?"

He murmurs this before lowering his voice to avoid being overheard by anyone around them.

"So you also think he's going to try something…?"

Both of us witnessed the grand performance he pulled off in the east. The current disposition of troops had to be a gamble of some sort. Tanya knows this well, having played a key role in the general's past schemes.

"Why, of course I do, Colonel. I believe the entirety of the Imperial Army is under the same impression. Oh…" Tanya catches herself. "I suppose that applies to the Federation as well. They'll catch on quick."

Unlike Ildoa or the Unified States, the Federation earned its knowledge the hard way. The ones who subscribed to pragmatism rather than the ideology of Communism would recognize Zettour's plot for what it is.

"They're one of General Zettour's countless victims, after all. As a fellow victim, I can promise you that anyone who's learned their lesson through bitter experience will be suspicious of whatever this is."

Colonel Lergen stares back in wonder before giving a light chuckle.

"It seems irrational at first, but it does make sense. You have quite the profound perspective, Colonel. I admit I must agree."

Naturally, Colonel Lergen still has his doubts.

"But…while I do believe this is all to sharpen his fangs, that is as about far as I can read into this. What is it you think the general is trying to do?"

"I can't really say for sure myself."

"Guesswork is fine, Colonel Degurechaff. I'm open to any insight into the general's mind."

Tanya begins to speak.

"In that case, to put it bluntly, military rationale dictates that the current strategy is an utter mess. Of our forces here in Ildoa, I'm assuming only the few who have seen action on the eastern front and have the general's devious designs instilled within them will understand what's happening here."

"Who knows where this is all leading?"

Tanya gives her own guess in response to Colonel Lergen's idle grumble.

"Perhaps all this chaos is necessary? I think we should look at it as the groundwork for what's to come."

"In a political sense? Ah, that would explain why we were stopped in front of the Ildoan Palace. If we interpret this as the general searching for a starting point to negotiations, then perhaps..."

Colonel Lergen stops short of saying "peace," but Tanya has her doubts about this speculation. General Zettour does have the end of the Empire in his sights. However, he isn't the type to quietly accept his fate without putting up a considerable fight. He came to Ildoa fists swinging.

"It's perfectly fine that we received the orders not to attack the city when we approached the capital. Not attacking the seat of Ildoa's royal family is a political decision."

This issue comes from the fact that such an important order wasn't given until the very last minute. From Tanya's perspective, this was abnormal. If the order to halt hadn't arrived in time, Imperial forces might have charged into the capital before the cease-fire.

Nevertheless, Tanya continues.

"Our orders to stop very well may be a part of the general's plan."

"What makes you suspect that? I'm not one to toot my own horn, but our swift advance to the capital was about as successful as we could hope for. Isn't it possible we simply exceeded expectations?"

Colonel Lergen's logic makes perfect sense, but Tanya is forced to retort.

"Were it the opposite—if we were ordered to make an unexpectedly early assault—I could understand."

Orders to expand an attack are to be expected. Being told to attack in order to capitalize on a fleeting advantage is part and parcel of war.

"However, we were told to stop our advance despite having a chance to capture their capital, which to me suggests there is trickery afoot."

In all honesty, Tanya would've gladly mounted an assault if she'd had the chance. She was trying to change her job, after all. Taking over the most important city would certainly look good on a résumé. Despite this, she was given the orders to halt. Losing such a great opportunity was a let-down, to say the least.

Either way, since she is a simple officer, it isn't Tanya's place to decide whether or not to take over the enemy's capital. Had she independently done so without authorization, she would've just been marked down as a dangerous soldier who doesn't follow orders—definitely not a reputation you want while looking for a new job. Tanya needs anything she can put on her résumé at this point. She considers different angles to find a good way to spin this.

It's now clear that there just aren't many opportunities to do that here. This is a point of pain for Tanya…though the intent of the top brass has become clearer.

"The way I see it is, the fatherland, or perhaps more aptly, General Zettour…is going to turn Ildoa into his own personal playground."

"A playground?"

"Doesn't it seem like a toy box? While the hostilities have yet to begin again, we're currently positioning a powerful task force to seize the enemy capital. Our enemies are also using this time to build up their forces. It feels as if the general is allowing his friends to come and bring their toys to play."

For such a well-mannered war, it would undoubtedly be a bloody one.

"There's a chance this may be more of a political display of power as opposed to a part of the actual war…"

Just as Tanya is about to agree with the colonel on this point, a young officer with the rank insignia of a major on his jacket rushes into the tent where the two commanding officers are in the middle of a meeting, offering the bare minimum of a greeting as he scrambles to collect himself.

"Excuse me, Division Commander!"

"I'm merely the acting commander. What is it?"

The young officer gives a slight salute before holding out a slip of paper. It appears the latest instructions have arrived.

"I brought this for you! They're new orders from the fatherland."

The overly enthusiastic major holds out the orders before sprinting from the tent as quickly as he appeared. Tanya already lost interest in the man and is more concerned with the orders.

"Speak of the devil. Is it from General Zettour?"

Colonel Lergen nods as he reads through the orders.

"These sound like the orders he'd give."

"So this means...," Tanya questions eagerly, which is met with a firm nod by Colonel Lergen.

"We are to take out the enemy field armies the very moment the cease-fire comes to an end. You will be leading your troops into combat against the enemy mages."

"Take out their mages and focus all of our strength against whatever the Unified States brings to bear? Is that his true plan?"

"Those are the orders for you. The entire army will attack with the intent to wipe out their field armies before they can regroup. It's a general offensive."

"It's time to give those newcomers from the Unified States their first taste of war."

We'll welcome our new guests with a nice initiation. We won't hold anything back. I'll make sure they learn just how nice our Imperial hospitality really is. This really is looking to be a well-mannered war.

At this point, Tanya is brought out of her excited stupor by a warning from Colonel Lergen.

"There is a note written here for you."

"For me?"

As she asks this, she remembers it is General Zettour that we're dealing with here. Honestly, an unnaturally long amount of time has passed since she's received orders for a tried-and-true front assault. The General Staff has continually used the 203rd Aerial Mage Battalion for his more personal, most abusive missions, after all. Tanya can only reminisce about the peaceful, good old days of her previous world, where she used to leave the office at a reasonable time every day.

Oh, how I miss peace.

How I miss going home at the end of the day.

How I miss my old life.

It was a good life I had back then. That is why I want to get it back.

"Yet another challenging task? My troops and I will see it through. We shall leave the Ildoan capital in ashes with a direct attack."

"It seems General Zettour knows you well."

"Excuse me, Colonel?"

"The note specific to your battalion demands you show restraint with your attack on the capital. This is a cut-and-dried order. There is even a limit on how close you're allowed to get to the capital."

Colonel Lergen offers a wry grin as he says this, prompting Tanya to check the text for herself.

"My apologies, Colonel, but…this means these orders are forbidding me to attack the capital, let alone take it over."

Surely this isn't this case, Tanya thinks as she watches Colonel Lergen affirm her suspicions.

"Effectively, yes."

The two share a mutual confusion regarding this point. The general's orders are essentially to leave the capital alone. These extra, clearly defined orders addressed to Tanya push this point.

"To think the general would ever give orders like these."

One can only wonder what craftiness is afoot behind these jarringly confusing orders. Whatever the case may be, one thing is for sure: This is only the beginning. Tanya and Colonel Lergen, the pawns of the General Staff, will likely be tasked with purely political restrictions.

"This changes the way we're fighting this war."

"Yes… Although, I can accept it without resistance. I will do whatever is necessary." Colonel Lergen dons a tired expression. "I do find myself wishing we could fight a regular war for once."

A lingering exhaustion can be heard in his tone as he utters this.

"This is war and politics. We must be careful about how we proceed."

This is true for everyone. How a person carries themself during a time of war is paramount. Tanya wants as many stars as she can get to secure a safe, successful future. Achievements look great on a résumé, after all.

"I honestly wanted to attack the royal capital, given the chance…"

Tanya's honest opinion makes her aspirations just a little bit too clear. She sees Colonel Lergen's expression tightening up a bit, which tells her that her superior understands the importance of restraint. Tanya, being fairly confident in her understanding of psychology, instantly recognizes that there is a misunderstanding that she must clear up.

"Please don't worry, Colonel. I am a soldier. I will follow my orders. While it's unfortunate that I'm so misunderstood, if I'm told to hold back, then I will do so."

"Ah, er… Colonel. Is taking out capitals a hobby of yours?"

"What do you mean? Taking out capitals?"

"First Dacia, then the Federation, and now Ildoa. You have a habit of going right for the jugular…"

"Ah…"

Tanya concedes this point. She recognizes that she has a quick trigger finger when it comes to taking out targets that could be considered significant achievements. Even now, the urge is strong when the royal capital is just a hop and a skip away. That being said, she isn't so irrational as to ignore direct orders. Foolishness is the last trait she wishes to accentuate on her résumé. Thus, she will play the part of the good officer—or at least the version of one in her mind—and stand at attention to confront Colonel Lergen's misunderstandings with an exemplary and impressively firm attitude of an officer who understands their duties.

"Colonel, don't be mistaken. Everything I've ever done, I was ordered to do. When duty calls, I will fly far and wide, and burn down all that I must before making my triumphant return."

"That's reassuring. I'll expect great things from you during this operation, then."

"But of course. Leave the enemy mages to my battalion. You'll find that our attack will prove highly devastating for their field troops as well."

"Good." The colonel always ends his exchanges with a polite response. The man is probably too polite to be a General Staff officer, but that's neither here nor there, as the colonel segues into his next question. He wants to know what the 8th Panzer Division can do to help. The answer Tanya von Degurechaff gives to this question has a wicked intent behind it.

"If I may, Colonel Lergen, I will take you up on your offer. Would you be willing to lend me the tanks we've acquired from Ildoa on this campaign so far?"

Those from the New World had a sense of admiration for the Old World. This may have stemmed from a place of prejudice, but the Old World's long history and vibrant culture were enough to fill any visiting youth with adoration.

Sadly, this was a sentiment that belonged in a different era. The Unified States vanguard that landed on the shores of Ildoa would be met by the monster that prowled the continent. The Imperial Army, both emaciated and battle-hardened by prolonged total war, was a spiteful beast. It may have been a product of culture, a by-product of continually fine-tuning the art of war. Atop a mountain of bones sat the world's enemy, a demonic chimera with the head of a General Staff officer and wings of hard-won experience.

These youths should be applauded.

They surely deserved to be recognized.

These ordinary people would become heroes in the fight against the Imperial Army, a monstrosity born from necessity.

》》》 **NOVEMBER 29, UNIFIED YEAR 1927, THE ILDOA FRONT** 《《《

The Empire's Aerial Mage Battalion has been reinforced with tanks. That's right, tanks.

They proceed to exude their mana signals in luxury for all to pick up on as they clumsily bring the line of tanks down one of the main roads in the most conspicuous way possible. The battalion follows the road in a leisurely manner, as if heading for a picnic on a nice cold day in a winter resort.

A female mage officer can be seen taking a bite out of a chocolate bar as she drives her motorcycle down the road, carefree. In her sidecar sits another officer—a small girl far too small to be a soldier—who happily pours herself a cup of nice and warm coffee from her thermos.

Honestly, the entire scene lacks the tension one would expect from a group of people heading to an active war zone. It looks more like a nice field trip. The reason for their brazenness in such a dangerous area? Well, this is the elite 203rd Aerial Mage Battalion.

They are currently borrowing the 8th Panzer Division's newly acquired tanks, with jerrycans full of plundered high-octane gasoline to fuel their trip. Incidentally, these are the same jerrycans the mages spent the entire cease-fire transporting, so there was a bit of a love-hate relationship going on.

The jerrycans are situated on either side of the standard-issue Ildoan motorcycles currently heading southbound toward the royal capital.

This is meant to be a diversion. We're acting like vulnerable bait for the enemy mages. Our main goal is to look so vulnerable that the Ildoan and Unified States troops can't ignore the Imperial carrot dangling before them. The premise is that the Imperial mages who wreaked so much havoc in the east have let their guard down in the faraway land of Ildoa.

I should mention that this plan has already hit a proverbial speed bump. Specifically, it's our disguises. Even more specifically, it's our mana signals.

Tanya's orders were to intentionally employ lackluster signal masking so that the battalion's mana would be easily detected. I explained to my subordinates that the intent was to lure the enemy. Everyone understood the goal and what they needed to do. There were no problems in this regard. The whole unit, from the commanding officer to the lowest foot soldier, everyone knew their role for this mission.

The only problem is that deliberately failing to mask their mana signals...has been more or less impossible. Their attempt to be lackluster is what's lackluster.

Our orders are to let everyone notice us, and yet, almost every soldier has kept their mana hidden. The problem became apparent when Lieutenant Serebryakov confessed in a strained voice that she couldn't let her mana leak.

I must recognize that I may have made an error in training my battalion. After all, the troops know that Tanya has never accepted anything less than perfection from them on the battlefield.

This much should be a given, I feel. When it comes to hiding mana signals, it's either fully blocked or not blocked at all. There is no point if even an inkling of mana gets through. Thus, mana signature concealment must always be perfect. To both maintain stealth and execute effective ambushes.

The 203rd knows this well, and that's putting it lightly. The members of the 203rd have achieved a level of emissions reduction so perfect that it has become second nature for them.

It's almost ironic. They're basically incapable of doing the opposite!

"There may have been an issue with my training methods. Perhaps I was too strict about mana signal leaks."

This is a huge blow to my confidence as a teacher. These are grizzled veterans. I can understand that their extensive combat experience makes it agonizing to even consider deliberately letting their mana signals show. It's become a habit for them while on the front lines. Any attempt by Tanya to make adjustments was foiled by the deeply ingrained habit of avoiding such an unforgivable offense. The more battle-hardened the veteran, the tougher it is for them to feign incompetence. In fact, it ends up being the newer recruits, such as First Lieutenant Wüstemann, who manage to fulfill Tanya's request.

That being said, this was basically the only problem worth noting.

Given enough time, a veteran could figure out a way to break their habits. In fact, that's what they've already done. More accurately, that's what Tanya made them do.

Thanks to this, small traces of mana signals are now slipping out—though not a satisfactory amount, considering their intended deception—as they zoom down the Ildoan roads.

The perfect weather today makes for a nice, peaceful drive. Thanks to their clear line of sight, the 203rd is able to spot the enemies first.

First to find the enemy, first to strike, and then a quick withdrawal. This is the ideal pattern of attack.

Of course, I'm constantly making sure my subordinates are fully aware of the strict orders to not go too far and to refrain from carelessly relying on their instincts.

"Salamander Leader to all units. Confirmation on two Unified mages above. They're flying at an altitude of seventy-five hundred in a pair. They appear to be a patrol, so we will ignore them. Hold your fire, understood? Also, refrain from tracking their mana signals."

In response to her orders, the first officer brings his bike up next to Tanya's and gives a small protest for the hell of it.

"02 to 01. Those two'll come back to ream us in the ass if we let them go."

"01 to 02. Keep the antics to a minimum."

"My apologies."

Major Weiss gives a salute and a quick nod, which earns him a grin from Tanya. It's obvious he isn't actually worried about them coming back to bite us in the ass. It's just a joke to try and lighten up the mood before battle. Humor is always good when danger waits in the wings.

I pour myself another cup of coffee while enjoying Ildoa's mild cold weather.

"Lieutenant Serebryakov, you always make the best coffee."

My adjutant is preoccupied with driving the bike, so as a sign of appreciation, I reach into her satchel and take out more chocolate for her. After politely accepting, my adjutant promptly takes a big bite out of the bar while I turn my attention to the two specs in the sky.

"It's impressive, really."

A smile jumps onto my face.

I watch as the pair flies in a straight line above us. It makes me take a jab at Major Weiss, who keeps his bike next to mine while appreciating the enemy.

"Look at their flight. It's very smooth. I'm sure it'd take a considerable amount of reeducation to get you and the rest of the troops to fly like that."

"Mercy, please. I don't think we can fly in such a military parade–like fashion…"

"Come now," I say with a laugh. "I'm sure if we searched long enough, we could find outdated primers on how to fly."

"I'm too afraid to follow an obsolete manual."

The first officer shudders at the thought. To think this man used to do everything by the book. That was back in Dacia. I still remember it. How nostalgic. I recall my first officer following the old conventions and withdrawing at the first sight of foot soldiers.

But look at him now. Major Weiss's experience has brought him so far from textbook combat that I very much doubt he can even maintain any of the standard formations shown in the training manual.

"It's funny how much people can grow, isn't it, Major?"

"What's that?"

"Oh, it's nothing. I just never expected you to disparage the training manual."

I'm reminiscing fondly, but Major Weiss blushes and waves his hand.

"That was a long time ago! I was young back then."

"That's true. Making those mistakes while you're young is the best way to learn. I should probably go easier on Lieutenants Grantz and Wüstemann."

I nonchalantly share this with my first officer before receiving an unexpected remark from Lieutenant Serebryakov while she drives the bike.

"You know, every now and then I'm struck by this strange thought..."

"What's that, Lieutenant Serebryakov?"

"Just that it's a bit strange for you to discuss age..."

"Oh?" An uncomfortable sense of understanding comes over me. Nevertheless, it's the first officer who jumps in to correct my adjutant's misguided realization.

"C'mon now, Lieutenant. Let's not kid ourselves here."

"What, Major Weiss?"

My adjutant gives a blank look while, with the most serious of expressions, my first officer continues to speak.

"The only years that matters are how many have been spent fighting."

"How many years you've spent fighting...?"

"That's right. And in that sense, the colonel is the oldest one here."

"Da-ha-ha-ha!"

Jovial laughter spreads throughout the friendly vehicular picnic.

As far as I can tell, Lieutenant Wüstemann still seems a bit stiff. Perhaps he still feels a bit of tension from being on the battlefield. The rest of her troops, however, seem to be enjoying themselves.

As for Lieutenant Serebryakov...she continues to gobble down even more chocolate. The chocolate I gave her is long gone. Who knows where she got her hands on so many sweets.

Juxtaposed with the wholesome conversation happening on the ground, our enemies above maintain a rigid flight path. They are definitely sticking to their manuals.

While munching on some chocolate, I keep one eye on the sky and let out a sigh.

"It's still a decent maneuver. Their obvious surplus of resources is making me a bit jealous."

The soldiers above are mage troops being used for aerial recon.

There's nothing particularly strange about this. It's the most basic of the basics. Basics, if you look in a textbook, that is.

They're using their aerial mages to patrol multiple air zones, after all. To cover a wide area would require a significant amount of manpower.

While the enemy may have the resources to do this, such a tactic would be far too luxurious for the current Imperial Army to employ.

"We used to do that back on the Rhine."

I mumble to myself while shaking my head. It's more than possible that our continual waste of human resources is what led to the manpower shortage we face today.

It's just like radar picket ships. The enemy spreads their scouts thinly throughout the area of operations and the main force sends reinforcements when they encounter something. This is a legitimate tactic that only the wealthy can employ. And if you can afford to employ such a tactic…it's safe and reliable.

In this regard, the Unified States is blessed, but the Empire still has the upper hand. For now, at least. We paid for our tuition in full with corpses because experience was our teacher.

Hmm…

As I eye the enemies above, something occurs to me.

"Clean movements. Both of them are maintaining their distance."

These two mages are doing their best, and their efforts are pointed in the right direction.

However…I'm delighted after confirming my suspicions.

These two still aren't afraid. Just like the Federation soldiers weren't.

It won't be long before victory is ours.

》》》 THE SAME DAY, IN THE SKIES ABOVE THE ILDOAN PENINSULA 《《《

Two young mages flew triumphantly through the skies of the Old World. They belonged to the Corinth 7th Aerial Magic Regiment of the Unified States Expeditionary Forces in Ildoa. The cold yet ever blue November skies were teeming with signs of the war, punctuated by the occasional cannon fire that was audible in the distance.

Bravery was a by-product of the pilots who breathed in the air of an active battlefield. Their deployment to Ildoa was sudden, but Corinth mages were beginning to gain confidence in their abilities after a handful of encounters with the Imperial forces. Their mission: interdicting the rapidly advancing Imperial army. In the small amount of time that had passed since the cease-fire ended, the Corinth mages had managed to push back the enemy forces they had met thus far. Their unit's casualties had been minimal, and the mages were slowly losing their fear of the Imperial Army.

Confidence was born from accumulating successes. They all fought bravely, with a sense of adventure in their hearts and a desire unique to younger soldiers eager to show off to their peers. For soldiers more comfortable on the battlefield, they even made room for pursuing their love interests.

This was true for Jackson, at least. He wanted his crush to see him do his job well. First Lieutenant Jackson was happy to learn that his flight partner for scouting the area that day was First Lieutenant Jessica, his fellow soldier he had feelings for.

Jackson was too serious for his own good, as the other soldiers would often put it. His seriousness manifested itself during their surveillance with him keeping his eyes off Jessica and fixated on the main road below him. Even his superior, who went out of his way to pair him up with Jessica, would've been proud of his professionalism.

It was this diligence that eventually allowed him to pick up on the faintest of mana signals coming from the ground below.

"Jessica! We've come into contact with a mana signal!"

"It's 02, John. Ah, I mean 01!"

The two shared an awkward smile when they both forgot to use each other's call signs after suddenly making contact. Then they started seeking out the source of the signal. There were multiple signals moving together.

"01 to 02. It appears to be a unit of mages. What do you think?"

"I think you're right. But the signals are very faint…"

As far as these two knew, the signals they were tracking were expertly disguised. They had heard that the Imperial Army was full of highly skilled mages, but this was more than they'd expected.

"Do you think they're Imperial mages?"

"That would explain why their signals are so hard to track. I think we've hit the jackpot this time."

First Lieutenant Jackson received a compliment from his counterpart, whom he had feelings for. While he took a brief moment to bask in the afterglow, he knew he needed to remain vigilant about his surroundings. Every moment needed to be treated like it was a battle. He took this to heart and always operated in a reliable manner.

The pair continued to observe the enemies below while making their report.

"CP, CP! This is Boxer 01! We have confirmation of Imperial mages in our patrol area!"

"CP to Boxer 01. We don't see any unknown mana signals coming from there. Do you have visual confirmation?"

Jackson was looking through his binoculars as he answered command's question in a firm tone.

"Boxer 01 to CP, I'm sure of it. Visual confirmation on mounted enemies! I believe their mages are traveling by ground, just like in training. They are a powerful unit using an extremely high level of signal concealment while advancing!"

Mages hiding their mana signals while attempting to lay an ambush was standard. For the Corinth Regiment, at least.

Corinth's commander had experienced the various tactics employed by the Imperial Army's elite mages in the east and thoroughly relayed what to look out for to the entire regiment, such as Jackson and Jessica, through meticulous training. Jackson knew in this moment that it was thanks to Corinth's organizational power that they would be victorious.

"We can't confirm from over here. Have you confirmed their mana signals?"

"It's very weak, but there's definitely a signal. It seems the enemy mages are trying to bypass our patrols by concealing their mana signals."

The faintest of signals could be caught between both Jackson and Jessica keeping a watchful eye out during their patrol. They knew that the Imperial Army would likely use these tactics, and the fact that they required visual confirmation could only mean one thing.

"Outstanding work, Boxer!"

"I think we got lucky on this one."

"CP copies. We understand the situation. The Corinth Regiment will deploy ASAP. Connecting you to Corinth 01. Relay the enemy's movements to them."

Friendly forces were going to act on their discovery. This single encounter might have an impact on the overall tide of this war.

Lieutenant Jackson was beginning to feel excited, but he knew he needed to keep his cool as he shared what he saw on the ground with regimental command.

"Corinth 01 to Boxer, what do you see?"

"Boxer 01 to Corinth Battalion. We have a battalion's worth of enemy mages in vehicular transit on the ground making their way into our defensive line. Our position is…"

Where is our position again?

He knew the position… It was on the tip of his tongue, but for some reason, he just couldn't recall the radio code for the airspace he was flying in.

Where are we again? Why can't I remember?

It was so simple, and yet he couldn't recall it for some reason. This was when he felt a tap on his shoulder.

"This is 02 to Corinth 01. We're in Airspace CV42. CV42."

Jessica's soft, gentle voice chimed in to answer Corinth command's question.

Jackson gave her a heavy nod, to which she responded with a wave and a smile.

"Corinth 01, copy that. You both did well, Boxer. We need to hit their mages to maintain the capital's defensive line. We're going to deploy immediately. Keep an eye on the enemy from the sky."

"Boxer 01, roger that!"

"So, what can you tell us about the enemy? I want details. What do you two see, Boxer?"

So far, everything Jackson had done had been by the book. Something he'd practiced over and over again. He had tried to get a better idea of who they were dealing with, but he had yet to come up with anything.

"The enemy mana signal is too faint. It's hard to get a reading."

"Boxer 02, the same goes for me. One thing's for sure. The strength of the mana signal is far too low for a unit this size. They are most definitely veterans."

Hearing Boxer's response, the regimental commander brought the two into another channel, where high command was waiting to discuss how the army would handle the skies.

"Corinth 01 to High Command. We doubt a single mage battalion would breach our line on their own. Requesting aerial reconnaissance from the rear."

"Affirmative, Corinth 01. One of the navy's planes just saw what we believe to be an enemy panzer unit."

While listening in on the discussion between their regiment and high command, it hit Jackson. The Imperial Army was about to make their move. Had he and Jessica not found this battalion, the enemy's elite mages may have struck behind their defensive line with the element of surprise. He glared down at the enemy, as his sense of duty slowly transformed into an intense desire to fight. Perhaps that was why he somehow knew the orders he was about to receive from the regiment leader were going to be of grave importance.

"You heard the man, Boxer. The enemy is likely the vanguard for a large-scale attack."

Now, the regiment commander spoke with an apologetic tone.

"I'm hoping you two can get more information for me… Is it possible for you to approach the enemy to confirm whether or not they're the panzer unit we're looking for?"

Jackson shot Jessica a look to see what she thought about regimental command's request. They were being asked to dive deeper into the enemy's airspace, without backup. This would be exceedingly dangerous, but they both recognized the need, given the circumstances.

"We won't be able to keep an eye on the mages if we leave our current airspace, but they are in the location we told you. If we can be of service elsewhere, then…"

"It would really help if you volunteered to do this…"

"Then of course we will!"

The pair showed no hesitation in accepting the new mission.

"We can do it! Even their mages failed to detect us… Their defenses may not be as tight as we thought. You don't need to worry about us!"

"Corinth 01, we appreciate you volunteering to help. But be sure to remain vigilant. One thing's for sure: The enemy knows what they are doing." The regiment commander maintained a serious tone. "You mustn't underestimate them. When you are in their airspace, remember the difference between courage and recklessness. You can abort the mission if you feel it's too dangerous."

"Boxer 01, roger that. 02 agrees. We'll go as far as we can!"

Lieutenant Jackson and Lieutenant Jessica volunteered knowing the mission would be dangerous. There was an innocence to their bravery, as they accepted the mission without the slightest idea of what was waiting for them. They would be alone in enemy territory. Even a veteran would show some hesitance, given the circumstances, but these two showed firm resolution in their desire to help the regiment.

That resolution would be what let them escape the jaws of fate.

When it came to luck, God was not on the Unified States Aerial Magic Corinth Regiment's side. Even though they were the epitome of what a regiment could be, the disregard for their safety by the heavens could only be considered cruel.

The regiment was made up of elites from the Unified States, who were hand-selected to be sent to the Old World. They numbered 108 and stood at the forefront of the army in terms of training, equipment, and natural ability.

In fact, historians would have no qualms recognizing that the Corinth Regiment was one of the most prestigious units of its time. This was especially true of its leader, who was prepared for anything. He was particularly enthusiastic about learning through combat, and his deep understanding of military topography was highly regarded by his peers.

Above all else, the Corinth Regiment commander was a mage who led from the front. He was a true leader, an intellectual, and a brave officer who cared for his subordinates.

His unit was filled with top-notch soldiers who were well trained and were able to take advantage of their high coordination in combat. Experts agreed that the Corinth Aerial Magic Regiment had everything that could be asked for in an elite unit, except for the fact that they had been abandoned by God.

Even the decision to deploy forward in order to bolster the Ildoan capital's defensive line was a sound decision.

They had a regiment's worth of mages waiting in the sky for their orders, who all deployed as soon as the call came. Although it was a bit overkill in terms of manpower, it was an extremely appropriate decision. When multiple mana signals suddenly appeared on the ground below, they were able to react without hesitation.

Those who lived to tell the tale would remark that it was just as they had expected. Enemy mages trying to sneak toward the capital by traveling along the ground had been predicted long before the Boxer duo found them. That was how the appearance of multiple explosion formulas on the ground was met with minimal confusion.

The Corinth mages handled their first contact with the enemy with expert speed and precision. They raised defensive shells while immediately climbing higher. This was a textbook response to enemy mages springing an ambush from the ground. It was like seeing honor students in action. Their follow-up was equally impressive, as they quickly returned fire to suppress those on the ground. These mages were different from those who knew their tactics only by the books. They were true warriors.

The Unified States mages in the Corinth Regiment carried out their commander's orders to the tee...only to meet their demise that day.

They made a single mistake.

These skilled mages were, unfortunately, up against a beast of war born from blood and iron.

For they knew not the danger of the man-eating demon that was the 203rd.

"Drop your formulas and charge! Charge!"

Before Tanya can even finish her concise orders, her battalion abandons the bikes on the ground as they shoot into the sky.

The initial explosion formulas were nothing more than a distraction. Tanya and her soldiers know that an explosion formula wouldn't have much effect against an enemy already expecting an attack from the ground.

They know from their experience in the east how ineffective they are against a proper defensive shell (this is especially true when dealing with Federation soldiers).

Only amateurs would make the mistake of thinking mages are soft enough targets to be blown out of the sky with a single explosion. Formulas don't do much more than bend reality. Just like bayonets, however, magic blades cut right through the problem.

"Rush them! Break up their formation!"

It isn't rare for melee combat to be the answer when individual soldiers are capable of holding their own against an opponent. The 203rd Aerial Mage Battalion is a powerful unit known for its hit-and-run tactics. Up against an entire regiment, it's best for us to stick with what we know.

Maintaining the bare-minimum defensive shell, they use the rest of their mana to increase their altitudes. There's a reason the Elinium Arms Type 97 is called an assault computation orb.

The dual core excels at acceleration above all else. Like an out-of-control mustang, the Type 97 is more than capable of bucking an unskilled pilot, paying no mind to what happens to its rider. Nevertheless, this is an excellent piece of machinery. With the right knight, even an unruly horse can be an incredible stallion. The unstoppable, menacing acceleration these orbs produce is akin to…the heavy cavalry of the past. With the right officer and right environment, the Empire's enemies would get the full experience of the orb's destructive power and force.

"Unsheathe your magic blades! Show these manual thumpers what real violence and mayhem look like!"

As Tanya barks her orders, she finds herself overcome with a poetic mindset. She decides to give a bit of a supplementary explanation to let her soldiers know the significance of this encounter.

"Let us show our friends from the New World the essence of war!"

When I turn, I find my battalion accelerating beautifully upward beside me.

I'm satisfied to see that even the newer Lieutenant Wüstemann is able to keep up with the more veteran members of my battalion, such as Major Weiss and Lieutenant Grantz.

Then I glance over at our enemies, who are putting on a more pitiful show.

They're caught completely off guard by the sudden assault and have halted in a moment's hesitation.

"It seems like our new friends were expecting a shoot-out!"

A wide grin appears on Tanya's face. Their assumption was a safe one. Nobody expects a frontal assault when the sheer firepower of an entire regiment can be brought to bear. It didn't take long for them to snap out of their stupor, but…a moment's hesitation is lethal when the Type 97 can bring Imperial mages within striking distance. By the time they come to their senses and try to maneuver away, it's already too late.

Could they stop the charging cavalry with their broken formation? And not just against any cavalry, but the battle-hardened knights of the Empire?

It's inhumane how clear the answer to this question is: unequivocally, no.

Were this possible, mages wouldn't be feared by foot soldiers, and the Devil of the Rhine moniker would be more cute than anything else.

Leaving my back to Lieutenant Serebryakov, I cut right through the shattered regiment's formation like a hot knife through butter.

This is just the natural way of things. It's war logic, in the same way the heavier side of the scale brings up the lighter side. These beasts are born from ration and necessity. They are fearsome Imperial monsters, with fangs sharpened by modern technology, and they will use their fangs with expert precision to consume people. Their opponents, the Unified States Corinth Regiment, are, for better or for worse, a solid and sound unit of mages. They respond to the sudden rush by the book they trained with.

"Corinth Leader to all units! Distance yourselves from the enemy! Then get back into formation!"

The regimental commander gives his levelheaded orders, which are appropriate by any standard. When on the receiving end of an ambush, an army should retreat as soon as possible. With enough distance, they could take the time to get back into formation and organize a counter-attack. This is a perfectly acceptable method for handling a sudden ambush.

The leader's decision to reposition his forces is a good one, but reality is cruel. As correct as his decision may be, his troops lack the experience to carry out his orders proactively, and they need more time to process their new orders.

Falling out of their initial position already created a lag in their reaction times. Some of them are able to move exactly how they trained. These soldiers, who follow their commander's orders precisely, fall back and form up without trouble.

Other soldiers take a bit more time to kick into action. The moment they process their new orders, they fear splitting off from their companions, who are already retreating. Thus, in order to catch up, they accelerate as quickly as they can.

And the rest…are too preoccupied by the enemies flying toward them with blades at the ready. Before they can process their new orders, they realize what's happened—they've been left behind by their allies and are in grave danger. The panic that hits them blocks out everything they learned in training.

Not a single one of them knows why this is happening. It doesn't matter, for while they spend their final moments in a confused panic, the enchanting glimmer of the Imperial mages' blades are the last thing they see as their spinal fluid spills from their bodies onto the ground below.

This is the moment the scale tips in the Empire's favor. The Unified soldiers are in disarray. Their once perfectly organized formation has been, ironically enough, thrown into chaos by a single optimal order, making their soldiers easy prey in the sky. Prey that has the misfortune of sharing the sky with this war's apex predator, the vile 203rd.

"Dominate them, comrades! Dominate! Dominate! Dominate!"

As unfortunate as the situation is for the Unified side, Tanya isn't going to let this prime chance pass her by as she waves her hand vigorously to urge her soldiers forward, barking orders, and even conducting an attack of her own.

A pursuit is always the ideal position to be in for a commanding officer. Nothing makes a better target than an enemy's back. This is especially true when the enemy is running after committing a grave error.

Though the orders I need to give are simple enough, a bit of creativity to spice them up and rally the troops never hurts. I'm always willing to go the extra mile as a good boss when it comes to improving my employees' work environment.

"It's party time, comrades!"

"What should we do for our main course, Colonel?"

Tanya shows the makings of a grimace at her adjutant's nonchalant question before deciding to go along with it. A party does need a main course, after all. And it's the host's job to provide a meal for their guests that suits the occasion.

Naturally, this would be easy enough to procure. They couldn't ask for fresher imported meat considering what was staring right at them.

"It's a bit late, but how about a nice Thanksgiving dinner? We have fresh turkey from the New World just waiting to be shot! Live game, if you will! Ha-ha-ha!"

I laugh at my own cheeky joke. Our forces are elegantly running wild through the enemy lines.

War is silly. Which is why I believe it's important to step back and laugh at it from time to time. As I do exactly that, I take this opportunity to check up on my subordinates.

"Tell me, Lieutenant Wüstemann! Are you enjoying the party?!"

"Y-yes!"

It isn't the most confident response I've ever heard, but he gets a passing grade for being able to answer in the first place during an all-out aerial brawl. It's proof that he's aware of his surroundings and not too focused on his enemy. I'd taken him for an inexperienced officer, but it seems he's grown into his role swimmingly.

"Ha-ha-ha, you've gotten used to this already. You should be proud of yourself, Lieutenant. We're up against the enemy's best and brightest textbook-thumping elites."

I plant my magic blade in the chest of an enemy mage, creating another red stain in Ildoa's blue sky while praising my subordinate's hard work.

"A single good deed is worth a thousand words. You're doing a good job for your first time. I'm looking forward to seeing you rack up your score and eventually garnering a name of your own."

Tanya's words of encouragement are interrupted by Lieutenant Grantz yelling out as he cuts down another mage.

"No fair! A new recruit's score shouldn't even count!"

The first lieutenant, who's worked hard for his score, complains loudly.

I remember how difficult it was for him to raise his score back on the Rhine and flash a big smile as I home in on my next target.

I take aim, adjust my weapon, then fire. As soon as I'm done, I offer Grantz some frank advice as I liquefy the enemy at close range with my submachine gun.

"Come now, Lieutenant Grantz! The times are changing! Nothing wrong with a little workplace reform, eh?"

"What?!"

"Resistance is futile! The workplace is always changing! For the better!"

Each time the survivors of the assault try to regroup in company-sized units, the 203rd immediately cuts them down. The 203rd, broken up into four companies, continues its coordinated assault to prevent the enemy from reorganizing themselves while constantly knocking more mages out of the sky.

What broke the Corinth regiment's morale the most was the Imperial mages' shared laughter that could be heard during the onslaught. And why wouldn't it? There was no way for them to predict aerial mages capable of flying at this speed, swinging their magic blades with smiles on their faces while their allies were turned to mincemeat.

This is their first time clashing with the unknown, and that unknown turns out to be a monstrous enemy who has come just to give them a bloodbath. Their will to fight all but dwindles as they stare into the jaws of this vicious beast of war.

Nevertheless, the Unified soldiers stand and fight. They take up their arms, just like they practiced in training, grip their orbs, and face their enemies.

Though only barely...it's commendable that the regimental commander manages to marshal his troops enough to put up an organized resistance.

Though the Corinth Regiment was dealt a severe blow by an enemy mage battalion, the chain of command is still operational.

"They're putting up a surprising amount of fight."

Even I can't help but notice their persistence. A smile appears on my face. Their resistance means little to the widely feared Devil of the Rhine, who can summon the Imperial Army's war knowledge.

I clap my hands before pointing at the enemy officer showing the best movements among his peers.

"We won't be needing him much longer."

My adjutant hears my murmur and nods.

"Thanks to their officer's hard work, we don't have to worry about any stragglers getting away."

"Precisely."

Tanya grins.

"He saved us the hard work of finding a regiment's worth of deserters."

It's no easy task chasing down a regiment with a battalion, but the enemy leader saved the 203rd from having to do this. Now that the numbers are about even, there is no point in delaying the inevitable any longer.

Time to finish them. I wave my arm.

"Let's show them a plunge!"

Everyone understands the meaning of those words. There is a principle of war that is pertinent even outside of mage battles.

The higher the ground, the better.

We're technically in the skies, but being higher is always the superior position. And with our Elinium Arms Type 97 Assault Computation Orbs...the Empire has the advantage in altitude. With the enemy huddling together in one place, we will plunge onto them from above. It's a simple maneuver, but as effective as it is violent.

With our plunge, the clear blue sky is quickly filled with crimson petals that rain down toward the ground.

〉〉〉   **THE SAME DAY, THE 8TH PANZER DIVISION**   〈〈〈

From Colonel Lergen's perspective, one's expression often told more than their mouth. Not that some things weren't worth being put into words anyway, but the smile of a certain young lieutenant colonel, wearing a cap stained with what was almost certainly the blood of her enemies, spoke volumes to him.

He knew exactly what this meant—that Lieutenant Colonel Degure-chaff had come with good news. It didn't take an Imperial engineer to figure that out. Her smile made it clear she had the news he was waiting for. Strangely enough, though…the young 8th Panzer Division major standing with her seemed a bit uneasy. He was a young officer, but even taking that into consideration…what had him so agitated?

Beginning to feel a little agitated himself, Colonel Lergen questioned the situation for a moment, only to soon stop himself. He looked at the small child, drenched in blood, smiling from ear to ear. This was, objectively, a bizarre sight to see. And yet, the sight wasn't unsettling for Lergen in the slightest.

"Well, this is a bit of a problem…"

It appeared he was utterly desensitized to the sight. Be that as it may, it wasn't something he could fix about himself despite identifying the problem.

He allowed himself a bit of a wry smile before looking Degurechaff in the eyes, who responded with a perfect salute. There was nothing else for Colonel Lergen to do or say. Why would the 8th Panzer Division reprimand the poor girl for a heroic victory?

The young major stood at ease while Tanya gave Lergen her report.

"We annihilated the majority of the enemy mage regiment. With friendly forces securing air superiority on top of that, nothing shall threaten our air superiority for the time being."

"Great work. That's fantastic news."

Air superiority. A phrase that was always pleasing to the ear. For a panzer unit that wished to move quickly, safe skies were an immense tactical advantage.

"All that's left is the enemy's field troops. Things don't look so well on this front."

"Colonel Lergen. Could it be that you're having a difficult time destroying their troops?"

"Unfortunately, yes."

"Why is that?"

Lergen paused for a moment. He questioned how much detail he should go into before concluding that he could simply excuse the young major from the meeting. Giving the young major simple orders to take care of did the trick. The two watched as he ran eagerly out of the room before Lergen gave his explanation with a sigh.

"We can't help it if General Zettour's political maneuvers will take precedent over military tactics, but the cease-fire has had grave consequences. While we managed to stockpile a bit of fuel and resources, the enemy has done far more with their time."

Not only did the Empire have a chronic lack of...everything, but their position wasn't great, either.

Lergen decided to share the main cause of the problem next.

"What's more, we clearly lack the soldiers needed to wipe out the enemy forces... Were we allowed to attack toward the capital, it would be a different story...but we have clear orders not to do that. This is a severe restriction."

"Is it a spatial restriction?"

"Yes," Lergen said, confirming her suspicions. Despite the many restrictions on where they could send their troops and how they could use them, they lacked the manpower to complete the many goals that must be met in each location.

"If we divide up your unit, do you think you could become a hammer, Colonel?"

"Would your troops act as the anvil?"

Colonel Lergen looked Lieutenant Colonel Degurechaff in the eyes for a short moment before shaking his head.

As they were both career soldiers, he and Tanya quickly came to the same conclusion: It wouldn't be possible. Tanya joined the colonel in a duet of sighs, which filled the empty command room with orchestral disappointment.

"As it stands, we were able to use our mobility to threaten the enemy to a certain degree. But at this rate..."

"You needn't say the rest, Colonel. There is a high probability that the advance on this front will completely stall... I can only wonder what the general's aim is in all of this."

The reason the two could share in their show of pessimism was that they were two commanding officers in the same room.

With this in mind, Tanya offered Lergen her thoughts.

"The Ildoan peninsula isn't that wide, geographically speaking. This is ideal for building a defensive line. Should the enemy set up their trenches, it will be hard for us to advance."

Geography was everything in a war. In Ildoa's case, the peninsula presented an extremely thin front, which made it much easier to defend. Leaving no space for an attacker to slip through, they could thoroughly cover the entire line with a minimal number of troops.

"Colonel...since it is you I'm speaking with, I'll share a bit more with you. We have a total of twenty-two divisions here on the Ildoan front. This certainly isn't small from a tactical standpoint, but it dwarfs our numbers in the east in terms of relative scale."

"I know. The general shared with me the disposition of our troops. It is clear to me that the intention was to gain an advantage using our high mobility throughout Ildoa."

"That's correct. In all honesty, we have a full army here."

Up until recently, Lergen had been going over the numbers back at the General Staff Office.

He'd done the final numbers for the east and the reserve forces, but it had been a long time since he'd seen a front as heavily loaded as Ildoa's.

"Six full panzer divisions, and five more mechanized divisions. The majority of these eleven divisions deployed at full strength, including my own panzer division, while the rest met the bare minimum needed for a division."

"So half of them are built for speed. It's clear that this is meant to be a mobile war. I'm surprised we're able to hold the line in the east while bringing this many to bear in Ildoa... So why the delay?"

Lergen knew the value of taking advantage of an opportunity to break out of a bind, and he had experienced the tragic consequences of coming to a standstill. For only a few days earlier, he successfully led the 8th Panzer Division south past the enemy's defensive line.

"It's quite frightening. We've put everything we have into this war and used it well, but I can't shake the fear that we'll let this chance slip by."

"It is strange. Is a supply problem causing our current delays?"

Perhaps the general was concerned about logistics.

"No," Lergen answered, accompanied by a firm shake of his head when addressing the question about logistics.

"We certainly are lacking in areas, such as fuel, but this is Colonel Uger and General Zettour we're talking about here. We have it much better here than we did in the east."

While they received only the bare minimum amount of fuel necessary, this much was to be expected.

They had bullets and fuel. Taking it a step further, they had enough warm meals with plenty of fat on them for at least two a day. Their logistics department was doing fantastic work considering how deep into enemy territory they had advanced.

"I'm still at a loss as to why we accepted the cease-fire in the first place. According to my sources, General Zettour used my name to approach our enemy?"

Lergen shot Tanya a look and could tell she knew exactly what he was talking about.

"Yes, I was brought along as his personal bodyguard for the talks."

General Zettour really did trust this girl. To an incredible extent, even. While appreciating the general's trust in the lieutenant colonel, Lergen asked a question that had been plaguing his mind for a while now.

"Why did the general stop our advance? Why did he authorize the cease-fire in the first place?"

"I haven't the slightest idea why he would do either of those things."

"Despite being there for the talks?"

Degurechaff answered his question by quietly shaking her head. Both she and the colonel shared the same thought.

Why did we need to stop a week ago?

The Imperial soldiers knew what would happen if they did: This front would get bogged down in trench warfare.

All it took was for the enemy to dig the holes to hunker down in, and considering how long and thin the Ildoan peninsula was…they didn't need to dig too many holes. There weren't many locations as difficult to attack as this one. The moment the battle devolved into trench warfare, it could easily turn into a stalemate.

Lergen was very apprehensive about the prospect of getting mired in hell like he did back on the Rhine front.

"The last thing I want to get us into is more trench warfare. Now is our only chance to advance."

"We have broken through a large-scale web of trenches before…"

"We can't pull another Open Sesame. It would take far too long to prepare the tunnels. No matter how you shake it, our current line of attack is designed to hit hard and fast. There's no reason to even consider anything else."

Lergen crossed his arms and then reached for some tobacco before sensing someone staring at him.

"What's the matter, Colonel? Is there something on my face?"

"I must admit, I'm a bit relieved to see you with such a troubled look on your face."

"What? Wait, what do you mean by that?"

"I would've been worried if I saw you with a wicked smile. The sort General Zettour shows when he is cooking up something wretched."

"Ah…," Lergen responded with a troubled chuckle. "A smile…"

That wasn't something he could easily show in a situation like this. It went without saying why. And yet, it was strange how the world worked sometimes. For whatever reason, it was just as clear to him that the General Zettour in question was most definitely smiling that very second.

Lergen put the tobacco back down and tilted his head to the side in thought.

"I have no intention of criticizing my superior, but I have no idea what General Zettour plans to do. Surely you must have some insight?"

"I can offer you only a sip of a fine liquor brewed from guesswork and secrecy. How would you like it served?"

"Dilute it with a bit of water for me. What do you think his goal is?"

"World peace."

Degurechaff stared straight into Lergen's eyes when she said these words. She spoke without the slightest hint of hesitation or sarcasm— she chirped her nonsensical response as if it were a universal truth.

"I believe that General Zettour is a pacifist that knows no peers."

"Perhaps you should look up the meaning of that word, Colonel."

"There's no need for that. If there is no aspiration more noble than peace in this world, then General Zettour is a true pacifist. That is what I believe, at least."

"Are you being serious?"

Lergen gave Degurechaff a dumbfounded look, but she continued as serious as could be.

"There is no one in this world who wishes for the Empire's peace more than the general. To do virtue to the transitive property, if we're able to accomplish world peace, it means peace for the Empire."

The Empire's peace. World peace. And the general's goal. As easy as these words were to say, they thoroughly stimulated Lergen's mind.

"So why do you suppose the general is having us attack Ildoa?"

"My best guess is that if world peace isn't possible, then he decided the next best option was to watch the world burn to a beautiful crisp."

"Come again…?"

Lergen stared blankly while Degurechaff calmly restated her opinion.

"He wants to bring an end to us and the world."

"Like a double suicide? Ha, ha-ha, ha…" He forced a laugh out, only to realize he wasn't laughing nearly as much as he had intended to. "Hopefully his wish doesn't come true… Hm?"

"Colonel Lergen?"

That was when the realization hit him, leaving him with no choice but to laugh.

What if we're fighting despite knowing his wish can't come true?

Lergen knew well the anguish of being a buffoon. He had experienced failure in his own struggle to secure peace. A path he wasn't able to pursue, and a point of true remorse for him.

The world was so vile that it made one want to vomit. Which was why it took everything the colonel had to keep his composure.

He crossed his arms and shook his head to relieve himself of his cruel imagination, but there was a thought that refused to leave.

It couldn't be. Could it?

His concern would eventually find its way to his lips.

"If our orders were to put pressure on the Ildoan capital, then it just may be viable diplomatic ammo. But what if we look at the situation with a total disregard for common sense?"

"What's that, Colonel?"

"Let's think this through, Colonel… We are currently at a standstill with the Ildoa troops, who now have the backing of the Unified States, despite having the enemy capital within firing distance."

"That is correct… Hm?"

Degurechaff then gave Lergen a look that suggested she knew where he was going.

With a difficult-to-describe expression about her, she continued.

"In normal circumstances, our current situation could be evaluated as stagnation. For we have yet to lay a finger on our should-be target, the capital."

This was what the situation would look like to untrained eyes, at the very least. The Empire had failed their mission and the Ildoan and Unified soldiers had successfully protected the capital. The newspapers would focus on the prior, without going into too much detail on the immense damage suffered to make the latter happen.

"Precisely. Even the enemy soldiers will view this as our failure to seize the capital."

"But the only reason we haven't done so is because General Zettour gave us clear orders not to. What if it's the opposite? Not that we lost our chance to attack the capital, but…?"

The two both engaged in examining the situation from a more demented perspective. What if, from the very beginning, their potential attack on the Ildoan capital was not the goal itself, but the means to achieve a different goal?

Lergen turned to Tanya, speaking in an attempt to organize his thoughts out loud.

"The Unified States will come to Ildoa's aid. The Empire will lose to the duo, who are filled with joy over the victory they earn."

This was the moment both of them realized a mistake in their train of thought.

They would experience victory, only to end in defeat.

Defeat. After the media told the world the Alliance had successfully defended the capital.

It would give them a taste of heaven before pulling them down to hell.

Essentially, the actions of a man with a wonderful personality.

"Colonel, I think I know what's going on."

"Oh? And what's that?"

Lergen's question was overshadowed by the sound of someone rushing into the tent. It was the same young officer who Lergen had sent out earlier on an errand.

"Colonel Lergen! We have emergency orders from Command…!"

"Thank you," Lergen said as he looked down at the note in his hand before telling the major to return to the communications room. Just as he was finishing reading the message, he realized Colonel Tanya was smiling to herself. "Colonel Degurechaff?"

"Let me guess. The orders are for a full-scale attack. Our target is the enemy field troops… And I'm guessing we'll be surrounding them from their flank."

Tanya easily listed her predictions, which made Colonel Lergen look from her to the paper in his hand, then back to her.

He then closed his eyes for a moment before expressing what had him so stunned.

"Did you already know these orders?"

She knew what he meant by this.

"So I am correct…?"

"You are, Colonel."

He passed her the note, which she read in a single glance before grimacing.

"He is the worst sort of con artist, isn't he?"

The general's plan was as crafty as could be, after all. According to the orders he gave, the field soldiers sent in to defend the Ildoan capital were unable to retreat for political reasons. Therefore, the Empire had successfully managed to use the capital as bait to trap the enemies in their current position.

With this in mind, there was only one plausible course of action the Imperial Army had left to take…and that was a full-scale attack. The Empire would likely allocate half of their armored forces to create an echelon to penetrate the enemy line south of the capital, taking out any field troops who would try to establish their base while posing a counterattack with any surviving troops. It was simple. Their enemy had spent the last week accumulating as much firepower as they could for one goal: to protect the capital. The Empire would, in turn, crush the culmination of all their effort in a single blow.

"We're going to crush their dream of protecting the capital."

"…We're going sweep their glorious victory right from under their feet…"

"It'll be nothing short of mental torture."

"You're right about that," Lergen agreed as he felt the lightening of his soul. "Our job is to show them this is a lost cause."

"That it's all a lost cause."

"Yes..."

Colonel Lergen then realized something unsettling as he gently shook his head.

"...So we're giving them a glorious victory, then taking it right back..."

"What's that, Colonel?"

He waved away Tanya's questioning look, swallowing the doubt in his mind before sending her off.

It wasn't something he wanted to say out loud.

That this...was exactly what had happened to the Empire.

When visiting an Ildoan Embassy:
Never ask them about their champagne
selection. This will be considered a
grievous breach of diplomatic protocol.

The Contemporary Rules of Modern Diplomacy
(Published Unified Year 1960)

Z: Hello. I'd like to make dinner reservations for tomorrow at the dining hall. Please bring your finest champagne for a celebration—something nice and bubbly. Do you have any recommendations? You know what, I think Ildoan wine would be appropriate for the occasion. I'd appreciate it if you could suggest a nice pairing for me. Let's start by hearing your recommendations for red and white wines.

T: I'm sorry, sir, but this is the Commonwealth Embassy. I believe you may have the wrong number.

Z: No, yours is the number I wanted to call. I'm calling to ask you to make arrangements for a feast tonight at the embassy. It's for the ambassador and me, after all. There should be plenty for us to discuss.

T: My apologies, but could I get your name?

Z: It's Hans. What's your name? You're on call for the embassy, and you don't know who I am?

T: Mr. Hans. I'm deeply sorry about this. Until we confirm your identity, I can't divulge any of our staff's personal information with you.

Z: You know what, I have no interest in your name. I'm simply asking to set up a dinner to commend this historic event. Is the embassy unable to host a party?

T: I'm sorry to say that our embassy in Ildoa is currently suspending operations. We're busy keeping our personnel safe and evacuating our citizens as the Empire makes their advance. Besides, I'm not even sure who exactly you are...

Z: Listen to me, boy. This is precisely why I'm trying to make a reservation. Have you no wits about you? Your teachers at secondary school would be crying if they heard this call. I feel pitiful just thinking about it.

T: What are you talking about? Are you a citizen in distress?

Z: No, no, no. Though that's what *you* may be right now.

T: Me? Is this some kind of prank call...?

Z: Goodness, not the sharpest tool in the shed, are we? Here, make sure this exact message gets to the ambassador.

T: I'm sorry, but this really sounds like someone is playing a joke on us. I'm going to hang up now.

Z: Really, now? You're going to hang up on Hans von Zettour of the Imperial Army General Staff when he's simply trying to make dinner arrangements?

T: What...? What?!

Z: This is Hans, a good friend of yours. I'm planning on having dinner tomorrow at the Ildoan Palace, and I want the ambassador to be the guest of honor. In fact, why don't you come along as well. Maybe I could teach you some manners then. Prepare yourselves to become our prisoners. Now then, I'll be seeing you tomorrow. Make sure to bring your best champagne, at the very least.

T: Excuse me? Hello? Hello?!

 DECEMBER 5, UNIFIED YEAR 1927, THE ILDOAN FRONT

General Zettour's entourage moved with incredible speed along the Imperial offensive line while on their visit under the pretense of an inspection. The group brazenly made its way to the front-most part of the line as soon as the cease-fire was lifted. Most of the officers, fearing the risk of being there, petitioned for the general to reconsider, but he paid them no mind. He had a small platoon of aerial mages guard his envoy as they continued south.

While this was no small task for the mages at hand, the fact that General Zettour was on the front lines was a sign to them that their army was in a position that allowed him to be there. His presence on the front lines was a huge boost to the troops' morale, as the Imperial Army held commanding officers who hung out in the rear in low regard.

Thus, the arrangements for his meeting with the many division commanders progressed swimmingly, and eventually, the mages charged with protecting him were finally relieved. On the other hand, his entourage of officers and those who went ahead of the procession were now busier than ever, running around to prepare for the big meeting that... they somehow managed to get done. They even managed to procure a building with a roof. Instead of a field tent, they commandeered an Ildoan school building for the meeting. With everything ready, the Imperial officers lined themselves up in the faculty room like so many elementary school teachers. As their seizure of the building was rather rushed, the room looked exactly like it had when it was a functioning school.

The aides and adjutants had cleared out textbooks and what were likely stacks of homework to make room for their maps, creating a decidedly strange setting for the war council. In what should be a place for shaping children's futures, the staff officers were ironically drawing up plans to use their own nation's youth as kindling for the bellows of war. Nevertheless, the meeting started with an upbeat tone.

"The annihilation of the enemy's field armies is progressing well."

General Zettour calmly addressed his staff from what was once the school principal's desk.

"Our forces launched an offensive the moment the cease-fire ended. We're currently silencing enemy resistance and advancing south while expanding our gains. The operation is progressing ideally."

The general's calm demeanor made it sound like he was discussing what was for dinner tomorrow, but the experts he had assembled nodded in agreement with his assessment. Each and every one of the officers in the room held General Zettour, who had all but single-handedly pulled off this unprecedented success, in the highest regard.

"The enemy numbers a hundred forty divisions on paper, but only around seventy of them are meaningfully functional. We've already attrited their strongest units with our initial assault. We gave them a week's worth of time, but it appears as if we were the ones who made the most of it."

General Rudersdorf's unforeseen postmortem attack on Ildoa was progressing surprisingly well. The confusion the higher officers had initially felt toward the strategy and command was completely absent from their faces. The fact of the matter was that the Empire was winning its campaign in Ildoa. Therefore, all General Zettour had to do for this meeting was lay out the numbers.

"We've witnessed overwhelmingly positive results by abandoning key positions and focusing purely on destroying the enemy. We have successfully reduced the enemy's strength to approximately seven divisions. In contrast, we have twenty-two divisions that are still in fighting condition. Experience is truly great, gentlemen. We are handily winning this war."

The listeners responded to Zettour's inviting words with ambiguous smiles that seemed to be a mixture of bitterness and joy. For warriors as seasoned as them, his words created an indescribable emotion.

Is victory this easy?

The attack on Ildoa was a strategic surprise. No one had foreseen the timing of its execution. Setting aside the difficulties with the seasonal weather, the Empire launched their offensive almost immediately after Ildoa announced its alliance with the Unified States, something meant to keep the Empire at bay. Stunned by the attack, Ildoa was caught off guard in the initial fighting. The weeklong cease-fire should have given the country more than enough time to reorganize its troops, and yet, the Empire still maintained its victorious position.

The secret behind the Imperial Army's success was their ability to retain the initiative while causing absolute havoc with limited resources, allowing them to devastate the enemy's forces without tying themselves down to any given location. This was a strategic victory for the Empire, something the generals were eager to praise, even if only on the inside. These gentlemen were, in the end, soldiers—generals, at that. Even if they were to allow themselves to bask in their current victory, they made sure to keep reality in the forefront of their minds.

"I have a question, General. While it's clear we've dealt the enemy field armies a crushing blow, isn't the seven divisions estimate a bit too... optimistic?"

"What makes you think that?"

"Time. It won't be long before the enemy's reserves inevitably mobilize. Furthermore, Ildoa, unlike the current combatants of this war that have exhausted a great many mages in previous battles, should have a considerable surplus of mage units."

"You're right about that. They are bringing in their reserves and deploying fresh mages as we speak. However, they will only raise their numbers."

The commanding officers showed a collective confused look at General Zettour's assertion. Evidently, his answer was beyond their imaginations.

"These new soldiers, gentlemen, will be completely unarmed."

"Unarmed? Is Ildoa having a hard time procuring equipment? Even if that is the case, it's only a matter of time before a problem like that is resolved."

"Precisely," General Zettour said. He already had the answer to that problem and gave the staff officers a light scolding. "You're right about time resolving the issue. *Somebody* will give them what they need."

This was where he corrected the gentleman.

"That time will not come as soon as you're assuming. I can promise this much, though I can't say exactly when it will be."

Now that he held everyone's attention, General Zettour paused for a moment as an easy grin appeared on his face.

"You see, we've commandeered all of their heavy equipment."

As General Zettour oversaw logistics and had a long-running insight into how his own nation functioned, he felt confident sharing his conclusion with his subordinates.

"We've taken the bedrock of their industry from them."

"Does that include their means of production?"

He nodded.

"Of course. We have secured more than ten divisions' worth of artillery along with their production lines in Northern Ildoa. We gathered enough during the cease-fire period to meet our own needs. Let's just say, it's a good thing we attacked the Ildoans before they attacked us." Though the general's eyes were roaring with laughter, he continued in a calm monotone. "If we include the outdated equipment and supplies the enemy left behind that we've destroyed, it's quite clear we acquired their newer gear."

Northern Ildoa was the nation's most developed industrial area. This applied to its infrastructure, factories, and people. Losing any one of these was a fatal blow to Ildoa's military-industrial supply chain. The Empire managed to obtain irreplaceable strategic resources that the Ildoans simply couldn't afford to lose. Their capture was more significant than it would be for the Empire to lose its industrial lowlands.

Were this any other war like the ones they had fought in the past, Ildoa's defeat would've been thoroughly decided at this point, but still they continued to resist. This was a dreadful fact—a fact that General Zettour knew in his soul that he alone regarded with true fear.

He had the misfortune of having no friends to share his concerns with, and what a lonely fate it was. He yearned for his old friend in moments like this, but this was the consequence of the crime he had committed. Therefore, the general was forced to keep his fear to himself, maintaining his composure as he pressed on with the meeting.

"We continue to enjoy local superiority."

General Zettour spoke arrogantly, just like he knew his friend Rudersdorf would have. He continued to speak with the confidence of the *fearless general*, an image he'd created for himself.

"From a purely military point of view, we have been able to enhance our ability to crush the enemy. This is a privilege that can only be capitalized on now. Therefore, we must use all our strength to cut down what remains of the enemy's field army."

Zettour paused, scanning the room for any objection. Were this politics, this would be the moment someone tried to stop him. Alas, such a sight was absent from this room. His peers watched with hopeful eyes, waiting eagerly for his next words.

Good, Zettour thought as he nodded with the slightest hint of resignation.

"Our objective is simple. We will ride this momentum to capture the Ildoan royal capital."

"Oooh!"

The room filled with a mixture of gulps and excited grunts.

Though maybe a bit repetitious, Zettour decided to drive the point home.

"Let me be clear about this: I need you all to understand that our goal is *not* to occupy their capital."

He paused, allowing the room to grow silent before sharing his intentions with them.

"Our true goal is what it has been this entire time—to defeat the enemy military. Therefore, it's important that the means serve the end. We must force the enemy into a defensive position, confining them within their capital. This is the key."

Confirming that his words had fully sunk into the minds of his commanders, General Zettour quickly shifted to discussing the situation at hand.

"As a result of repelling our reconnaissance in force elements, the enemy forces have bitten into the forbidden fruit of *belief* in their ability to defend their capital. Judging by the newspaper reports, they believe they're winning this conflict."

The Ildoan Army had managed to gain a foothold against the advancing Imperial Army. This alone was more than enough to give them a perception of impending victory. This went double for the Unified States, whose military was new to war… Its soldiers wanted to see a dream of victory.

"They snatched the bait right up from our excellent trap. The poison known as pride should be settling in their guts right about now. It's nice to know that all it takes is the wave of a hand to please these people."

They had made sacrifices for their "hard-earned" victory, so it definitely wasn't something they would give up easily. These coalition members had already won the war in their eyes, and no one was willing to let go of a victory they believed was rightfully theirs.

General Zettour was sure that both public opinion and the enemy's ego were under the intoxicating influence of the sweet ale of victory. That was what his experience in the Empire told him was happening. Even Ildoa, which adhered strictly to its raison d'état, could not escape succumbing to the monster known as public opinion. With this knowledge in mind, General Zettour was practically bragging to the staff officers.

"For the enemy, the capital is their white elephant."

It was a masterful trick the general was playing. The royal capital, in all its sanctity and status, wasn't something the enemy could allow themselves to give up without a fight. The illusion of honor was nothing more than a *nonperforming loan* that their opponents refused to abandon and would ultimately lead to their demise. History holds a wealth of knowledge to be learned from.

"The enemy will go to great lengths to protect the irreplaceable. This will prove quite painful for them, so it's only humane that we put them out of their misery."

No army would abandon the royal capital they fought tooth and nail to rescue. It was a well-known fact that soldiers were reluctant to even reorganize the front line if it meant abandoning a position they believed they were holding on to. The Imperial staff officers knew this well, which was why there was no room for misinterpreting General Zettour's intentions. Their goal was to destroy the enemy field army, and the royal capital was nothing more than a prop.

It turned out to be a younger, sharper officer who first raised his hand in question.

"I have a question."

"Go ahead."

"Will we be withdrawing from the capital once we take it over? If our primary targets are the field armies, I feel as if abandoning the capital early may be prudent, depending on the scenario."

"Ahh." Zettour gave the young commander a warm nod. "That's a fantastic question."

It was a highly applicable question, given the parameters the commanding officers had to engage with the problem, one that showed Zettour that his war experts were brilliant in their own right. At the same time, such a question appeared to be the best they could come up with, so Zettour simply gave them the answer he already had in mind.

"To be square with you, it's hard to tell at the moment."

"Do you mean to say you're trying to have it both ways if you can, sir?"

The younger commander gave Zettour a dubious look, which was met with a shrug of the shoulders and jest.

"Withdrawing after our occupation is something I am indeed considering. Ultimately, if it comes down to deciding between land or troops, we will prioritize defeating the enemy's troops. However, taking their capital would be akin to taunting the world with a red matador cape. This is something I want to take advantage of, if possible." The general maintained his composed tone. "That's why we're merely going to run the auction on the city, as far as I'm concerned. If the enemy takes the bait and is willing to place a high bid, we'll squeeze every last coin out of them before handing over the remains. We want to sell for the highest price possible."

Zettour then took out a cigar, as if to signify it was time for a smoke break. He took a few moments to scan the room once more to be certain that his words were settling in before proceeding once more.

"Everything depends on whether or not the enemy is willing to place a bid in the first place."

Zettour spoke as if he was a detached observer.

"If the New World, namely, the Unified States military, shows no interest, then there is no need for us to be a stickler about holding on to an empty capital. The city will have its peace, and it will amount to a slap in the face for us."

The most important thing for Zettour was that his opponents took this bait. If the enemy showed no interest in the capital, then he would have to figure out a way to *make* them interested.

It was his strategy against the world. He would lie and con every single person on the face of the planet if he had to. In the name of love and duty, Zettour would commit any deed necessary for the sake of the Empire.

"Whatever the case may be, the overarching objective of this campaign is to solidify the Empire's borders."

This was a big, fat lie, of course, but it came out smooth as silk.

"And our army has already achieved the first step toward this goal. We've already won."

Thieves tend to be liars before ever becoming thieves.

Zettour knew that his words were brazen lies—that they were empty. He thought about how much his imbecile of a friend Rudersdorf must have acted the part...about how vulnerable he must have been behind his always-tough exterior. Zettour felt so alone.

What caused the general the most fear and sadness was how deeply moved he could tell his commanders were just by looking at their faces. He met their shower of compliments and commendation with what could only be described as a vague expression. He had no qualms about fooling the world, but it was different when he had to deceive his own family. Nevertheless, this was his sin—his duty—to shoulder. He swallowed his doubts and continued to speak without batting an eye.

"We've delivered a heavy blow to our enemy, particularly the Ildoans. Our occupation of the north will impact not only the strategic depth of our campaign down the peninsula, but also the Ildoan Army's industrial foundation itself."

This campaign was the Empire's first success in a long time, which must've been why his speech was being received so well by the commanders.

Perhaps it was a sign of their confidence when it came to the realm of pure military tactics. Their expressions caused Zettour to let out an ever-so-slight yet strained smile.

"What's this? You're grinning, General."

Zettour waved away the jovial remark.

"Sometimes it can be difficult to keep everything bottled up inside."

He and his audience shared big smiles with bright and shiny faces. Was the mood due to their presence in Ildoa? If that was the case, then Zettour worried he might really end up harboring a true hatred for this country…even if this attack was his own fault.

"I'm glad we came here."

"General?"

"The air is clean. It's quite refreshing. And the weather makes you remember when we used to come out here to escape the Empire's bitter winters. But best of all, there's a war for us to win. I can't imagine there's a better place for us to be right now."

The entire room burst out in laughter. These grown men guffawed like young children. The general sat down in the school principal's chair, watching his comrades engage in friendly banter. Nobody made an attempt to hold back their unbridled laugher in the school building. It was a good spot for the middle-aged military men to share a dream of victory, this school building in a faraway land. Would these men—the Empire—be able to defy the laws of nature?

Ah, if only I were younger…

Zettour wore a wistful smile. It was clear to him that he had pretended to be human for too long—he hardly considered himself a person anymore. He didn't know whether to grieve, sneer, or laugh about this.

So instead, he simply shook his head and banished those unnecessary thoughts. He reached for his army tobacco and began smoking. The puffs of smoke he exhaled conveyed an annoyance he couldn't express with words while he waited for the room to calm down before rising suddenly with the cigarette still in his mouth. Once he had everyone's attention, he spoke again.

"Now that we've won the first phase, the goal for the second phase is to establish a defensive line."

The assembled commanders gave him a knowing look. They all nodded to show they understood. To put it plainly, now that the threat to the south had been greatly reduced, the Empire needed to firmly secure its new territories. The problem was what came thereafter.

"We shall secure a deep foothold in the Ildoan peninsula. I'd like to create an environment where we can focus purely on the eastern front."

They were going to transfer their military from Ildoa to the other front after their victory. The dogma of the interior lines strategy was certainly familiar to military generals who had served in previous wars.

"That said, I won't hesitate if we can cut down our enemy when given the chance. It's always ideal to make the enemy pay dearly with minimal sacrifice on our part." Zettour intentionally showed his commanders a wicked grin. "That's why we'll be sure to teach the Ildoan upstarts a lesson before we head back east. The same goes for our friends from the New World. They must learn firsthand why the Empire should be feared. Therefore, I wish for each of you to understand that our attack on the Ildoan capital is nothing more than a small bonus for us."

It was a little treat for the Empire while they solidified their southern border. They would use their power to menace their enemies—that was all, really. Though it sounded simple, this would challenge each commanding officer to carefully weigh when to advance and when to pull back...a challenge each of Zettour's staff officers would be more than willing to take on. He could tell there was no need to be concerned after giving the room a quick scan before taking his seat in the principal's chair yet again.

He continued to smoke his tobacco while answering a few follow-up questions. With that, this meeting came to an end without a mountain of ash piling up in the ashtrays. The empty ashtrays marked a peaceful meeting, one without shouting, anguish, or idle complaints about difficult tasks. Nothing like victory and quick progress to bring people together. It was evident that victory was a panacea that solved all problems. That was why it was so alluring during times of war. A military victory relieved an array of maladies and soothed otherwise unendurable pain, even if that comfort was fleeting.

That being said, it could be difficult to swallow a victory at times. From General Zettour's perspective, much of what he claimed to be in the name of victory was nothing more than a secondary objective plastered in a veneer of military rationale. Sweet, sugar-coated logic that made the pill easier to swallow for Imperial soldiers. The medicine they needed to take was a far cry from true victory. The reality was that Zettour personally sought to dig deeper into the abyss to establish a foxhole from which he would launch a much craftier assault.

He had no interest in whether or not the attack on the royal capital was a success. His only intention was to entangle the Unified States in this war to create a convenient, new enemy. He knew most of his commanding officers wouldn't be able to understand why. This was because it was more of a swindle than a feat of military might. A cool, wicked plot that would invoke an emotional response from his enemies...a political ploy.

Soldiers, especially Imperial soldiers, who knew little of politics, refused to pay any attention to the very politics that determined the fate of their nation. That was why their smiling faces seemed so bright to Zettour. He loathed the sight, though he didn't know why... Perhaps it was a manifestation of his own weakness.

After the meeting came to its end, the officers left the school building in groups of twos and threes, while General Zettour walked toward a vehicle that had come to pick him up...alone. Neither his adjutant nor any other staff officer was with him. Even his security detail of mages had been sent home. It wasn't a sight befitting the deputy director.

The car he was being driven around in was a small, civilian vehicle that he had one of his orderlies scrounge up. The Ildoan car he had commandeered was built for comfort and certainly wasn't poorly made. It was not, however, the type of car one would expect the grand, wicked ringleader of the Imperial Army to be riding in.

It was like a game of pretend, where the army made use of what it had available to act out a campaign of military intrigue, and *this* was the supposed mastermind who was shaking up northern Ildoa? He didn't want to imagine how they would ridicule him in the history books. The military needed to do something about their chronic lack of funds, even if only in appearance.

I need to show history…the world…an illusion…

With that, Zettour realized that he was going to need to fool himself before he did the world. And the amazing road they were driving down certainly didn't make it easy! He sat in the back of the small car, pretending to enjoy his cigar while feeling utterly disgusted by the comfortable road he was being driven down. The pavement. The immaculate townscape. The beautiful, colorful buildings. Everything was different from the Empire. Different from the burnt-out Reich over which the sun was quickly setting.

He hated to admit it, but…

"Why is it so different? Where did we go wrong…?"

The Empire was good at one thing—the military—which left the fatherland in a bland shade of gray. The Ildoans' military was weak, riddled with waste. But their towns? Compared to the military superpower that was the Empire, they were incredible.

There was a time, once, when this color could be seen on Imperial streets as well. Zettour and his ilk had drained all the color from the fatherland.

Had they, the military, made a grave error in judgment when it came to prioritizing what needed protecting? The general was overcome by a chilling emptiness as he had this thought. The Ildoans used what little military power they had for politics. Conversely, the Empire used its oversized military might without paying politics any heed, and this was what had brought the two nations to where they stood today.

Zettour, sitting alone in the back of the comically tiny car, wondered whether or not the other staff officers realized the difference in color.

"Nobody questions this…"

He grumbled this to himself, but he knew it needed to be said aloud.

The Empire needed to know that all that effort it put into war was coming back to bite it in the ass.

"It's worse than that…"

Imperial soldiers weren't idiots. If push came to shove, they could grasp the importance of politics, on a surface level at the very least. Even then, that was only if they were forced to. It would never occur to them to use politics on the battlefield.

"This is proper for an Imperial soldier."

Zettour refrained from saying any more in the presence of his driver, but he couldn't help but lament how unfortunate the situation was. It was okay to be wrong on occasion! The ability to know what was wrong, to allow for error, was what made everyone human, and what allowed them to live in peace.

He couldn't stop a sigh from escaping his mouth. The entire world was far too entwined in this war. With the Empire being long past the point of no return, Zettour was forced to focus on his countrymen facing a national crisis back home. Things were getting far too out of hand. The military experts he had around him were focused on nothing more than how to win the battle at hand. War, however, wasn't fought purely on the battlefield.

"This is total war, after all…"

The general sighed and shook his head. Total war. Totality included public image, mythos, and especially acting—when necessary.

"We have the numerical advantage and enjoy local superiority…"

The Empire was in a superior position all around the country, a fact that left the general feeling a nihilistic and cruel emptiness. In the east, the balance of power was critical. In the west, they had been forced to go on the defensive. As their enemies pinched them from either side, Zettour couldn't think of a single way to flip the hourglass that counted down to his nation's demise. Objectively, the localized superiority they enjoyed meant little to nothing in the grand scheme of things.

The general folded his arms.

Then again, objectively speaking, the inner workings of the Imperial Army weren't out in the open for a third party to judge on the Ildoan front.

"The Ildoan front is one of our last stages, and world news agencies are always looking for more juicy stories."

The general was ready to trick the entire world. He was going to be the clown that twisted the world like one big animal balloon.

"I need to put on a good show for them."

His casual monologue perfectly captured the situation he was in. He had come up with a new idea, the sort born from raw necessity. Knowing now what must be done made what he would do next unavoidable. The general spent his ride back to headquarters obsessively thinking up what kind of dastardly trick he could play.

This was a tall task but…there was a good precedent for what he wanted to do. Though it was a bit of an embarrassing memory for him, he decided to take a page from young Lieutenant Colonel Degurechaff's book and *announce* his attack.

The same way she did back in Moskva. This was ideal. He chuckled as he remembered the announcement she made to Dacia. He would take a page from her book, combining the two attacks.

All General Zettour needed to do was play his role well, and it would be perfect. Well, more like his clear insight forced him to accept the sad fact that *playing the part* was the only option left for him.

With this resolution in his heart, he finally returned to the temporary headquarters, where he was escorted by guards to his next location. There he found his trusted subordinate, Lieutenant Colonel Uger, waiting with everything prepared perfectly for his return. There was so much moving around on the front line, and despite sudden changes in plans having become a daily occurrence, the temporary command headquarters was fully equipped with all the necessary functions to smoothly operate the army's command system, and this was all thanks to none other than Colonel Uger.

"Colonel Uger, perfect timing. I need you to set up an itinerary for me."

"Okay, I'm assuming there was a change in plans?"

Uger's honest response to please his superior was met with the casual dropping of a bomb on Zettour's part.

"Send a message to the commanders on the field. Tell them to begin operations. Let them know that I will be on the field as well. That is all."

"Y-you'll be on the field…?"

Uger had learned to have certain expectations for what the general was going to ask. His intuition was right about it being trouble, to say the least. The order made him visibly wince, something he knew wasn't appropriate. He quickly collected himself, putting on his best face for the general.

Zettour watched the show he'd put on for him, laughing it off.

With resolution in his heart and a false sense of playfulness, he was going to toy with the world.

"Get me a telephone."

He picked up the transmitter with a grin and called the operator. He made sure to follow the rules set by the military, though his call was hardly going to be official business—not for the army, at least. Zettour was using the phone for something personal. Seeing as it was a part of his grand scheme to deceive the world, his personal call could be seen as patriotic—superficially, at least. That said, could a personal call like this be placed while he was on duty? Even during times of peace, this was certainly breaking a litany of rules and regulations—this was during an operation in wartime. The call definitely wasn't something that would ever make it through the system.

But the general was allowed to proceed.

"Headquarters? Yes, it's me."

A request was all it took. He didn't even need to explain himself. The usually particular phone operators didn't say a peep when it was a general—the deputy director, no less—on the line. Zettour was in charge of communications, after all, which was why they didn't pry into his business, and why General Zettour was allowed to proceed with his soon-to-be historic phone call.

"Do you have their number in Ildoa? Yes, thank you."

He asked them to transfer him, and his request was fulfilled without hesitation. He was placing a call to the Commonwealth Embassy in Ildoa.

"I wonder how the ambassadors will react."

To be frank, while Zettour recognized how childish he was being, he placed his hopes in the wit of whoever ended up taking his call—the same kind of hope a child might have when they go see what's inside a toy box. He would try to stand out even more than he probably needed to, given the circumstances. The Commonwealth diplomats having a little awareness shouldn't be too much to ask for.

General Zettour, however, placed the phone back down with a bored look on his face.

"The Commonwealth has been at war for far too long. To think that lot of tea-chugging gents would ever lose their sense of humor."

The general grumbled to himself. He knew it was arrogant for him to think his fun trick would play out smoothly, without a single issue. Either way, he left the call learning one thing: that he didn't have the power to govern fate. A single call was all it took for him to understand this.

He could move freely through the bureaucracy of his own army. His prowess and skill allowed him to turn the military officials and their regulations upside down as he saw fit. Even then, heaven had forsaken him. For even if by coincidence, his foreign counterparts never seemed to meet his expectations.

"Well, that man sure was a stickler for the rules. Must still be wet behind the ears. I hope he's there tomorrow…"

The person he had spoken with was one of the Commonwealth's bureaucrats—a group once known for their quick-wittedness—and yet, not even they could supply him with entertainment.

He let out a sigh upon this sad realization, before Colonel Uger, who'd been watching this entire time, finally exclaimed to the general.

"G-G-General! You just divulged classified information by telling them we're going to attack!"

That was arguably the correct reaction to have at a time like this. It was clear to Zettour that Uger was being completely serious by the look on his face. Though he was a highly capable officer, he was still naive when it came to things outside of his area of expertise.

"Are you familiar with theater?"

"What's that have to do with—?"

"It's important to understand the meaning of plot, or perhaps I should call it the intricacies of human psychology."

"General?!"

Colonel Uger's panicked shout was met with a casual shrug. The colonel was acting so human and naive, with his obsession over always being serious and sane. The colonel's lack of experience almost made the general want to laugh.

At the same time, in comparison to Hans von Zettour, his purity almost shined like a bright light. His subordinate's ability to maintain his sense of right and wrong made Zettour feel a bit jealous—even if it was out of inexperience.

The general had been whittling away at his own soul all day long, so he opted to shake his head and stop himself from thinking any deeper about the subject. Instead, he explained the context of his actions in a way that Colonel Uger would understand.

"I, a well-known con artist, called the enemy's supreme commander. And not even to Ildoa, but to the Commonwealth Embassy."

"I have no idea what you're trying to do…"

"Exactly. And neither does the enemy."

"What?"

Colonel Uger stared blankly; he was likely very confused—the same exact response Zettour intended for his enemies to have as well. He could only hope that was exactly how they were feeling at this moment.

They needed to think of him as an eccentric, inscrutable figure.

"It feels strange to not understand something, I imagine. Doubt is a breeding ground for more questions, and more doubt."

This was how anxiety was created, and anxiety gave birth to fear. Zettour wanted them to fear him—not the Empire, but he himself.

"It's the Commonwealth we're dealing with here. They take pride in their espionage. With the ghost of possibility haunting them, their thinking will grow rigid."

It was a small trick in his enemy's territory of expertise, as low-budget a production as it was. Nothing more than a quick con, and a dirty one at that, not something a respectable general would ever employ. But for Zettour, who loved his nation, he needed to use any card he could play. Logic and logic alone defined his actions. He gave a self-deprecating laugh to Uger and continued.

"The goddess of fate has forsaken me, after all."

"General?"

"As long as I leave nothing to luck, then I can win."

It was hard to tell if he said this in self-admonition or deprecation. It was an unconscious confession of how he truly felt. Though, after saying it aloud, he had no choice but to be conscious of it. Zettour took the resentment that had become pent-up in his heart and cursed his enemies.

"I'm taking out my frustration on those damn Albion diplomats."

"You are?"

"In the way a gentleman would. They do love their espionage, so I gave them something to think long and hard about. Mighty gentlemanly of me, if I do say so myself."

Colonel Uger, showing a look of utter defeat, had many things he wanted to say. This was no mystery to General Zettour, who carried on before the colonel could get a word in edgewise.

"Well, we can't let them have all the fun now, can we? We have to enjoy ourselves, too."

Zettour invited the staff officer, who looked appalled by all of this, to play a nasty game.

"And what do we do best? War is to the Empire as espionage is to the Commonwealth. Let's have some fun with this."

Colonel Uger squinted at Zettour as if his eyes were out of focus, which was when Zettour nonchalantly announced...

"I'm going to see the battlefield for myself, and I have the best seats in the house. I'll be a spectator as well as an actor on the stage of history."

Though Colonel Uger's confusion was reaching a boiling point, talk of seeing the battlefield was clear-cut enough for him to get an idea of what the general was getting at.

"I'm sorry, but what exactly are you trying to do, General?"

Zettour smiled widely as he gave his subordinate the declaration of intent he had been asking for.

"The front lines need to be visited every once in a while."

"Do you realize what you are saying, General?! Without you, the chain of command will...!"

Again, this was the correct argument to make, for the correct reason. Zettour's logic affirmed Colonel Uger's words in the fullest. But, alas, the times were changing. With the flames of total war burning away at the general, there was no argument to be made. Words and rationale didn't matter—the general needed to shock the world.

"We need to kill what people call fate. It is man who creates history, and we're going to let that damn goddess know it."

Which is why I ask you, world, to fall for this trick. I need you to recognize me as the enemy.

>>>>   THE SAME DAY, AT THE SALAMANDER KAMPFGRUPPE IN   <<<<
                                THE IMPERIAL VANGUARD

When problems occur, it's almost always out in the field. However, the root of the problem may lie elsewhere. In fact, those out in the field are oftentimes innocent victims. Major Weiss wrestles with this strange sentiment in real time when he hears the dreadful news. And how does he receive said news? Well, his expression alone is worth a thousand words—the major's agape mouth is the picture of disbelief.

"What?! He's coming to…rally the troops…?!"

"That's right," I say with a nod. I've never seen Major Weiss this thrown off by anything before. Evidently, he's having a hard time accepting this is happening. His reaction makes sense, since it really is unbelievable. I'll have to lay it out for him as clearly as possible.

"General Zettour wishes to inspect our forces. Here, with us."

"Wh-why here?! We're as far forward as you can get?!"

The first officer's doubts are legitimate. The Kampfguppe has continued to advance to stay close to the Ildoan troops, poised to attack whenever the orders arrive.

We're standing in the eye of the storm. A bad place to be for a certain someone who is trying to come at a time like this. If only this were a scene out of a novel. It's almost difficult for me to maintain my composure as this disaster is about to befall Tanya and her troops.

"Calm yourself, Major Weiss. I'm well aware that this isn't some military parade back at the capital."

"Then you need to change his mind! If anyone can convince him, it's you!"

"I won't be able to."

My first officer isn't going to give up easily, but a wave of my hand is all it takes to let the major know resistance is futile.

"You must remember this, Major. General Zettour is a completely different species."

"You make it sound like he's an animal... Either way, coming to the front lines is far too dangerous."

"You're not wrong about that. Scouts are a daily occurrence where we are. A sniper would cry tears of joy if they caught a glimpse of the general." I cross my arms and sigh. "But tell me, do you think that means anything to the man? Do you honestly believe he'd change his mind over something so glaringly obvious?"

It's easy for me to picture the general dancing his way to the front lines fully aware of this fact. General Zettour is an intelligent and understanding man. On top of that, he's always given Tanya a fair shake. This makes him a superior who's hard to come by.

He has but one fault—and a critical one at that—in the form of his overbearing love. He loves his nation, the fatherland, and other imagined communities far too much. From my perspective, this isn't rational by any means. Which is why, on occasion, it is difficult for me to understand General Zettour's motives. Being unable to discern my superior's thoughts is a point of distress. There are times when she just can't come to an agreement with his actions.

"We must accept the fact that there are people out there willing to dive even deeper into the front line than us if deemed necessary."

The general is, in effect, a warmonger. In fact, he may well have morphed into something even more severe by now. Honestly speaking, I've always thought of General Zettour as an intellectual associate on a personal level... Has the stress finally gotten to him? This is yet another testament to the cruelty of war. Be that as it may, Major Weiss disparaging the top of their organization is disrespectful, even if he is Tanya's number two. Realizing that there isn't much use in trying to pull the wool over his eyes, I take on a tone that won't sound too severe.

"I, too, have a hard time believing a man of his intellect would ever do this... Something tells me he wants to see live combat as opposed to a conventional inspection."

"I just can't believe it. Does he think he can leisurely walk into the front line like this?"

"Remember the eastern front. There's a chance he'll happily pick up a gun."

Chapter **III**

"It's scary, but I think you're right."

I nod, fully in agreement.

"It's the general we're dealing with here. If there's a stage and a podium, there's a good chance he'll take it."

Major Weiss winces. He looks like he has something more to say but swallows it. Perhaps he's finally facing reality. With that, my first officer and I silently accept our predetermined fates and mobilize to get things done.

First things first. We hold a meeting with the officers who share the responsibility of hosting the general. This much should be obvious, but none of the officers are elated to hear the *worst news of the day*—that General Zettour will be inspecting the front line. Captain Ahrens gazes up at the sky in disbelief while Captain Meybert keeps himself propped up on a cannon. First Lieutenant Tospan distracts himself from reality with meticulous plans to fortify the current positions. Perhaps each of them represents their branch of the army with their different reactions, but regardless, they're still soldiers. Knowing the inevitable gives them the chance to steel their nerves, at the very least.

Tanya von Degurechaff is a being from another world. She has a second set of values that she can compare and contrast with the Empire's militarism. A set of values constructed in a peaceful, civilized society, with exceedingly unremarkable norms. This set of values is what allows her to be certain that if she has to choose between going to war and placating her superior, then ten out of ten times, she will choose her superior. That isn't to say that it is ever enjoyable to have your work schedule thrown for a spin, but she understands that freedom isn't something a person who is part of an organization can enjoy forever.

Everything comes with a price. For the army during a time of war, the sad fact is that freedom is far too extravagant to afford. When it comes down to the two options of combat and entertaining a superior, it isn't a difficult choice; of course Tanya chooses her superior. Who wouldn't? Entertaining a boss is ten billion times easier than assaulting an enemy base.

This is why I have a smile on my face when it's my turn to see the general. My people and I stand up as straight as we can to welcome him. It isn't too big of a deal for an upstanding member of society to line up with my subordinates to welcome guests.

This is what I tell myself as the general and his entourage appear, traveling surprisingly light. There aren't even that many of them to start. His security detail consists of nothing more than a few military police on bikes. As for the bike the general is riding, it appears to be a civilian vehicle. It isn't difficult for me to imagine the gastrointestinal pain his entourage collectively feels. I can almost feel it just looking at them.

The scariest part, however, is the general's expression as he dismounts the bike. With a smile on his face that is comparable only to the bright Ildoan sun shining down on us, General Zettour appears to be as happy as can be.

"Why, hello there, Colonel. I couldn't be happier to see you on this fine day."

He offers a wave with the same friendly smile. What's more, he practically skips right up to me. Something about it all feels like an act. I can hear an alarm going off in the back of my mind. It's the same level of danger I feel when an air control operator suddenly changes his tone and calls for an emergency scramble to respond to the highest threat level.

"How have you been? It feels like a nice spring day, despite it being winter."

"Why hello, General!" With every cell in my body on high alert, I answer in the most diplomatic way possible. "It must be this amazing weather, but you look so vibrant. It makes me so happy that you're here to see us!"

An eye for an eye, a tooth for a tooth. A smile needs to be met with an even bigger smile, and empty, flowery words will be met with more over-the-top gestures.

"Well, that sure is nice of you to say. How have things been lately?"

"We have a lot to worry about due to this incessant sunshine. The unfortunate lack of clouds makes for great artillery weather."

General Zettour quietly listens and acknowledges Tanya's concerns.

"I suppose even good weather comes with its disadvantages. Though, you must admit that it is beautiful here, is it not?"

"What do you mean?"

"This is the prettiest time of year, just before the flower petals begin to fall."

This comment is so jarring that it becomes incredibly difficult to maintain my smile. What an ominous thing to say. There certainly is an elegance to the falling of beautiful flowers, but it's a bit strange coming from the man wielding a chainsaw in Ildoa's proverbial garden.

"The flowers we're here to pluck? It makes me sad to see them go."

"So sentimental. You're an elegant little flower petal on the battlefield yourself."

The only way I can respond to the light teasing is to act dejected.

"I'm nothing compared to you, sir…"

"Why do you say that? I'm trying to pay you a compliment."

"And it is an honor! But I'm merely one more soldier. A cog in the machine, loyal to my nation's will. I'm nothing in your presence."

I bear no responsibility for this! I'm simply following my legal orders! Anyone who's studied law knows these words hold little water in a court. Anyone who's studied a bit of law *history*, however, benefits from knowing how the laws changed over time.

For example, the phrase "I was only following orders." This was used by both sides of the First World War as a justification by various people on trial for war crimes. It was used so much, in fact, that it created the need for a court where such an excuse wasn't enough. A court that wouldn't be established…until the *next* major war. Which is why I, currently mired in the first of said wars, am not too worried about it. My use of this phrase is perfect. An ounce of prevention is worth a pound of cure.

While I mull over all this as a form of escapism, General Zettour ruthlessly forces me to face reality.

"I'm glad it's an honor for you. This may be the last beautiful flower season Ildoa sees for a while, but that's none of our business. I want you to really rough them up."

The gaze he shoots me makes it clear there's no way to worm my way out of this one.

Yes is the only acceptable answer. Keeping this insight to myself, I maintain my dignified posture, standing at attention exactly the way it's shown in military textbooks.

"Just give the command, sir."

"And so I shall. The orders should be on their way now. Our priority is to devastate our enemies."

When it's put as clearly as that, the boots on the ground aren't left with much of a choice. I prepare to accept the unavoidable orders.

"Understood. Well then, General, I must go command the vanguard."

Now, if you excuse... Before I can say goodbye, the Empire's highest-ranking general appears to hold his left hand out toward me with a smile.

I stare at the extended empty hand, and Zettour grins.

"Before you leave, there's something I want from you."

I don't even have time to get a *huh* out.

"I need bodyguards, Colonel Degurechaff. For my security detail... I understand it's a bit unreasonable to insist on something so difficult, so I'll make do with a single mage company. Please make the necessary arrangements."

Bodyguards.

An entire company's worth.

At a time like this.

The words appear in my brain with a size and intensity that's equal to the shock I'm feeling. This is an earth-shattering request.

"What was that officer's name...? Ah, Grantz. Lend me the first lieutenant. It should be easier for me to work with him as he understands my temperament."

"General, if I may... I've only just received orders from you to attack the enemy. You made it clear that their destruction takes priority over all else, correct?"

I object... Even if there's only of a fraction of a chance of him changing his mind...I need to take it. I'll do everything in my power to resist this. Such is the nature I've acquired resisting with all my might in a futile war.

"That's correct. I need you to accomplish both orders."

I let out a sigh. I know how these things work. These are orders, and he is Tanya's superior. This explains why he came here without much of a security detail. He planned on acquiring one at his destination, which is why he brought the bare minimum for the trip here, and it falls on Tanya to provide it for him, as per direct orders.

In the Imperial Army, General Zettour's orders are law. Thus, there is only one thing a middle manager in Tanya's position can do, and that is deliver promptly without question.

It only takes a glance up at the general to realize that, in contrast to the big smile on his face, there isn't a hint of a smile in his eyes.

This isn't an environment where she can cry out, "Nein!"[1]

As much as a headache this is for her, she must comply.

"Bring Lieutenant Grantz to me! General Zettour is calling for him!"

Lieutenant Grantz, who'd been studying the war map, was suddenly overcome by a hard-to-describe chill that caused him to let out a strange cry.

"Whoa!"

The first lieutenant felt the chill creep down his spine. Even if this was Ildoa, it was still almost winter. While the time of year could have explained the strange feeling, there nevertheless was something ominous about the sensation as he took his eyes off the map and reached for a warm drink.

"Lieutenant Grantz…? Are you all right?"

"Ah, yeah. I felt strange for a second there. I'm fine, though."

Grantz waved off First Lieutenant Tospan's concerned look while he drank the warm tea.

"It was just a shake. The sun may be warm, but the air's still cold outside."

"Maybe you should see the doctor."

"It's just a random shiver. If I went to see the doctor every time I felt cold, I'd be stuck in the medical tent."

---

[1] Tanya wants to say *NO!* but she knows she can't. Not to her boss. She's his sycophant, like a true-blue middle manager.

"Nothing wrong with spending a cold winter in bed now, is there?"

"The only real winter threat is the Kampfgruppe leader."

"Good one!"

Ha-ha-ha. The two first lieutenants shared a brief laugh before focusing on the map once more. It was important for them to keep the map as updated as possible since the battlefield continued to change by the minute. It was their duty to keep the freshest version of the map memorized at all times. It took quite a bit of focus to do this, which the two maintained by sipping the cheap tea that came with their rations, making sure to load it with sugar while they scanned the map. This time, however, it didn't seem like there were any major changes since they last did this sugar-charged ritual. They didn't expect the enemy to move anytime soon.

Once they finished updating the map, they would have some time to themselves. They could enjoy some of the snacks they'd purchased with their own money to go with the tea rations, and maybe even play some cards if they could find enough people. In this way, their job was easy. Once they were finished with the map, only Captain Meybert and Captain Ahrens would need to bring it to the headquarters.

The first lieutenants had a bit more leeway in their schedules, which was nice as they could take some time to relax.

This, of course, was bearing in mind that General Zettour was visiting the Salamander Kampfgruppe—there was a unique tension spread throughout the camp. Grantz, who had no aspirations to rise through the ranks, was resigned to letting the higher-ups deal with the general, though.

The majors, colonels, and generals would be in charge of tending to the general, while Grantz and Tospan hung back and handled the rank and file. They had no business mingling with the nobility, save for the off moments at military parades. Even then, they would only see them from the parade lines.

There was no need to go out of his way to see the general unless he was particularly keen on brown-nosing.

Grantz took another look at the map, committing each and every geographical feature to memory... As bland a job as it may be, he found comfort in it.

Chapter III

In a word, it was tranquil. In more words, he was a man who liked structure, and he couldn't ask for anything more predictable than a post like this! The good soldier that he was, Grantz was even able to find a sense of fulfillment in this position. Which was only natural, as this comfortable job was his and he made sure to do it well.

Being able to mess around with Tospan over some card afterward was just a bonus. After finishing up, the two of them set out to find the other soldiers to join them in a game, but they ended up being stopped by a single soldier, who came right over to them. For Grantz, who motioned to invite the soldier to their card game, what came out of the soldier's mouth was like a bolt from the blue.

The soldier came with orders for Grantz to report to the Kampfgruppe HQ. Orders like these were usually given over the radio if they were urgent. The fact that a soldier relayed the message verbally usually meant that it wasn't too high priority. What was strange was that the soldier came on a bike with a sidecar to bring Grantz back with him.

"Did something happen to the colonel?"

He asked the driver of the bike, but he was informed that it was the colonel who called for his presence. Being the experienced officer he was, this was enough for Grantz to know that either new enemy troops had arrived in their area of operations or there was a change in strategy. There was also a chance their battalion was volunteering to participate in a major offensive.

Whichever the case may be, there was a reason the wise Lieutenant Colonel Degurechaff chose not to use the radio to contact him. Something big was happening. This much was certain. Whatever that may be, Grantz's experience allowed him to predict that he would need to be ready for it.

His long-sought peaceful sabbath would have to wait. Grantz could feel that an intense job was coming on the horizon, and being the impressive soldier he was, he wouldn't retreat from his duty. He took a deep breath. This was all it took for him to steel his nerves. No matter what the task was, he refused to falter. It was his way of preparing himself for battle; nothing could shatter his mental armor now.

Ready for whatever trials and tribulations awaited him and his companions, he entered the tent only to be immediately met by a wall of tension that could be cut with a knife. What shocked him the most was the stiff expression the commander showed, as if she had an intense decision to make. This was enough to terrify Grantz.

What could possibly make Colonel Degurechaff look like this?!

It was only her and her first officer, Major Weiss, in the room. It must be something highly classified. And yet, while these thoughts ran through his head, a new question tugged at his mind.

If this was the case, why had someone like him been called here? Why not Captains Meybert or Ahrens, or any of the other first lieutenants?

Just as the confusion was setting in, his superior turned to him with a smile.

"First Lieutenant Grantz. Congratulations."

"What?"

"You've been selected by my superior… He's taken a liking to you."

Grantz stared blankly at his own superior when he felt a hand clapping onto his shoulder. Startled, he turned to find the face of an older gentleman. He must've completely hidden his presence, because Grantz didn't realize there was anybody behind him until that very moment…which only added to his confusion, but this was when he realized he recognized this face.

And before his brain could even fully manifest an answer, it instinctually shifted to reject whatever reality this was in an instant.

Sadly for him, soldiers are a part of an organization with strict standards. He averted his gaze, only for his eyes to fall on the gentleman's lapel, which clearly showed the rank insignia that decorated it.

With the *general* insignia triggering his instincts, Grantz stood at attention. This conditioning was likely a product of Lieutenant Colonel Degurechaff's training.

He turned his entire person around on his heel, standing up straight in attention. This much done all on autopilot, Grantz's consciousness itself finally caught up to who exactly the gentleman was.

"Hello there, Lieutenant. I haven't seen you since the eastern front. How have you been?"

General Hans von Zettour addressed Grantz with a smile, which would be a blessing for anyone with aspirations to climb the ranks.

Aspirations First Lieutenant Grantz didn't have.

"Ah, I, uh…"

Perhaps having pity on her subordinate, who was clearly at a loss for words, or maybe as a friend, Degurechaff jumped in to take the focus off Grantz.

"General, please try not to bully Lieutenant Grantz."

"I'm simply greeting an acquaintance of mine. You know, there aren't that many pleasantries left for a man my age to enjoy. I have to keep my nerves sharp somehow, don't I?"

"As I am still young, I tend to sympathize with the trials of the younger soldiers."

Grantz had seen his superior's heroism on the battlefield many a time, but seeing her fight like this in an official capacity was deeply moving. Watching her provide cover fire like this made her seem like a shining beacon of light—her back imposing and powerful despite her small frame.

"You've got me there. Well, let us get to the thick of things."

The general nodded nonchalantly—his easygoing attitude suggested this whole exchange was well practiced…which quickly brought Grantz back to his initial question.

Why had he been called here? He had an inkling…and if he was anywhere close to the mark, then Grantz would have to pray that his worst fears wouldn't come true.

This short-lived hope that this was in any way possible was ruthlessly shattered by his benevolent superior.

"Even among my battalion, First Lieutenant Grantz is one of my most capable mages. That being said, he leaves much to be desired in terms of attentiveness and organization. He is not fit to be an attendant or first officer, in my opinion, which is why you should perhaps reconsider…"

"Are you recommending against using a hunting dog as a sheepdog?"

"This particular hound is a bit too finicky to be a sheepdog."

"Oh? It sounds like you wish to say…that Lieutenant Grantz isn't fit to be my personal guard?"

Grantz, who couldn't flat out say he didn't want to do it, could only stare hopefully at Lieutenant Colonel Degurechaff, who was evidently willing to go up against the nobility for the sake of her subordinates.

"I do question whether or not he is suitable for the role. The mages who make up my battalion are more like the tips of spears. Even when it comes to defense, they use not a shield but their honed points."

"That's fine by me."

"Different mages have different aptitudes, is all I wish to say."

The proud commander of the Salamander Kampfgruppe made a heroic display of resistance. First Lieutenant Grantz's adoring eyes watched her as she stated her case. Her bravery made her back seem much larger than any child could possibly possess.

"He is a necessary part of my battalion, General. He is most useful to our nation on the vanguard. I only wish to have the right soldiers in the right posts."

"So you're against lending him to me."

"I am unable to fully agree with your allocation of our resources."

It took immense bravery for a field officer to say words like this to a general—to disagree, object, and resist. Nevertheless, Lieutenant Colonel Degurechaff proceeded to do everything in her power to defend Grantz as he watched from the rear. The gratitude he felt knew no bounds.

He knew she was a superior who wanted the best for her subordinates, but never had he imagined she'd go this far!

He was immensely moved by the whole scene, and her efforts would prove successful…in helping him accept his inevitable demise.

"Colonel Degurechaff. I'll make *note* of your advice for the *record*. Now, is there anything else?"

The general's authority gave him an overwhelming advantage.

"General, as the commander of the General Staff's mage battalion, it is our duty to serve the Empire and our nation, and not—"

"I'll bear in mind that you were down a single company when reviewing your performance during this campaign. That said, I somehow doubt missing a single company will have that large of an impact on your battalion's results."

"Every single man counts, General."

"Sadly, this is a war. We must make the most of what we have."

"And I believe it is my job to do my best to maintain what I have."

General Zettour gave Lieutenant Colonel Degurechaff a stern glare, but she continued to fight for Grantz nevertheless. Honestly, she was up against the general. With there being nothing Grantz could say or do at all, he was expecting her to give up much sooner than she did. The grave reality, however, continued to loom over them as this exchange went on. Lieutenant Colonel Degurechaff was a lieutenant colonel, and General Zettour was a general. One was the subordinate, and one was the superior.

"Do you have any other concerns? I apologize, but I'd like for you to understand that this has already been decided."

The lieutenant colonel fell silent. She gave Grantz a glance, her eyes filled with pity, which made the situation all too clear—there were no reinforcements coming. For the first time in his military career, Grantz was cut off and alone.

As if to announce the results of the negotiation to the dumbfounded lieutenant, the old gentleman with glittering stars lining his jacket turned his attention to him with a glaringly forced smile.

"Well, Colonel. It seems all that's left is getting the lieutenant's consent."

"Yes… You are correct."

Grantz's superior gave a reluctant but clear nod. His last and only line of defense had fallen, and no reinforcements were coming. Standing before Grantz was an eerily smiling general. He beamed at him from the pinnacle of his organization, the army. The gaze with which he waited for Grantz to speak was like a sharp blade wrapped in cloth. He knew from experience that this was it. That resistance was futile… It was time for him to raise his white flag.

"I—I look forward to being able to accompany you again and help in any way I can!"

"That's the spirit, Lieutenant Grantz. I expected nothing less from a man such as yourself. I'm glad you're willing to volunteer yourself for the important task."

He had no recollection of volunteering for this, and he was overcome by amazement. The general's hand felt heavy on his slumped shoulders.

"Let's try to enjoy ourselves, Lieutenant. There's nothing to worry about."

"Do I look worried?"

"I intend to add to your achievements with this assignment, not leave a black mark on your career."

The moment the man walked through the door of the Ildoan Army General Staff Office, he realized an undeniable difference between the current state of affairs and what the office once was.

"Look what this has done to the world..."

After stepping into what was once his office, Colonel Calandro lamented to himself.

"The insanity that is total world war..."

The Ildoan Army used to laugh at the Imperial Army. They thought the Empire must've been insane to ever engage in *total war*. It was what the soldiers used to talk about at the salon, with a glass of wine in hand. It was hard for any of the soldiers to imagine their nation engaging in something so idiotic, given its raison d'état. To them, war was just an extension of politics, and to fight a war for the sake of fighting a war was completely out of the question. If they had to fight, then it should be in the interest of their nation. The opposite—a nation becoming a slave to war—was a sick and twisted concept.

That was what the colonel always thought, at least.

"The world looks different when you're the one at war."

So what happened to their army in an actual war? Ildoa, which had once ridiculed the Empire, was now being burned by the flames of its war... The office's aloof outlook, which had been like an elegant fragrance that lingered in the old General Staff Office, was completely gone. The expressions of the civilians and soldiers who came and went through the office doors were as grim as could be. They were the expressions of people forced into oblivion roaming aimlessly through the world.

From an observer's perspective, their looks garnered unbearable pity. The Ildoa of plenty was no more.

"But...it's understandable."

Calandro muttered to himself about the dreadfulness of their inescapable reality.

The core of their military had been devastated, and they lost the equipment needed to arm their reserves before they could be mobilized. It was difficult to reckon with what was happening, but there was no fooling himself about it. This wretched reality was Ildoa's.

Chapter **III**

As a result of the vicious Imperial attack, the Ildoan Army was on the verge of collapse. The colonel didn't even want to imagine what things would've looked like without the weeklong cease-fire.

Given that most of the immediately deployable divisions had already been lost, they used their very limited time to scrounge up enough troops for some twenty-odd divisions. The sad truth was...that these divisions were hardly battle-ready. Whatever they had was a shell of what it should've been.

The oft-ridiculed, warmongering Imperial Army that fought on for no reason was continuously proving that it was indeed good at one thing— war. What was happening to Ildoa was the result of its silent ridicule.

The colonel didn't even want to think about that monster Zettour. The fact that he spoke with the general only a short while ago was still mortifying. That man and his army were going to do what they did to the Federation to Ildoa.

"I thought I'd built up an immunity to him in the Empire's eastern front, but I guess not."

It was clear to Calandro that he'd lose this battle before it started if he let his enemy get to him. He also knew that it was more than just his problem at this point. The situation was grave. The Empire was rampaging down their peninsula with the momentum of a victorious army, and the Ildoan Army was stuck fighting with less than half their regular numbers.

The only reason their collapse hadn't already happened was thanks to their largest hope at the moment—their alliance with the Unified States. The presence of the expeditionary force that had quickly reached Ildoa was cause for relief for the Ildoa officials. They simply needed to bide their time while they waited for the rest of the Unified forces. Which would be their strategy from the moment the cease-fire ended on out.

Colonel Calandro shook his head.

"We're going to need confidence in our forces if we're going to bide our time."

Calandro had seen the devil known as Zettour in action before... He doubted whether his countrymen had the fortitude to endure that devil's viciousness.

"Do the higher-ups know what it means to go up against the devil himself...?"

Needless to say, Calandro told his superiors this as soon as he returned from meeting the general. He warned them in every way he could.

Sadly, however, he was always met with the same answer: *"We understand your concerns."*

In actuality, under the leadership of General Gassman, the commanding officers charged with defending the capital did manage to heed one of the colonel's strategic warnings in their own way. When they noticed the Empire's advance slowing, they committed to stopping it by setting up fortified defensive positions. Using what was left of the shattered divisions, they set up bases along the defensive line. This was arguably the correct decision. The planners had a solid grasp of what their current army was capable of and did what they could.

The soundness of the decision was what left Colonel Calandro alone in arguing against the idea. His reasoning was that it was far too dangerous to *defend territory.* Calandro even made his case to General Gassman himself.

"We don't have the strength to fight back if it comes down to a pitched battle. Putting down roots is essentially giving the Imperial Army free time they need..."

Colonel Calandro's appeal was shot down by conventional military logic. Holding the line took priority over all else. The Ildoan Army chose to defend what it thought needed defending, and both military and political reasoning supported this plan of action.

Thus, Colonel Calandro was left to become Ildoa's Cassandra. He was the prophet of tragedy. No matter how prescient his warnings, they would not be heeded by his peers.

 DECEMBER 6, UNIFIED YEAR 1927, THE ILDOAN FRONT ◀◀◀

After offering a living sacrifice in the form of Lieutenant Grantz, Tanya and the rest of the Salamander Kampfgruppe officers finally have the freedom to return to business as usual. They still have the grueling order to give the enemy a bloody nose, but now they can carry these orders out on their own terms, without the watchful eyes of a high-ranking officer peering over their shoulders.

With that, Tanya assembles her officers to begin the final confirmation of the operation before carrying out the orders. First Lieutenant Serebryakov acts as her assistant, with Major Weiss, Captains Meybert and Ahrens, and First Lieutenant Tospan representing each of their respective branches of the army. Together, the group collectively gives a difficult look at the war map laid out before them. Tanya has Lieutenant Wüstemann sitting in on the meeting, too, for his own studies.

"Tell me, my Kampfgruppe officers. What do you think of the enemy?"

It's Captain Ahrens, heading the panzer unit, who takes the initiative to answer my question.

"It's the same every time we look at it. Judging by the map alone, their strong points are dug in and leave few openings."

Captain Meybert nods in agreement and continues.

"The enemy has prepared well for this engagement. It's likely that they have positioned their artillery units in the rear for concentrated support fire. The challenge lies in their camouflage, making it difficult for our reconnaissance units to pinpoint their exact location."

Though likely unimpacted by the difficult assessments made from the armor and artillery perspectives, Major Weiss shows a similarly difficult expression as he lets out a sigh.

"What do you think, Major?"

"Full frontal assaults are never easy, but…the more recent bases we've encountered have proper anti-mage countermeasures in place, making them harder to blow through."

"I see… And what about you, Lieutenant Tospan?"

The man in charge of the infantry simply shakes his head at my question.

"I have nothing to add. We'll see what we can do, but I believe charging a base is always going to come with hefty sacrifices."

More pessimism. While it's never good to underestimate your enemy, this shouldn't be a blanket outlook. I look at the three of them with a grimace.

"You three sure are cautious… You mustn't forget that it is human beings who carry out war. Taking this into consideration, we should look at the Ildoan soldiers."

I'm a former HR expert and I take pride in my ability to communicate sincerely with modern man. My lifetime's worth of experience is what tells me that my interpretation is correct.

"Ildoa's war council is made up of intelligent planners. Luckily for us, however, they have little experience when it comes to actually fighting a war. You should all be happy."

"We should?"

The first reply I get is a dubious look, but I shrug it off. Good and bad luck are two sides of the same coin.

"First, Ildoans have lived a life without war. Second, their lack of experience combined with high intellect will make them easy to defeat."

"Uh…"

My officers silently try to find words to reply with, but I calm them down with a wave of my hand.

"It isn't that hard to understand. Our enemies have spent a lot of time studying this war from afar. That said, there are many things one simply can't comprehend without actually experiencing them, such as the momentum defeat carries with it."

This is true whether talking about organizations, humanity as a whole, or just individuals. In other words, the enemy doesn't realize they're in a downward spiral.

"An army that goes on the defensive while it is on a losing streak has already lost the battle."

It doesn't even have to be a big battle to start the streak. A single random encounter is enough. Had they a small victory, something to stir up a sense of bravery in their soldiers, then the defense laid out before them would most definitely be something as impenetrable as steel. But if their forts are filled with hiding badgers…? Then they are weak, and their weakness needs to be capitalized on.

I know this from experience.

"The only cure for defeat is victory. An army full of soldiers who don't believe in themselves is surprisingly weaker than what numbers alone would suggest."

Even the most well-built base will amount to nothing if its soldiers are hiding inside it, protecting themselves until the end of the battle.

The Seige of Odawara is a good example of this. The same goes for

Osaka castle. After losing their will to fight back, the defenders of Odawara simply surrendered its castle to the attackers. Even with all the planning and effort that went into raising the grand Osaka castle, it fell due to having subpar defenders. Soldiers who are certain of their victory are hard to contend with, but soldiers fearing their impending doom will often crumble on contact.

After thinking for a moment, staring at the well-made enemy fortifications while I imagine the mental state of its soldiers...I reach an easy conclusion. The soldiers inside are most surely a mess. If this is the case, then we only need to amplify their fears and destroy them while they are a panicked mess.

"Captain Ahrens, I require you to undertake a difficult job for this operation."

"Seeing as my orders for most operations fit that description, what will you have us do this time?"

There is an honorable resignation in his casual response. It seems these soldiers have adapted to unreasonable demands in a way that is helpful. As Captain Ahrens's superior, and more importantly, as a good middle manager, I'm proud of the fact that this is the level of trust we've established.

After a brief chuckle, I give him orders in a deliberately calm manner.

"I want you to have your tanks really make some noise."

"Why, may I ask...?"

"Ideally, they'll mistake you for Colonel Lergen's 8th Panzer Division. We'll scare them with a false sense of numbers."

Dummies and decoys. There are entire chapters on this diversionary tactic written in the military textbooks.

"It will use a lot of fuel and artillery..."

"That's fine. I need it done, Captain. If the enemy mistakes the armor formation for our main forces, then it is a small price to pay. I want you to throw everything you've got at them!"

If the enemy believes there is a panzer unit at their doorstep, then their defensive line will most certainly falter. To put it simply, the soldiers will get scared, and their commanding officers will show hesitation.

The base will surely grow disillusioned by the division.

"Captain Meybert! You'll be charged with covering Captain Ahrens with support fire. I'm expecting you to use just as much of your arsenal as the division does."

No bars shall be held to maximize the enemy's fear. We must take the initiative to do what the enemy fears the most.

"Major Weiss and Captain Tospan, you'll be given the lofty task of accompanying the tanks. You'll be going on a quick drive with me."

The two men nodded before Weiss took the lead to ask a question for both of them.

"Where will we be driving to?"

"The enemy base. It's almost suppertime, and something tells me Ildoan bases are much tastier than whatever's in the Federation and the Commonwealth."

》》》　　THE SAME DAY, THE ILDOAN ROYAL CAPITAL/ILDOAN ARMY　《《《
GENERAL STAFF OFFICE

The commander charged with overseeing the capital's defense had a clear understanding of the largest problem at hand.

"They chose the wrong man for the job."

The commander—General Gassman—mumbled to himself. The general was well aware of how unsuitable he was to defend his nation's capital. He knew himself well and would be the first to admit that he was more suited for military administration. The first thing he did when he was put up to the task was acknowledge that he belonged in the rear, and a strategist belonged in his position—something he even tried to relinquish. Sadly for him, however…General Gassman was too skilled a military administrator for his own good.

Perhaps it should be said that the heavens abandoned him, in a sense. Namely, over the course of his career, he had successfully gained the trust of his nation, its government, the palace, and the people, almost too well. The politicians saw him as an honorable general, the palace a general that knew the ropes, and among Ildoans, there was a general consensus that he seemed like a trustworthy man.

It didn't help that General Gassman looked good in his suit as well. The outfit he wore to acquire funds and make political arrangements during a time of peace offered an easily understandable sense of security in Ildoa's time of need.

So what happened when he tried to transfer this power to somebody more capable than himself? His letters of resignation and recommendation were both seen as a form of modesty, and the position of high command was more or less forced onto him.

Which brought him to his current predicament—being worn down by a never-ending chain of decision making he just wasn't used to.

The worst part was that he had absolutely no clue what the enemy was thinking. Every strange turn the Empire took amounted to a terrifying fog that only grew thicker with time.

"I have no idea what they're doing..."

General Gassman, alone in his office, moaned to himself.

"My usual strategies just aren't going to cut it."

He'd asked his staff their opinions and reviewed countless reference documents on the war front, finding several different assessments, each *correct* in their own way, which he compiled into one...like he always did. Somehow, however, this didn't translate into a clear strategy.

What he was doing was administrating. A process that was taking far too long for somebody who needed to make immediate decisions. Gassman was good at coordination and administration, but it was clear to him that he had no talent when it came to being decisive. He knew this better than anyone else, but knowing this didn't help him—it wasn't as if he could ask someone else to make the decisions for him. He was the leader, and he needed to make the decisions on his own accord.

That was exactly why Gassman was conflicted. Were he up against a more regular enemy, this much wouldn't have been a problem for him. In this regard, his biggest mistake was trying to learn about his enemy. He tried to understand what made the crafty Zettour tick, thinking from the perspective of the Empire...but he had absolutely zero clue as to what they were trying to gain from all of this.

"Do they really intend to attack our capital? Or is it merely a threat to obtain more leverage in negotiations, just like the cease-fire? Or perhaps...they're after something else?"

The general wasn't convinced by what he saw. He stared at the map, but his opponent's attacks made less and less sense as the reports came flooding in from the front lines.

There were two powerful panzer units that were making their way toward the capital. These two units were powerful, but only in the sense of individual strength.

"This alone won't be enough to truly threaten the capital. The Empire knows better than any of us how poorly tanks fare in urban warfare."

These units were a threat out in the open and certainly had the potential to break the Ildoan defensive line, but...two units operating independently could be handled.

Gassman took into account the comparative weakness of his own army, and considering the multiple, in-depth warnings his subordinate, Colonel Calandro, had provided him with, he had no intention of underestimating the military threat of the Imperial Army.

Even after taking all this into account, military logic brought him to the same conclusion every time.

"It feels fair to say we shouldn't be in too much danger."

They were fighting a defensive war, after all. Between their intricate contingency plan, posing counterattacks when appropriate, and initiative within their camps, things seemed to be going according to their plan. At least, enough for them to keep the Empire at bay.

"They've learned their lesson on the Rhine and in the east. A frontal assault against a fortified position requires numbers, and always comes with great sacrifice."

Going on the defensive gave the attacker the initiative, but the defender a positional advantage. In other words, a defensive war was a difficult war to lose. This reality was something the general knew from countless analyses of the reports on the Empire's war in the Rhine...or at least this is what the general told himself.

"Calandro's concern seems fairly ungrounded. He's an excellent soldier, but his time in the east must have clouded his judgment."

The general felt regret for having subjected his subordinate to the Empire's vicious onslaught in the east while going over the numbers in his head.

The Empire had been engaging in total war for a long time. It was facing severe shortages due to chronic losses of blood and iron. The Empire had fought the world for far too long. Even if it was a military powerhouse, it was surely on its last legs as a country.

Going over this in his mind brought up a new question. After using what felt like an unlimited amount of their resources in the east... what could the Empire possibly gain from shedding even more blood in Ildoa?

"Colonel Calandro's concern for a *frontal assault* is likely a red herring, a trick they're trying to pull, knowing how we operate. Which may mean...that the US experts are correct in that the Empire will bypass the capital and attack the field troops."

Bypass, surround, and destroy with mobile warfare. They will go around Ildoa's bases, cut the base off from the rear, then attack the isolated base. This was a tactic the vicious Empire, and General Zettour in particular, had employed frequently in the east.

"It all depends on what their target is... Are they after Ildoan and Unified States troops? Or are they trying to bottle up our field armies in the royal capital?"

What would happen to the troops when they had no place to run?

"For the Empire, who's desperate, having an enemy army trapped in a city could make for a good bargaining chip."

They could kill all the troops or use them for negotiations. Their fate would be in the Empire's hands, and with General Zettour in the picture, General Gassman was almost certain that he could think of several ways to use their lives for political purposes.

General Gassman, murmuring this all to himself, finally let out a wry chuckle.

General Zettour... It was the first time in a long time he'd recognized an Imperial general who could think politically, if at all, when it came to anything unrelated to war.

"And if Colonel Calandro's concerns prove legitimate..."

The capital would fall, and confusion on a grand scale would ensue. This much the general wanted to avoid at all costs. The odds, however, favored heavily that this threat was nothing more than a diversion.

"The fog of war, eh...? You hear about it all the time, but it's an eerie feeling to be unsure what the enemy is trying to do based on the map."

What exactly was their primary target?

"The capital? The field troops? If they're bloodthirsty warriors, then they will turn the capital into rubble. But would that sly con artist really charge a matador's red cape so simply?"

What if he was trying to trick Ildoa into believing that he was? Or what if they were going for both? General Gassman let out a large sigh.

"I haven't the slightest idea what they're thinking over there. What could they be after?"

The general folded his arms and thought about the problem once more.

"What is General Zettour doing right now?"

What was the enemy general focusing on? The general had a timeline of what he had done so far and was fairly certain he knew what his end goal was.

According to Colonel Calandro, defeat wasn't even on the man's mind. The colonel was just letting the enemy's intimidation get to him, though. But that said, it was likely the case that General Zettour had no interest in occupying all of Ildoa at the very least. So there must have been something else he was after.

Gassman's thoughts were collected up until this point.

"What on the surface looks like a violent tirade may actually be him occupying the north...? It's hard to imagine he would want to take the entire country."

Ildoa was neutral. That is, until they formed one too many alliances, tipping the Empire into aggression and creating a desire for a buffer in the north. It was an irrational notion, but consequential in that the Empire had actually attacked Ildoa.

From General Gassman's perspective, though it was a heavy blow... it was nothing more than to keep their nation in check. A jab to scare them, not knock them out of the picture completely. Although the general did believe that when the enemy stopped their advance, they would've hunkered down in the north.

"Which means...they'll attack the capital to cause fear. Or maybe it is to draw in our field troops and take them out there?"

It wasn't clear what Zettour was going to do, but it was logically one of these two. It was likely a jab to contain Ildoan forces near the capital and away from the north, and it would be foolish for them to take the jab head-on. For the Ildoan Army had already suffered tremendous losses, and they simply hadn't enough divisions left to fight back.

Were they to lose what was left of their forces, Ildoa would be left defenseless and at the mercy of the Empire.

And then… General Gassman mulled over concerns for a problem unique to the capital.

"We still have the royal family to worry about. Should I have the king evacuate the capital? Or would it be better for him to stand his ground…?"

Argh. The general grabbed his head as he continued to think about the far too many problems that were happening all at once.

》》》   THE SAME DAY, THE IMPERIAL ARMY VANGUARD   **《《《**

Things are simple on the battlefield. The rule is, when things get complicated, surviving always takes the highest priority.

Even a Nobel Prize–winning brain is just like any other brain in physical terms. The brightest mind will explode just like the dullest if hit with a bullet, and every second you spend thinking is just another chance you'll end up shot. Even the minds that created nuclear weapons would splatter when met with a single bullet, and there's no wisdom to be shared by a brilliant mind if it's mush in a corpse. This is yet another reason why Tanya is such a large proponent of peace.

"People can do such amazing things if they aren't busy fighting a war."

I make this comment from atop an advancing Imperial vehicle before reaching for a phone. Incidentally, this phone connects to the inside of the tank that I'm sitting on top of. A phone is necessary for the passengers enduring the bumpy ride on the top of the tank to communicate with its drivers, who are deafened by the delightful sound of a revving engine. It should also be mentioned that these aren't standard. A bit of ingenuity to make things easier on the field, and though making such modifications is technically a violation of the rules…there just so happens to be a few open spaces in the tank's armor large enough for a telephone cord to pass through. With enough ingenuity, anything is possible.

Anywho, I'm using the phone to talk with the leader of the panzer unit, Captain Ahrens.

"Any signs of enemy's reinforcements?!"

My shout is almost as loud as the battlefield, which is so muffled by the tank's roaring engine that Captain Ahrens must yell over it to be heard.

"According to reports, none have been sighted! The enemy may not be falling for our diversion!"

"It seems that way!"

The air nearby warps as I respond. A mortar round must've landed a bit too close for comfort. The enemy soldiers are doing a decent job putting up resistance. The artillery that falls upon them seems incessant.

Examining my shell, I find it hard to tell what kind of shrapnel is lodged in there. Was it a cannon round, a missile, or anti-aircraft artillery?

Tanya gives her defensive shell a nudge with her finger before showing a wry smile. Surely the foot soldiers on the ground with neither a protective film nor a defensive shell to shield themselves with must be at their limits. Unlike them, Tanya and her battalion, however, had the privilege of being a part of the tank desant...!

While I have no qualms about using human shields, it's definitely strange for me to shield a tank with my own body. I wonder who came up with such a ludicrous idea before that chain of thought comes full circle and I realize it was me. Should I question my own sanity or blame the absurdity of war?

"The world is a tough place for a pacifist."

Setting aside who's at fault here, the enemy's impressive volume of fire and lack of a reaction to our diversion would normally be the signal for us to hightail it out of here to save fuel and ammo.

The enemy reacts with nothing but artillery fire, or at least that's what it seems like. It's almost strange how little movement there is in the base itself.

Though I question whether my intuition may be misguided, there's also a rush of anticipation.

"Captain Ahrens! We must bear in mind the fear they must be feeling. What if they aren't ignoring our diversion?! What if they are simply ignoring our assault as a whole?!"

"I'm sorry, but what did you just say?!"

"I'm asking what you make of this if they are ignoring our assault."

"That can't be right, can it?!"

I want to agree with him. If the enemy is keeping themselves cooped up in their base… If they are trying to fend us off with artillery and not even venture out…

The Kampfgruppe needs to capitalize on this chance and fast. The proper response would be to fly in, blow them to bits, and scatter the survivors. To do so would be a large gamble, though.

A frontal assault on an enemy base bears significant costs. If they have a thoroughly thought-out counteroffensive prepared, the Empire could easily be fended off.

I want to believe in my instincts. After factoring in my personal desires, it's no longer a very objective decision…but…

Whether it be a regiment or a division in there, whatever's in that base isn't showing any signs of life. The utter neglect to take initiative in their counterattack shows that they're cooped-up badgers in there—or fish in a barrel. Blowing a single hole in their base may well be all it takes for it to fall apart. Maybe even worse than falling apart. The Empire could absolutely dominate the base.

I close my eyes for a moment and mentally weigh the potential returns against the heavy risk. The possibility of dominating this base, and the dangers of attacking a well-defended base.

The idea of going out on a limb and risking it all is agonizing, but my hunch is supported by experience—the blood and sweat I've paid in tuition tell me that this is a chance worth taking.

We need to take our shot, and it needs to be a big shot.

It's time for a recon in force. That's what mages do best.

"Mage battalion! Prepare to charge! I say again, mage battalion, prepare to charge!"

Clear orders to start up the instrument of violence. My battle-ready battalion of mages grip their rifles and rev up their orbs, as they each shoot Tanya a questioning look, the answer to which she'll give in her next address to them.

"We're engaging in recon in force. Our target, the enemy base! I say again! Our target is the enemy base!"

The 203rd is a bloody mage battalion—drenched in the blood of their enemies—and its commander, who embodies this the most with her Rusted Silver moniker, grew up fighting in the trenches on the Rhine front. In an age where veteran soldiers are rarer than diamonds, this mage battalion, which honed its fangs in the north, south, east, and west, is a precious strategic asset for the Empire—and Tanya is going to bet this precious asset on one single attack.

"They think they can hide in their base?! Well, we'll just have to pop their war cherries for them! Aerial Magic Battalion! We are proud comrades! Our battalion of Named mages shall devour the world! The time has come for us to show the world what we are capable of!"

Yes, mages excel at anti-tank warfare. The tough exterior of a tank means little against a top attack.[2]

Even against anti-air attacks, they could manage, though not without more difficulty. Mages are capable of taking an entirely different trajectory than conventional aircraft, with their ability to almost instantaneously change directions and lift off or land at the drop of a hat, giving them a much better defense against incoming AA fire.

Support fire is another strong point for mages. Needless to say, explosion and optical formulas lead the pack in quick and effective aerial fire support. We're essentially flying artillery. When used in tandem with actual artillery, they become artillery observers that can also fill in the blanks.

That being said, the Imperial Army's aerial mages are, in essence, hunting dogs. Their ultimate raison d'être is to chomp down on their enemies. Concealing a sense of repugnance and resignation for what I've become, I rally the troops.

"My Imperial hunting dogs! Follow me! I'll lead the charge!"

I bark more orders before taking flight, and her troops need nothing more than a commander willing to commit and lead them. They follow Tanya, with her adjutant covering her rear as always.

With Lieutenant Serebryakov at my side, most challenges can be overcome. My other subordinates? There's no need to worry whether they

---

[2] Evidently, tanks and other armored vehicles are vulnerable to attacks from above, which means attacking their top section is an easy way to take them out. It's also a magic word that is cause for many typos in the Carlo Zen-o-sphere, with myself being a culprit that frequently ends up with Top Down Attack/Top Up Attack. My publisher, though, takes the cake with a random Top Down Up typo.

will follow, either. There isn't a chance in hell my officers won't perform their duties. This is where aerial mages excel the most! Chipping away at the stalwart fortification that blocked their path, perhaps even flying in and dominating it alone.

I shouldn't have to explain all this. This much has been driven home to the leaders of each company, and three of the four that were conducting a tank desant came together as soon as the orders to charge went up. In their current wedge formation, they keep close to the ground as they hurtle toward the base. Suppressing fire from enemy rifles and machine guns does little against our defensive shells, and it's a simple matter to add a little evasive maneuver to make it harder for the enemy to hit us in the first place. Think of it as an Imperial Mage Panzerkeil.[3]

As I lead the charge, I take out the Elinium Type 95 usually kept tucked away. In exchange for sullying my free will, this device provides the thickest of defensive shells.

"Lord and savior, guide my way. I walk with you, in pursuit of hardship. I will climb a mountain of thorns and praise your glory from its bristly peak."

Littering the Ildoan soil with verbal rubbish, I manifest optical decoys one after another. That, combined with the speed of a fighter plane, should be enough for a successful assault.

The shellshocked enemy doesn't even have time to keep up with the sudden action, and as glittering spells fill the sky with explosions, they will soon be reunited with the shit they soiled their pants with.

"Dominate them! Dominate everything! My battalion! Dominate!"

Explosion formulas pepper the base, with a single penetration formula blasting through its wall, turning the part of the base the mages come into contact with into a hell on earth. The outer wall of said corner easily caves to the attack.

Intent on causing fear for whoever is in the base, be it some mythical hero or whoever, the 203rd Aerial Mage Battalion, a battalion that specializes in raiding, penetrates their walls.

---

[3] A wedge-shaped tank formation made for advancing. This is primarily used when attacking heavily fortified positions with anti-tank defenses. Apparently, tankers hate fighting dug-in enemies. Incidentally, it turns out anti-tank gunners hate fighting tanks, so the feelings are mutual.

The good soldiers of the Ildoan Army take out their handguns with quivering hands as the horde of Named mages come piling toward them with shells that would require at least a cannon to penetrate.

Those who actually get a shot off are real modern heroes. Those who try to aim first, wise sages. But neither of their fine efforts amounts to anything in the face of the rich experience that has gone into honing the pinnacle of the Empire's art of war in its aerial mages.

Now, with this fearsome threat before them, just how intense is the utter shock they must feel watching their brave brethren be crushed? How intense is it, to watch the base they believed to be impenetrable be demolished?

The result is simple. The second line of defense watches as its first line falls in a single fell swoop.

"So this is what happens when you throw a scant thirty mages at the problem."

Tanya sighs to herself and turns to find her adjutant smiling awkwardly.

"I mean…it is us we're talking about here. I think it would be different against any other group of mages."

"Veterans we may be, for them to crumble like this says a lot about their forces."

Ignoring Lieutenant Serebryakov, who looks like she has more to add, Tanya takes a radio that she seems to have acquired from the base and listens in.

"Chaos, confusion, and no composure. Mm-hmm, sounds like the momentum of a losing army. Ah, it's so easy on the ears."

Tanya grins widely.

A firm defense is only effective if the defending side seeks taking initiative in defending itself. Even the dogmatic and rigid Federation showed a hunger for taking the initiative from the onset of the war.

"The enemy is mistaking a defensive war for defending its line. It seems they've forgotten what it means to defend."

With this attack, on top of the fact that enemy forces have yet to try and recapture or destroy taken land in retaliation, This gives me a general sense for the enemy's will to fight.

Defensive wars are retaliations, attempts to cause stagnation, and the exchange of space for time, and no bars should be held to do so. But look at these fools.

"I think I may like the Ildoans, Visha."

"Then I guess I, and the rest of the battalion, will like them, too."

"I bet you're right! Judging by Captain Ahrens's response earlier, it seems we do, in fact, share our own common sense."

A shared common sense is a beautiful thing. Two coworkers getting along is worth celebrating. Everything is going well.

Well, it's about time to call the troops.

"Captain Ahrens, can you hear me?"

"How was the assault reconnaissance?"

"We ripped apart their defensive line. Sorry, there's nothing left for you."

"Oh, lord…"

The loud tank engine that can be heard over the radio isn't enough to drown out the captain's surprise. His reaction is limited to that outburst, though, as Captain Ahrens has worked with this battalion long enough to know not to verbally question news like this.

"Then…I assume now is our chance to pursue the enemy?"

Instead, he responds with a question about the situation. He's a good officer, who knows when to pitch ideas. I appreciate his enthusiasm to create more value in our operation and admires him for the fine human resource he is. Setting aside his delightful response, though, I must correct the slight misunderstanding he's making.

"Not exactly, Captain. We can't expect to pursue them."

"Is the royal army on their way?"

"No, not quite!"

Tanya ends up grimacing at her own giddy enthusiasm while she relays the unexpected sight that is unfolding before her to Captain Ahrens so he can enjoy the news as well.

"It seems enemy command doesn't intend on letting go of this position. They're hunkering down at a different part of their base. It appears we won't need to pursue them after all. Not if they're just going to stay here for us."

"What? They're not going to retreat and reorganize?"

"Common sense dictates they should, but evidently, we don't share the same common sense as the Ildoans. They're digging their heels into this base to fight."

This time, the captain cannot hold back his doubt.

"That can't be true, Colonel."

"Why is that, Captain?"

"They have a city right behind them! Even a civilian can hold out and stall a battle until reinforcements arrive by escaping into an urban area. But you're telling me they're going to stay out in the open to get surrounded?"

The enemy shows no signs of heading for their city at all. For a soldier with ample experience, yes, it makes sense that not doing so is out of the question. It's clear from his voice that Captain Ahrens is in utter disbelief at how the enemy is handling themselves.

Which is why I've taken it upon myself as a civilized person to teach him the glaring truth.

"Calm yourself, Captain. Escaping to a city is out of the question for most armies around the world."

"What? No, I'm not saying I would ever actually want to fight the Ildoans in their own city or anything, but..."

No, no. I signal with my hand even though I'm on the radio. He's not understanding me.

The captain's opinion is correct for *someone who's been fighting in this great war,* but he's forgotten a truly basic part of being a civilized person.

"These people do not understand total war."

"What do you mean by that, Colonel...?"

"The Ildoans still have their sanity. Their too afraid to bring tanks, cannons, or Gatling guns to use against mages into the places where civilians live."

What is common sense for the great war is utterly out of the question for the rest of the normal world. It reminds me of Colonel Calandro when he came to see the Imperial forces as a military observer. He was trembling. Trembling at the current state of the war in the east.

Tanya and the rest of the Empire have long accepted what it means to fight in this war, but for the rest of the world, it must look like the deepest part of hell. It's almost possible for her, as an objective observer of this reality, to feel a personal benefit from their relative difference in values.

"The enemy is too civilized."

Chapter **III**

And that's exactly why…

Tanya chuckles scornfully.

"We have to give our civilized friends a much-needed dosage of the violence machine."

Now that Tanya has peered into the minds of her enemies, there is no longer a need for her to hold back.

"Salamander leader to the 8th Panzer Division. Break through the enemy line at a point of your choice and surround them."

>>>>   THE SAME DAY, THE 8TH PANZER DIVISION   <<<<

General Zettour, who was with the regiment under the pretense of rallying the soldiers, had been walking around with a natural gait greeting each and every face he knew well—and it was now the substitute commander Colonel Lergen's turn.

As if fighting the enemy wasn't enough of a stomachache on its own, having to sit with the general while he eagerly awaited the report that they'd made a breakthrough gave birth to a whole new kink in his digestive system. Colonel Lergen, who for better or for worse, routinely wore the iron mask of a military bureaucrat, knew that the time he spent pretending to look at a map while he kept his facial expressions under control would amount to mental torture. Which was why the colonel was praying for relief to come as soon as possible.

As fate would have it, a higher power seemed to have pity on his poor soul, as his prayers would be answered in the form of a running communications officer. The excited officer held out a message for the colonel, which had incredible news that had come straight from the front line— the news he had been waiting for. The colonel read it and nodded to himself before happily handing the message to General Zettour.

"Break through the enemy line at a point of our choice and surround them?"

The general finished reading Colonel Lergen's note and rubbed his chin with a grin.

"So this is the vanguard unit's decision."

It could be said that Lieutenant Colonel Degurechaff possessed a truly grand outlook. The Empire was in a superior position. This was on top of the fact that the enemy's main forces, its aerial mages, had already been removed from combat. The skies were clear as well. Having pulled as much as they could from the east and west, the Empire had managed to maintain aerial superiority so far. They had a good hand of cards, but even then, reports from the front lines that penetration could be made at will was about as splendid as things could get.

General Zettour had a choice to make. He folded his arms in thought. "Yes."

There were holes made up and down the enemy line, so he agreed with the report that they could penetrate any one of them. The general was caught off guard by the prospects of surrounding their bases, though.

Naturally, he was the first to take urban warfare into careful consideration when thinking about taking over the royal capital. It all depended on how the Ildoans fought their defense. Worst-case scenario, he could accept having to abandon their conquest on the Royal Capital altogether. But if they could surround the enemy field troops outside the city? Then it was free rein for the Imperial Army. In fact, he could even go to their capital for dinner just as he had phoned the embassy the night prior.

"What do you think, Colonel Lergen? It seems that Colonel Degure-chaff, with that fine hunting dog nose of hers, has picked up the scent on a fantastic chance."

"I agree, General."

The colonel answered with a quick response and nod, prompting Zettour to display a satisfied grin.

"Then, Colonel. I believe it's time you go out for a run as well."

"I'll do everything in my power to make this work! Now, please excuse me!"

Colonel Lergen gave a salute, then gallantly trotted out of the command center to give the orders to advance. The entirety of the 8th Panzer Division, which had been waiting for the orders, kicked into high gear on his orders.

The sudden change of pace almost looked like a panic, but the collective of soldiers doing exactly what they were supposed to do was like a well-tuned orchestra. Him offering a salute to the soldiers and officers waving their hats was a product of preestablished harmony.

Chapter **III**

The general knew it wouldn't be long until he heard the results of the attack. They were going to win a complete victory.

"It's funny. When the enemy falls, it's always all at once."

The enemy was unable to fight against the brunt of the Empire's attack. Zettour couldn't help but mutter to himself his sense of dissatisfaction in the show they were putting on for him.

"The defensive line established by the Ildoan-Unified troops appeared firm, but that firmness is only determined by the soldiers inside the bases."

It reminded him of a time when he was a young officer who had been assigned to be an observer. To the best of his memory, he'd debated with Rudersdorf on the importance of a will to fight when engaging in positional warfare.

"I argued the defenders held the advantage, and he argued it was the will to fight that mattered above all else."

Judging by these results, it appeared both sides of the argument were true.

A base with soldiers who hid inside it without a strong will to fight could not persevere against a determined attacker. That said, defenders within a base who had a strong will to fight were nigh impenetrable. It could be considered the obvious conclusion. Although, no matter how willing to fight the defenders were, or how solidified their base was, in the end, fire and national power prevailed. Power had the ability to mow down any defense, and in conclusion, national strategy was the be-all and end-all.

"Argh."

Zettour grumbled. He was the supreme commander of the Imperial Army and a lone man foolishly challenging the world to war. There was no amount of effort he could put forward to garner a national strategy that could actually defeat the world. How lonely it was to be in such a powerless position.

"The Empire and its army are undoubtedly powerful."

What his nation did have was fists capable of pummeling Ildoa as well as the soldiers the Unified States sent to help. Centered around its panzer units, the Imperial Army's exercise of power was like something out of a textbook.

It was a feat that had been made possibly by Lieutenant Colonel Degurechaff and Colonel Lergen. The Imperial Army surrounded the Ildoan Army, who insisted on holding their positions outside the capital. Once they had the enemy surrounded, they came under attack from US forces who came to relieve their allies, which the Empire purposefully allowed to penetrate their encirclement before closing the hole up behind them and continuing their siege.

If this had been a boxing match, then that maneuver would have been a perfectly executed counterpunch. A single counter used to knock out the enemy in the ring of the century.

What became of the soldiers the Ildoan citizens watched from the city with hope? They were facedown in the ring, unconscious, leaving the capital defenseless.

By the time the citizens realized that their defense had crumbled away, the Imperial Army 8th Panzer Division had already set foot in the heart of the Ildoan royal capital. Of course, this rapid pace was something the Imperial Army needed desperately. To take control of a city full of civilians, both domestic and foreign...there was very little margin for error.

Colonel Lergen brought the command center into the city and immediately began administering the occupation and dealing with the many new problems that were cropping up...which a person at General Zettour's level had no business meddling in.

Instead, the general was plucked out of the base and brought to his car by his entourage. In stricter terms, it wasn't as if he was actually leaving the colonel to do his job, but...his purpose for being there—namely, the soldiers he was there to encourage—had made incredible gains. Most of the officers assumed that his guards were getting him out of there after a *job well done...*

Zettour, however, felt no need to fall in line with their assumption. He appreciated his security detail finally giving him some relative privacy and took the time to think while he enjoyed a cigarette.

The situation was good. The enemy had lost their will to fight with a swift attack. There was a chance that survivors would re-collaborate to pose a counteroffensive...but he had a good bodyguard sitting right next to him.

Weighing the risks against the merits in his mind, Zettour came to his conclusion: that since he had the aerial mages led by Degurechaff with him, his scheme was worth a shot.

His scheme to leave his name in history, that is.

His name would be the one left in history books for the world to peruse. Unless he was desperate to prevent this from happening, it would be irrational for him to hesitate at this moment—the moment he claimed Ildoa.

There were times, after all, when military rationale must kneel before political and national demands.

"Lieutenant Grantz. Do you have a moment?"

The young mage lieutenant ran up to the general. He likely intended to show a stern face, but his expression was just stiff. The young man had good instincts, but Zettour was in no position to show any mercy. Thus, he would cajole the young lad in terms a soldier could understand.

"Bring me toward the capital. We must make haste. Hesitation could lose us this prime opportunity."

"Yes, sir!"

Grantz nodded and got straight to work, obedient soldier that he was. He didn't make an effort to prolong the preparations or play any tricks to stall. Instead, the convoy set out soon to head to the Ildoan capital.

An easy trip it was, on the nation's beautiful roads. Setting aside the company of aerial mages defending his vehicle, it was a pleasant day for a drive.

"My guards aren't giving me any lip. Finally, some time to myself."

General Zettour enjoyed a cigar in the back of his car as he savored this moment of peace and quiet. Although it wasn't long before First Lieutenant Grantz, being the good soldier he was, grew curious about their exact destination.

"Do you mind if I ask where we are headed?"

"You'll find out once we reach the capital."

The general answered in vague terms, though it was more difficult to keep up the facade when they entered city limits.

"General, are we going to the palace, or a government facility? Or are we set to convene with Colonel Lergen at the new headquarters?"

"Hm? Ah, this isn't an official advance."

The young lieutenant was utterly confused by these words. He likely assumed he was advancing the general into the city for official business related to its occupation… Keeping him confused kept him quiet, so it wasn't too big of a problem.

"I suppose we've come far enough."

Zettour gave Grantz a wide grin. This was enough for the poor boy to realize the dire straits he had landed in. The first lieutenant immediately stiffened up. Seeing this, Zettour, as his general in command, politely asked him:

"What do you say, Lieutenant Grantz. Are you in the mood for a walk?"

"Sir, you don't intend on stepping out of the car, do you?"

First Lieutenant Grantz did everything in his power, even shooting an overtly cautious glance outside of the car, begging his superior not to do so. Though unable to talk back to his superior, he made his concern utterly clear. He was a good young man, but this didn't amount to anything.

"Look how wonderful the street is. Is it unrefined of me to want to go for a little stroll? Let's go outside."

It wasn't as if First Lieutenant Grantz's concerns were lost on the general, of course.

An urban environment was a nightmare for those charged with keeping him safe. There were blind spots in every direction inside this concrete jungle, with tall buildings offering enemy snipers countless vantage points. Given the hostile civilian populace, everyone was a potential threat.

Even for the elite aerial mages who made up his security detail, defending him in this environment was a tall task.

But this was where the general wanted to go.

"General Zettour, are you truly going to go for a walk here?"

Grantz appealed for the general not to. He needed the general to change his mind at all costs. He was just a first lieutenant, though. It was outrageous for him to even give his opinion to the general.

"Did you not hear me? The falling of the royal capital is a historic event. We should take this rare chance to march through the town triumphantly."

"March…? Uh, due to cautionary reasons, I—"

"Cautionary? You're a soldier, man, toughen up. Do you want the world to think I was some sort of scaredy-cat?"

Grantz began shaking when the ill-tempered General shot him a nasty glare. He could feel the sweat dampening the collar of his uniform and even began to feel a bit dizzy. Nevertheless, he needed to fulfill his duty as the general's bodyguard.

"I'm sorry, General, but we're in enemy territory! This is the capital we've just seized! It's far too dangerous out there! Please...stay in the car!"

"You're got it backward."

"What do you mean?"

"Do you want it to look like the deputy director of the Imperial Army was hiding in the back like a coward? It's more dangerous for me to stay hidden away."

This sort of angry reaction from a general was a nightmare for a lower-ranking soldier.

"Understood... We'll be surrounding you as you walk."

"Are you dull in the head? Maybe I should've listened to Colonel Degurechaff when she said you weren't fit to be a guard. Listen, the whole point is that I don't want to make myself look like a coward. Guard me from far away."

And just like that, the general whimsically opened the car door and stepped onto the Ildoan road. To start off with, General Zettour, as natural as could be, stretched his back. He then stretched his arms before taking a cigar out and blowing smoke toward the beautiful Ildoan sky.

With the simple expression a man makes when he enjoys a good cigar, he began walking. He stood up straight as he walked, blowing out more smoke.

His nice and shiny shoes clacked as he made his way down the stone road, and his freshly starched pants were picture perfect, as if this were a military parade, thanks to the diligent orderly who had prepared them.

Looking dignified, he walked down the road in leisure. His swagger told a story of a man who hadn't a fear in the world.

Historic landmarks seemed to line this road in particular, and every now and then, the general would stop and read the metal plates mounted here and there that explained the spot's significance, like some stereotypical middle-aged civilian tourist.

This was enemy territory, and the old tourist was a general. As if the rank insignia that lined his lapel didn't stand out enough, there was a civilian car heralding his insignia on a flag that followed close by. The sheer fear caused by the sight made his bodyguard, Grantz, dizzy with nausea. What if there was a sniper in one of the buildings? It didn't matter, the general was out in the open. It wouldn't require an expert sniper to take him out.

"Would you mind walking a bit faster?"

Grantz murmured to himself, but his concern was all but lost on General Zettour, who made no effort to speed up his stroll. He seemed more interested in the historical spot he'd stumbled upon and even went to fetch a camera from the car.

The general gathered his security detail for a picture, even making them pose, as if this were a commemorative photo. Grantz was falling apart on the inside, but the general paid him no mind as he took a small break where he stood. Mingling with the soldiers was what good officers did, but having said that...even if Grantz was an officer, he was also in charge of the general's safety, which was why he was horrified.

The smiling general, offering cigars to the other soldiers, was like a literal sitting duck. A first-year soldier who'd only learned to fire a gun that day could easily have taken him out with the urban camouflage of the city streets.

With the scenario at hand, the general was acting like a daredevil. It was as if he was trying to provoke the enemy into doing so.

"Whenever...wherever..."

He could hardly think as he watched. The sheer uneasiness was burning away at Grantz, who saw an enemy at every street corner. But the general?! He was just waltzing around, leisurely as could be! Without his guards there defending him, what would this look like?!

General Zettour's guards, too, must've been enveloped in his leisurely disposition, because they were starting to show no signs of caution.

For better or worse, the surrounding Ildoans didn't look on their group with vicious eyes...but it was hard to guess when a person would try to kill someone. Grantz knew this from his experience in the Rhine, in Arene, and in the east. He knew that Ildoa, no matter how blue its sky was, was no different.

Moved by his sense of danger, Grantz finally ran up to his superior's boss.

"Oh, Lieutenant Grantz. Do you want a cigar?"

"I—I appreciate the offer, but I need to take care of my lungs. We regularly fly at high altitudes, so it's critical we refrain from smoking."

In the spur of the moment, Grantz gave an honest response when he rejected the cigar, but the problem at hand was much more severe than his respiratory health.

"General Zettour, the longer we're out in the open, the more likely someone bad will find out. Let's not stay in one place too long."

"Oh, Lieutenant. You're so pure. Take a look around for yourself."

General Zettour placed his hand on Grantz's shoulder and spoke with a magnanimous tone.

"Where exactly do you see a threat? There's nothing threatening about where we are right now, if you ask me."

"Well, we have defeated the enemy field army."

"Then what's there to worry about?"

"I don't mean to step out of line, but while we've defeated their army, the reality is there are still potential enemies lurking about. When it comes to keeping you safe, this situation is far from ideal."

Grantz thought as he said this.

We're way too out in the open. You're an Imperial general, the highest-ranking general there is! What if someone is out for revenge? Or a surviving soldier who knows how to take the perfect shot, or some rabid patriot just waiting out there?

"You're such a worrywart. You would've brought me to the front lines in the Federation had I ordered you to, wouldn't you? Was I misguided in placing my hopes in a company as excellent as yours for my defense?"

"We're willing to follow your orders, no matter what they are."

"Then if I order you to stop bugging me about this, will you stop?"

Grantz was more than prepared to do battle. He'd throw himself in front of a stray bullet to cover the general if he had to. But there were too many angles he couldn't cover where they were in the city.

"I don't mean to be difficult, but us mages aren't as all-powerful as you think we are."

While a mage could use their magic and defensive shell to protect others...they couldn't move faster than flying bullets. The soldiers in his company weren't even proper guards in any sense of the word. Elite though they might be, Grantz's lack of experience made him anxious. What's more, a company simply didn't provide enough manpower to protect someone in an urban environment.

They needed to search all the surrounding buildings to confirm the general's safety, but he just didn't have the numbers. Sending out the handful of soldiers he had was like pissing in the ocean. The most he could do was have a few of them walk ahead while the rest of them followed. Though Grantz himself didn't have the authority to order the foot soldiers to do anything anyway.

It was going to be the general who had to give them their orders, but he seemed to have no interest in his own safety as he simply walked down Ildoa's streets. Streets full of people!

Grantz almost wanted to cry at the absurdity. General Zettour, as if having found fault in the lieutenant's grim expression, let out a loud, ostentatious sigh.

"Lieutenant Grantz. You're still young. Why don't you take this day to celebrate a nice victory?"

"The colonel taught us to tighten our helmets after a victory."

"That's wonderful advice. Although it isn't the advice a person should ever have to give."

His superior's superior could say whatever he wanted, but Grantz couldn't allow himself to agree or disagree. Grantz found himself recalling an old expression.

Silence is golden, and eloquence is silver. It was something people used to say.

"Your superior is a monster who believes others can do exactly as she can. Am I wrong, Lieutenant?"

"The colonel is an incredibly capable person, after all…"

"They say the Imperial Army is made of many faces, but she is several cuts above the rest."

General Zettour rubbed his chin with a satisfied look. He then adjusted the cigar in his mouth and took a moment to enjoy it again.

"That said, one must rejoice when the time calls for it. It can be quite taxing on your mental health to neglect making the most of every opportunity to do so."

"Does good progress warrant dropping everything to rejoice?"

"I want you to look at this capital. We've acquired so many munitions and crushed so many enemies. And now this beautiful capital is ours."

The general was being theatrical in his speech, but there was a truth to what he said. Grantz even reminded himself how easy it would be to simply agree with him.

However, Grantz refused to look away from the harsh reality, as he was taught to. Even with the general, he wouldn't allow himself to daydream.

"General, the enemy forces have only lost on one flank."

Reality was reality, and the world was the world.

Grantz had been made to realize that the world never was the way one *wished for it to be*—that they lived in a strict and cruel reality.

This was why, even when speaking with the highest general of his army, Grantz would not falter in defending his perspective.

"Today's victory was, at most, a small one."

"You're precisely right."

The general spat his cigarette on the ground and stamped it out while tightening up his soft expression and glaring into Lieutenant Grantz's eyes with dead seriousness.

"What you said is accurate and correct. I thank you for your unvarnished words."

As he said this, he grabbed the lieutenant by his collar and pulled him closer with impressive strength.

"Which is why I need you to shut your damn trap."

He whispered in Grantz's ear with a chilling intensity.

"I...what?"

"You mustn't bend the knee to sound logic."

The general's stark determination in his actions could be heard clearly in his chilling tone

"Now smile, Lieutenant."

The general's friendly demeanor disappeared, and his words were strained.

"I said smile; it doesn't need to be real. Smile like an idiot. That's an order."

"You want me to...smile?"

"That's correct. Do not show them your weakness. I don't care if it's fake, you mustn't allow the enemy to know what dire straits the Empire is in right now," General Zettour whispered in a subzero tone to Grantz, who would swallow whatever he was about to say. "Throw away your pretensions. You don't need to act well, just do what I need you to."

Grantz stared right into the general's eyes, something he regretted immediately.

"You are a conqueror. Say it to yourself, *I am powerful.* I don't care if you have to trick yourself about this, either. Just make sure you never let anyone watching get the opportunity to figure out if it's true."

Staring into the general's eyes, he saw the depths of true nothingness. It was like staring into an abyss.

"You must trick the world. It isn't much to ask, to put on a nice face. Go on, do it. Trick yourself."

What was he saying?

Soldiers, your peers, and regular people all set their eyes on two things. Your rank and your face. This is something they teach you early at the academy.

"I'll k-keep that in mind."

"Never forget it. Smiling is a part of an officer's job. Haven't you learned anything working under Colonel Degurechaff?"

At that point, General Zettour caught himself where he stood. He rubbed his chin once before offering a wry chuckle. From what Grantz could tell, this was the first actual, non-twisted smile he'd shown all day.

"Your superior, she may be laughing earnestly. She may find what we're doing here genuinely entertaining."

"She is the colonel…"

Grantz found himself in agreement. It was true, she always had a smile on her face. Whether it was a self-deprecating sneer, or her happily humming a war song, he never once saw her panic before. Strangely enough, whenever he struggled at his limit, looking at his superior would always bring a smile out of him. He had never seen her show distress when backed into a corner for as long as he could remember.

A part of him questioned whether this was the case for her adjutant, Visha, but it was nothing more than speculation.

"Whatever happens, I want you to smile, Lieutenant. Smiling is important."

General Zettour wore a smile of his own.

"The Imperial Army will kick the daylights out of our enemies. You'll see, in the newspaper. Our power will go down in history."

There would likely be articles and caricatures in the newspaper describing it. The majesty of the Empire, its power, and the menace it was.

Which was why the general would whisper a final thought into the young lieutenant's ear.

"We're going to give the world a good taste of our boot leather, you hear?"

The soldiers executed a mock battle
on the front lines but ran out of
ammunition, so they went to the enemy's
base to procure what they needed.

A Legend from the Salamander Kampfgruppe

Tanya von Degurechaff is a firm believer in an in-depth training regimen. I know the value of constantly drilling seemingly mundane movements and committing them to muscle memory.

Training is always important.

At the same time, training that's impractical for actual combat is useless. It's just as bad as using nothing but actual combat as a soldier's *only* form of training. Now, it goes without saying that combat experience is valuable, but it has its limits.

Can a soldier who fights well in the trenches replicate their skills in a tank battle or when conducting maneuver warfare? Does it let them understand deep operations? No, and that's precisely where training comes in—it allows soldiers to broaden the breadth of their experience.

Actual experience is undoubtedly precious by nature, but those who hold such experience above all else are bound to suffer immense consequences.

I believe two things are paramount on the battlefield: uninhibited critical thinking and the gumption to seize the initiative. Additionally, I place great importance on cost-effectiveness.

"Yes, experience is wonderful. But first and foremost, the tuition is too high."

Far too high, at that!

And yet, experience can only provide empirical knowledge. Relying purely on magnificent experience is what leads commanders to mindlessly march their troops into machine-gun fire and call it military doctrine. The reverse is true as well. Staying on the defensive because the prospect of attacking is too frightening is what the French army did during World War II after learning from their experiences in World War I.

There's no denying the value of combat experience, but soldiers can't afford to stop thinking. It's crucial to always strive for improvement by thinking critically.

Luckily, it's possible to iron out the kinks in training. Better to learn those lessons somewhere other than the battlefield, where mistakes are paid for in blood.

In any case, this strange lull in the fighting with the Ildoan and the Unified States forces is the perfect chance to evaluate how well the Kampfgruppe can adapt to positional warfare during the peninsular campaign.

To put it bluntly, the results are bad. Really bad.

I'm at a loss as I watch my unit make fools of themselves for the first time in a long while.

"What is this disgrace?!"

I've been a little anxious about this for a while now. That's why I wanted to confirm my suspicions with an exercise, and I thought I knew what to expect, but…there's a limit to what's acceptable.

"You're supposed to be our army's elites! Have you idiots forgotten the sacrifices of your comrades on the Rhine?!"

I'm livid at the performance of her officers, the ones I've placed so much faith in. It might have been worth a chuckle if they were still pretending to be inept. These are the unstoppable soldiers who led the way in securing the Ildoan capital and then drove south to seize additional territory, but even they can't be good at everything. However, if their fundamental soldiering skills have grown dull, then it's a massive problem.

This Kampfgruppe is always the tip of the spear in blitzkrieg and maneuver warfare. My subordinates are masters of mobility—the same men and women who've held the line in the east. But when it comes to a little Rhine-style trench warfare? *Wretched* is too generous to describe the crap job they're doing!

"It's supposed to be a defensive position! Even moles can dig a hole! You're supposed to be humans! Use your brains! Make *trenches*! Make them right!"

Lieutenant Serebryakov is close by, so she has a front row seat to Tanya's shock. Of the entire battalion, the only ones doing a somewhat acceptable job are the mages under Major Weiss's command. All I can do is complain to my ever-faithful adjutant.

"This is just appalling. They've been deployed so long that they forgot everything they learned in training."

"Our experience in the east was…something different. It's also worth noting that the majority of our Kampfgruppe didn't see action on the Rhine front. For most of them, this is probably their first real taste of trench warfare."

I shake my head in disbelief.

"Even if that's true, everything they need to know is written in the manual. NCOs and officers should have read it."

"The standards have fallen dramatically since the war started. Not to mention, the soldiers have their hands full just going about their daily duties…"

I let out another sigh. The Ildoans seem perfectly capable of erecting proper fortifications without ever having experienced war. Their devastatingly poor morale and lack of will to fight are major problems, but at least they look the part!

Biting back another sigh, I reluctantly agree with my adjutant, at least on the surface.

"I know that. I also know my desire for the troops to perform beyond their actual capabilities is unreasonable, but a commanding officer's inaction is paid for in body bags."

Tanya's adjutant starts to respond by saying, "That's…," but Tanya stops her with a wave.

"The Kampfgruppe's manpower is not limitless, and there's no hope of getting replacements. The Empire can't afford to squander the lives of these soldiers. Our nation is completely broke, whether we like it or not."

I shake my head as I peer up at the blue skies of Ildoa. I was so confident in the training my subordinates had undergone. This is unacceptable. To think we'd lose such crucial organizational knowledge.

"I may have put too much faith in my Kampfgruppe."

"For what it's worth, we have consistently produced results…"

I nod, acknowledging her point. Indeed, the unit's accomplishments can't be ignored. However, no organization or company can be judged by results alone, nor should it. There are always potential risk factors that must be thoroughly investigated, which is precisely why I'm putting the unit through its paces like this in the first place.

The primary cause for my foul mood is the construction of what are supposed to be trenches. The holes being dug are just "good enough," and the complete lack of intent to turn any of it into a permanent defensive position is apparent.

It's possible that the troops see little purpose in trenches after plowing through the enemies' defenses so easily. Things wouldn't be so bad if only a handful of soldiers shared this sentiment, but it's the same no matter where I look...

I question some soldiers digging nearby.

"Who ordered you to dig eastern front trenches? Was it Lieutenant Tospan?"

"Yes, Colonel. We're following Lieutenant Tospan's orders."

Just as I expected. It's painful to see veteran-enlisted and NCOs alike mindlessly accept orders to construct eastern front–style trenches. Setting my disappointment aside for the moment, I give a formal response.

"Good work, soldier. Sorry for interrupting you."

Letting them get back to work, I raise my voice to call for my officer.

"Tospan! Where is Lieutenant Tospan?!"

Tanya's voice can cut through even the din of an active battlefield. There's no doubt the infantry commander heard it because he jumps out of one of the trenches and comes running. Tospan is met by a menacing glare and a barked order fit for the battlefield.

"Start over. Right now! And do it right this time!"

"Colonel? Is there a problem...?"

"There's nothing *but* problems, Lieutenant! That's my problem!"

Usually, Lieutenant Grantz would have been able to flawlessly provide the lieutenant with some much-needed support, much like how his unit protected Tospan's infantry during combat. However, he and his company have been confiscated by General Zettour—a point of pain for everyone here. I shoot a brief glance at my adjutant.

"Colonel? Shall I...assist Lieutenant Tospan?"

"Negative. The Kampfgruppe is already running thin on commanding officers."

This is the downside of a Kampfgruppe. The structure of an ad hoc task force places most of the command and control burden on the commanding officer. The headquarters is painfully understaffed. There just aren't enough officers, given the unit's size.

This wouldn't be a problem if it was only a temporary combat formation, like originally intended. Unfortunately, the Salamander Kampfgruppe seems to be, for all intents and purposes, a permanent unit, and the overwork that comes with this is cause for yet another headache. If only Lieutenant Grantz were here, then I could leave command of Tospan and Wüstemann to him and maybe send some of my paperwork his way as well. No point in wishing for what I can't have, though.

The hundred people under Tanya's command are better than the million she doesn't have.

While taking care to keep the exasperation and disappointment from showing on my face, I turn to Lieutenant Tospan—who seems utterly oblivious—and address him in the gentlest tone I can muster to point out what the issue is.

"Listen, the determination to hold this position at all costs is good and well. I have no intention of belittling your resolution. But that is precisely why I can't have you dying meaningless deaths."

After acknowledging his effort and motivation, I say what must be said. Even if the troops are prepared to die, it doesn't mean they should for no reason. Such luxury is unaffordable during wartime.

"Constructing strongpoints will not work here."

"But we used it to great effect in the east...?"

"You have to bear in mind the differences in terrain, Lieutenant Tospan. The eastern front is vast. Meanwhile, on a front this narrow, it's far too easy to concentrate fire. The enemy artillery could obliterate us in the blink of an eye if we stack up like this."

Even the Federation Army's overwhelming firepower has to be dispersed to a certain extent due to the immense size of the eastern front. Up against the Unified States, the same country that has so much ammunition it can lend-lease the Federation and still have enough for itself, there's no telling how much firepower they can bring to bear on the narrow front. Just imagining it is terrifying.

That's why I have to reproach my subordinate's lack of foresight and point out that he's relying too much on past experience.

"Do not underestimate our enemy. Even if it is a pain, prepare multiple trenches for defense in depth. Make sure they form one continuous line of defense. It's an old-fashioned strategy, but this battlefield calls for elastic defense."

A correction is in order.

"In other words, remember to secure an escape route."

"Won't that make our soldiers want to retreat?"

"Lieutenant Tospan, just what do you think your subordinates are?"

"I... Well..."

I let out a deep sigh in front of my subordinate, who appears to be caught in a big misunderstanding.

"I appreciate your readiness to die for your country in this trench. However, it isn't your duty to die. Never stop using your head. None of you are allowed to die pointless deaths. Only after you've struggled with every last bit of strength you can summon does your death have any meaning."

Lieutenant Tospan nods in understanding as I leave him behind and move on with my inspection. Unfortunately, the problems don't end there. Up next is Captain Ahrens. I wind up having to explain to the tanker that he needs to prepare for situations where going around enemy fortifications won't be possible.

"This is not the east. It's much narrower here. Too narrow."

"But a frontal assault will result in casualties that—"

"It's the opposite. Rather than attempt to avoid the unavoidable, you must think about how to minimize our losses in the event of a frontal assault."

"Y-yes, Colonel."

"Good. It's more or less the same as our raid on the Ildoan capital. Come up with a plan. Never stop thinking."

Once Captain Ahrens also nods in understanding, I seek out the Kampfgruppe's artillery. After a quick scan, I call Captain Meybert over.

After confirming a couple of things with him, I'm finally able to unwind a little.

"Well done, Captain."

While the individual soldiers have varying levels of skill, it's clear that the officers and NCOs know what they're doing and form a strong core for this group. The expertise and professionalism of the artillery crews are alive and well.

"It makes sense that the gunners would remember their trench warfare."

"In all fairness, Colonel, much of what the artillery unit does derives from fighting in the trenches. It would be difficult to forget."

"I wish the other units could hear you now. Good work, Captain Meybert."

While it doesn't do much to lighten my mood as a whole, it always feels good to see a professional at work.

"Thank you, but there are still a lot of issues. Even if we train and train until we're a well-oiled machine, there is only so much we can do without supplies."

"Spoken like a true artillery officer."

"Math and physics are our bread and butter."

I can't help but chuckle at Captain Meybert's matter-of-fact response as I lend an ear to his plea.

"So what are you running low on?"

"Everything."

This answer is nothing if not predictable. It's practically a running joke at this point because my response is the same as always.

"Such is the fate of the tip of the spear."

"You must be used to this by now, Colonel."

I shrug.

"Hardly. Our mission is too demanding and our support is too lacking. There's a limit to how many times I can laugh it off as a matter of pride or honor, but I shan't let my soldiers hear these qualms."

It's more an idle complaint than anything else, but a superior showing some weakness makes it easier for subordinates to open up about their own qualms. This communication technique seems to hit its mark, as the captain immediately reveals his most significant problem.

"Cutting to the chase...we don't have enough shells."

"Is it that bad? I was under the impression that we brought the minimum amount necessary."

"Unlike on the eastern front, we don't have a reliable way to replenish our stocks. We can't rely on acquiring supplies from the enemy, either."

A lack of rounds...isn't something I can fix, which is incredibly frustrating. Nevertheless, since I am a superior officer, it's my job to provide my subordinates with a solution of some sort when they come to me with their problems. Failing to offer anything constructive would be a sign of incompetence.

I cross my arms and mull it over before eventually responding.

"What about using captured Ildoan artillery? There should be plenty of ammunition for those."

"Actually, I thought we could maybe use them, too."

"Then we should... Wait, what do you mean you *thought* we could?"

My eyes ask, *What stopped you?*, and Meybert emits a tired sigh in response.

"It's because of their equipment procurement."

"Their procurement? Ah, I see."

I slap my knee in realization as Captain Meybert lets out a sigh.

"They use a variety of different calibers."

"Specifically...?"

"The Ildoans use a mix of different guns sourced from their many allies with absolutely no standardization. Just looking at their ammunition feels like walking through a military museum."

"Thank you, Captain. That is a great analogy."

A military museum is a nice place to see an expansive collection of armaments, but it would be a mistake to try and use the displays to fight a war. It seems the equipment they seized wouldn't be of much use.

"Perhaps we could acquire what we need from the Unified States?"

"Well, I believe that could work, but their artillery has yet to show themselves since our last encounter."

"They'll come eventually."

"I'm sure they will."

"But, yes, they're of no use to us until they come... Saying that makes it sound like I want them to come."

I cross my arms and ponder about the shortage of shells.

The value of cannon shells has practically exploded because of how hard they were to obtain on the Ildoan peninsula. Were the market functioning correctly, an ocean of munitions would pour into the country...

"If only there was a market for artillery rounds. Ugh, this isn't something I want to think about during an active war."

Supplies are scarce. The supply routes are unstable. And there's little hope for increased production or new supply lines. We'll have to make do with what we have on hand.

"Let us change our thinking, Captain. How far can our current stockpile take us?"

"If I'm being honest, I doubt we can adequately suppress the enemy. It may be more prudent to disregard the potential losses and use our guns in direct-fire missions on the front line."

"No, our gunners are precious human resources. We can't afford to waste them."

The artillery unit is full of engineers and technicians—in other words, they're high-skilled workers.

"I want our gunners to focus on shelling... What if you had mages operating as forward observers to improve your accuracy?"

The solution Tanya thinks up on a whim draws an enthusiastic response from the captain. He looks at me with a beaming expression on his face.

"We could work with that!"

I've never seen him look and sound so excited before. It seems this problem has been bothering the artillery officer for a long while now.

"If we have eyes in the sky, I can show you what a well-trained artillery unit is really capable of!"

"Then let's test out the idea. We'll conduct an exercise."

A military exercise is a high-level learning event. It would be carried out, reviewed, modified, then held again until the movements were mastered.

And so the Salamander Kampfgruppe began splitting into two teams—near the front line, mind you. In peacetime, the very idea would be utterly baffling, but Tanya's subordinates have grown numb to irregular orders and no one raises so much as an eyebrow. The Salamander

Kampfgruppe officers, convinced they are the only sensible people left, obediently follow their orders and reorganize their troops for the exercise.

As an ad hoc task force, our identity is synonymous with temporary formations and quick reorganization. The officers don't even notice just how incredible a feat it is to execute a military exercise so close to our enemies, even considering our slightly advantageous position.

"Begin the exercise!"

With those orders, the Salamander Kampfgruppe that has split into two groups begins the war game.

It should go without saying they are using live ammunition, and both sides are firing at each other. Of course, while the bullets are going in the correct general directions, no one is aiming to hit anyone directly. Still, for the infantry in the trenches, live rounds are flying right overhead.

The soldiers have nothing to worry about so long as they keep their heads down in the trenches. Compared to the standards on the Rhine, this is a rather mild exercise.

"This is trench warfare! Stay low!"

I can't help but sigh at the panicked shouting of the NCOs in the trenches below. From my vantage point high up in the sky, the performance of the elite Salamander Kampfgruppe is surprisingly disappointing.

"Damn it! Did you all become exhibitionists in the east?! Get down!"

"Move, move, move! Are you *trying* to get hit by friendly fire?!"

"No! Pull back! Pull back now! Did you forget the basics of positional warfare?!"

Each of her officers barks at the veteran NCOs to get them moving but…it's all very unwieldy.

They're too slow.

Much, much too slow.

I sigh and fold my arms.

"We've spent too long in the east. Going from a wide front to a narrow one is quite the headache."

The only silver lining is Captain Meybert's artillery fire. With the assistance of mage aerial observers, their shells are landing with impressive accuracy. Still, it's a meager showing compared to our time on the

Rhine. This being an exercise, no one is trying to drop any shells on top of the infantry, but with every round that goes off, the lack of flying lead is very palpable.

With our current stores, they wouldn't last more than a few days in an artillery slugfest. Back in the glory days on the Rhine...the constant bombardments may as well have been a part of the daily weather report. Such a stockpile no longer exists in the Empire.

Between the east, the west, and Ildoa, our dwindling resources are spread so thin that there isn't much to send to any individual front. It shows how reckless it is to go up against the world. It surely doesn't help that the Empire's labor force and industrial production have reached the heights of exhaustion due to protracted total war. Just how many more drops of water could be squeezed from the dusty cloth that is our nation?

Each unit participating in the exercise is first-class, but it doesn't matter when they lack what they need to function properly. Were these regular times, a group of professionals such as this could find a workaround or acquire what they need from the market. Sadly, there is no market; it's collapsed, and the war won't let it bounce back.

I heave yet another sigh, unable to suppress my frustration.

"I'm growing tired of this endless war..."

Right as I grumble, I notice a change in pace in the battle playing out below. Once the two groups close in on each other, a series of flares go up, signifying that the soldiers must change from live ammunition to dummy rounds. Cries of acknowledgment go up from both sides.

This appears to be the moment the tank unit has been waiting for, because they spring into action.

"Captain Ahrens is charging in. That was quick."

This show of initiative is impressive, and the infantry under Lieutenant Tospan respond by hunkering down in the intricate trenchworks, then mounting a counterattack.

Protected by their defensive shells, Major Weiss and several other mages are acting as referees and declare several tank kills. That was an ideal response to being charged by armor.

However, Lieutenant Tospan's unit lacks the weight of numbers. At the end of the day, a Kampfgruppe can't hold ground with the same resilience that a division can. Even in the event we can plug the hole of a break-through, we don't have the numbers to properly counterattack in strength.

On top of that, the artillery split up to provide both sides of the exercise with support fire, but…the entire thing is quickly devolving into a mudslinging contest.

I've seen enough, especially considering the fact that this is all taking place near the front lines.

"End the exercise! End the exercise!"

I look down at the troops from above, a scowl on my face as I make the announcement. The results of this exercise leave me with nothing but concern for the future.

The disappointment and regret put my thoughts in a tailspin, hurtling down a labyrinth of confusion. It is her adjutant, however, who breaks me out of this depressing mindset.

"What did you think, Colonel?"

"Do you even have to ask? You were watching it with me, after all."

"In all fairness, I think most would give them a passing grade in terms of competency."

"Don't forget, this is *after* we gave them instructions on what to do. If the troops need us to order them around to properly conduct something as elementary as trench warfare…we won't be able to hold this position…"

I close my eyes as if struck by a painful headache. The performance of my troops would be acceptable at best if they were a regular infantry division, but it's clear that they're out of their element.

This is the Salamander Kampfgruppe—the General Staff's trump card. The only battles we see are the worst of the worst—the fieriest depths of the war. These soldiers may be experts at maneuver warfare, but now they have to become experts at trench warfare as well.

"We've become far too accustomed to the eastern front."

"It was always run, duck, and run again back on the Rhine. That muscle memory goes away if you don't do it for a while."

"You're absolutely right, Lieutenant Serebryakov. We didn't have the chance to experience fast-moving, nose-to-the-ground trench warfare in the east."

Despite the persistent headache, I try to remember my subordinates' movements. They are mobile and can maintain their mobility for long periods of time. Even if this is only an exercise, their movements alone are quite nimble. They aren't afraid to advance when they need to and can maintain unit cohesion even while withdrawing.

But this is the same as what they did in the east. There are still many problems when it comes to conducting deep battle in the trenches, which will be necessary in Ildoa.

While not overcommitting to defending the trenches is a point worth considering, Lieutenant Tospan's decision on how to meet the tank advance was lackluster. He needs to coordinate with the artillery more. On the other hand, while Captain Ahrens did make good use of a Panzer-keil formation...it's clear that his soldiers aren't used to mounting frontal assaults on fortified positions.

"Our troops are in bad shape. I had them repeat some small exercises because we have the time, but I still fear for the future. We need a way to teach them..."

I'm still murmuring to myself about what the next steps should be when the slightest of sensations commands my full attention.

There's a faint signal, off in the distance.

Most people would overlook it, but my experience as a veteran war mage helps me notice it.

"Hm? Is that a mana signal?"

"I don't feel anything."

"It's coming from between our ten and eleven o'clock. Almost directly behind our unit. The altitude is somewhere between one and two thousand. They seem to be alone."

After focusing on the area I point out, Lieutenant Serebryakov nods, apparently picking up the signal as well now.

"Is it a messenger from Lieutenant Grantz's company? It's much too soon for them to be rejoining us."

The company that General Zettour stole away won't be returning for a long while. We shouldn't be hearing from them anytime soon. What's more, everyone knows Tanya places great stock in traveling in pairs. Lieutenant Grantz would never dispatch a lone messenger.

"Everyone should be on guard. Just to be sure, let's have Major Weiss…"

"It's all right, Colonel. That's a friendly mage."

"Wait, how do you know?"

"She's a childhood friend of mine from school. I recognize her signal."

"Ah, I see," I say with a nod to Lieutenant Serebryakov. "It's good that your friend is still alive. Very good. But why is she flying alone?"

"I'm pretty sure she's attached to HQ. She's their messenger mage, I believe."

Upon learning that, I suddenly plunge deep into thought.

Headquarters. Using an officer as a messenger. And sending them alone to the front lines?

"It must be an urgent message for them to use a mage! But why now?"

Mages are scarce as it is. This is on top of the fact that General Zettour is using a whole company of them as a security detail. Deciding to send a mage despite all this speaks to the gravity of the message they're carrying.

I'm certain it's definitely nothing good. Though this is always the case, something tells me this time will be especially bad.

Acting on my instincts, I raise the alarm.

"All units! Return to your positions! Return to your positions at once!"

It takes only a single order from Tanya to end all ongoing exercises and send the soldiers running to their posts. The Kampfgruppe does a magnificent job changing their posture to combat-ready in an instant.

The tanks are covered in camouflage nets, the infantry flow into the trenches, and the artillery all but disappears from sight.

Thanks to this, by the time the approaching Imperial mage arrives, she sees no one but Tanya and her adjutant.

With a look of slight confusion, the young, dignified mage gives a firm salute before holding out a sealed envelope to me as I return the courtesy.

"I come on the orders of the General Staff to deliver this message. Please take it."

The young mage officer is holding a document case. As per the strictest protocol, the case is sealed and will be handed over only after the recipient signs for it.

It should also be mentioned that a self-destruct device is attached to the document case to prevent it from falling into the wrong hands.

"Good work, Lieutenant. I have indeed received your delivery."

I sign for the dispatch and remove the automatic combustion device before realizing that my adjutant is a bit restless. I glance at the mage who has just arrived, and it finally dawns on me.

"Ah, right, of course. You two were classmates. Adjutant, I will return to the ground. Who knows when you'll get another chance, so please, take some time to catch up with your friend."

"Oh… Is it really all right?"

"Of course. Feel free to chat over some tea, if you'd like," I add, demonstrating the qualities of an excellent superior that I pride myself on being.

Afterward, I fly over to my private area on the base.

Before doing anything, first I drink a glass of water. Then I set my eyes on the envelope—it's just like the ones I've seen in the General Staff Office.

"I'm assuming it must be from General Zettour."

Naturally, a sigh escapes me. This is General Zettour I'm dealing with, after all. I can tell from the messenger mage alone that this one will be a doozy, so I steel my nerves before reaching for the envelope once more.

"What's this about…?"

With one final mumble, I open the envelope and find a single, flimsy sheet of paper.

I take a deep breath.

Then I read through it. As soon as I finish, I find myself cradling my head in this corner of the field camp. Even if I remain silent, there's no hiding the anguish of a struggling middle manager that appears on my charming, adorable face.

"Ah, fuck. Why…? Why would this…?"

Despite only having just downed a glass of water, an intense wave of thirst hits me. The urge to chug the entire pitcher makes me reach for it. In fact, I have a fleeting urge to dump it over my head.

"Secure the area around the royal capital…? He wants us to do *what* now…?"

Orders are orders.

No matter what the order may be, there are no exceptions.

Still cradling my head in anguish, I moan to myself.

"I always get asked to do the impossible... I thought I was used to it, but it seems General Zettour is on a whole other level..."

The truth is that just capturing the city was already an insurmountable feat in itself and wouldn't have been possible without the Salamander Kampfgruppe leading the charge.

"To think he could possibly expect more from us... Wait."

I take a moment to reconsider the situation.

The Ildoan capital was never meant to be occupied permanently, just temporarily at most. And yet, when we did successfully take the city, it was done with seeming ease. It makes sense that the need would arise for the Empire to flaunt their new acquisition. From a military standpoint, the army must announce its superiority to the world to preserve the facade of strength.

"Th-this isn't what we signed up for..."

The capital city was never meant to be anything more than a pit stop. That was the plan, at least.

"We're supposed to be leaving by now. How did things turn out this way...?"

Thankfully, none of Tanya's subordinates are here to see this outpouring of stress and frustration.

The orders say to secure the area around the Ildoan capital. It appears as if the general has a strong desire for the army to take a forward position while holding on to the city—despite lacking the manpower, firepower, and armor to get the job done!

"Perhaps Santa is going to bring us reinforcements this year?"

As I scoff to myself about the impossibility of that, I review the current situation.

The recent exercises have convinced me that positional warfare can't be sustained. So how exactly are we expected to secure the capital? Orders are orders, but some things simply aren't possible...

I stand from my seat and calmly begin to consider our options.

Pacing back and forth, sometimes crossing my arms or waving them around, I eventually come to the conclusion that I'm all out of tricks. After all, the mage battalion is beyond the point of terminal exhaustion by now!

"How does he expect us to pull this off? Seeing as how the enemy is slowly pulling back, I suppose we can advance if that's all we need to do."

They could move forward in tandem with the enemy's retreat. It's certainly possible, though it would gain the Empire nothing more than a modest foothold, and to do so would come with a grave price.

"It seems unlikely that we'll have much choice in deciding where the battle will be fought. And retreating will be complicated, to say the least. We'll essentially be handing the initiative over to the enemy. The risk is unacceptable."

If the weaker force allows their enemy to attack them as they please, total destruction will follow soon after. Initiative is the main factor that determines who wins any given encounter.

"Do I want to fall victim to an enemy counteroffensive?" I pose this question to myself, only to laugh.

Of course not.

"Using Open Sesame against our enemies was brilliant, but it's not something I ever want to be on the receiving end of."

I recall Operation Revolving Door with a degree of trepidation. No matter how big or how strong an army may be, the cost of losing the initiative will always be paid in blood and tears. The Empire encircling and destroying the Republican field army was a recent example of this. The Republic had a powerful military that was fully capable of keeping the Empire at bay on the Rhine front. They only forfeited the initiative to General Zettour and General Rudersdorf a single time, and that cost them the war.

I don't want to repeat their mistakes.

"Initiative. Yes...initiative."

How are we going to maintain the initiative in the first place, given our limited manpower? It's a complex puzzle, and the pieces are the Salamander Kampfgruppe's lives, honor, and assets. Things can't get much worse than this in terms of corporate exploitation!

I refuse to fail here—a job change is still on the board. With renewed determination, I reassess the situation.

"Let's think this over. We don't have the intel to conduct a surgical strike to decapitate the enemy. Moreover, going on the offensive always comes with risk."

The fog of war is thick, and the danger is real.

"At the same time, even if we focus solely on establishing defensive fortifications, hardly anyone would consider that successfully securing the area…"

We're understaffed.

We don't have the troops to spare for an assault, and a prolonged defense will only wear down what few forces we have left. This is a worrisome predicament. While our army may enjoy a temporary local advantage, concentrating forces here puts immense strain on the Empire's other fronts. It's only a matter of time before the panzer divisions must return to the east. In fact…there's a strong chance that we might be sent back to the east as well, right after exhausting what little we have here in Ildoa.

"We can't afford to take any losses and there are no prospects for reinforcements…"

Is it even possible to secure the capital in the first place…? My brain is reaching its limit. No matter how much I puzzle over the hopeless situation, no solution is making itself apparent.

Secure the capital…

Secure the capital…

Secure the…

These words are a persistent source of worry as I continue mulling over them. There must be some way to make these seemingly impossible orders a reality. There has to be…

With a series of moans and groans, I allow my mind to entertain even the most fantastical scenarios as a means of escapism before a new realization hits me.

"Hey, wait a second…"

Is there any reason to mindlessly keep a hold on the capital? General Zettour was the one who originally said he had no intention of being tied down in the capital, after all.

I repeat my orders out loud.

"Secure the area around the capital."

That's it. Nothing more, nothing less. In fact, the orders very specifically mention the area *around the capital*. Securing this area will, in effect, secure the capital itself, which would be the usual intention behind orders such as these…but this isn't how the orders are worded, specifically. Conversely, the orders could also be interpreted as *ignore the capital*.

"Our orders are to establish a forward base and ensure the area surrounding the capital is pacified…and yet, there's no mention about protecting the capital itself."

Maybe I'm overreading this. Were these not General Zettour's orders, I would have promptly secured the capital itself without a second thought…

If only things were that simple.

"General Zettour doesn't mention the capital specifically in these orders. If his wording is intentional, then he has no intention of focusing on the capital at all…"

Maybe it's meant to be some sort of diversion or a ruse to distract international observers. Anyone who sees the Empire secure the area around the capital and set up defensive positions would assume that the Imperial Army is adopting a defensive posture.

But what if this is all a deception?

"Then our true goal is something else… Wait, what is our true goal then?"

I'm fairly confident in my ability to read my superior's true intentions, within reason. I honestly can't imagine General Zettour pushing for the Empire to occupy the Ildoan peninsula in its entirety.

So what is he hiding?

What is his next move…?

I just realized another notable fact about this operation.

"He had us do something like this before…"

It was back on the Rhine front. More specifically, it had to do with Operation Revolving Door. I'll never forget how we were thrown deep into enemy territory to camouflage the Imperial Army's massive withdrawal.

It's almost uncanny how similar this is.

"Does this mean the general is planning to abandon the Ildoan capital?"

Despite proposing the idea myself, it seems ridiculous.

Chapter IV

"We've only just taken the city. Normally, securing it is the obvious next step. When it comes to the capital, the political significance is tremendous."

Setting aside the suddenness of the orders, securing the surrounding area would usually imply securing the capital itself. This much should be a given. Would the Empire ever voluntarily abandon such a strategic point?

I'm having a difficult time wrapping my mind around the idea. If it were anyone else giving these orders, my unit would already be preparing to secure the capital, despite it being nigh impossible.

So it makes sense that the rest of the world will most definitely make the same assumption: The Imperial Army is fortifying its defenses in Ildoa.

What would that mean for the war?

A smile crosses my face as I remember something.

This is precisely the same as it was on the Rhine front.

"It's easy to retreat now, isn't it?"

The general is obscuring his intentions: a strategic reorganization of the war fronts.

"But we'll need to buy time...for a few days?"

That time on the Rhine was also grueling. I sit back in my chair with a sigh and let my body go limp as I stare blankly at the top of the tent. I still don't understand the point of occupying the capital for a few days, only to retreat right after. Is it political? Or is there a military goal? Either way, I'm sure it comes down to how the rest of the world will interpret what we do here.

Perhaps it's an appeal to the Empire's strength, as if saying that we're still powerful enough to capture the capital.

If that's the case, then the answer is simple.

It's important to behave in a way that is easy for others to understand. We have to demonstrate our intent to defend the capital and be as brazen about it as we can. Whatever we do, it needs to be overt and forceful enough that there's no room for misinterpretation.

It's all an act. A performance.

But the show needs to be bombastic.

The world needs to hear the clamor of battle and thunderous explosions.

"That settles what we have to do. The question is, how?"

It needs to be a huge uproar.

Rather than a simple commotion, we need to shock and awe. We need to sow chaos. Our job is to manufacture a crisis. Ideally, without spending too much of our already dwindling resources.

"In other words, this is a PR stunt."

The Empire needs to carve its terrifying public image into the minds of the public. That means the power of mass media will be essential. It goes without saying that outlets with global reach and influence are preferred.

"Our best hopes lie with our guests from the New World."

If the main objective of this operation is riling up the Unified States media, then the US troops should be the primary target. There's just one problem. I doubt my Kampfgruppe will be enough to scare them straight.

"What to do?"

I pour another cup of water from the pitcher and take a moment. The cold drink helps cool off my overheating brain, but it sadly doesn't tease out a new brilliant idea. Where can I borrow units from? At the very least, I'd like to get some more fire support, unless there happen to be soldiers just lying around somewhere.

"We'll have to borrow what we don't have. I wish I could consult with Colonel Lergen or General Zettour about this…" I shake my head. "No, we don't have any reserves to call on even if we wanted to, and the 203rd being overworked is business as usual."

But then something occurs to me.

"We need firepower, eh? Instead of borrowing it, we could just… procure it…"

Procurement.

"Should we use captured equipment? No, that's not…oh! I've got it! That's it!"

I clap my hands together. We lack firepower. If you don't have something, you just need to borrow it. And it doesn't necessarily have to be borrowed from our friends. How could I forget that I can always ask our enemies? They always have what we need!

"In the free market, trust is currency. But in war, violence is the primary means of exchange."

And the Empire has some of the best violence there is to offer. When it comes to capturing arms, we're neck and neck with the Feds.

What a simple solution that I managed to forget.

"All we need to do is capture a Unified States artillery battery, then use the cannons paid for by their hard-earned tax money to blow the US-Ildoan forces to smithereens."

There isn't even a need to defeat the enemies. Hell, the trenches can be left unfinished. All they must do is harass the enemy with their own weapons.

"If it's just one base, we should be able to do it. As for our gunners... we can either have the mages airlift them to the camp or have Captain Ahrens give them a ride."

While carrying all of the artillery unit's equipment would be challenging, the soldiers themselves aren't too much of a burden. The mages can also carry any extra shells and help defend the new position.

We need to show the Unified States and Ildoa how it feels to have your own artillery turned against you. Ideally, we broadcast it to the entire world through the media.

As the plan starts to come together, I examine a map to hash out the details. It isn't long before my adjutant reappears after finishing her talk with her old classmate, which is perfect because I was just thinking about how I could use a pick-me-up. There are times when a good cup of coffee can provide great inspiration. By the time I finish my drink, the broad strokes of the plan have already taken shape.

Our target should be a moderately sized artillery battery. It honestly doesn't really matter which one, but spend enough time in the command post and the ideal candidates will show themselves.

"Hmmm, this looks promising..."

Just as I find a good spot, my subordinate's voice grabs my attention.

"We've picked up a new batch of mana signals. A company of mages. Lieutenant Grantz has returned."

Lieutenant Serebryakov has been on guard duty while I've been working away on my plan. It seems that my subordinate has returned during my intense brainstorming session.

"Ah, perfect timing."

"Are you going to use them for the operation you're currently planning? I'm sorry, but…they must be exhausted."

My adjutant is concerned for her comrades. Though that may be the case, I have no choice but to mercilessly use them.

"It is regrettable to ask them to go right back to work, but I need people. As necessity demands it, I will have them play a role in this operation. We can't spare anyone."

We need to use whatever we have. I can't afford to let a company's worth of experienced mages sit this one out. It's a superior's job to make tough calls like this.

That said, I can't help but sympathize with Grantz, for I am also at the mercy of an unreasonable superior. Nevertheless, it's my duty as a good manager to ease Grantz into the news. This is an important part of preventing wear and tear on my important subordinates.

Benevolent superior that I am, I tell my adjutant what orders she should pass on.

"Let's make sure they get what rest they can. Extra rations as well. Ah, also make sure to give Lieutenant Grantz something that'll be easy on his stomach."

"Why is that?"

"He was with General Zettour, after all. I have also spent a long time accompanying the general, so I have an idea of the poor man's struggles."

"So there are things that stress even you out, Colonel?"

"What do you mean by that, Lieutenant Serebryakov?" I fold my arms and question her further. "If there's something you wish to communicate, I'd like it if you could write it up and submit it formally."

"Oh, no, I didn't mean anything by it!"

I shoot the lieutenant a glare, and she immediately corrects her posture. Visha sure has gotten tough as of late. A slight grin crosses my face, and I just shrug.

"Every superior needs to pay attention to their subordinates' stomachs."

"I will see to it that he eats something easily digestible."

"While you're at it, if there isn't any urgent news, make sure Grantz knows he doesn't need to come to the command post. He can give his report to whoever is on duty and dispense with the formalities. Make sure he and his soldiers eat up and get some rest."

"Understood," Lieutenant Serebryakov says with a salute before turning to leave the office. On her way out, I tack on a tougher order.

"Ah, Lieutenant. One more thing. Make sure to take care of Grantz's paperwork for him."

"Huh? Uh…you want me to do it?"

With a nod, I say, "That's right. It's for the unnecessary remark you made. Looks to me like you have more than enough energy to get the job done."

"Uh, I…"

"Don't tell me you'd abandon a comrade in need?"

"I—I will do my best."

"Good," I say with a nod.

Once Lieutenant Serebryakov leaves the room, I return to the task at hand—figuring out what must be done.

Defeating the enemy—much easier said than done.

Tanya's been given the freedom to act independently, but such freedom is always accompanied by high expectations. Specifically, General Zettour demands just under the limit of what's humanly possible. Unfortunately, my subordinates have been deeply influenced by their experience, and they lack the know-how necessary for this. I am both a participant in the operation as well as its overseer, and shouldering both roles comes with a negligible reward, only solidifying my desire to change jobs. That said, I'm not about to let this chance to pad out my résumé pass me by.

And so I set into motion my modest plan I've privately decided to name Operation Harassment. Standing before the gathered officers of the Salamander Kampfgruppe, I get straight to the point and inform them of their next objective.

"What do you think of a nice hike, comrades?"

This is their invite to a pleasant outing.

The officers immediately know what this means and chuckle to themselves. Nothing to be concerned about.

"The plan is simple. We will go to our campsite, start a nice fire here, cook some meat there, splatter some bloody meat everywhere, then help ourselves to whatever canned goods we can find. Everything we need is already at the campsite, so it'll be a great time."

The camping metaphor seems to get the point across without problems. Major Weiss even adds to the joke, mentioning he hopes there'll be beer.

This should be an easy job. The Salamander Kampfgruppe, which can go toe to toe with an entire division, will hit a single artillery emplacement with everything it's got. And we've already located the base via aerial reconnaissance.

I'm taking point for the attack. The aerial magic battalion finds the base and launches an all-out assault. Obviously, there are defensive lines surrounding the target base, but these are relatively easy to fly over and ignore.

The 203rd, making the most of the fact that they are essentially infantry who can fly, quickly closes in on the base. Evidently, the US artillery gunners didn't expect to be the target of a direct attack because the resistance was...sporadic, at best.

"Suppress the enemy! Keep their heads down!"

By the time the mages used their magic blades and pistols to wipe out the handful of brave enemy defenders, our own gunners were already being airlifted across enemy lines.

The members of the artillery unit find it baffling to be carried by mages, so they're understandably apprehensive at first, but...it isn't long before they take over the Unified artillery battery that has been vacated.

The abandoned position is somewhat messy when they arrive, but heaps of artillery shells are just sitting there, ripe for the taking.

I grin as I ask, "What do you think, Captain Meybert? Look at all these artillery pieces."

"We haven't had a chance to calibrate them yet..."

"I don't expect great accuracy. Hell, if you land one direct hit in every hundred shots, I'll be more than satisfied. These shells are free, after all." Everybody likes free things. That thought brings out a chuckle. "Our taxpayers certainly won't mind any missed shots."

"While that may be true...an immobile artillery position is a very attractive target."

That's true.

"If Captain Ahrens can't break through the enemy defenses, then withdrawing…"

It goes without saying that it would become incredibly dangerous.

Captain Ahrens and the majority of the Kampfgruppe are currently engaged in fierce fighting as they approach this artillery position. That said, I do have a backup plan just in case he fails to reach us.

"If it comes down to it, you can hoof it to the extraction point, right?"

"That's written in the infantry handbook. We can act like infantry if we need to, Colonel."

I give the captain a firm nod.

"Good. Let's begin, then. Fire everything you can get your hands on."

"With no restrictions?"

"There's no need to be stingy, Captain."

We're shooting on someone else's dollar, after all. A big smile crosses my face, and it seems the gunners are just as happy, since they normally have to be very careful about when and where they use their precious ammunition.

With a perfect salute and a big grin, Captain Meybert and his artillery crews spring into action.

The process starts with checking for booby traps. Once the coast is clear, they fire a few test shots. Of course, they have the veteran mages of the 203rd Aerial Mage Battalion acting as their observers. Lieutenant Grantz and his company, to be specific.

They work slowly, shooting one shot at a time. This is to learn the peculiarities of the cannons. They shoot, then adjust their aim, then shoot once more.

After a short series of singular explosions, the roaring cadence of repetitive fire can be heard. It's a good tempo—bracketing shots crescendo into a rolling bombardment of heavy artillery. That's the sound of a healthy country at war. Each booming explosion is more Unified States tax dollars being pissed into the wind. It's nice to fight a war on someone else's dime for once. Just as I'm beginning to enjoy the pleasant symphony of cannon fire that's come free of charge, Lieutenant Grantz's shouts reach my ears.

"Enemy mages sighted!"

Numerous mana signals appear in the distance, but it's only a battalion at most.

"They're the same strength as us, no need to worry."

It's the enemy mages who can respond the quickest to the unexpected development. The lack of familiarity with any of the given signals suggests they are still wet behind the ears. There's a good chance that they lack the proper training as well.

"I can't tell if they are US or Ildoan soldiers, but...they will make good prey."

I lick my lips as I think about the emotional damage this encounter will cause. Not only did their base get stolen, but the mages they sent out are about to be chewed up. As the Empire's PR agent, Tanya should definitely knock these flies out of the sky.

"Let us give them a light searing!"

Now that they have their orders, the mages all lift off at once. As they form up in the skies above, the sight of the approaching enemy mages is a massive letdown.

"Well, this is disappointing." My shoulders drop as I continue, saying, "They're certainly motivated, but it's clear they are all beginners."

Major Weiss agrees with the assessment in a bewildered voice.

"Their formation's full of holes. You can tell just by looking at them that there's nothing to fear. The US soldiers we fought before were in much better shape."

"Don't underestimate the enemy, Major. Keep in mind that there's always a chance they may be pretending to be greenhorns."

"With all due respect, Colonel, I think it would be a bigger problem for us to be overly cautious of...*that*."

Honestly, he's probably right. There's no need to be overcautious without cause. Still, it pays to be vigilant about their potential.

"While the Ildoan and US soldiers may still be newborns when it comes to battle, time, experience, and training will soon change that."

"For now, we can thank God they still lack those three things."

Saying this, Major Weiss begins to lead his mage company into the fray. As always, the dual-core Type 97s offer us Imperial mages maneuverability and the defense of a tank. Even the protective barrier of distance is quickly overcome when we move at speed.

I don't intend to sit back and watch as my troops do all the work. An optical formula should provide some cover fire. Hoping to suppress the enemy, I crack off a few shots.

Stopping a mage or two in their tracks would have been more than enough, but my suppressive fire has a much greater effect than I expected.

A few of them fall right out of the sky... Now we know for sure these are a bunch of baby chicks. Major Weiss's company is more than enough to handle them. I watch this all unfold with a smile on my face—until an unpleasant remark reaches my ear.

"It's all thanks to God's protection. We can knock these mages right out of the sky, Colonel."

Since he's doing a magnificent job trouncing the enemy, Major Weiss is free to think whatever he wants, and a part of me wants to respect this. The other part of me cherishes the separation of church and state.

God, he says...bah!

"You're wrong about that, Major Weiss. Either we have the devil on our side, or our enemies should curse whichever god has forsaken them."

Look no further than Being X. If there really is such a divine being, then why must a world this wretched exist to begin with? For a rational creature such as myself, the present state of this world is nothing but a source of grief.

"Fight as if you are this world's god."

"I'll do my best, Colonel."

"Good."

For some reason, I'm starting to feel a bit bad for the enemy mages. There's no need to eradicate all of them. If there is a way to end this without needless bloodshed, then that has to be the best option.

"Lieutenant Serebryakov. Come here for a moment."

"Oh? What is it?"

"Send a message recommending their surrender. You should make it sound like a civilian contractor from the rear. If necessary, you can pretend to be a common typist who just happens to speak the Commonwealth tongue."

A knowing look appears on Lieutenant Serebryakov's face as I dictate the most convincing announcement I can come up with.

"This message for the Unified States commander comes from a direct subordinate of Colonel Lergen of the Imperial General Staff. The winner of this battle has already been determined. It is out of chivalry that we ask you to consider a quick surrender and avoid wasting any more young lives!"

"I'll send this straightaway."

The response we get is, well...

"From the US commander to the Imperial commander: Eat shit and die! I say again, eat shit and die! Over!"

Well, there it is. Our call seems to have had little effect besides bolstering their morale. They still have some fight in them yet.

"Damn... They're surprisingly tough."

The enemy has survived initial contact and continues to hold. I quickly take stock of our opponents. Despite the heavy blow we inflicted, this is the worst possible reaction. I had hoped they would be routing by now, but they're far from defeated. If they can respond this tenaciously, then their unit must still be in decent shape. Soldiers who still have a functioning commander are much more resilient.

The sign of a true commander is the ability to instill the desire to fight in their subordinates.

"Well, well, well. Looks like they have a talented leader."

Convincing them to surrender is no longer an option.

"We've already maximized our gains from this little excursion. Let's do our best to make the enemy mages a bit more reluctant to challenge us next time."

This small-scale encounter has been fiercely fought. Technically speaking, this is nothing more than a recon-in-force mission. One where Tanya's Kampfgruppe just so happens to seize an enemy artillery position, bat around some enemy mages, and then plunder whatever they can before triumphantly returning to base.

In the grand scheme of things, this single incident likely won't have an enormous impact on the outcome of the war. It's more harassment than anything else, using the enemy's own munitions against them. However,

if there is one thing that is gained from this minor kerfuffle, it is time—something the Empire and the Imperial Army General Staff desperately need.

So when the small excursion is over and we're finally heading back to base, I find myself groaning internally.

Today was a success...but only barely. This tightrope walk will have to come to an end sooner or later.

Given the choice, I would change the way we do things, but the Empire is currently living hand to mouth and is constantly demanding I do the same thing over and over.

It's all so predictable.

That's when a telegram arrives for Lieutenant Colonel Tanya von Degurechaff. Fresh orders to prepare for redeployment to the eastern front.

I tremble as a single thought crosses my mind.

"How...how much longer do I have to keep this up?!"

 DECEMBER 13, UNIFIED YEAR 1927, THE ALLIANCE HEADQUARTERS, THE COMMONWEALTH AREA

When Colonel Drake finally comprehended the orders, he plummeted into a swirling vortex of despair.

Why did this have to happen?

He peered up at the clear blue sky. It was so wide and open that it felt like he might fall in. For a second, Drake thought that if he reached out with his hand, he'd be able to touch it. The beautiful weather almost made him forget about the war.

"Now I get why there are so many paintings of Ildoa's sky."

Drake murmured this to himself as he gazed at the stunning expanse above him. Were it not for the heavy weight on his shoulders, the scenery would have moved him deeply. Unfortunately, Drake's mind was elsewhere.

"Why are we the primary forces?"

As a gentleman, he shouldn't be grumbling like this. Drake was perfectly aware. He didn't need someone to tell him how a commander should act, but resorting to these minor complaints was the only way he could stifle his seething rage.

As always, things happened suddenly.

It started with redeployment to Ildoa.

Drake had a hard time accepting the orders; he knew that being transferred to Ildoa meant he'd likely be on the roughest, toughest parts of the front. At the same time, a part of him recognized that his unit amounted to nothing more than propaganda fodder.

In a way, the multinational volunteer unit being sent to Ildoa made perfect sense.

The only problem was whether they would be able to bring along their friends from the Federation. While Drake's boss had promised everything would be taken care of, he wasn't going to take his word for it. He fully expected to be stopped at every step of the way. Of course, it turned out that he didn't need to worry. Evidently, a certificate from the Commissariat for Internal Affairs was enough to make miracles happen in the Federation.

Everything went as smoothly as could be, and just like that, the multinational volunteers found themselves in Ildoa. The person in charge of accommodating them seemed to understand the troubles Drake had gone through and quickly prepared lodgings for the unit.

He was pleasantly surprised with good treatment; each soldier even got their own room. When it came to food, the Unified States provided the mages with all the high-calorie meals they could ask for. It wasn't as if they were treated poorly in the Federation, but it certainly was a pleasant surprise to receive every consideration, given the Unified States had only just entered the war. Unfortunately, this great treatment would play a role in leading Lieutenant Colonel Drake to misunderstand the state of the war being fought in Ildoa.

When the Commonwealth diplomat came to see him, Drake was genuinely impressed by how smoothly everything had gone up until that point. In hindsight, this was carelessness on Drake's part, and he wouldn't realize his mistake until he saw the look on the diplomat's face as he paced back and forth in the room he was called to.

Drake straightened his already alert posture before speaking.

"May I ask a question?"

"Go ahead, Colonel."

"Thank you, Ambassador. I'm curious as to why I'm receiving a briefing from an ambassador."

The ambassador answered Drake's question in a calm manner.

"Great question. It's to make sure there's no room for misinterpretation regarding your very important mission."

"According to my orders, the multinational volunteer unit is tasked with supporting the US-Ildoan mages."

"Ah, yes. Feel free to forget those orders."

The ambassador laughed off Drake's question with a gentle smile and warm tone.

"The situation has changed a bit. Your position within the multinational volunteer unit has changed as well."

"I see. Is it for political reasons?"

Drake watched the ambassador nod with a grimace.

Argh, more politics.

"Then...why were we called here?"

"While your command is known as the multinational volunteer unit, it's technically a part of the Commonwealth military. We'd like for you to operate independently while in Ildoa."

"I see..." Drake gulped. "And would you do me the courtesy of telling me why?"

Drake looked at the ambassador intently, but he responded quickly, as if the answer wasn't something he'd ever intended to hide.

"It's to preserve public opinion in the Unified States."

"And that means what, exactly?"

"We have to be mindful of their anti-Communism sentiment. Photos of US soldiers fighting bravely alongside Communists would be... problematic, so we would like the Federation troops to support the Ildoan forces."

"Understood... Somehow, that feels a bit irrational."

"You're right about that. It's quite stupid, honestly."

The ambassador nonchalantly shifted his tone to let Drake know that the decision had already been made and this was inevitable.

"Even so, we must be cautious of anything that could spawn conspiracy theories in the minds of the public."

"Conspiracy theories? I don't know what you expect from us. War is a breeding ground for all sorts of rumors."

"I know these things can only be prevented so much, but the higher-ups are wary, nonetheless. I'm sure they'll keep an eye on public opinion and things will settle down eventually..."

The ambassador let out a big sigh before bemoaning the situation.

"Mr. Drake, I'm sure you have an inkling of what I'm talking about. There are times where necessity brings people together and times when it rips them apart."

"Are we simply pretending to be friends while fighting a war?"

"I also made the case to the higher-ups that this is all pointless. It will take a bit more time before the gentlemen back home and those in the colonies warm up to the idea, though. But, hey, the world is a cruel place. They'll figure it out for themselves before long."

Drake could tell the ambassador was trying to reassure him.

He heaved a sigh on the inside. It was apparent to Drake that the ambassador was trying to push the problem off until later with another empty promise. That's all it ever was with these people—empty promises. They opted for procrastination at every turn! The idea that time would solve everything was more or less the same as never dealing with the problem. It was why the Commonwealth was involved with the multinational volunteer unit in the first place. Politics demanded the country affiliate with Communism in the east.

Politics also brought the multinational unit to Ildoa, and politics would keep them segregated from their allies.

"So, Ambassador, is there anything I should keep in mind about the political situation?"

Wars couldn't be fought with only colorful words. Drake was used to this by now, and he was ready to accept another precarious task or two.

He stared intently at the ambassador, who responded with a soft chuckle.

"Try to relax. I won't bite."

He offered Drake a chair as if he had a choice. Once the lieutenant colonel took his seat...the words the ambassador hit him with rocked his world.

"Let's start with some good news. I need to congratulate you. It seems Christmas has come early for you, *Colonel* Drake."

"Ambassador, I am still a lieutenant colonel for His Majesty's Marine Mages."

"Save me the modesty. You've been promoted."

Drake gulped and steeled his nerves before asking.

"May I ask why?"

"For starters, it isn't ideal that the highest-ranking soldier in the multinational volunteer unit is a Federation soldier. We need to maintain a careful balance, which is why you're officially a colonel now."

Drake could feel the cynic deep inside him grow restless at the remark. *I'm being promoted for balance?*

Everything always came down to politics.

"So this is a political promotion... That's not something to celebrate. It makes me feel like an idiot for fighting this damn war so seriously."

"Your accolades factor in just as much as concerns about balance."

"If only that were all that mattered."

"It's just how those back home view the issue. Sending a lieutenant colonel to stand next to a colonel puts us in a disadvantageous position, does it not?"

Politics. Dirty, rotten politics. Nevertheless, Drake was well aware that this was how the world worked.

"I can't help but feel dissatisfied with the promotion..."

"Come now, this is a good thing. Let's talk about something less serious for a bit."

Drake had a hard time viewing the promotion in a positive light, but the ambassador's expression suggested he was being sincere.

"Less serious, you say. Let me guess. More politics? And therefore troublesome by nature, I assume?"

"Right on the money. I'm sorry to have to burden you further."

"I assume it's about my unit's assignment, yes...?"

"You're quite perceptive."

Whatever it was, it required Drake to be a colonel like Colonel Mikel. Probably more of the usual petty squabbles of nations. Ultimately, it compelled the soldiers of the Federation and Commonwealth to fight separately.

Drake imagined that this would be a doozy of an assignment. It didn't help that the Ildoan Army was losing the war by a wide margin.

Everyone back in the home country always focused on the most pointless things. Drake had an idea of what they were thinking: that it wouldn't look good for the Federation to swoop in and save the day.

"While it's mostly a formality, you've been granted a wider range of discretionary powers. Your unit will be allowed to act independently."

"What unit will we be attached to? Are we operating separately from the combined mage headquarters?"

The ambassador took a moment to think before responding to Drake's bewildered question.

"Technically speaking, it's a little different."

"In what way?"

"Your assignment in Ildoa will not be under the joint mage unit as we initially informed you."

Drake's confusion deepened at the unexpected answer. He was under the impression that all mages fought under a single command in Ildoa, but this wasn't the case anymore, evidently.

"Did they reorganize the headquarters?"

"Only formally. The Commonwealth and Federation forces will be added to form one big alliance. The headquarters overseeing operations will be called the Allied Joint Mage Command."

I see, Drake thought as he began to grasp the situation.

The impact of defeat was far more immense than he'd ever imagined.

Considering that the presence of ground troops from the Commonwealth and the Federation was nominal at best, almost all the infantry present was provided by the Unified States and Ildoa. Setting aside the name, the Allied Joint Mage Command consisting of four different powers significantly reduced Ildoa's role in deciding war policy.

Ildoa was practically forfeiting its sovereignty. The Empire must have been pushing them to the limit for this even to be considered. The implications were clear to Drake. This war must have placed immense strain on Ildoa for them to agree to these kinds of concessions despite their strong sense of pride.

"The war must be taking quite the toll on Ildoa. I knew things were getting hot here, but I only just realized how hot."

"I'm glad to hear you're up for the challenge."

Drake gave a vague nod in response.

"Hearing this makes me quiver in my boots. What sort of impossible tasks are coming my way? I just hope I can get along with my superior."

"You needn't worry about that. You're your own boss now. Again, congratulations. It's quite the honor."

"I'm sorry, what?"

"It's a part of your personnel change. Your new appointment is an independent command heading up the First Combat Group of Allied Mage Command. Give it your all, Supreme Commander."

A big title accompanying a grandly named organization—it reeked of more senseless bureaucracy—but what did he mean by "independent command"?

The Allied Mage Command was probably nothing but a facade. While Drake knew that there were times when it was worth establishing something in name only to get it off the ground, he was quickly realizing that the organization had little substance.

He couldn't hold his tongue with the ambassador.

"It's quite the honor, but I only command a single battalion. Even if I have the authority to operate independently, we won't be able to execute any meaningful operations, given our scale. Somehow, this feels like a change that will do nothing but increase paperwork."

"Now, hold on... If you work together with the Federation army, it should increase your numbers, shouldn't it? It should be politically acceptable so long as you request their assistance and have them operate under your command."

The ambassador had just told Drake not moments ago he needed to keep his forces separate from the Communists, only to turn around and ask that they work together when it was convenient.

Drake was aware that diplomacy involved various expressions and formalities, so he laughed bitterly and did the math once more in his head. However, there was a limit to what could be done.

"We'd have two battalions, at most. Though considering our losses, they wouldn't be at full strength."

The Federation troops were worn down from intense fighting in the east. To make matters worse, most of the troops they did have were mostly fresh recruits. There were at most sixty mages who could be mustered for action.

"Hmmm, well, that won't do. The lads back home made their calculations based on the multinational volunteer unit having the fighting strength of two regiments."

Drake couldn't believe his ears.

"We couldn't pull that off even if every single one of us did the work of three soldiers."

What a joke. Talk about counting your chickens before they hatch—hell, they're already eating the damn eggs.

No matter how badly Ildoa had been weakened, they couldn't fill the gap with soldiers they didn't have.

Soldiers aren't simply numbers on a page.

Combat strength is measured by a unit's coordination and integrity. Trying to calculate that from figures in some report was something Drake had to comment on.

"Combat-effective units don't grow on trees, you know."

"We need people, Colonel. You do understand, yes?"

"If we combine the Federation and Commonwealth troops, then mix in some outside help...the best we could do is a single watered-down regiment. That's the absolute limit of what's remotely possible."

Drake shared his honest perspective based on what he knew about the multinational forces. His intent was to be sincere, but his numbers simply couldn't satisfy the ambassador.

"I see. Well, that won't do at all."

The man let out a big sigh and peered up toward the ceiling in open displeasure. Drake could guess what this reaction meant. The Commonwealth felt a need to maintain the facade that it was a major power, just like Ildoa and the Unified States did.

And yet, they had only sent a single regiment to support the war effort.

Drake could imagine how this quickly became a matter of pride. As meaningless as saving face seemed during wartime, his country would go to great lengths to maintain its international standing. It couldn't bear falling behind other countries.

If that was the issue, then Drake had a plan.

"You don't need to worry about it too much, Ambassador. While we may only be a single battalion, we can support our allies in a meaningful way. We certainly won't be a hindrance to the Allied Mage Command by any means."

"My apologies, Colonel, but there seems to be a slight misunderstanding here. Your job isn't to support the main forces."

"Then what is our assignment? Do you honestly want us to conduct raids independently? That doesn't sound like an efficient way to divide command..." Realizing that each sovereign nation operated under their own set of rules, Colonel Drake ended up offering something falling between advice and a warning. "Breaking up each nation's forces just isn't a good idea. We run too much risk not running them all under a single unified command. We won't be able to contend with the Empire divided like this—"

The ambassador raised a hand, cutting Drake off.

"You've got it all wrong, Colonel."

"What do you mean?"

"You're right that we can't afford to break up our forces. That's because you are now commander of the main forces, Colonel."

"I don't think I follow you. I command but a single battalion. That's not nearly enough unless the Commonwealth is planning on sending me reinforcements..."

When Drake responded with visible confusion, the ambassador only offered him a lonely smile.

"No, no. What I'm saying here is that what you have is everything, and you're commanding it, Colonel."

"This has to be some kind of joke. We don't even have enough officers. How is the Commonwealth, with what little we're committing at all, charged with commanding the main—"

"I'm afraid this is the truth, Colonel. Yes, a few days ago, your forces wouldn't have been considered a major portion of our strength here. But that's changed."

"So we're the main…forces…?"

An alarm blared in Drake's mind. Then a chill ran down his spine—the same chill he felt when he came face-to-face with the Devil of the Rhine. Something terrible was going to happen.

"The Ildoan and US mages are no more."

At first, this sounded like something he'd just heard, but then Colonel Drake began to fully parse the sentence, word by word.

No more? Weren't they reorganized? The ambassador did mention the reorganization was only a formality…

"Wait. So the mages here weren't reorganized into the Allied Mage Command forces, but have been completely wiped out…?"

"Yes, the entire US expeditionary force has been annihilated."

What is he saying? It was hard for Drake to follow the conversation. He only barely squeezed out his follow-up question.

"What happened to Corinth Regiment? They were good soldiers with excellent gear. Even if they took heavy losses, surely we can salvage at least a battalion from the survivors?"

"Colonel, I'm not using the word *annihilated* figuratively here."

"Is that even possible?"

"It's what happened," the ambassador said with an expression that spoke volumes about his deep exhaustion.

"We'll be lucky to get even a company out of what is left."

"But the US Marines and their navy should have separate mage units. According to the reports I've read, there should be a whole division's worth of mages stationed in Ildoa…"

"The Corinth Regiment has fallen, and the US Navy's mages are busy defending the seas. To make matters worse, the newly deployed replacement mages have already been devoured by the Devil of the Rhine. She's quite the glutton."

Finally understanding the severity of the situation at hand, Drake let out a long, weary sigh.

"Can we have our navy send some mages?"

"Have you already forgotten the Inner Sea incident? The Empire took out several capital ships and aircraft carriers with some strange combination of mages and torpedoes."

"So they're afraid of a second attack if they send their mages here…"

Drake had watched the attack unfold himself, so he understood better than most that the navy had no intention of ever repeating the same mistake again—the navy's mages weren't going anywhere no matter what.

Despite sinking into utter despair, Drake didn't give up.

"What about the Ildoan mages? This is their home. Surely they're more willing than anyone to fight now that the war has come to their doorstep."

"They lost the majority of their equipment up north, and the initial fighting claimed many of their mages' lives. While Ildoa is working hard to mobilize any mages they have left, there's a serious shortage of orbs."

"We can bring them the orbs they need!"

"We thought about that."

The ambassador seemed to be holding himself back. He spoke each word reluctantly.

"But we need to get the orbs first. We don't even have enough for our mages back home. We're already importing every orb we can get our hands on."

"Well, import them and send them here."

"You need to face the music, Colonel Drake. They can't be imported fast enough from the Unified States. What's more, the Yanks are gearing up as well, meaning there won't be enough orbs for the foreseeable future."

"This is preposterous… Any US orb would be better off in the hands of a veteran Ildoan mage than one of their raw recruits."

"Militarily speaking, yes, you're correct."

The diplomatic phrasing of the ambassador's remark made Drake scowl.

"So it all comes down to politics in the end… Right, Ambassador?"

"The Unified States has suffered a heavy blow, and they're already reconsidering the scope of their involvement as a whole. That's why there won't be any large shipments of orbs to Ildoa." As he finished that explanation, the diplomat pleaded once more with the man he'd forced into being a colonel.

Chapter IV

"Colonel, please."

"Some things simply cannot be done…"

"You and your mages are now the only western forces in the Allied Mage Command. We can't allow the Federation to swoop in and save the day. It needs to be you, Colonel."

"So you want me to go up against the entire Imperial mage corps with a single battalion…?"

"I'm sorry."

The ambassador looked as if he was on the verge of tears as he apologized. It was likely his attempt to show his sincerity, but Colonel Drake wanted to cry just as much as he did.

"We just don't have the numbers. I need you to understand that we literally don't have enough…"

"Colonel, politics demands that we see it done."

"I'm sorry but we're limited by what is and isn't possible."

No matter how many times the ambassador pleaded with Drake, the answer wouldn't change.

"We were sent here to support a friendly force four hundred mages strong as a sizable detachment. If I follow your request to operate independently from the Federation mages, there won't even be thirty of us left." The number was utterly insignificant by any standard. "Listen, Ambassador. If those are my orders, then I will do what I must as a gentleman who loyally serves His Majesty."

"I know it will be difficult. Thank you."

Colonel Drake had only one final remark.

"You can consider these daffy orders delivered loud and clear, Ambassador. My only request is that it be a fellow gentleman who drafts my next orders."

》》》 **DECEMBER 9, UNIFIED YEAR 1927, THE IMPERIAL ARMY'S** 《《《
ILDOA INSPECTION COMMAND CENTER

Officers who've made a career out of their military service are generally used to receiving sudden orders. Anyone would be caught off guard by them at first, but this is the only time it surprises them, as after the second, third, and so on, it simply becomes the norm. Once it happens all the time, it's easy to accept it as just another part of life. Experience comes with the resignation that orders are orders, and this *is* the military.

It was usually the same story for Lieutenant Colonel Uger. As the most thoroughly overworked railway worker for the duration of the long war, he regarded a sudden change as an everyday occurrence. Even so, there were still things that managed to catch even him off guard.

"Welcome back, Lieutenant Colonel. I apologize for calling you here, but I'm canceling all orders I've given you thus far."

"You're what…? Excuse me, what I meant to say is, if you have new orders, I'm happy to oblige."

General Zettour grinned as he handed a slip of paper to Uger, who was standing at attention.

"Congratulations, Colonel. You're being promoted."

The single slip of flimsy paper had the details of his personnel change, but he didn't get a chance to read any of it.

"It's about time for you to experience leading a regiment, Colonel. Seeing what it's like on the front lines is part of your duties. In an appropriate position, of course."

General Zettour wasn't technically wrong. Commanding a regiment was a core part of climbing the ladder in the military, and there was more than one issue with rear echelon officers who had never set foot on the actual battlefield.

"While it pains me and the General Staff to have to let you go, personnel matters must be handled fairly. As regrettable as it may be, now that our campaign in Ildoa has settled down a bit, it's time for you to move on to a new assignment."

"If that is what's expected from me as a staff officer, then I…"

Colonel Uger tried to read between the flowery words. To him there was only one thing he needed to confirm.

"I'm honored to be given the position, but I must ask if it was you who made the arrangements for this."

"Of course, Colonel Uger. It would be nothing short of treason for me to keep a man as capable as yourself stuck at the rank of lieutenant colonel. While it was a tough decision for me to make as deputy director,

I'm thoroughly pleased with your achievements and loyal service under me, and this is your reward." The general grinned, smoking a cigar as he continued. "You'll be leading your regiment as a colonel."

With things put in terms as plain as this, it was clear to Uger what was happening. He was simply no longer needed by the general. The moment that thought crossed his mind, he accepted his new fate and saluted General Zettour without hesitation.

"Thank you for everything, General."

"Don't be so dramatic."

"It's just sad to think my service as a railway officer is coming to an end."

Having been the general's subordinate for so long, Uger knew that there was little faith placed in his ability as a strategist. He was also aware that he likely wouldn't be much use on the front lines, so this new posting was placing him somewhere he wouldn't perform well, effectively demoting him. This was a sad realization, but Lieutenant Colonel Uger accepted his fate without complaint and offered the general a deep bow.

"I see. To think you'd be this broken up over being separated for a scant few days. I didn't realize you liked working for me so much."

"A few...what?"

"Ha-ha-ha, you're always so serious."

General Zettour grinned the way he always did when he was playing a good-natured joke. Though he was all smiles, Uger could've sworn that he caught a glimpse of two sharp fangs peeking out.

"Many do consider me a con artist, but I'm not the type to treat my subordinates as disposable tools."

"Given how long I've worked under you, I thought I understood you better than most."

"*Thought*, you say?"

Uger gave an uncertain nod and continued.

"I thought I understood your character when you were still a lieutenant general."

"So you think I've changed since Rudersdorf's passing?"

Uger nodded without hesitation this time. Though he had no intention of saying it out loud, there were actually moments when Uger felt uneasy around the general as of late.

"I'm aware of my shortcomings as a staff officer, but when compared to the other staffers, General, I also think you—"

"Deviate from the rest?"

General Zettour rubbed his chin with a satisfied look about him before eventually shrugging his shoulders at the lieutenant colonel.

"I'm glad to hear you say that. I think the Empire needs more wise perspectives such as yours."

The general's expression transitioned to a more annoyed look.

"Unfortunately, there aren't many people left these days."

"We've been at war far too long."

"Which is why I take every capable subordinate I can find and work them to the bone, grinding them down until there's nothing left. So long as you're a skilled railway officer, then I must send you into the mire of the front lines."

Lieutenant Colonel Uger took a small breath as he accepted his superior's compliment.

"Lieutenant Colonel Uger. From today, you are a colonel who will be commanding the 103rd Railway and Transportation Regiment, and at the start of the next year, you'll be transitioning into a new post: section chief for the General Staff. Congratulations."

The general's well-wishes were offered incredibly casually. The fact that Uger was receiving his next two assignments at once was not a good sign.

"I'm sorry, but—"

"I hate to say it, but commanding a regiment is just a temporary, do-nothing job until you return to the General Staff."

All staff officers desired to become a regiment commander at one point or another. Regiments were easy work. All an officer needed to do was sit in a chair and the glittering path to becoming a general would open. Regiment commander was never anything more than a temporary assignment.

However, Uger was an old-fashioned soldier, and without putting too much thought into it, he spoke up.

"If I may, General, the position of regimental commander is one of the pillars of the military... For it to be used like this... Were it not for the prolonged war making promotions easier to come by, I'm sure my predecessors in the regiment wouldn't accept my promotion quietly."

"For sullying the sacred position of regimental commander?" Zettour scoffed at the thought. "Colonel Degurechaff rejected a similar offer, saying she didn't want it."

"She did...?"

"Because Personnel kept nagging old Rudersdorf about it, he went and recommended her for the position. The lieutenant colonel was adamant about not being separated from her unit, even if it flew in the face of the general's recommendation."

Strangely enough, it was easy for Uger to picture the scene.

Having studied alongside Tanya at the war college, he thought she seemed like someone who would reject the position.

"Colonel Degurechaff prizes honing her skills on the battlefield. She knew what was truly important. I'm moved by her commitment to her duty."

"That's for sure. And it's an honest outlook, to desire to act where one is needed. All Imperial soldiers should aspire to be like her."

Lieutenant Colonel Uger found it hard to disagree. Unconditional devotion and service—these were virtues that made for a great officer, but... Strangely enough, an idea worked its way into Uger's mind as he recognized this. That the quintessential ideal soldier was inhumane in its essence.

"While I agree with you on that point, General, can a person really be rigidly proper all the time? I know you only mean it as a joke, but..."

Uger let out this remark with a sigh, and the general responded flatly.

"Ranks, posts, and what have you—all of it comes with a corresponding duty that must be fulfilled. During a war, the ideal officer ends up embodying their post."

You're wrong, Uger wanted to retort, but he stopped himself. Whether he liked it or not, a part of him knew the general was speaking the truth.

As Uger struggled to find the right words, Zettour continued with a smile.

"You're free to think about it how you will. Either way, I expect my subordinates to do everything that's required of them. Do you follow me?"

Feeling the general's eyes bore into him, Uger straightened up his posture again. Seeing this, General Zettour nodded slightly before asking the colonel once more.

"Do you understand what I'm saying?"

There was only one response to this question. Uger gave a hurried nod and answered.

"Doing my duty is a matter of course. I shall treat my time as regimental commander as a vital mission if that's what is required of me."

"That's good, because your orders actually will be quite important."

Uger wasn't sure what to make of that.

"Now, Colonel…"

"I'm still technically a lieutenant colonel."

"I think it's good to get used to your new title sooner rather than later."

Hearing this really drove home reality for Uger. He would soon be leading a regiment, something he would've been proud of before this war broke out.

"We've managed to seize the Ildoan capital. This is a key moment for the Empire."

"What are you going to do?"

"We're going to take everything…"

The general's intentions were clear to Uger, whose entire career revolved around logistics. That was precisely why he felt conflicted about the remark. A part of him hoped it wasn't what he knew it meant.

"Everything, sir?"

"Come now, Colonel. Don't be coy with me. The evil army has captured the holy city. What else is there for us to do besides pillage?"

That was exactly as Uger feared.

"That being said, we're civilized people. We will conduct our pillaging in a civilized manner."

"And I'm to oversee said pillaging…"

With grim resolve, Colonel Uger lowered his head in acceptance.

He hadn't visited the front lines yet in this war. If this was where his country needed him to dirty his hands, then so be it…

"You're joking, right? Someone like you would probably end up giving in to the enemy's pleas and letting everything slip through your fingers."

Uger straightened up to look at General Zettour. He understood why the general thought of him that way and couldn't really deny it. Uger was...too compassionate to be the coldhearted soldier he needed to be at times.

"You know me well, General..."

"No need to be down on yourself, Colonel. Your skills make you an irreplaceable cog in our organization, even if your edge isn't quite sharp enough to spearhead the instrument of violence."

The general's words made Colonel Uger recall something. It was Lieutenant Colonel Degurechaff who had advised Uger to stay in the rear for his family's sake. This was likely her way of being considerate to her war academy classmate, despite being the rigid monster of righteousness many considered her to be.

"Then...I will do what I can as a proper part of this organization."

"Well, let's get you started with the ruthless task of whipping up a logistic schedule for me. I'll take care of acquiring what we need from the capital, so no need to worry. There'll be plenty that needs moving."

"You can leave that to me."

"Perfect. I have high hopes for our railways. I need you to move my bounty north."

>>> DECEMBER 16, UNIFIED YEAR 1927, THE ILDOAN ROYAL CAPITAL <<<

The Imperial Army officials quickly made themselves at home in the Ildoan capital, setting up the base for their occupation in the most lavish hotels and government facilities they could find. The Empire's bureaucracy is already rearing its head.

Tanya, following orders to appear at the base in the capital, is shockingly required to go through three checkpoints and two separate, mind-numbingly bureaucratic sets of paperwork before finally gaining the permission to set foot on the base itself.

I immediately motion to question the officer on duty about arranging a meeting but get caught off guard by something unexpected.

"Where is the general?"

"He just finished his inspection and has left the base."

"So I missed him."

What unfortunate timing. I wanted to speak with him to maybe find out what were the chances of being sent to the east once more. That being said, it appears General Zettour didn't forget to leave me a souvenir before departing.

"This is from the general."

The duty officer holds out an envelope.

"An order to return home...? I see, so we really are withdrawing from the capital."

The Empire still has the eastern front to worry about. Compared to the east, the campaign in Ildoa is winding down, with the most pressing matter being the shift from attack to defense. Wherever we end up next, this is it for my days under the Ildoan sun, and my gut tells me that we'll be slugging through the muddy ground in the east before long. That's where the real battle is happening.

Unfortunately, there couldn't be a worse place to search for my next job than the eastern front. Given the choice, my first pick would be getting stationed in the west, and Ildoa would be my second choice. The one place I don't want to end up is the east, but getting worked up over it won't help. All signs are pointing in one direction.

Now that I'm ready to accept my fate, I stand up and head for the hotel café. I may as well get one last cup of good coffee. If nothing else, Ildoa still has some of the best beans around. Evidently, I'm not the only one who thinks this.

Both the lounge and the café of the hotel that currently houses the Empire's command staff are overflowing with Imperial soldiers, making it impossible to get any peace and quiet.

All I want is some time to myself...

Just as I get ready to leave, I spot a familiar face who also just gave up on coffee after seeing the line snaking out of the café.

"Oh, if it isn't Lieutenant Colonel Degurechaff."

"Hello, Lieu...er, sorry. Colonel Uger. Congratulations on your promotion."

"Oh, right."

Colonel Uger gives a wry chuckle as he pats the new insignia on his shoulder.

"I'm only a regiment commander for show."

"It is still a tremendous honor, regardless of the circumstance."

A promotion means advancing in your career. Even aboard a sinking ship, it's only natural to feel somewhat envious of an acquaintance's promotion. Of course, Uger's promotion means a more influential connection for Tanya. What's not to love about that?

"Are you free, by any chance?"

I would never let a chance to mingle with powerful coworkers pass me by.

"Of course. I'd love to join you."

"Great. General Zettour left behind his car for me. Let's take a quick drive."

I happily follow Uger out of the hotel and into a parking lot where his civilian vehicle is parked. He offers me the passenger seat, which I find a bit strange at first, only to realize that Uger will be driving. Looks like there aren't enough people to assign someone to driving duty.

In the meantime, I'm a bit excited about where this conversation may take me. The Ildoan city roads whiz by as Colonel Uger drives along. After a short while, he eventually speaks up.

"It really is a beautiful city, isn't it? This might sound strange to say as this city's occupiers, but looking at these streets reminds me of a time before the war."

Colonel Uger flashes a smile as he says this.

"Make you wish we could keep them, eh?"

"I'm sorry, Colonel… I'm sure you're the last person who needs to be told this, but do you think we could preserve this beauty if we were to fully occupy the city?"

Colonel Uger nods slightly with an indifferent expression on his face. He holds on to the steering wheel, facing forward, but eventually feels a pair of eyes waiting for the conversation to continue.

"What are you suggesting?"

"A city as big as this consumes a vast number of resources. It would be a nightmare for us to keep it supplied if we kept it under military control." I stare out the car window at the cityscape. "Take a look for yourself. The vast amount of rations and other aid being passed out to refugees… We have somewhere around five hundred thousand soldiers in Ildoa right now, but the city's population is easily double or triple that number, if not more."

And those people consume endlessly.

"I can understand the need for distributing provisions to maintain order while we take what we need, but we cannot maintain this for long. The army will cease to function as an organization before it even comes down to a fight."

Logistics seems mundane at first glance, but people need to eat to live. If they can't, then they will fight to survive. This is why the Empire needs to keep this city fed. Failing to do so will create a massive nightmare for the army.

"This isn't a problem we can afford to deal with right now. The Ildoan peninsula may enjoy a bountiful harvest, but with its supply network as good as dead, we can't get the food the land produces to the people who need it."

"Ha-ha-ha. You never change."

Colonel Uger gives a vague nod and rubs his neck.

"I'm glad you are able to keep logistics in mind while you lead from the front lines. Honestly, it would make my job so much easier if we had more commanders like you."

"People need food to live. It isn't that difficult of a concept."

"That's the truth. Even the toughest of soldiers are helpless against an empty stomach." Colonel Uger, the man who is in charge of the Empire's railways, clenches his jaw after he says this.

"Considering the entire surrounding region is essentially a battlefield, it isn't our place to insist the city's people fend for themselves. We need to keep these people fed, even if it's getting increasingly difficult for us to provide for our own people."

"I figured a frontline commander would be one of the last people to suggest willingly surrendering such strategic ground."

"It requires too much to hold and defend the capital. With how tight things are in the east, it isn't sustainable to have our forces here for too long."

"You really haven't changed. I always feel jealous of how smart you are when we talk."

Chapter **IV**

After offering that compliment, Colonel Uger continues to drive. Ildoa's central train station is coming into view. Despite the heavy security, Uger is let through as soon as the guards see his face. In fact, the military police stationed near the checkpoint where they are checking cars stand at attention and salute as the car passes. Thanks to this, we can move freely without being stopped by anyone. Once inside the station, we walk to the train platform, where Colonel Uger points to a freight train.

"What comes to mind when you see this?"

I take a moment to size up the train before answering.

"That it's fully loaded."

The freight train is packed with containers. It's the only notable thing about the train, and it seems to be the right answer because Colonel Uger responds with a satisfied look.

"It's loaded with Ildoan goods. We've taken their gold and silver, their raw resources, their machinery, weapon parts, and everything else a country needs to fight a total war. The payment is those provisions you were talking about earlier."

"The city still seems quite beautiful despite all that."

Colonel Uger gives an awkward smile as he continues.

"We made sure not to break anything, but make no mistake—we're taking everything of value. We have a requisition team going through the city like a bunch of looters."

I nod in understanding.

"Ah, so we're systematically pillaging their city."

It's certainly the most effective way to steal, and something countries around the world have been doing since the dawn of governance. It's also somewhat of a specialty of the Empire's. We're pros when it comes to scrounging up what we need in faraway lands we've occupied. The Empire will, without a doubt, find and acquire whatever it needs from every place of note in the city over the next few days.

"Like a swarm of locusts."

"Well put. We've hit not only the banks and the palace, but are raiding all of the art and historical museums as we speak."

"So we are the destroyers of culture. They're going to hate us for this."

Colonel Uger gives a slight wave of his hand and corrects my remark.

"Sorry, I didn't mean to give you the wrong impression. We're not actually stealing any cultural artifacts. Anyone caught pilfering art or cultural objects will immediately be court-martialed and turned over to Ildoan authorities."

Now that I wasn't expecting.

"Why is that...? I mean, it's always good to respect culture, but is there a reason...?"

"It's the general's courtesy toward this nation, or so I've been told."

"General Zettour's?"

Somehow, I find that hard to believe. It isn't difficult to understand why someone would want to respect cultural artifacts for political reasons or a personal sense of honor, but this kind of logic doesn't apply to General Zettour. That man operates on a completely different level.

"How magnanimous of General Zettour. But...we soldiers tend to look at things from a practical standpoint. I doubt that he's the kind of person to exempt cultural items out of the goodness of his heart."

Colonel Uger's grimace suggests he agrees with my sentiment. It likely isn't possible for an officer who's worked directly under the general to reject the idea outright. We both know that soldiers are logical creatures who loyally serve a master known as *necessity*.

"Well, if there are cultural items left behind in the city, it will make it harder for our enemies to attack it."

"That may be true, but I feel like there's more to it." I ponder the possible reasons for a moment. "Perhaps serves as bait with poison in it."

"That's an interesting idea, but what makes you think so?"

"A beautiful, empty city. The Empire has nothing to lose even if the city is destroyed. Is the plan to make it seem like the enemy caused the destruction through urban combat?"

A pleasant smile appears on the colonel's face.

"It's good to learn that even you make mistakes."

Colonel Uger chuckles to himself. Seeing Tanya get something wrong is a first for him.

He's genuinely amused, but I notice a hint of darkness behind his expression.

"You're correct about this being poisoned bait. But regarding the cultural artifacts, it's nothing more than a matter of priority—stealing art and historical items won't impact our ability to continue fighting this war."

"What...?"

"Sure, they could be worth something if we can sell them, but who is going to buy anything from us? We are prioritizing raw material, food, scrap metal, and heavy machinery. Cultural goods aren't worth anything to us right now."

When I hear this, I heave a deep sigh. The Empire, isolated and alone, can't afford to waste its time on anything but food and resources. I'd laugh if it wasn't so heartbreaking.

"How terrible."

"We're not even at the worst part yet. You didn't hear this from me, but...the general wants to turn the capital into a gorgeous pile of ashes to lure the enemy ships to the peninsula."

"The enemy...what?"

This I did not see coming. He wants to bring the enemy ships here? To attack them?

"I'm sorry, but is this meant to be a ploy to raid their merchant navy?"

"Ha-ha-ha. You sure are making guesses with more regular common sense today."

I scowl at his response. It seems I need to reconfirm how exactly Colonel Uger sees me. Just as a precautionary measure.

"Colonel, I..."

"Oh, I didn't mean anything by it. Honestly, I had the same reaction when I first heard the general's plans. But it makes sense when you think about it. With the capital's broken logistics network, the city has essentially been reduced to a resource-hungry market of consumers."

"That's true," I say with a nod. "You're the expert, so I shouldn't need to say that the incredibly laborious task of feeding this resource-hungry city falls on our army's logistics department."

Colonel Uger nods, then offers up some new information in a distressed tone.

"Right now, the Empire has some special trains running."

"Special trains? For logistical purposes?"

"In a way, yes. They are running from the north to the capital. They're bringing refugees down here."

"The Empire is transporting refugees…?"

The capital is a funnel for resources, difficult to defend, and carries many of its own logistical issues due to its current population. Why would the general want to bring even more Ildoan refugees here?

"I'm sorry, Colonel, but are we doing it against their will…?"

"No, the refugees are given a choice to take the train. That said, occupation is despised up in the north of the country, so it isn't difficult to convince them to leave."

"Ah, I see now!"

All these consumers and no supply chain to fulfill their demands. Hearing that the army was bringing more people here paints a very clear picture. It is beginning to make sense why the general wants the enemy ships to come here.

"There will be a mass migration to the capital, which we will return to the—what are they calling themselves, the Alliance? Though southern Ildoa is a major agricultural region, I doubt they will be able to feed the entire country without fertilizer and grain from the north."

General Zettour is sending the unneeded masses down south, in a way that makes the Empire seem humanitarian. By letting the people escape martial law by transporting them to their nation's capital, he's removing potential partisans from the north. It also allows the Empire to pressure the enemy, but…there's something I need to point out that seems too good to be true.

"One wrong step and we'll be committing a war crime."

Assuming the enemy will care for these people could be a grave mistake.

"We need to believe in the Unified States."

"Are we expecting them to use ships meant for munitions to bring food for the refugees?"

When I see Uger give a small yet firm, affirmative nod, I fold my arms and consider what I've learned.

It's a good plan. A sort of attack on the enemy's supply lines. It could even be considered a strategic attack. It isn't rare for military tactics to come in the guise of humanitarian acts, and fortunately, there is a good chance the enemy will oblige us. No sensible person would stand by idly while the people of this city starve, and the Ildoan and US forces are run by sensible people.

At the very least, their sense of reason hasn't been charred by the flames of war yet. Not the way the Empire's has been. The enemy shouldn't have the capacity to ignore the result of the Empire's foul tactics and still fight a regular war. That's what the Empire is relying on.

"It would seem that we are betting a great deal on this hope. Moreover, we're hoping that our enemies will act accordingly... That doesn't feel great to hear."

"Nope, it sure doesn't."

It's honestly a terrible thing to have to consider. What's most aggravating is the likelihood that the enemy can and will comply. If one thing's for sure, it's that Uncle Sam has no lack of resources!

I'm sure that the Unified States will probably give Ildoa all the food it needs. And it'll probably make it happen without any real planning. They'll just brute-force the problem thanks to their inconceivable wealth and resources!

"What a miserable state of affairs."

"So you feel the same way...? This is a bad time to be a good person."

"That's for sure. It's the worst for those of us struggling to keep the fight up on the battlefield."

The Empire is running short on everything. In this war of attrition, the so-called Alliance is backed by the biggest sponsor. Talk about an unfair competition.

Feeling particularly resentful, I can't help but speak my mind.

"I'm hoping I remain a just person through all this, but war ends up justifying even the most unreasonable of things at times."

"I commend your sense of righteousness."

The colonel lets his shoulders drop as he pays me a compliment—the compliment seems genuine.

"This war has been hard on us all. As someone used to seeing his coworkers burned out by it, I respect you a great deal."

"There is nothing righteous about what we are doing."

I know he's speaking from a place of envy and self-pity, though I would never say that out loud. I also can't reject his comments outright due to his rank.

After a brief moment of thought to find the right words, I mutter softly.

"As a human being, I don't want to give up the desire to improve."

Colonel Uger winces, as if he fully understands the sentiment.

"That's right. That's how people are supposed to be."

"Yes, people never stop striving to improve themselves."

To become more intelligent.

More righteous.

More capable.

I am a firm advocate of lifelong learning. Standing atop the shoulders of giants is possible only after those giants have been built. This is the essence of the civilized world and human society, which were born from curiosity and hard work!

"You're right about that. Thank you, Lieutenant Colonel Degurechaff. You always teach me the lessons I need to learn."

"No, I only said what I believe is appropriate."

When he hears that, Colonel Uger smiles warmly.

"Sorry for having you make the trip out here with me. I'll have a car take you back. Stay safe."

"No, it's been my pleasure. Until we meet again."

Lieutenant Colonel Degurechaff, the tiny giant herself, showed a perfect, textbook salute before making her way out of Ildoa's central train station. She climbed into a new vehicle Colonel Uger had arranged to take her back to her troops.

Seeing her go, Colonel Uger returned to his own temporary place of work, where he would continue to wrestle with numbers and figures.

"It's going to take forever to figure this all out."

It was a job the colonel took upon himself, primarily because his current job was, as General Zettour so blatantly stated, a temporary position.

His plan to requisition Ildoa's freight trains and locomotives had already been drawn up. He'd already devised multiple theoretical plans while he familiarized himself with the Ildoan railway network. Other personnel from the railway department had also been dispatched to help acquire what they needed.

While the occupation of the capital and the subsequent requisition plans were all very impromptu, knowing that this position was only temporary allowed him to power through it. Most of it was routine work anyway. Honestly speaking, if Colonel Uger really had at it, he could get through it quick enough to get a few days to himself before he returned to serve under General Zettour once more.

Uger wasn't the type to allow himself that privilege, though. Even if he was nothing more than a colonel for show, the work he was doing was real. He didn't resent the work he had to do to ensure the trains ran smoothly—that was his pride as a railway worker.

Uger quietly laughed at himself. "We may be fighting this war...but we can't allow ourselves to lose what makes us human."

Uger stared at his palms, looking at the white gloves he wore. There were small ink stains on them. These were considered badges of honor in the rear. But how many stains were there that couldn't be seen? The same hands that held his wife and children were treating the Ildoan people as numbers on a page, using them as a weapon against the Alliance.

Was it right for the military to do this? Uger knew it was what the Empire needed in its current state. He understood this intimately, but he also knew that it was wrong, and it was only out of necessity that he was promoted.

"General Zettour... I...I...never wanted to be promoted like this."

Uger felt compelled to complain out loud, something that was happening more and more as of late. He hated that he had become a colonel. When he heard that Lieutenant Colonel Degurechaff had rejected a similar promotion, he thought it was out of a pure desire to remain on the front line, being the warrior that she is, but...

"It must have been a matter of morals..."

Yes, she's a fighter, but...

Lieutenant Colonel Degurechaff had a firm sense of what it meant to be a just person that she refused to stray away from. She was far better than the supposed colonel, who let those around him decide everything. These thoughts may have been born from jealousy of the person whom he considered the manifestation of righteousness.

"Orders are orders, but…your heart is your own."

Uger straightened his hat before firmly saluting toward the deep blue sky. He knew that the young lieutenant colonel wouldn't see it. This gesture was for his own satisfaction, but even so, the soldier known as Uger wanted to believe in a greater good.

There is so much to learn about the world on a field trip.

——— Lieutenant Colonel Tanya von Degurechaff ———

Not even a perfectly executed job is finished until you're safely back home. I recall this fact while reminiscing over something I learned in my past life, back when I was a regular, lazy student living in a more peaceful world.

My class was on a field trip, and my teacher—exhausted after a day of taking care of children—was wheezing while he explained to the class that the excursion wasn't over yet so everyone was supposed to go straight home. I remember how I had to hold back a chuckle while I watched him say this with barely any breath left.

Now, however, I have more respect for that teacher. I grimace when I realize how immature I was back then despite feeling so clever all the time.

There isn't much to be said about such a notion going over a child's head. I likely saw meaning only in the trip portion of the field trip. A clear mistake, as there are no one-way field trips. Though belatedly, I commend the teacher in my mind for going to such lengths to teach an important life lesson.

It's paramount for a responsible member of society to make a quick trip home without detour so as to avoid any unnecessary injury or mishap en route. To think I would finally come to this realization at such an age in the faraway land of Ildoa.

"There are so many things a person must learn in their lifetime..."

Which is why a systematic education apparatus is to be cherished above all else for a functional society. While the education system of her original world and country was not without its flaws...no effort was spared when it came to providing children with the knowledge needed to survive daily life. A progressive, civilized culture is an advantage enjoyed by a peaceful society of plenty.

This is yet another moment where I find myself reminiscing about the greatness of peace. If going home is a part of the field trip for children… then so is the commute home for adults.

Accidents on the job, especially during the commute, are a very serious matter. My teacher once offered more words of wisdom on a separate occasion—*learning is the job of a child*. Pairing the two notions together, the train of logic is as follows: Field trips are a part of education. Thus, they can be considered work for children. Although…this brings into question the lack of labor laws for a student. This notion is somewhat frightening to think about. A person is left very vulnerable in the absence of the law's protection…

Though not without logical flaws, a sense of nostalgia for my student days washes over me. As a soldier, and as a mage for the General Staff, I can only wish to once again escape this darker-than-black corporate culture and relive the peaceful life of a school student. This wish is for naught, though.

Oh, how I long for peace. Wonderful peace, amazing peace. Irrationality incarnate…Being X seeks to destroy peace, to turn it on its head. He's probably jealous of peace itself as a concept!

Regardless, I will not yield to that offshoot of the devil. Logic and the market should be prized above all else, and that's where my obligations lie. To return peace to this world, at all costs, and to show the world that the market always wins.

Which is why Tanya must survive. I'll oblige General Zettour's orders to return home with glee if it will help me achieve this. Even if I know I'm returning to the capital only to be shipped off to the east, at least I'll get to spend some time at home.

Hopefully, at least the tail end of the year will be spent in the Imperial capital. Surely there is still some residual culture left there for me to enjoy.

That's what I'm hoping as I pack my bags for the trip home. A random encounter with Colonel Lergen on my way to the HQ to discuss the train schedules makes me think I'm lucky, but that notion is quickly dashed.

After exchanging salutes and brief updates about our recent deployments, we soon discuss preparations for our return home. This was all we were *supposed* to discuss, at least. When this proves not to be the case, I have no choice but to question the absurdity of it all.

"What...? What did you just say, Colonel?"

"That your return orders have been canceled. You're staying here."

At least he looks apologetic when he says this. His tone, however, is as firm as can be when the devastating news rings in my ears.

"You're deployment has been extended, Colonel Degurechaff."

"You're sure about this."

"I am. I'm sorry to have to ask this, but I'll need you to stay here and conduct another operation or two."

"Y-you want my battalion to do what...? But my Kampfgruppe has already received orders from the general to leave Ildoa..."

"I'm well aware of that. As much as it pains me to hit you with this sudden change in orders, I need you to comply. It's what the campaign needs from you. These new orders take precedent over your orders to withdraw."

Said orders are written on a thin sheet of paper. To think a single sheet of paper can have such power over a person's destiny.

"Your mages stand head and shoulders above the rest, after all. I want you to savage the front lines for us. You know, to put on a show—just until our troops have reorganized the line."

"A-are those my orders?"

"They are."

The colonel's words couldn't be more explicit. It's almost cruel.

"You'll be tasked with the important job of protecting the troops while they fall back. That being said, you'll only need to keep the mages here. The rest of your Kampfgruppe can return home as scheduled. I'll make sure they get home safe."

With a heavy thud, I drop my suitcase to the floor. If I were in a more regular state of mind, I probably would've registered the sound of it opening up when it hit the ground. Usually, I'd slap on a smile and jest about my clumsiness, but I'm in no state of mind for that now.

The stress of having my well-deserved time off poof into thin air and be replaced by the curse of more work has left me struggling to process what's happening.

The colonel's words play over and over again in my mind: *Canceled. Extended. Only the mages.*

"I'm really sorry about this, Colonel, but it's what must be done. We need you to agitate the enemy. Distract them while we fall back."

I'm stock still. I haven't even realized my bag is on the ground yet. The word she loathes most—*overtime*—flashes in my mind. Just when I was looking forward to going home, I'm hit with this. Needless to say, returning home for some time off is all that has kept me going these past few weeks!

"Colonel Degurechaff? Are you all right?"

"Ah, yes, please excuse me."

My brain, finally overcoming the stress, registers that I've been given new orders. Despite my utter exhaustion, I speak almost reflexively.

"This news is shocking, to say the least, but I will do what I must. If we're to use only our mages, then we will be conducting raids primarily. Is it fair to assume that I will have full authority over how I conduct my troops in order to do so?"

"Of course. As you may suspect, we have plans to make a full withdrawal from this position. Depending on how quickly the trains can move, we will be abandoning this spot soon."

The initial policy to refrain from fixating on the capital is still in effect, it seems. Within the span of less than a month, the rulers of the capital will change once more. It sounds simple, but given that the Empire will be abandoning the capital, it makes the timing of the withdrawal exceedingly precarious.

"So when exactly is it going to happen, Colonel Lergen?"

"I can't let you know yet. It is why we need you mages to hold the line in a deceptive way. You can make a swift withdrawal when the time comes."

"If our troops are too slow in their retreat, it could very well place too much of a burden on us in the rear…"

Tanya shares this deep concern of hers, which is met by a reassuring nod from Colonel Lergen.

"We'll be in debt to Colonel Uger when all is said and done. He's done an incredible job of keeping the trains on a tight schedule. Although counterintelligence is proving to be a massive hurdle in all of this."

"Has the enemy picked up on our withdrawal?"

Colonel Lergen gives a strong nod before lowering his voice.

"It's why we need you to create a diversion. We need the enemy to mis-interpret our intentions. We don't want them to pursue us as we leave."

"So we must use aggression to mask the withdrawal?"

"That is correct. They must perceive us as a perpetual threat, at all costs."

I'm just barely able to swallow a groan that tries to escape my throat as I listen to the colonel's explanation. Sudden orders are never easy to handle.

My mages are supposed to execute feint attacks to hide the army's movements. While it makes sense, given our true goal, it was only a few days ago that we destroyed the enemy mages and then engaged what seemed like their newly mobilized reserves. These two operations were also all in service of making the deception more convincing.

"We've been doing as much as we can to deceive the enemy, but there is only so much a single Kampfgruppe can do…"

"If your mages cannot do this, then who else in the Empire can?"

Colonel Lergen is being sincere when he says this, but it still strikes me as something that's easy to say for the one giving orders. This will be a highly risky task, no matter how the colonel slices it. Having already dealt lethal blows to the enemy forces, they are already thirsty for Impe-rial blood. It isn't the ideal situation to conduct further agitation under.

With a mental emergency protocol kicking into gear in my mind, I begin constructing a counterargument.

"Colonel. I will follow the orders I am given, but I wish for consider-ation to be made for my soldiers. They are all people, too, at the end of the day."

"I understand. When this operation is complete, I will use my author-ity to get you and your subordinates the extra rations and time off they've earned. I promise to make the direct appeal to General Zettour for you."

It's clear that Colonel Lergen isn't lying— he will almost certainly use every ounce of authority to try and get Tanya whatever she needs—but Tanya isn't so naive. No matter what reasoning Colonel Lergen presents the general with, it is necessity and necessity alone that will determine the future.

In other words, the colonel's promise is empty. While he can promise that he'll spare no effort on her behalf, he cannot promise her the time off. This is fraud, in the purest sense, which elicits a moan—albeit an internal one—on my part. Speaking of fraud, General Zettour is the greatest con artist of the era. Colonel Lergen of all people should know that there's no use placing any faith in him.

I heave a little sigh. What does the colonel have the power to *actually* provide me? I'm the one who's been charged yet again with an impossible mission, and I have no intention of becoming the lone sacrificial lamb.

With a fresh resolve, I promptly make my demands to the colonel.

"Colonel Lergen. Since you are willing to go out of the way to make such special arrangements for me, I'd like to request you lend me some much-needed equipment and personnel."

"There isn't much for me to lend out. What do you need?"

"I want to borrow your air support. As much as you can spare."

"What do you have in mind for them, Colonel?"

Tanya wears a confident grin.

"Drawing on inspiration from Colonel Uger, I want to play a little trick. I will create a bottleneck and fix the enemy in place."

"And by that you mean...?"

"I'm going to cut off the Unified States' seaborne supply route."

Colonel Lergen is clearly interested in hearing more.

"But how do you plan on doing this, Colonel? Raiding their shipping lanes? I somehow doubt we can expect to deliver a strong enough blow to disrupt their supply lines."

"No. It would be difficult to seek and destroy all their ships...but we know exactly where Ildoa's ports are."

"I never thought about it that way. Ports are very stationary targets."

"I remember being restricted in maneuverability when fighting on the southern continent due to how long it took us to get supplies out of the water. Should we destroy the enemy's port facilities with an aerial assault, it should keep them quiet for a while."

Colonel Lergen reacts to Tanya's words with a firm nod.

"Very well. I see your point, Colonel. Tell me what you need."

"I hope you can understand that I'm going to need a lot."

Though there is resignation in my tone, my comment is met with a reliable smile.

"I'll see what I can do, and expect results that match what I give you."

Tanya's request is fully accommodated, with Colonel Lergen arranging for the army to get her everything she asks for. He even manages to get the General Staff to lend her one of the larger transportation airplanes—a testament to his powerful connections and negotiation prowess. Thus, with the Imperial Army backing Tanya's plan in full, a significant segment of the air fleet scheduled to return to the capital changes course for Southern Ildoa to support the assault. I'm guessing that General Zettour took a liking to my plan.

The fact that my plan has been well received translates into enthusiasm that I can share with the troops.

"Comrades! The Empire has placed great hope in us!"

I'm addressing them at what was once an Ildoan air field. With the air fleet lined up along the long runway behind me, I brief the assault squad that I'll be leading into battle. I place immense trust in my aerial mages and their capability to wage war—if anyone can successfully execute this mission, it's them.

Their mission is simple: to incapacitate the enemy's ports to create a logistical bottleneck. It should be simple enough. They will travel by air to catch the enemy off guard, a relatively orthodox tactic for the Imperial mages.

"It's almost time."

After watching a series of fighters take off from the runway, Tanya and her soldiers board the massive transportation plane. Once in the sky, they couldn't have asked for a smoother flight. A plane this big at this point in the war is essentially an endangered species, but thanks to its skilled crew, the flight feels like a leisurely trip through Ildoa. The soldiers sip coffee as they watch the peninsula go by below them while also being sure to fill up on ham and bread before the big mission.

"This would be so perfect if we weren't in a war right now."

I mutter this to myself, earning an amused look from my adjutant, who is munching on some chocolate in the seat next to me.

"What would you be doing right now if there was no war, Colonel?"

"Me? I'd be living out my life as an upstanding member of society."

Lieutenant Serebryakov displays a bit of a confused look at this response.

"A member of society…?"

"What's this, Visha? Have you been at war for so long that you forgot what civilized life was like before?"

"No, it's not that… Wouldn't you still technically be a…"

"Be a what?" Tanya politely inquires her adjutant, but the conversation is cut short by a loud buzzer. The mages all look up, alert, only to be addressed by the calm voice of the pilot.

"This is the captain with an urgent sitrep. According to air control, the bomber squadron flying ahead of us has encountered enemy fighters and is under attack."

With that, the entire battalion of mages all grow tense. The mages are able to infer a lot from this report. It's clear to them that the enemy's anti-air capabilities are still fully operational. The group of mages are hit with the unsettling feeling of the unknown that is to come. With the mood growing heavy in the cabin, the pilot continues to share what he knows.

"Air control has weighed in on the situation, and it has been decided that we will use all available air assets to defend the bomber squadron. Every unit besides this plane's escorts will engage the enemy as a diversion." The captain calmly continues, "Should they down this plane, I'll have to ask you mages to fly the rest of the way. You don't need to worry about us. That is all."

Mages can fly. This plane's crew cannot. There's a clear asymmetry in the risk both parties are shouldering, and the professionalism of the air force personnel is deeply moving.

It isn't just their professionalism in how they carry themselves, but also the quality of their service that moves me, as the crew brings my mages to their destination without a single mishap. When they announce that we're over the target point, I stand in front of my mages with an intrepid grin.

Chapter V

"It's the same as always. Let's do our job."

I step out of the plane into the blue sky and let gravity take over.

Free-falling toward the ground unassisted by magic, I fix my eyes on the spot where we'll conduct our ambush—but there is something off. I can't quite put my finger on it, but a chill that only someone who's experienced combat could recognize quickly runs down my spine. I'm not one to take the fog of war lightly, so I decide to act on my instincts. Time to change the plan.

"All units, use your magic! Descend at full speed!"

Even if it means allowing our mana signals to be detected, it's better for the troops to have their defensive shells up. Not even a few seconds pass before my intuition proves correct. Before the transportation plane even has a chance to leave my field of vision. It's our multinational friends. Evidently, they've been lying in wait for Tanya and the Imperial mages.

The sky around us is immediately filled with incessant AA fire. The roaring of machine-gun fire rings loud as large swaths of the sky become impassable. There are likely mages waiting for us on the ground, too, given the explosion and optical sniping formula mixed into the barrage. It is an incredible display of anti-air defense. A show of intense and overwhelming force that is reminiscent of the notorious American imperialism from my old world. Even the veteran mages who've seen the Rhine are taken aback by the sheer volume of munitions being hurled into the sky. This is a level of firepower the likes of which they've never seen before.

"What the fuck is going on?!"

"There's nowhere to fly?!"

"This is insane?! Where is all of it coming from?!"

"Are we the ones getting ambushed?!"

The level of confusion that can be heard over the radio, too, is a first for me. It seems my battalion has been dropped off in a very tight kill zone. I'm the only one here who's read about this happening in history books, but not even those accounts could aptly describe what's happening right now. I have a hard time imagining the United States military of my own world ever made a fusillade of bullets and artillery shells of this scale in this time period.

"Damn it! They've already advanced this far?!"

Personally, I had hoped I wouldn't have to deal with something like this until the distant future.

Instead, my unit has found itself trapped in a deluge of steel. This method of area denial relies on filling the sky with as many shells as possible.

The enemy isn't bothering to conserve ammo.

They're simply throwing everything they have into the air.

It is a way of fighting only the Unified States, one of the world's leading superpowers, could afford. On top of that, there's additional fire coming from the Ildoan base as well.

"Damn, do the Ildoans keep *all* their ports this heavily defended?! The US soldiers are here, too!"

Almost in disbelief at the sheer scale, I also recognize that on some level, I should've expected this. Even a layman such as myself was able to determine the potential of a port becoming a bottleneck. For a country as experienced in global logistics as the Unified States, they really do spare no expense to make sure their supply lines stay open.

Tanya already experienced the Ildoan Navy's AA defense firsthand before. Now both countries are working together to seal off the sky. It is as simple a solution as it is brutal, posing a serious threat to even the most veteran members of the 203rd.

The roar of exploding cannon shells is accompanied by shockwaves that hit the mages and sear their defensive shells. The explosions alone, while undeniably loud, are nothing more than the anthem of the battlefield. What's truly frightening is the shrapnel flying in every direction.

It's quite aggravating, really, the absurd volume of metal being flung our way. Some of the shrapnel is managing to chip away at our defensive shells, and each new round brings a fresh hail of razor-sharp fragments. Being in their effective range is already quite dangerous. If any land a direct hit on one of the mages, it may completely pierce their shells altogether.

The clicking of Tanya's tongue is almost loud enough to hear above the deafening chaos. The enemy poses a far higher threat to the skies than we predicted.

"Damn those New World bastards! And damn the Ildoans!!"

At this rate, we'll be shot out of the sky long before we reach the ground. We need to move now, before they whittle down our forces.

"Battalion! This is the big leagues! Kick those orbs into high gear!"

As I channel mana into my Elinium Arms Type 97 Assault Computation Orb, I start preparing an optical camouflage formula when I realize something: The enemy isn't even aiming. They're literally firing into the air at random.

"Damn it! How far are they willing to go?!"

An optical camouflage formula wouldn't mean anything within this fiery baptism of bullets and cannon shells, which leaves me at a loss. Should we just beeline for the ground? We can't even if we want to.

"Disperse! Break formation! Pair up with whoever you can and move independently!"

Better to spread the enemy's potential targets rather than concentrate our forces in one place. Thankfully, my mages are well equipped to think and move on their own. They understand the meaning behind the orders, and everyone moves accordingly. Individuals come together to form a group, and groups merge to become an army. Since every mage under my command knows our mission is to destroy the port, I leave it up to them to decide how to carry out the task.

"All units! Prioritize your descent and move in pairs!"

Tanya barks her orders and raises her voice to add one more.

"Comrades! Do not falter. Getting shot at is business as usual! There aren't enough bullets in the world to stop us aerial mages!"

The 203rd is both fast and capable of defending themselves. None of its soldiers should be taken out of the sky, so long as they don't try to do the impossible. Although, as the aggressors, we have to find an opening to mount our counterattack.

To my great agitation, the situation only worsens.

"Damn it all! If we're stuck in the enemy's cone of fire, then this will devolve into a battle of attrition. Just how much firepower do they...?"

Wait...

Hoping to encourage the troops, I fire off formula after formula at the enemy below when I remember something and suddenly slow down.

"Colonel?! Don't stop flying!!"

"Wh-whoa?!"

Immediately heeding my adjutant's warning, I panic and reaccelerate just in time to avoid a massive volley of bullets that fly through the spot I was occupying moments ago. It takes every ounce of oxygen in my lungs to push through the rain of fire.

"This is no joke!"

With no oxygen left, I'm gasping for air and taking deep breaths to steel my nerves once more. Right now, nothing could be sweeter than the tasteless oxygen I generate with magic.

While I just managed to avoid getting hit, had I reacted even a single second later, I'd be Swiss cheese falling toward the ground right about now.

Tanya escaped by the skin of her teeth this time.

"You saved me! Thank you, Lieutenant Serebryakov!"

"A-are you all right?!"

"I'm fine!"

I catch my breath before scoffing at myself. While it's true this is a dangerous place to not pay attention to where you're flying, that momentary captivation lapse earlier gave me a hint for a new plan.

Remember, our goal is to neutralize the enemy port, and we don't necessarily have to be the ones doing the hard work.

"All units, follow your leader! We're dive-bombing toward the ground. Make your defensive shells as hard as you can!"

"02 to 01! Do you have a plan?!"

Major Weiss practically shrieks his question, which Tanya answers confidently.

"We're going to get up close and personal!"

With that, I fly to the front of the scattered formation before descending as fast as gravity can take me toward the ground below. Of course, our enemies don't sit idly by. They're clearly marking me as their new target, but…their response solidifies my confidence in the new plan. The enemy shows no sign of letting up as I and my mages use our Type 97 orbs to plummet toward the earth.

A mage flying this close to the ground, peppering it with formulas as they go, is like a vicious beast that's been let loose. The enemy is brave to continue fighting in these circumstances and meet the full-frontal assault with high-caliber AA fire aimed almost parallel to the ground.

It would be dangerous for a mage to take a direct hit from a round that's capable of piercing the heaviest tank armor head-on. This won't be a problem, however.

"Just as I suspected! This is a ragtag alliance we're dealing with here!"

I unconsciously grin as I shout this. Closing in on the enemy makes their unexpected weakness apparent. And that weakness is their coordination.

If these armies from different nations are working together without any real coordination, then we must simply cause friction in the space between them. Flying at a low altitude, I draw fire from either side.

The decision reveals Ildoa's fatal mistake: Their soldiers trained too meticulously.

"I mean, going all out is a good thing, I suppose."

Using her defensive shell to brush off the hail of AA fire, Tanya ends up chuckling at the Ildoan Army's determination. They clearly understand the danger posed by these mages who fly mere feet off the ground and deserve praise, as they've studied well. Things have been tough for the Ildoan Army so far. They were tormented by the Empire's most elite battalion, the 203rd, since the dawn of this campaign, and now are almost too familiar with the threat these mages pose, which translates into a lack of hesitation when it comes to aiming their cannons horizontally. They understandably want to destroy the mages at all costs, no matter who or what gets caught up in the blast.

This is the right decision, in a military sense. It is White Silver—better known by now as Rusted Silver, the Empire's deadliest Named class of mages—that is bobbing and weaving desperately through their cannon fire as we speak, after all.

By acting perfectly logically, the highly diplomatic and politically aware Ildoan Army ironically fall for Tanya's trap.

"Thank you, my Ildoan friends! Your cover fire is a true lifesaver!"

Tanya shouts with gratitude. While it may be true that AA guns are highly effective against mages who are flying straight at them, without enough time to unify their respective chains of command, and operating under different doctrines, Ildoan cannon fire hits their allies on the ground instead of Imperial mages in the air.

"Ha-ha-ha-ha! You guys are terrible hosts now, aren't you?!"

Combined, the Unified and Ildoan AA fire is a force to be reckoned with. But what happens when they end up on the receiving end of each other's cannons?

The result is most of the fire meant to stop Tanya and her troops ceases, but not without some stray shells finding their way to the port they came here to destroy.

"This is rich!"

Using the enemy's firepower as leverage against them proves to have a bigger effect than she could've hoped for.

"We must send our thanks to the Alliance!"

Tanya shouts to her mages while waving for them to review their handiwork.

"Cause chaos! Make them fire those cannons! They'll destroy the port for us! That's the way! Destroy the port!"

With their defensive shells protecting them, the mages act like powerful Apache helicopters that fly just above the ground to cause tremendous chaos. The enemy could perhaps fend them off if they fired everything they had, but when it became obvious that they were as likely to hit their allies as they were to hit the enemy mages, they couldn't help but hesitate. This is the correct choice for a good person, and it shows that even in total war, these soldiers all have good souls.

The goodness of their souls, however, will end up costing them their lives, as without a means to attack, the soldiers stop their hands. This moment's hesitation quickly transforms into a deep panic when the Imperial mages make their way to the camp and begin cutting them down en masse.

Should this panic spread throughout the enemy forces, a handful of mages is more than enough to cook the entire pot, but it's an eye for an eye and a tooth for a tooth on this battlefield. Just as man is man's greatest nemesis, there is nothing more formidable for a mage than a fellow mage.

While Tanya and her small group of elite Imperial mages wreak havoc around the Ildoan port, a presence in the sky above can be felt closing in at an incredible speed.

"Mana signals incoming!"

When the call is heard over the radio, the 203rd quickly gathers to assume a new formation. Their low altitude, however, puts them at a tremendous disadvantage.

With a curse, all attention shifts to the incoming foes.

"Enemy mages! And they're…?"

I immediately recognize several of their mana signals from the eastern front. With a few notable signals that are exact matches, one of which has been ingrained into my memory, it's clear that we've fought against these mages before.

"Not that damn pervert! Son of a bitch! Why do I have to deal with that deviant all over again?!"

Had Colonel Drake known that Tanya was referring to him as a pervert behind his back, he would likely make liberal use of his expansive Commonwealth lexicon to craft a strong rebuttal—though it should be mentioned that he reacts to her presence on the battlefield the same exact way.

"It's the Devil of the Rhine again…!"

The two of them both curse each other from across the battlefield. In the sense that they are both middle managers overseeing their units in tough times, they both carry similar concerns and tribulations. There is one other person on the battlefield who is concerned with something entirely different.

"There you are! Blasphemous Devil of the Rhine! I will end your wretched existence!"

The sheer resentment in her voice is like something straight out of hell. Her voice, which bears a baleful tone that cannot be ignored, rings out over the radio for allies and enemy alike to hear. This goes for Tanya as well, whose ears perk at the mention of her name. She looks up to the sky at the specs flying around and sighs.

"Adjutant. I'm not the type to bring my emotions to work, but…I truly do curse the fate that has brought me up against this wretched opponent once more. This is growing all too cumbersome. I can't stop sighing."

Lieutenant Serebryakov watches her superior from the side as she says this. Tanya does indeed look weary as she lets out continuous sighs.

"Just listen to these insults."

"She must really detest us…"

Tanya grunts.

"And for no good reason. It's the Empire who is their enemy, not I."

"Well... Uh... I'm not sure if..."

"I know, I know. There's no use whining about it, nor is there any point in trying to understand how they think. They don't act logically."

Tanya dons a lonely grin as she unleashes a formula.

"This is a battlefield, and as we don't enjoy the privilege of choosing our enemies, let's shoot the pervert and raging bull out of the sky."

With another long sigh, Tanya curses her bad luck once again while chanting the spell for a three-pronged explosion formula. Reshaping the world to physically manifest a formula of this scale is second nature at this point. Within the next instant, the entire sky is filled with balls of fire. It seems they aren't going to give us time to breathe. After casting a similar formula of her own, Tanya's adjutant asks a strange question.

"Who are the pervert and the raging bull?"

"The pervert is their commander. The Albion chap who tried to suicide-bomb us using his own mages as meat shields. That's about as deviant as it gets, no?"

"I suppose it is, in a way..."

"And then we have the raging bull. You see her there? She's the one flying straight toward us. Can you believe your eyes?"

Tanya winces as if she bit down on a stink bug while watching the rogue mage come flying toward them.

The mage has gone rogue and left her formation, something that would leave any other mage a dead duck. What's keeping this duck alive, however, is a defensive shell far too thick to be blown out of the sky.

An idiot though she may be, the powerful shell she has deployed can easily take a penetration formula meant to be used against stone walls, let alone an optical sniping formula, even if the caster is one of the 203rd's elites.

Tanya's only saving grace in this situation is that this mage is more or less an idiot.

With this in mind, Tanya calls out once more.

"Can you believe this! I must choose between the pervert and the bull!"

"You really dislike these types, don't you, Colonel?"

"I do indeed. It's hard to tell what those whom you can't understand will go and do."

Tanya wishes to believe that the world will be a better place without these two menaces in its sky. With this in mind, she knows that she'll have difficulty taking on the pervert who's been following her around the war front, and she makes her decision.

"Major Weiss! I'll leave the pervert to you!"

She can simply push the problem onto someone else. It's her prerogative to do so as the commanding officer.

"Understood! What will you be doing?"

"I'm going to dance with the bull. You needn't show restraint on my behalf, though. Once you've rid the world of another pervert, you can come to have a bite of the bull, too."

"That's assuming there's anything left of the bull once you're finished with it, Colonel."

"It's first come, first served. Just like everything else in the world!"

The two share a laugh before Major Weiss acknowledges the orders.

"Then I'll be off!"

With that, Major Weiss, who was flying barely a meter off the ground, makes a swift ascent. The Type 97 orb shows that it still has a comparative advantage on the battlefield with its rider clearing a vast altitude in a matter of seconds. His impressive speed allows him to probe the enemy's reaction while getting into the best position. The orb, excelling in both top speed and acceleration, truly is an Imperial mage's best friend.

"Attack! Don't cling to preconceptions or past experience!"

With Major Weiss leading his unit, they begin shrouding the Commonwealth mages with a wall of offensive formulas. Tanya turns to Lieutenant Serebryakov.

"Time for us to go! Today is the day we push these swine into the sea!"

"Yes, Colonel!"

The always reliable pair mobilizes for battle in well-coordinated tandem. Using the facilities at the port as a shield from above, the two mages weave around the obstacles on the ground, bringing them closer to the enemy ground forces while keeping their eyes on the target. There are ways to fight from the low ground if you know how to do it.

"Let's get the drop on her! Give me three rounds of disciplined fire!"

The spell manifests. Together the two of them conjure a highly complex optical formula that has a homing function worked into it. The highly calculated attack hurtles straight toward the enemy, striking true.

A raging bull makes for an easy target, but an attack that would usually have Tanya grinning leaves her shaking her head instead, because the target is still in the sky.

"Damn it. I can't say I didn't expect her to survive the attack, but she just shrugged it off! Just how hard is that shell of hers?!"

The pair of mages share a groan, but the bull isn't going to give them much time as she comes nosediving straight for them. Keeping her eyes on the vicious target, Tanya opts to use a less subtle attack. One that relies on pure firepower.

"Change the spell! We'll pierce that shell of hers!"

The choice to do this could be made only with the current distance between the two. To capitalize on the moment, Tanya takes out a Type 95, pouring as much mana as she can into the orb. Though the process of channeling the immense amount of mana takes its toll on her, making her brain feel like it's being consumed by worms, the tremendous spell it creates is well worth the risk.

"O Divine Light! Illuminate my path, everlasting glory. Come forth, song of eternity! O the glory of our magnificent Lord!"

Drawing on aspects of a long-distance offensive optical formula, Tanya chooses a piercing formula to penetrate the thick, Federation-style defensive shell. Both she and Lieutenant Serebryakov, with their breathing in sync, unleash a spell powerful enough to pierce the hull of a battleship.

Confident in their spell, the two watch as it connects with their target. The spell they put all of their power behind hits its mark, but the results are not what they had hoped for.

"I-is she still flying…?"

The awe can be heard in Lieutenant Serebryakov's voice as these words leave her mouth, and they accurately describe how Tanya feels as well. The beam landed a direct hit. It was the perfect angle, too. That attack would've downed Tanya without a doubt had she been on the receiving end. It would've sliced right through a Type 95's defensive shell like butter. And yet, the enemy was still in the air.

Chapter V

The spell that could've knocked out a heavy tank—and perhaps a battleship—left nothing but a small crack in the mage's shell.

"We can't treat this one as human. It's time to slay a monster."

And who is it that defeats monsters in a story? A hero? How absurd. Solitary monsters are always defeated by a well-run organization. One must look no further than the history of man to know this. Knowing that numbers are the only way to bring down this behemoth, Tanya immediately calls for her subordinates.

"Lieutenant Grantz! Lend me a hand! When we crisscross, we'll pincer her!"

"Roger!"

There isn't time to give in-depth orders. Asking for his help was enough. Tanya and Lieutenant Serebryakov feign a retreat to lure the charging bull toward them. She takes the bait, and they draw her deeper into the port complex.

The two are practically coughing up blood with the intense flight pattern it takes to force her into the killing zone.

"We've got her, Colonel!"

"Do it!"

That quick call is all Lieutenant Grantz needs to know exactly what to do, and he immediately leaps into action.

He leads his company on the hunt.

In perfect unison, the company unleashes a barrage of penetration formulas that all fall on a single point.

The focus fire pierces the physical world between the company and its target.

What should have been enough to leave even the thickest part of a battleship in shambles, however, is fully absorbed by the raging bull's defensive shell.

The shell itself did crack, of course.

However, the mage that it housed is completely unscathed.

The blow knocked her off course, but she's already back up, and a new shell is forming.

"You've gotta be kidding me?!"

"Lieutenant Grantz! Keep firing!"

"R-roger!"

While Tanya manages to calm down her panicked subordinate, a part of her recognizes his concern.

"Damn, she managed to survive even that. This mage really is becoming a monster."

Tanya glances to her side, and her adjutant agrees with a nod.

"She's more than a nuisance. Her shell is far harder than what even Federation mages can muster."

Tanya agrees wholeheartedly. That said, she isn't in a position to throw in the towel and give up.

"Lieutenant Grantz! Can your company hold her off?!"

"No way! We can't suppress her for long!"

Hearing this, Tanya turns her attention to Major Weiss. If one company isn't enough, then she'll use two. It's simple math, but surely focus fire from two companies' worth of mages should be enough to bring down the bull.

Unfortunately, her first officer is still engaged in a cutthroat dogfight with the pervert. Tanya shrugs. There is no use in placing hope in reinforcements that won't come.

"Lieutenant Grantz! We're going to do it one more time! Just one more time!"

"We can't! We can barely keep up with this mage! She's fast, tough, and fearless!"

"Come now, Lieutenant Grantz. You mustn't overestimate your enemy. She's less intelligent than a Federation mage, less cunning than a Commonwealth mage, and she's flying alone."

"Then I take it you have a plan to defeat her in one fell swoop?"

Tanya answers a hopeful Lieutenant Grantz's question with a grim tone.

"I don't appreciate you underestimating the enemy, either, Lieutenant."

"You really do have what it takes to become a general one day, Colonel…"

"Oh? Has my wisdom impressed you that much? Makes me glad that I've always acted as a model commander for you."

Tanya, throwing every formula in the book at the raging bull, is beginning to feel her submachine grow uneasily hot when she picks up on a new sensation.

"Wait, something is coming."

"What?"

"From the sea… What is it this time?"

As far as Colonel Drake could tell, the situation could only be described as miserable. The enemy was unperturbed by their AA fire, diving right into it toward the ground.

"Lord, we're up against mages who can fly in a perfect, tight-knit formation and then leap right into a firefight and raise absolute hell!"

To make matters even worse, a lone company was more than capable of keeping Drake's mages at bay. A small part of him hoped that First Lieutenant Sue's tirade would pull through as a last-ditch effort, but she was easily countered by a pair of enemy mages and then ended up on the receiving end of focus fire from the enemy mage company. While she was still in the sky, it was only a matter of time before she fell to an attack this relentless.

Things were looking bad. Drake wished from the bottom of his heart for more soldiers. Allies who would save his ragtag task force of mages and keep them from charging in alone.

"But just look at this godforsaken company of mages go!"

It was difficult for him to watch the enemy mages fly with such perfect coordination in comparison to his own.

"If only we still had the Corinth Regiment."

His lamenting over this, however, would come to an unexpected end when an innumerable amount of mana signals appeared from out over the ocean. In the next moment, all eyes on the battlefield shifted toward the sea to find multiple specs coming their way. The mages were wearing blue uniforms suited for aerial combat and were flying in attack formation.

They were Allied reinforcements—desperately needed reinforcements.

The timing of all of it was so miraculous that Colonel Drake pinched his cheek and winced at the pain. Realizing that this was actually happening, Colonel Drake called out to his troops.

"Reinforcements! Reinforcements are coming!"

He shouted and waved his hand in the sky so that everyone could know—so that their will to fight would be rekindled.

"It's the marines! The marines are here!"

His words caused a ripple to spread through the ranks, a ripple that quickly turned into a tidal wave of triumphant cheers. Light returned to the eyes of the Allied forces who had been dominated by the Imperial mages so far.

The Imperial mages, who had been running amok around the battlefield, also showed a quick reaction by increasing their altitude and assuming a formation that showed they were ready to continue the fight. Though they had already caused tremendous havoc, the enemy now had a clear disadvantage in numbers. There wasn't much they could do from a tactical standpoint.

This was no reason for Drake to go easy on them, however. If they were going to abandon their tight-knit position near the ground, then the AA crews were more than happy to oblige them with fresh fire from below. Of course, even when up against impossible odds, the Imperial mages were a relentless enemy.

"Damn it all! I hate to admit it, but they know how to fly all right!"

Colonel Drake grimaced at how skilled his enemies were. Genuinely impressed, he decided to send them his regards in the form of a spell. Unleashing his little present for them, a massive explosion blossomed in their air space. His sincere effort to kill them, however, would come to nothing as the enemy effortlessly evaded the explosion's area of effect.

"Criminy. I can't believe they can still fly like that."

"Do you think they're on something, Colonel?"

"Like some kind of drug?"

Drake gave the remark some consideration for a moment, but there were no obvious signs of impaired judgment or reckless aggression to be observed in their well-calculated and coordinated movements. Though they lacked numbers, they were flying circles around the Allies. What's more, despite having been doing this for the entire battle, they only seemed to be speeding up. Speaking of things with tremendous momentum, it appeared that First Lieutenant Sue had attempted a second charge, only to be fended off once more by the enemy company's focus fire.

"Glad to see Lieutenant Sue is still full of energy... I'm jealous. I'm already fighting for every breath."

Colonel Drake clicked his tongue and tried to refocus.

The enemy was a bunch of monsters capable of fighting First Lieutenant Sue head-on. If this was the case, then they would need to slay the beasts like any other humans would—with a well-coordinated attack.

"We'll capitalize on the marines' support! Let us push the enemy back!"

They needed to concentrate their fire.

Backed by AA guns and mages on the ground, their friends from the US Marines who had arrived at the perfect time rushed forward to deliver a devastating blow to the Imperial forces.

"I can't believe it! Out-fucking-standing!"

Drake ended up admiring his new comrades, for the moment the marines hit the battlefield, they unsheathed their swords and charged. These mages were true warriors of the seas.

"Cover them! Cover them! Don't let their courage go to waste!"

Shouting, Colonel Drake commanded his troops to give the charging US Marines mages cover fire. They continued to position themselves to support the naval mages while pinning the Imperials with suppressive fire and diversionary attacks, allowing them to hold off the Empire's mages long enough for the naval mages to arrive in a tight formation and unleash their spells from close range. They carried with them what seemed like a new weapon, which scattered their magic fire like a shotgun blast, completely dominating the battlefield.

Though heavily suppressed, the Imperial mages weren't giving up that easily, and they returned fire while holding firm. That wasn't enough to stop the brave navy mages, though, who continued to pour it on the Imperials.

It was an exchange of visceral yelling and gunfire that overwhelmed even the Named imperial mages. Unable to bear the pressure any longer, the Imperial mages began falling back.

"But they're still in the fight."

The sight made Drake moan. Though obviously withdrawing, the enemy's perfect formation left little room for pursuit. While the marine mages continued their magical barrage, they were never given the opportunity to give chase as the Imperial mages systematically retreated in good order. The Empire mages were...the picture of well-trained, well-practiced pilots.

"I suppose we should be happy we managed to make them back off at all."

Grateful that luck was on his side that day, Drake muttered this to himself while keeping a keen eye on his enemy. With them effortlessly veering at the slightest of angles to avoid the relentless Ildoan and Unified States AA fire, it was hard to call them a defeated battalion.

"Damn it, even their retreat is flawless. If we're not careful, they may turn this around and mount a counterattack."

There was tension in the air. The Imperial mages still had an arrow nocked to their bow, aiming straight for Drake's forces. Even in retreat, they were a formidable foe. Their mere presence was terrifying.

"Colonel Drake! We've received an emergency transmission from the enemy!"

"What? They're contacting us? What are they saying?"

One was to expect the unexpected during a war. It wasn't uncommon for something to make absolutely no sense. Accepting this fact of life was something all soldiers eventually did after enough experience. Despite this, Drake couldn't avoid the utter confusion he felt when he heard the report.

"Yes, they...are issuing an urgent complaint."

"A complaint? What could it possibly be about?"

Drake took the transceiver and tuned into the general broadcast. What he heard was a reading, spoken aloud without encryption. The person speaking sounded like a female officer, perhaps? In a calm voice, she repeated the same sentence over and over. It was read first in Imperial, then in Commonwealth. The officer finished in fluent Federation as well. All she needed to speak was Ildoan for everyone on the battlefield to understand. It was clear that the reading was sincerely trying to communicate the Imperial Army's sentiment on the matter, but...

"What are they saying?!"

Drake was left floating in the sky, dumbfounded by what he heard.

Chapter V

"That the use of shotguns goes against the law of war? They're protesting because it's inhumane…?"

Colonel Drake reconsidered his analysis on the matter from before. Just what in the hell was the Imperial Army trying to communicate at this stage of the war? The colonel was truly at a loss for words.

"I may have been wrong about their sound judgment. What possessed them to go and contact us about something this trivial?!"

"Colonel! They're asking for an answer!"

Drake's subordinate shouted this at him but was cut off by the colonel shouting back.

"What the hell do they expect me to say?"

The mid-combat sideshow was making the colonel dizzy. He cradled his head in an attempt to stop the sudden and intense feeling of vertigo.

"Colonel…? Are you feeling all right…"

"No, I'm fine. I'm starting to wonder, though…"

"Wonder what?"

"If the Imps really aren't on something."

Drake chuckled at the idea while he kept his aim locked on the retreating Imperial mages. He would send them a well-placed formula instead of an actual answer.

"Those damn Imps. They're the last ones who should be talking about inhumane acts…"

Drake was visibly annoyed but would be caught off guard once more by an enraged announcement made in Commonwealth with a thick Imperial accent.

"They've contacted us once more. It's the Imperial commander. She's addressing the Alliance commander!"

The slightly shrill voice of a child could be heard shrieking over the radio.

Despite the speaker's high-pitched voice, there was nothing cute about what she had to say.

"Your army's flagrant disregard for the international laws of war is a grievous offense that cannot be ignored! Even amid the chaos of battle, we are bound by a code of conduct that upholds the dignity and humanity of all involved! Your brazen violation of this treaty is unacceptable, as it not only dishonors your own troops but also stains the reputation of the entire human race. In the name of justice, I implore you to put an end to these barbaric practices, such as the inhumane use of buckshot against fellow human beings and restore the honor and integrity to the battlefield!"

It wasn't quite clear if she was being serious or if this was all a joke. What was he supposed to say? Both sides were doing their damnedest to kill each other. The entire situation left Colonel Drake utterly bewildered.

"Is she being serious? Is that what she has to leave us with after this battle? She's in the middle of a retreat, and she's worried about the rules?"

Mouth agape, Drake shook his head and shrugged. Simply put, he just couldn't process what was happening.

It would be fine if the cause of his confusion were just some unknown unit, but this was the Empire he was dealing with. The enemy he'd been fighting this entire war. The colonel had done everything he could to learn about his enemy up until this point, and yet, they still managed to surprise him.

"I don't know what to think anymore."

The exchange left a bitter taste in his mouth. He sighed, exhaling into the Ildoan sky. Just what percent of the sky was sighs? Drake couldn't help but wonder.

Had he the time, he could probably ponder this physiological question for over a day, but reality didn't give him such a leisurely opportunity. He had a massive aftermath to deal with after this brutal battle. Though at most, some intense paperwork was the extent of his problems since his side was able to push the Imperial forces back, but it was hard to consider this a silver lining.

It started with him drawing up a written report and apology for First Lieutenant Sue's rampage along with some other cumbersome multi-national unit–related bureaucracy. Regarding the friendly-fire incident between Ildoan and Unified States forces, Drake effectively pretended not to know about it and let them sort it out themselves.

Even setting this aside, the Alliance consisting of Ildoa, the Commonwealth, the Unified States, and the Federation was being incredibly unproductive. Drake's experience in negotiating with Federation authorities certainly came in handy here, but when confronted with a torrent of bureaucracy, such as translation, consensus-building, and brokering compromises, even an experienced officer couldn't help letting out an endless series of sighs. Until now, he could rely on Colonel Mikel to handle all of this, but due to the recent political adjustments, he and Mikel were the same rank.

"This is tough…"

The result was that the colonel found himself cooped up in camp dealing with a mountain of paperwork. At least a kind Federation official brought him some tea.

Despite having survived the battle, he questioned whether he could survive the sheer volume of paperwork. Drake was genuinely daydreaming about this fearsome outcome when Colonel Mikel, exhaling loudly, caught his attention.

"Is something the matter, Colonel Mikel?"

"No, it's nothing. I think it must be a bad joke…"

Drake watched Colonel Mikel try to hide a slip of paper, but considering his position in the multinational forces, he couldn't allow his Federation counterpart to hide things from him. Colonel Mikel was a good friend and fellow mage, but…Drake was still a Commonwealth officer. Thus, he reached for the paper before the colonel could put it away.

It was a single page with a format he'd seen before. It was the standard form for a message, but the contents tested Drake's nerves to their limit.

"There's seriously something wrong with the Empire."

My stomach is really starting to kill me…

From: An Imperial mage Battalion Commander
   To: The Commonwealth Army Commander

It is thanks to the unexpected but invaluable contribution of your army's mages that our operation to destroy a key Ildoan port has achieved a historic and unprecedented victory, the likes of which even the highest-ranking Imperial military officials could not have foreseen. Despite the highly unusual nature of the battle, its results have led this officer to recognize that accolades must be distributed with fairness and justice. It is my fervent hope that you will reveal the names of the courageous mages who provided us with crucial fire support that destroyed both your transport ships and the Ildoan port facilities. I swear on my honor that I shall petition the Imperial military authorities to recognize their well-deserved decoration.

VI

The Logistics of War

What the Unified States expected: War.
Those bastards' primary weapon: Refugees.

The truth is, we came into the war expecting to fight the Imperial Army, and a fair fight at that. But in hindsight, we were painfully naive.

We completely misread the circumstances: The Empire was an expert and many years our senior when it came to the wickedness of total war, and we were a bunch of wet-behind-the-ears newcomers who went in thinking we would get a direct confrontation, fair and square.

With such a misguided expectation setting us up, it's no wonder we missed our mark. Though it makes plenty of sense when you go back and think it over after the fact. Our nemesis, Zettour, never had any intentions of fighting fairly from the very start of his invasion—something I can now say with utmost confidence.

The man was faithful to the fundamentals of war. Particularly when it came to *using his own army's strengths to exploit the opposing army's weaknesses*. It was crucial for him to create battlefields where his army held the advantage for him to draw out opposing forces.

This was the principle he followed when he set the stage for the war in Ildoa. The bastard made sure to never lose the initiative there.

We went into battle thinking we were the protagonists, when really we were just playing a two-bit part in a script the Empire had prepared for us.

The abomination that happened in Ildoa was a historical sleight of hand that duped the Alliance. Even worse, the important lessons that we needed to learn were neglected instead.

In the minds of the public, the Empire won the battle, but we won the war. This may be true, in a sense, considering the ultimate outcome. Historically, the Empire did lose against the Alliance, an outcome that offers us the slightest bit of pride and confidence.

Chapter VI

But what of it? I always found this such a narcissistic way to view the subject. There's nothing constructive about ignoring glaring problems in light of a single victory. Forgive this old man's lecturing tone, but as someone who lived through the war, I can only remember the days spent on the Ildoan peninsula with a sigh.

The Empire was tactically superior? Their soldiers were highly skilled and could fight better than ours? They had Named mages and ace pilots? This much is all common knowledge. None of these individual episodes was totally inaccurate, and there certainly isn't a lack of anecdotes, myths, or legends on the battlefield. Someone could easily pen up an interesting novel or, at the very least, have fun with old comrades in a bar.

Sadly, though, those things are mere details.

What I want to discuss is what really happened.

The reason that we lost on the peninsula was that…we failed to adapt on a fundamental level when it came to total war.

When the rules of conflict change, an army needs to adapt to them as quickly as possible, and the cost of being unable to do so was tremendous.

Although, there are many other factors that I need to mention. A big one being, for example, the fact that our enemy was a bunch of rotten bastards. Maybe I'm just too old-fashioned, but this above all else was why I couldn't stand that scum. While it would be disingenuous to argue he wasn't a one-in-a-million general…that bastard Zettour's use of refugees to burden our logistics was as morally repugnant as it was ingenious. It was more insidious than a tactical bombing, and since he painted the attack in a veneer of righteousness, he pulled it off while the whole world was watching.

He tried to bring our army to its knees using the stomachs of Ildoa's refugees. This single attack alone was more than enough to earn him the con artist moniker we all know him by. While it would be their tactics-above-all policy that would eventually do the Empire in, the Ildoa campaign led by Zettour was its own monster. He had calculated every turn of the entire campaign, through and through.

Do you know how they used to siege castles in medieval times? Back when there weren't even bombs, let alone magic, the stone walls of a castle were about as impenetrable as a wall could get, and an incoming attacker's biggest concern was how they could take the castle down.

The dominant tactic of the time was to chase those living in the surrounding area away from their homes and into the castle, a method to win without actually attacking that medieval tacticians likely borrowed from their predecessors.

For better or worse, the history of man is a story of war, and the tactics employed by the Empire in Ildoa were a simple revival of historical methods that were tried and true. It could be said that, in this regard, the Empire was an outstanding successor in keeping the classics alive, and it seems that General Zettour, in particular, was well read.

It's something often pointed out by scholars now, but the tactics employed by General Zettour—commonly lauded as fantastical and bizarre—were, more often than not, sound tactics that drew on knowledge from the past.

A good example of this was Operation Revolving Door from the Rhine front. While it is commonly upheld as a dramatic use of maneuver warfare, it was primarily tunnel warfare that did the heavy lifting in causing the collapse of the defensive line—yet another classic example of anti-castle warfare from times before explosives were commonplace. Even his staggeringly aggressive style of maneuver warfare on the eastern front is yet another example, taking the classic war theory of luring, encircling, and destroying an enemy in a field battle and stretching the concept to its limits. Decapitation tactics, something people often see him as an innovator of, also have ample precedent in the many assassinations found throughout history. There is no shortage of examples of armies succumbing to chaos after losing key commanding officers.

If there is anything that must be recognized about General Zettour's implementation of these tactics, it is that he adapted them to modern warfare in an incredibly refined manner. This could also be said about the Empire as a whole. Bastards, the entire lot of them, but they had an incredible knack for war. They were like a pack of ferocious beasts who could think.

If we, the marines, were ordered to engage the enemy in direct combat, we would've won. If our nation said the word, we would've seen it through. The issue was, there was no enemy to fight when we got there.

Why? Because our enemy was that son of a bitch Zettour. He never intended on fighting us from the get-go. I can say for sure that con artist never saw the entire theater in Ildoa as anything more than his own toy box. It was his to do with as he pleased, a catalyst for stroking the Empire's ego.

Which was why he played games to his heart's content there, flipping the country upside down, only to return to the north like it never happened. He left it to us, the adults, to clean up the mess he'd left behind.

He never had any interest in Ildoa. It was nothing more than a way for him to gain time, and a spot to force us into.

There's good reason why this point of view is valid, too. Look no further than the records on logistics and supply—they tell the story.

Sadly for us, the public oftentimes sees our deployment alone to be heroic and the apex of the war. Countless historians have exhausted an ocean's worth of ink detailing pitched battles, and it is no different for major naval engagements. It is only the initial battle that will make it into any of the history books. In contrast, the world of logistics is, frankly speaking, quite bland. There's a rigidity to it that lacks the spectacle necessary to woo the masses. This is why history books are filled with heroic battles, which they explore down to the finest detail, while barely ever discussing victories of the supply line.

They may touch upon the success of an attack on an enemy's supply line in the frame of a larger battle, or even discuss examples where the lack of provisions was the determining factor in a certain strategy's success. Any such examples, however, are for the more well-informed readers. They are difficult to understand. The less-informed masses tend to find the age-old story of a small group of soldiers overcoming the odds through bravery and ingenuity to snatch victory from the jaws of defeat far more glorious.

This isn't to say that commanders who are able to pull such a feat off don't deserve their accolades. It is, however, highly irresponsible for a nation to expect this much from its commanders as the standard. The *hero* scenario entails that its actors lack the support they should've had in the first place. If we're to praise those who have gone far above and beyond their call of duty, we must also rebuke a nation that neglects to fulfill its own.

What's needed isn't just some flowery words of praise but proper training and equipment. To get even a single glass of water to the front lines means that somebody somewhere in the rear must carry it there. This is what we're dealing with here.

In times of peace, access to a drink of water is as simple as turning on a faucet. Your options become much more limited during a war, however, where you either need to bring that water from its source to the battlefield, treat water found in the field, or neglect your soldiers' needs entirely.

Armies are massive groups of people, and people get hungry and thirsty. To expect soldiers to die fighting when they are already dying of starvation and dehydration would be the height of callousness.

To prevent this from happening, the army needs to function as an organization. The amount of food, water, and bullets a single hero can bring with them into war is paltry, which is why teamwork is essential to victory, and why we should do away with our habit of focusing solely on the glory of the vanguard charging gallantly into battle.

The colossal number of people it takes to support the war from the front is something that should never be forgotten. It is what gets people the things they need, when they need them, and where—something that in times of peace is taken for granted. This is something that is truly great—the people and system who make it possible—and it's a lesson that the Unified States learned all too well when it answered a historic humanitarian call of epic proportions on the Ildoan peninsula.

》》》 **DECEMBER 20, UNIFIED YEAR 1927, THE GENERAL STAFF OFFICE AT THE IMPERIAL CAPITAL** **《《《**

The Ildoan HQ made it clear they would take in the refugees from the north. General Zettour could finally release the tension in his shoulders after confirming that Ildoa avoided mass panic, thanks to systematic support from the Unified States and the rest of the Alliance.

"I'm glad I placed faith in their sense of reason."

Though Zettour never fancied himself a gambler, he'd won this particular bet. And it was the gamble of a lifetime. One that pitted the lives of Ildoan citizens as forbidden bargaining chips against the rationality and humanity of his enemies. And he had bet correctly.

"Yet another evil, detestable deed that will forever be associated with the name Zettour. It seems this will be my only legacy—one of evil."

Zettour chose this path for himself, and he knew what he was doing by doing so. Though he could trick those around him, there was nothing to be gained from tricking himself about it.

Which made it strange. Despite having convinced himself he was ready to play the villain, there was a part of him that felt vindicated by the outcome.

"How…sentimental."

His soul felt at peace. It felt as if he was exempt from feeling guilty. With a sigh, he reached for a pack of cigarettes to fill his lungs with some much-needed tobacco, when a strange idea struck him. Just as he'd murmured to himself only moments prior…having been saved from his guilt felt so sentimental.

But what exactly was saved? Was it his own conscience? Or was it the strategic interests of the Empire? With a nasal grunt, Zettour gave himself a self-deprecating chuckle.

"I'm no longer…my own man."

I am the state. It would be easier if he truly thought this highly of himself, but he knew he would never be anything besides a humble career soldier. That said, there was a good possibility he was currently transforming into the ringleader of a military coup…but he was still a pathetic individual who was watching the sun set.

Zettour couldn't become the sun. He was well aware of this, more than he wished to be. The most he could hope for was that the world would mistake him for it. This was the sole reason he was in the position he was in, and why he enacted the evils he did.

Zettour had sent large swaths of Ildoa's refugees down south. His tactic, which turned the nation's population against it the same way sieges forced castles to capitulate in the past, was as straightforward as it was cowardly and evil.

It was Zettour's idea, and Zettour was the one who ordered it. In other words, it was all Zettour's doing. Not the Empire's.

"I can only wonder if I still have the compunction to genuinely pretend I was ever concerned about the well-being of the refugees."

He chuckled... Since he was a soldier who had crossed the line, this was the only attitude he could have about it.

"But to think my variation of human wave tactics would take shape in such a heinous way and target the enemy's stomachs. I am so wicked. God must truly despise me."

Zettour was the offender. The honor and glory of being an Imperial soldier had dissipated. He knew they would—such was the only logical outcome, seeing as the Empire's inevitable defeat was clearly looming on the horizon. The very foundation of his nation was unstable.

"Will I be able to finish my tread down this tightrope? The apprehensions that eat away at me are already such a massive burden on their own. There's no utility in taking on more to worry myself over."

A puff of smoke left Zettour's grimacing mouth, carrying his sentiment with it.

"I only ever wanted to be a good person."

He even thought he was, or at least, he once did.

"But these are the times we live in."

A gun hung at his waist. All he needed to do was bite down on its barrel...and with a simple pull of the trigger...

"I'm sure it would make things easier."

No more worrying about duty...

Then Zettour shook his head to dispel the thought. He was more surprised by his own weakness than the thought itself—surprised that he still had thoughts like this from time to time.

 THE SAME DAY, THE UNIFIED STATES HQ IN ILDOA ◀◀◀◀

On the Ildoan peninsula, where the conflict between the Empire and the Alliance raged on, outside help was necessary for replenishing the constant outflow of supplies, gunpowder, and lives. The war was truly avaricious in this sense.

Weapons needed constant maintenance, and ammunition, naturally, could only ever be used once. Before anything else, soldiers were living, breathing humans. It wasn't as if the US troops stationed in Ildoa under Truger's command could defy the laws of nature. That made it necessary for them to request that supplies be sent from home.

The men and women fighting the war needed both weapons and ammo, as well as other essential resources such as food and water. Luxuries, too, were important for a healthy, functioning army—almost indispensable. These soldiers, who longed for nothing more than a simple letter from back home, were risking life and limb on the battlefield. Was some amusement, be it in the form of food or entertainment, too much to ask for? A lot went into keeping spirits high despite their perilous circumstances.

In this regard, the Unified States did well for its soldiers, meticulously learning from past mistakes to ensure that those stationed abroad were treated well.

"Everything is perfect. We can even get our troops on the front lines ice cream and steak."

A logistics worker would aptly make this remark on the job one day. They took pride in the strong supply lines they had established.

It went without saying that ammunition was readily available. The nation had a tremendous stockpile for its well-established worldwide lend-lease program, which allowed it to keep its soldiers well fed and armed to an extent beyond the Empire's wildest dreams.

What's more, their distribution network was perfect. With many boats for transportation, each guarded by escort vessels, and an expansive air force, it had the seas and skies of the world covered and enough easily transportable fuel to fully maintain it.

It was a standard for distribution never seen before. What the Unified States considered a perfect system had Tanya screaming, *"Cowards!"* Where the Empire had most of its supplies still being transported by horse, and even had to resort to having its mages use tugboats to tow its tanks across rivers, the Unified States' transportation network was completely motorized. The nation had so much of a surplus that it could keep the other members of the Alliance thoroughly supplied on top of this. It was the picture of excellence.

There are few methods as tried and true as sound logistics to bring a country to infallible victory, which was why the Unified States made heroic use of its seemingly limitless resources to make sure that the front lines had everything required to win.

While the front line was bolstered with the best people and equipment for the job, fate had a different plan for the country. When the Unified States reached the peninsula, it underwent its own baptism in total war, and it was the dreaded General Zettour who bitterly, evilly, and relentlessly poured the holy water over the helpless newborn US Army's forehead.

Were the US generals and officials incompetent? No, not by any stretch of the imagination—both Ildoa and the Unified States had studied the *con artist Zettour* in exacting detail.

The two forces went into the battle with both a clear strategic and tactical advantage to defeat their crafty nemesis: sheer numbers. As simple as this may sound, it should've been the correct answer to the problem. The Unified States, the Commonwealth, and Ildoa were all major maritime powers with control over the seas, ample forces on the ground, and a combination of mages and planes that could achieve aerial superiority. Putting it plainly, the three nations did everything right, and their military leaders were confident that they would be able to put up as strong a fight against the Empire and Zettour as any other forces could.

Incidentally, many said that General Zettour admired his enemy.

"One must be jealous of our enemy. Look at their massive army, bountiful resources, and endless supplies. It is difficult to call this a fair fight. It's almost immature of them, really."

The dreaded Zettour was widely considered a crafty tactician and a one-of-a-kind strategist. The US officials behind the creation of a flawless military-industrial complex should be proud of the fact that they had made him concerned.

They were going to destroy the enemy with their superior resources. A simple, effective approach that the US could have faith in. A losing army that lamented over losing due to a lack of resources never should've gone to war in the first place. This would ultimately be what led to Zettour going down in history as the defeated general he became.

However, it's well established by now that the dreaded Zettour will go down in history as one more thing: a con artist. This reputation of his has established itself not only in the eastern front, but in the west as well.

By the time the Unified States had prepared its forces in Ildoa for an epic counteroffensive against the Imperial Army, the bomb laid at their feet by the expert of total war would explode. An explosion that would have the Unified bureaucrats practically fainting over the newest reports.

"We don't have enough boats! Or goods! What the hell is going on?!"

Reality was nauseating for the planners overseeing logistics, who lamented over the hopeless status of their merchant navy.

What in the world could've led to this?

They could understand the cause.

It was all due to a surge of unexpected demand, for which there were two reasons. First, the Ildoan Army's lack of critical resources. And second, the geographical impact of total war in Ildoa.

Had it been only one of these problems the Unified States had to deal with, it probably could've met the challenge without issue. Both of them culminating together at the worst possible time, however, made for one massive dilemma.

General Zettour's blitzkrieg invasion of Ildoa led to the occupation of the nation's heavy industrial zone to the north by the Imperial Army, which would go on to be described as one of the more catastrophic events in the war.

Having lost its industrial base, armory, and even its stockpiles, Ildoa was in no position to remilitarize on its own, and outside support—which in this case fell on the Unified States to provide—was vital.

The Unified States had a contingency in place to resolve this, of course. They would simply send all the weapons, equipment, and ammunition the country needed.

If the Ildoan youth had been willing to fight the Empire so the youth of the Unified States didn't have to, then sending them what they needed would have been an easy decision for US politicians. From a long-term perspective, Uncle Sam was more than willing to help keep the Ildoan Army fighting on the front lines. Although it was also true that this posed a short-term problem. If they needed to keep dozens of mobilized soldiers armed...then it meant that the Unified States would have to reduce the allocation of resources for its own army.

There was also the nightmare of having to actually send everything its ally needed. A person in charge of the Unified States provisions who was ordered to make this possible would aptly remark:

"What, do they think these weapons grow on trees?!"

While the nation had a massive surplus of weapons and bullets, these were still finite.

Even for the massive manufacturing base boasted by the Unified States, it was no small task to arm the armies of the Commonwealth, the Free Republic, and even the Federation, all while keeping its own quickly expanding army well geared.

On top of having to do this, it was expected to send over a dozen divisions' worth of supplies for the Ildoan forces.

Just procuring the arms would be a lofty task on its own, but getting them across the sea as soon as possible was truly a nightmare.

Anyone would lament over the orders.

"We're going to have to reduce what we're sending to the Commonwealth and Federation, and lower the pace of our own army's expansion..."

It was with a collective sullenness that those who oversaw logistics made such a grave decision, for they knew they had a lot of work ahead of them.

While it was tough for those who had to make the cuts, it was far tougher for those on the receiving end of those supplies. When the Federation, Commonwealth, and Free Republic learned their allotment was being reduced, officials from each nation worked fervently to secure their own portion. The strong mutual distrust among the three supposed allies intensified as they entered this new prisoner's dilemma. It would later be discovered that behind the curtain—when begging, demanding, crying, and relentless attempts to entertain ambassadors weren't enough—the foreign diplomats even resorted to bribery and extortion.

Chapter VI

The number of backroom deals and underhanded tactics that would take place was utterly detestable. This should've been more than enough to undo the jerry-rigged bond the nations had in their *Alliance*. Though before the cut-and-dried separation between the thought camps would take root in the east and the west, a clear wedge had been driven between the two sides. Were it not for the existence of an overt and obvious mutual enemy, this change in supply allocation created more than enough hostility to spark a new conflict.

As such, the Unified States made a decision that all the stakeholders could reluctantly agree on. While it was a noble decision for the nation to prioritize the nation in crisis, Ildoa, much of the effort that went into launching their initiative would fall flat. Despite the Unified States' best efforts, the Ildoan Army simply lacked a distribution network that could adequately handle the amount of supplies they needed. Until new domestic supply lines could be established, the Ildoan Army was fully dependent on the Unified States for every last bullet and morsel. And even then, the question of supplying weapons to Ildoa was...one of the easier issues the Unified States would face as a nation.

The worst problem manifested was the national food shortage—a vital resource Ildoa's citizens needed to live. This was a complete blind spot for the Unified officials and cause for a major headache.

That wasn't to say that they had no considerations for food shortages. They had plans set in place to provide food for refugees in locations they might occupy, and they were more than capable of *bringing* food to such locations as opposed to having to acquire it at their destination.

The Unified logistics officials even had a structure set up in case they invaded the Empire and had to provide for its people under military rule. The same went for the François Republic's territories. They could establish a temporary rule there while they waited for the Free Republic or its bureaucrats to take over.

Thus, the possibility of unforeseen civilian demand was something that was considered by the logistics officials. What they couldn't have predicted, however, was just how much grain they would need to hand over to the civilians when they reach their allied nation!

Any predictions they had made going into the war were only for military support and equipment. Thus, their initial decision to prioritize Ildoa was more of a slogan than a firm policy.

While they knew they would have to reduce support for their other allies going into the war, it was only a matter of by how much, not all at once. The logistics team figured they could primarily support Ildoa while maintaining the rest of its supply network.

This miscalculation would be dispelled at a moment's notice upon receiving word from the Ildoan ambassadors of the possibility that the country could need a large quantity of wheat—a request that would have anyone doubting their ears. The very concept went against all common sense.

"This is Ildoa we're talking about!"

The officials blurted out their doubt.

"It's an agricultural exporter!"

"How does a nation that produces so much run out of food?!"

It was exactly as the government officials were exclaiming to each other as they fell into a panic: The nation of Ildoa was traditionally known as an agricultural powerhouse.

The country had a rich, world-famous culinary culture that spanned from the north to the south.

As rich as this culture was, it wasn't without its own idiosyncrasies. The climate of Ildoa was different in its northern and southern parts, allowing the nation to harvest a wide variety of crops.

Specifically, the north produced a majority of the nation's staple grains, while the only grains grown in the south were purely for *self-consumption*, with tree crops being the main commercial product. Their agricultural products included a wide variety of produce, such as olives, grapes, and citrus fruits, as well as wines and other processed derivatives. It also included the milk and meat of sheep and goats.

Ildoa had a plethora of produce that it was well known for, and there were few nations around the world that matched the nation's scale in agricultural exports. If there was any difficulty with the nation's agricultural foundation, it was that the vast majority of its commercial produce was difficult to use as a staple food.

Were this a time of peace, this wouldn't be a problem. The nation enjoyed a comparative advantage that would've made Ricardo proud.

But this was total war.

With all imports having been ceased due to the war, the nation was receiving an influx of refugees from its north to its south.

The hotels that were empty due to the war quickly found themselves overflowing with refugees. It wasn't as if the southerners didn't try to help their northern counterparts out in their time of need, but no amount of desire to help could fill the void created by a dearth of resources.

Supply had diminished, and demand had increased dramatically. Prices began climbing faster than even the notorious Imperial mages, and while it wasn't anyone's fault, the country reached it breaking point when the US military arrived.

When the multinational volunteer unit—consisting primarily of US and Ildoan troops—deployed to defend Ildoa, the Ildoan authorities naturally provided the army with its stockpiled food while also trying to replenish said stockpile with food from the market. At the same time, by force of habit, the Unified States tried to establish its own local stockpile—using foreign currency to buy up what they could—and they directly contributed to the astronomical rise in food prices in southern Ildoa.

By the time officials picked up the situation, the prices were already growing out of anyone's control. It was clear that food could be sold for more tomorrow, and then even more the next day, resulting in a reluctance for farmers to sell crops too early due to the ever-increasing prices.

Regardless of the prices, there just wasn't enough food to feed the nation due to the stockpiles in the north, which were prepared for times such as these, falling into Imperial hands. The result: The Ildoa-Unified HQ was up against a new, unforeseen enemy—a difficult-to-believe sudden rise in food prices on the civilian market. In addition to this, it didn't help that citizens of both the Unified States and Ildoa both enjoyed a prosperous standard of living long into the Great War.

In any case, one of the major impacts that total war had on the nation was a food shortage without precedent. Everyone back home was foaming at the mouth with rage, cursing the heavens while they fell to their knees.

"Southern Ildoa is on the brink of a famine?!"

From an objective perspective, it wasn't as if the Unified States Army's presence in the nation was the trigger for the new development. As with any shortage, prices rising was only a matter of time more than anything. It was just as likely that those living in the south would end up causing a rise in prices due to bulk panic-buying out of fear of further invasion, but any potential causes were simply that—causes that never had the chance to happen.

What the people of Ildoa, and the world, saw was a tremendous rise in food prices the moment the Unified forces hit Ildoan shores. It left the Unified Army with the unfavorable criticism that they were *buying up all the food*. In actuality, the dent that twenty, thirty thousand soldiers would make on the feeding of millions of civilians was insignificant, but it was the optics that mattered.

The world's opinion on the matter had solidified. It was around this point when the officials, already in a deep panic, would receive even worse news: that a key port in southern Ildoa had lost its function due to an Imperial assault.

The fact that all the large port facilities in the south were within range of an Imperial attack also posed a new, serious problem for the Allies in terms of ensuring the safety of transportation routes. Although this much could've been solved if the Allies could expel the Imperial Army from the north.

"But that's a big *if*."

It was as one of the bureaucrats so aptly articulated: *If* they could expel the Empire, there would be no problems.

With that, the expeditionary forces brought to Ildoa under the command of Lieutenant General Truger were engulfed in the logistical chaos. His initial plan, seeing as the ground forces that had been urgently deployed to the outskirts of Ildoa's capital had already been defeated by the Empire, was to fortify the positions in the south as quickly as possible before heading north to raid the enemy holdings and help stabilize Ildoa's lines…but this plan quickly fell apart.

Everything was going smoothly when he reached his position in a southern Ildoan city and established his HQ, but his schedule would be turned upside down when he received word that an Imperial task force was attacking a military port to his south, forcing him to immediately deploy mage reinforcements to help protect the supply ships.

With his forces exhausted afterward, and there being no food to feed them, Truger knew he was in no position to mount a counteroffensive. The general was in his office, dealing with the administrational aftermath of the attack, when his subordinate would come with a new report.

"Sir, we've received a maximum-priority message from back home. Please read this."

"What is this insignia?"

From behind a mountain of paperwork, Lieutenant General Truger expressed his confusion.

"I've never seen this, either. What's it say here? *Integrated Form 1*?"

"With the Department of War being reorganized as the Department of Defense, the navy and army are now both under the same command. I heard they were going to reformat all our paperwork."

He waved his hand and sent his subordinate away, sighing deeply while he read over the paper.

"So the folks back home are quick when it comes to whipping up shit like this to send over with the highest priority."

Where provisions wouldn't find their way, mundane problems reached him with utmost haste. Lieutenant General Truger read over the report with regret in his eyes.

The paper his accountant was so kind in bringing him spelled out in the most direct of terms the supply issues that were occurring across Ildoa.

"We could win in an all-out battle, but it's taking us too long to get to the battlefield."

They had the firepower. They had cannons and shells. Observational equipment and trucks to get these around. All the fuel they could ask for.

If he gave the order, his brave soldiers would head north without question. If he followed navy doctrine, there was little reason for him to keep his forces in the south, but moving north now meant the Ildoans would starve.

"We came here to fight the Imperial Army. What the hell is this?"

Truger let out a large sigh.

"The shipping problem is far too severe. If only we didn't need to distribute the Ildoans' food for them…"

The man bit down on the cigar in his mouth and looked down on the strategic map left on his desk.

"Currently, the Imperial Army has thirteen divisions and three panzer divisions."

The equipment for these units were, as far as he could tell, still in good condition. Conversely, the Alliance was in poor shape.

While Ildoa boasted thirty divisions, plus the Unified States' infantry divisions and a single naval squadron...with the exception of the Royal Guard units, these were mostly weaponless.

"We could arm them, but..."

They didn't have enough ships to bring the weapons they needed to Ildoa. While ships were being built as fast as they could back home, it wasn't possible to bring everything they needed right now.

The New World and the Old World were separated by a vast amount of space. Just bringing this number of soldiers along with the immense provisions to keep them supplied across the great sea that divided them was a feat in itself.

"If our boats weren't being used to carry wheat, I could ship twenty of our own divisions along with a couple of Ildoan ones to the north and execute our Plan B to surround and destroy the main Imperial forces."

The Unified States had two choices: to bring wheat to Ildoa or bring its forces north. There was no choice for the good soldier to make, no matter how much of a warrior they were.

"If we send our soldiers north...the starvation of those in the south will be pinned on us."

Was a military victory worth the lives of civilians? It was a military dilemma that a democratic nation never wished to face.

"The folks back home won't let us do that... And we certainly can't let innocent people die."

He dropped his cigar into his ashtray and signed the papers before looking at a new set of documents that similarly described limitations due to deficiencies.

They had the boats. These boats were carrying what the nation needed.

"Just look at this mess."

Being forced with the laborious task of taking care of southern Ildoa had the Unified States writhing in pain and left Truger chuckling wryly to himself. He had an idea of what the Empire was going to do next.

"Judging by the current situation...the moment we seize the Ildoan capital and any major cities in the north, our supply lines will be forced to carry an even heavier burden."

The capital and some of the northern cities were where most of the population lived. As the Unified States entered the conflict, its chief concern had been urban warfare, but it now looked more and more like advancing north would tax their supply lines more than their own military.

UNIFIED YEAR 1927, THE LOVE NEST FROM WHICH LOVE SHALL BE SHARED WITH ALL DURING THIS SEASON OF LOVE

A date was an outing. Loria knew that he and he alone was suited to go on a date with his precious fairy, and that those who sought to interfere with his love deserved nothing but death by his own hands. This much was fact, and yet, he was conflicted, for there was little he could do against that wretched Zettour!

With this in mind, Loria's sworn enemy—a little shit that needed to be killed, a stain that needed to be purged from history itself—had wronged him and the world once more. In Ildoa, this time. Knowing that the unforgivable, utterly detestable Zettour was greatly cherishing the precious fairy Loria had such pure feelings for filled him with a blistering rage that erupted from the depths of his soul.

Were it any other enemy, simply killing them would be enough to end all this...but dealing with a wicked evil that sought to so overtly interfere with his path to love made this a war.

It was all in the name of love and purity that the man was towering with rage and passion. Each and every breath he took was an unabashed protest to the irrationality and injustice that plagued his worldview.

Each breath Loria took was, for him, a curse against his unforgivable, sworn enemy for taking his precious fairy away from the eastern theater. In this way, Loria's worldview was undergoing a grand shift.

It was almost genuine of him, in a sense. Loria saw himself as a pure man experiencing pure love, pushing forward in his pursuit of that love.

As a higher-ranking official for the Federation, he had any given number of options available to him, along with their varied potential outcomes, but he wouldn't act so rashly.

It should be obvious, but he was capable of handling any amount of work in the name of love. In the name of his future. *Our future!*

With profound resolution, Loria diligently made arrangements from within the Federation until the fateful day came for the big meeting, where with great vigor, he would sound the cautionary alarm warning of the Imperial menace to his peers.

"As you can see...the situation in the Ildoan theater has taken a turn for the worst. It's due to yet another one of the Empire's evil and inhumane tricks. The dirty bastard Zettour—rotten to the core—in all his impulsiveness, has done away with all logic and morals and is trying to fool the entire world to—"

"Comrade Loria. While I do appreciate you calling together today's meeting, I fail to see the point of this statement."

"Oh, right, Secretary General. My deepest apologies... It seems that the sheer absurdity of the matter at hand has made me a bit overzealous."

Loria shook his head and took a moment to correct his breathing. It was paramount that he maintain his composure to face the unjust world he was subject to. Even if the room he shared with the party secretariat for this secret meeting was chillingly cold, he still needed to exert tremendous effort to cool his own nerves.

"Allow me to clarify myself... The Empire is using Ildoa as the stage for a trick."

With a loud smack, Loria gestured toward a tuft of documents he held in his other hand as he spoke.

"These papers spell out the crafty, yet highly logical scheme to embroil the Unified States in Ildoa. Despicable stain he may be, our enemy has devised quite a plan."

It was all as plain as day. Loria's peers didn't need to be as crafty to understand, but nevertheless, it was somehow lost on them, forcing him to tell those who knew not of love what he saw.

"Yes, yes. Now quiet down, there's no need to get riled up about it. While it does indeed at a glance seem as if the Empire initially dug its own grave by pulling the Unified States into this war...it was not without unexpected merits for the Empire, however exceedingly short-term they may be."

It all comes down to this.

Loria raised his voice once more.

"The US aid for Ildoa, primarily regarding their humanitarian aid, will inevitably put immense pressure on their overseas shipping. This results in our nation being able to receive less help from the outside. Not even Imperial raiding on our commerce could've dealt a blow this heavy."

A few of his peers looked up, showing a shared pain in their own expressions. The Federation, too, was in dire straits when it came to acquiring much-needed resources. They could likely get along without the support should they need to, but seeing as total war was taking its toll on their nation, it was better for them to have access to support if they could.

Loria took on a brighter tone when he spoke next.

"Looking at a more positive point, our new allies will force the Empire to split its war front in Ildoa. The presence of a second war front should lighten the burden on our end. This is a fact. This is also something we've requested from our fellow Alliance members, including the Commonwealth, many times."

Loria took a short pause before continuing. He felt as if he was being cheated. It was painful for him to say this out loud, but he needed to.

"They've yet to fully answer our requests in a meaningful way. The reason for this is due to the narrowness of Ildoa. To truly pin the Empire there, they need more land to maneuver."

There was no need to look at the map to imagine this. Geography was everything in war, and the fight in Ildoa was being fought on a long, thin peninsula, stretching from north to south, and incredibly narrow from east to west. Compared to the massive expanse of land that the Federation and Empire shared, the divide between north and south in Ildoa was but a smidgen of land.

The width of the peninsula was the maximum size the front could ever reach.

It was far too ideal for building an efficient defensive line. Despite this, it was also very easy to gain depth in the long peninsula. It was a geography that was easy to defend and difficult to attack.

Loria let out a sigh as he continued to lament.

"This is a truly wicked con he's pulling. The Commonwealth, Unified States, and Ildoa will fight with the Empire here. As if they are the lone protagonists of this heroic tale."

It was easy for him to imagine the repeated advances and retreats the other nations would make while acting as if they were brothers in arms with the Federation, but the reality of all this?

Loria didn't attempt to hide his astonishment as he continued.

"What they're doing is entertaining the Empire's game of cat and mouse. All while we're engaged in a much more intimate dance here, which has brought us to the brink of exhaustion."

Loria's only wish was to dance as intimately with his fairy. For him, he needed to enjoy the fruits of his adoration for his precious fairy before her purity expired. They needed to dance together, sing together, lament together, pant together, and feel each other's love. Despite this, there was nothing happening in the Federation where he was stuck. As a hunter and teacher of love, Loria was sure that if there existed a true evil in this world, it was Zettour. It fell upon Loria to stir up rage among his fellow comrades for the man who knew no shame.

"And thus, my comrades, on top of having the resources that were meant for us sent to the new war front, we're in danger of the Alliance members in the west taking credit for winning this great war."

With resentment in his eyes, Loria gave the members sitting in on the meeting a stern look before shouting out his denunciation of the injustices befalling them.

"It is akin to them stealing a lover right from a bed that we have so diligently prepared."

Just imagining this was enough to make Loria's own heart pound in his chest.

Oh, my fairy. My precious, precious fairy. You deserve nothing more than to kneel before me and chirp your graceful song! Here, where you belong! It is my duty to pluck this flower before it fully blossoms and its petals fall to the ground!

"We cannot allow this injustice to occur! It must be prevented at all costs! You hear me? At all costs! We must stop this!"

"Comrade Loria, I really must point out that your final statements somewhat…lack composure."

"Please forgive me. I can get excited when it comes to my anxiety for the future of the Federation, and when it comes to propagating the ideals of socialism and how the world should be."

"Of course. Now, tell me on behalf of Internal Affairs. How do you see this coming to an end?"

Ask and you shall receive.

This was a simple decision for Loria.

"We fear the Imperial Army will soon abandon the Ildoan capital it currently occupies."

"This is…assuming the Unified States successfully takes it back, yes?"

"That's correct, General Secretary. While we do the real fighting here and slowly advance along our front, the US forces, only having recently entered the war, will claim what the ignorant masses will interpret as a dramatic victory. That poses a considerable problem in terms of propaganda."

Love was omnipotent.

That's precisely why it always won.

That's why Loria, who lived only for love, could see through the hackneyed act that Zettour was putting on with Ildoa as his stage.

"That rotten bastard, Zettour, is a first-class con artist."

"This is well known by us all."

"General Secretary…" Loria shared some advice from the heart. "If we do not cut off the hands with which he sleights, cut out the tongue with which he slithers, and remove the eyes with which he winks his signals… then the world may very well fall for his trick."

"Comrade. While what you say makes sense, it is far too conceptual."

A concept. Yes, it was understandable that men who lacked love in their life wouldn't fully comprehend Loria. It likely wouldn't make sense to a man not intoxicated on the cocktail of love and passion. Loria, who was awakened to true love, felt sympathy for his superiors who lived only for their work.

Out of humility, he straightened his posture before staring the secretariat right in the eyes and, after a brief pause, spoke up.

"Yes, I apologize. The true threat is that the Ildoan war front has garnered too much of the world's attention. Currently, there is a growing chance that the plight of the Ildoan civilians will spread to third-party countries where the Imperial Embassy maintains relations, resulting in the relief activities shifting even more toward Ildoa."

When it came to using media in propaganda warfare, the Empire was hardly a threat up until this point, but this was because the nation only ever tried to use media in the realm of justifying its own military actions. The anti-Empire sentiment in the media was as solid as stone, so it would be impossible to keep the media from running a story about the Empire treating its occupants inhumanely by driving them to starvation. The dirty devil Zettour was trying to take advantage of the propaganda machine that the Federation poured so much blood and sweat into.

"This will lead to a drastic decrease in supplies being sent to our forces who are locked in true battle with the Empire. The US forces are doing nothing more than allowing the Empire to buy time, while playing it off as if they are the true heroes of this war."

The Federation couldn't allow such injustice to occur, and it fell on Loria to bring his comrades together to firmly reject the adultery afoot.

"We must claim the initiative in the east for our own and use it. The world must know it is the Federation that defeated the Empire. That the party led the Alliance to victory and was the greatest contributing factor to it."

Which brought Loria to his proposal.

"I suggest we attack during the winter."

 DECEMBER 25, UNIFIED YEAR 1927, THE OUTSKIRTS OF THE ILDOAN CAPITAL

Spread thin throughout the Ildoan capital, the Imperial Army's 203rd Aerial Mage Battalion and its leader, Lieutenant Colonel Tanya von Degurechaff, currently serve as the rear guard for the Imperial Army. It is with shivering hands that each of the mages holds a single cup of eggnog that was included in their Christmas rations this year.

The bulk of the army has already left the capital. The same goes for the majority of the Salamander Kampfgruppe, too, as Colonel Uger made special arrangements to transport Captain Meybert and all of his heavy equipment, which should already be en route for the Empire's capital.

Tanya and her mages are left behind to act as watchdogs to head home last.

Strictly speaking, there are still a few Imperial units remaining in the capital as quote unquote *occupants*. As far as I can tell, the arrangements have also been made for these select units to make their full retreat before long. They'll all head north the moment the orders are given, and Tanya's orders are to protect them while they are on the move. Worst-case scenario, the Salamander Kampfgruppe still stuck here will have to fight their way north.

Thus, it is only natural for the less experienced mages like Lieutenant Wüstemann to be a bit anxious about our current deployment. Even my left- and right-hand officers, Lieutenant Serebryakov and Major Weiss, have tenser-than-usual expressions.

My mind, on the other hand, is plagued more with a question than it is anxiety.

It's good that we've made preparations for a swift retreat should the enemy attack, but I can't help wondering if there is a need to wait for the enemy to make the first move.

"Hey, Major Weiss."

"What is it, Colonel?"

"I was just thinking that, seeing as the lion's share of our forces have already left, don't you think it is about time we roll out the red carpet for our enemies?"

My first officer responds with a confused look.

"I believe it's our duty to prevent an attack."

"But what of the intention of our duty? Is it not to give our allies time while they retreat?"

"Well, yes, that is correct."

Her first officer nods, but not without a doubtful look, which I address frankly.

"Why not invite them here?"

"Is it okay for us to do that...?"

"The plan is to abandon this position either way, and I'm certainly not a fan of surrendering initiative to our enemies. Feigning a Christmas party or some kind of commotion while we retreat would make for a much better scenario in my mind."

A small clap rings out as I come up with a new idea on the spot.

"Was it the Alliance forces that showed up around the capital outskirts?"

"Yes. It appears to be a combined task force made up of US, Ildoan, and Commonwealth forces."

"If we ran a little recon in force and made it evident that this area is empty... Do you think they'd follow us back?"

Major Weiss crosses his arms and thinks with his eyes closed for a brief moment before eventually nodding.

"I think we could lure them out. It won't be hard to convince the Ildoan soldiers."

"Ideally, we would draw out a US unit."

Major Weiss cocks his head at the remark.

"May I ask why?"

"For political reasons. We want it to look like the Unified States is swooping in to save the day."

Major Weiss says, "I see," and though his tone makes it clear he doesn't quite follow Tanya's logic, he rubs his chin as he gives it some more thought.

"I believe their base is nearby, too... We know where the US Marines have set up. They have mages stationed there, so I'm sure they would try to intercept us."

While this is the answer Tanya is looking for, she can't help but sigh.

"They are the same mages who broke the international rules of war and ignored my complaint."

For people like Tanya, the navy types are always the most difficult to understand. The marines volunteer for the job out of patriotism but at the same time use shotguns against humans. According to the Imperial interpretation of the laws, it is stated pretty implicitly that the use of shotgun-style weaponry is inhumane because it causes unnecessary suffering by maiming its targets.

Chapter VI

"I hate that it has to be them who are the heroes."

"I don't quite follow…"

My first officer gives me a confused look, which prods me to take a firm tone as I inform him about my current concerns.

"Listen, what we need is a hot-blooded idiot that we can lure into this place. Hot-blooded as the marines may be…they're a bit too disciplined to play right into our hands."

I let out a sigh and shake my head.

"Maybe we should steal their flags. Yes, a nice little game of capture the flag might be just the ticket."

"Capture the flag…?"

"I bet if we raid their base and steal a big flag, they'll almost certainly chase us back here."

They'll chase us like it's a bullfight.

Although, these are some dangerous bulls, and we'll receive far less honor and prestige than the matadors. Alas, 'tis but another aspect of a bleak work environment.

I swallow my last sigh and steel my nerves while I make the decision.

"Alert the remaining troops in the capital. We are going to draw the enemy in!"

"Roger!"

"Let us make this Christmas a merry one."

⟫⟫⟫ **THE SAME DAY, THE ALLIANCE MAGE TROOPS** ⟪⟪⟪

Justice would prevail. It was how justice worked, and why those who were just could win. Always. This was how the world needed to be. Not because of logic or reason. It was just how things were meant to be, and First Lieutenant Mary Sue knew what she, a just person, must do.

"Our allies are under attack?!"

Mary was the first to stand up upon hearing the terrible news.

As a mage for the multinational volunteer unit and as a mage who fought under the Commonwealth, she felt indebted to the US Marines. It was their mages who came in to fight alongside the multinational volunteers a few days prior while they defended the port. They were reliable allies who had managed to make the Imperial mages send over a formal complaint after the battle was over.

Mary could not sit idly by if they were in trouble.

Moved by impulse, she ran straight for the command center.

"Colonel Drake! Please send me!"

"First Lieutenant Sue…"

Sue's commander looked dumbfounded. Clearly upset by the motion, he glared at Mary before letting out a sigh.

"First Lieutenant, the only report we've received is that there was contact with the enemy. They haven't sent a request for reinforcements."

"Are we to remain here while our friends are attacked?!"

Mary retorted with the most earnest of expressions, to which Colonel Drake lazily responded with his cigarette in his mouth.

"We're the reserve forces, First Lieutenant."

"So the reserves are here to watch our allies perish?!"

"You need to listen to what I'm saying, First Lieutenant. We are the Alliance's strategic reserve forces stationed here in Ildoa."

A big puff of smoke left Drake's mouth as he spoke.

"Do you know what that means? That we can't just up and go when we feel like it. You learned the importance of maintaining reserves back during training, didn't you?"

He spoke as if he were speaking with a child. Despite Mary's best attempt to show her objection with her eyes, it was clear Colonel Drake had no intentions of hearing her plea while he smoked that cigarette of his, something that rubbed Mary entirely the wrong way.

"Colonel, ever since you've been promoted to your new rank, you've grown complacent."

"What are you trying to say, First Lieutenant…?"

"Does your rank really matter to you that much?! So much that you can sit and watch your friends die?!"

Colonel Drake furrowed his brow at Mary's shouted verbal attack and shoved his cigarette into his ashtray before slowly getting out of his chair.

"First Lieutenant, do you understand what you're saying right now?"

"I'm asking if you have no shame!"

"I don't expect you to understand politics, but it's high time you learn that the army isn't a place for you to pretend to be some hero! If you can't get this through that thick skull of yours, then you can go back to your country!"

"I'm in the multinational unit to reclaim a country for me to return to!"

With a loud slam, Colonel Drake hit his desk and shouted back at Mary.

"Then you need to understand this! And if you won't, then leave!"

"I fancy I will then!"

With another loud slam, Mary shut the door behind her while letting out a loud sigh. Filled with so much rage she didn't know what to do with, Mary took flight and left the command headquarters.

She was told to leave after all.

If he wanted her to leave so badly, then she would be happy to do him the favor.

It was time for her to do the right thing with the right people.

Mary calmed herself before heading to the barracks, where she hoped to find like-minded people.

She didn't know what to say, or if anyone would go with her.

Would everyone understand that she was in the right here?

Mary knew that as long as she was sincere, then everything would turn out okay.

There had to be people who agreed with her—people who could be her true companions. Of course they would. She was doing the right thing, after all.

When Mary opened the door to the barracks, she mustered up all the courage she could to speak up.

"Everyone! Please, listen to me!"

Mary started by making her case to her peers.

Her words hit their ears and penetrated their souls.

Each and every one of them was a good person.

They all had the desire to do good.

To do what was right, with courage in their hearts.

Was it a curse? Or was it a blessing?

Not all of her peers would accept her plea, but not all of them would reject it, either.

However they felt, the majority chose to follow what they believed in.

Some chose to follow Mary into battle to save their allies.

Some were more reluctant, ultimately declining.

One thing was for sure, though.

That Mary Sue's calling was akin to a curse, not unlike a spell, and her words were spoken with utmost sincerity and a devotion toward helping the world.

And many would answer her call.

Thus, she took flight.

And just like she had been told to do, she left.

She flew straight for her allies who were under Imperial attack.

With her like-minded companions in tow, she flew toward more companions who were in danger.

"There they are! We have to cover them!"

Without fear, Mary and her peers flew straight into the raging battle between an aggressive Imperial mage squadron and the navy that viciously fended them off.

She was ready for a bloody battle. They all were, but she and her peers, having come here to fight for a just cause, were able to push the Imperial Army back with incredible ease, the likes of which they'd never experienced against the Imperial forces.

The Empire had been putting up a fierce fight up until that point.

The moment Mary and her fellow mages flew in, glimmering as they cried out for justice, the enemy line crumbled and quickly fled in a complete rout.

The enemy was so frail in their retreat.

Shocked by the sudden change, Mary and her fellow mages began firing off formulas to keep them from escaping with their lives, but the enemy mages were able to evade their attacks by the skin of their teeth. Despite the angry roar of the enemy commander demanding they stand their ground, the Imperial mages fled like cowards.

Mary, assisting the navy's counterstroke, charged straight into battle without a trace of fear in her heart. Where usually Colonel Drake would be barking for her to fall in line, she knew it was her duty to act as the spearhead of justice and chase down their vile enemy.

It didn't take long for the Empire to shift into a retreat formation. Perhaps some sort of spoils of war, a Unified States flag unraveled from behind one of the mages as they pathetically fled from Mary. The other mages seemed worried for her safety, as there were calls for her to stand down. She felt thankful for their concern but knew this was her chance to defeat her sworn enemy.

With her steadfast companions in tow, she would save Ildoa and the world from the Imperial menace. Having a clear goal in mind made fighting much easier. When normally there was more to be concerned about, even anguish over, by removing Colonel Drake from the picture, the world was so much simpler.

Mary charged with all her might. Through the clear, blue Ildoan skies, she chased down the wicked Imperial mages and delivered them the punishment they deserved. Every now and then, the Imperial Army would stop to try and fight back, but the sight of Mary was enough to send them fleeing once more.

"Do not run! Treacherous cowards! You shall receive swift justice!"

With rage in her heart, she let off multiple explosion formulas. The world, contorted by the magic and heat, manifested a lethal series of explosions. The sight of the Imperial mages thrown into such a pathetic panic at the blazing fire was exhilarating.

They chased their fleeing enemy. There was nothing else to consider. They had the enemy right where they wanted them. Eventually, it seemed the enemy commander gave up on trying to get her mages to hold their ground. Mary watched as her sworn enemy, the wretched Devil of the Rhine, fell into a panic similar to her subordinates and fled for her life.

The unbridled acceleration with which she flew away told the story of an enemy fleeing in fear. Mary and her mages, on the other hand, were already at their limits. Trying to shoot an enemy out of the sky took a much larger toll on a mage than fleeing for one's life did. Nevertheless... learning that she had successfully driven the enemy away quelled the flame in Mary's heart.

Fighting as the sword of justice felt good. Mary took in the moment, noticing that below her was the city. In fact, there were buildings and houses for as far as the eye could see. She pulled out a map and there was no mistaking it.

"This is…the capital…?"

This was the city that was being occupied by the Empire. She had followed the enemy mages into the city and driven them off. This city, however, was supposed to be under Imperial occupation. And yet, there were no AA guns firing at her and the other mages.

Mary, immediately overcome with suspicion, called out to those who followed her here. The group took a quick flight around the city to see what was going on. That was when she realized what she was looking at.

"There's no one here…"

The buildings that had housed the Imperial soldiers were all empty. Left behind were collapsed piles of documents written in Imperial and abandoned vehicles. There wasn't a single wretched Imperial soldier to be found. What started as a sneaking suspicion quickly turned into conviction after a few more laps around the city.

Then, it finally dawned on Mary what she had accomplished—her expression brightened immediately. She hadn't realized that they had pushed back the entire Imperial Army. Those cunning, wicked soldiers who always used their cowardly tricks to win. Mary had never had the power to fight back before. There were nights where she cried herself to sleep over her powerlessness to stop their evil deeds.

"Did we liberate…the city?"

Justice always prevailed. Pride, dignity, and determination always triumphed over the darkness. Doing the right thing, no matter how impossible it may seem, was possible for her and the mages who fought alongside her.

Mary soon regrouped with her fellow mages and found one of them had seized the flag that had been stolen from the Unified States. There were many soldiers who came from the Unified States in the multinational volunteer garrison.

"Let's hold this flag that we've reclaimed up high!"

Mary decided to march the US flag through the center of the town. The town was a ghost town at this point. Despite it being Christmas

night, there was nobody to be seen outside. It was no mystery why, seeing as how the city had been occupied up until just now.

It was easy to tell just by moving through the city that it had been, too. At every corner, there was a poster or sign that seemed to be of Imperial origin asserting its detestable dominance over the poor city. What was most loathsome…were the Imperial flags that flew high for all to see in the city square.

These were the symbol of evil.

The flags, arrogantly flown over the peaceful city the Empire had dominated, sparked a rage in Mary's heart.

"This is wrong."

Mary felt she must right what was wrong.

That the existence of something wrong mustn't be tolerated.

That which must not be tolerated, that which must be done away with.

The Empire, and all evil, should be eradicated from this world, and Mary needed to do it.

This was the only way for her to correct the evils of the world, and to bring back the peace it once knew.

Mary raised her flag.

The right flag.

The flag that banished injustice.

As the liberator of Ildoa, she held it high in the city center.

It waved gloriously in the breeze.

It let the world know the Empire's end was nigh.

That the Ildoan capital had been reclaimed.

"We will not lose!"

She would bring justice to the world.

"We will destroy the Empire!"

》》》》   THE SAME DAY, THE IMPERIAL CAPITAL   《《《

It didn't take long for news to reach the Imperial Empire.

A telegram was placed on the desk of Zettour, who was enjoying a pleasant smoking break with Counselor Conrad at the time.

Chapter VI

A large puff of smoke escaped his mouth. He held one of Rudersdorf's tucked-away cigars in one hand and a cup of coffee in the other while discussing diplomatic matters. It was Colonel Uger who would have the misfortunate of having to barge in during the conversation.

"Sir, there's urgent news."

Colonel Uger slightly knit his brow as he waded through the thick fumes permeating the room to hand the general a sheet of paper. General Zettour took the sheet and, without looking at it, asked the colonel.

"Have we lost the Ildoan capital?"

The colonel gave a small nod, which caused Zettour to smile.

"Thank you."

"Yes, sir."

The general watched as his subordinate left the room before folding his legs where he sat. He smoked in glee, occasionally looking up at the ceiling and laughing to himself—a scene that may never appear in any history books, but will certainly be described in novels.

"What, was this meant to be your Christmas present for the Alliance? You really are a criminal."

"It wasn't something I planned."

"Maybe not the date, but maybe the event."

"Counselor Conrad, it makes me sad to hear you say that."

General Zettour rubbed his chin and squinted his eyes while he bragged.

"The world wants to dream."

"And that makes you a nightmare, I presume?"

Counselor Conrad murmured this to Zettour, which warranted a wry smile from the general as he nodded in agreement.

"You're probably right. I feel the same way, after all."

"So why did the so-called Alliance fall for this?"

"It is the opposite, you see. I didn't trick them, but it is they who wish to be tricked. Everyone desires simplicity."

General Zettour took the cigar out of his mouth and held his hands out.

"It's as simple as this: Justice will prevail over the evil Empire. Pretty simple, eh? Which is why…they fooled themselves and fell for it, too."

Don't you agree? The general smiled. A gentle smile, so filled with glee.

General Zettour was so happy, in fact, he was practically singing when he spoke next.

"And if the world so desperately desires to be fooled, then I shall fool them."

(The Saga of Tanya the Evil, Volume 12: Mundus Vult Decipi, Ergo Decipiatur, fin)

Appendixes

Broken Scale

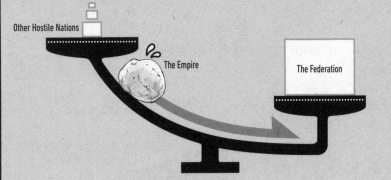

Other Hostile Nations

The Empire

The Federation

In this scenario, the Empire and the Federation are effectively locked in a one-on-one fight, with the Federation being the main actor in the battle against the Empire.

This means that the Federation will get to determine the Empire's fate once it is defeated. Unless the Empire does something about it...

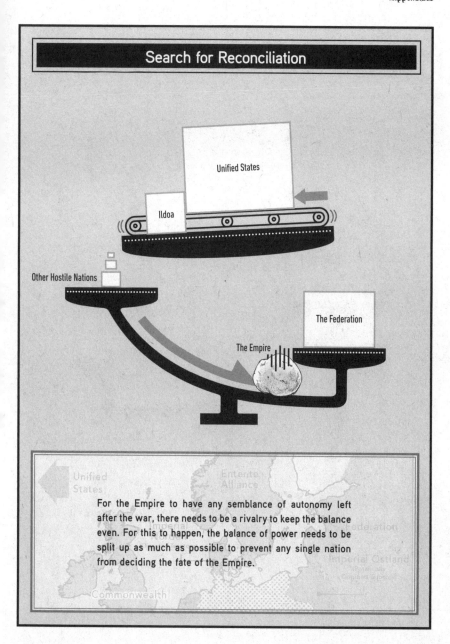

Search for Reconciliation

For the Empire to have any semblance of autonomy left after the war, there needs to be a rivalry to keep the balance even. For this to happen, the balance of power needs to be split up as much as possible to prevent any single nation from deciding the fate of the Empire.

Interference of Ildoa

Unified States

Ildoa

Other Hostile Nations

The Federation

The authorities in Ildoa made the mistake of mistiming when the Unified States should enter the war *for the benefit of the Empire*. Thus, they must take responsibility.

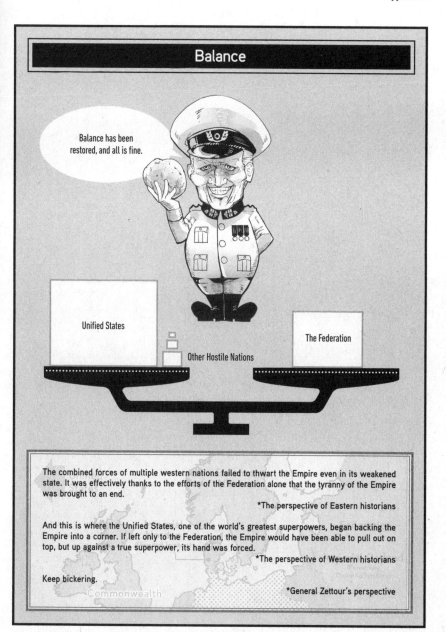

Balance

Balance has been restored, and all is fine.

Unified States

Other Hostile Nations

The Federation

The combined forces of multiple western nations failed to thwart the Empire even in its weakened state. It was effectively thanks to the efforts of the Federation alone that the tyranny of the Empire was brought to an end.

*The perspective of Eastern historians

And this is where the Unified States, one of the world's greatest superpowers, began backing the Empire into a corner. If left only to the Federation, the Empire would have been able to pull out on top, but up against a true superpower, its hand was forced.

*The perspective of Western historians

Keep bickering.

*General Zettour's perspective

Afterword

I understand some of my readers may be buying all twelve volumes in bulk to read them all at once. You. You are the real heroes. And for those of you who have been following me throughout this journey—hello, it's good to see you again. Carlo here, and I was able to pull off the incredible achievement of being published two months in a row. No, that's not a typo, but the truth and nothing but the truth.

I can now claim without any reservation that my work has been published twice in two months. That's an objective fact now. Although I suppose I should mention it took a year of preparation to make it possible. This was, of course, for good reason. A reason that I feel compelled to share with you all in detail as I want you to understand why you were forced to wait so long for this.

I'd like to start by saying that 2019 was a very hot year by all official records. I was planning on finishing this volume before summer, but it was just so, so hot all through the year that, in my pursuit of a summer finish, the heat fooled me into thinking it was summer until the very last minute.

I'm very confident that the majority of my faithful readers will be satisfied with this explanation, but if I were to supplement this with an off-the-record explanation, I should add that I was also a bit busy on top of the unprecedentedly long "summer."

This is something that can be said of all those involved in a creative career, but we are similar to elegant swans. The hurried patter of our tiny feet underwater isn't something we have many chances to show the public. Eventually, all creators, too, must take flight...which isn't necessarily always the case and can make things tough. What I'm trying to say by this is, well, without going against my NDA, let's just say I'm prepared for some of you to somehow misconstrue this as the second season of the *Saga of Tanya the Evil* anime being canceled.

Getting asked when the second season is coming out on Twitter and other social media is something that makes me both happy and very impatient. You see, I, too, am one of the many people waiting eagerly for the second season. I'm writing these books looking forward to the day when I can have my characters meet you all again in animated form. With me being busy with various things, it is still difficult to get a bead on the date, but please bear with me.

Which brings us to this book. What did you think of it? I feel it was a more generic light novel. One about a boy phoning his friends for a nice dinner, talking about champagne. You know, slice-of-life stuff. I hope you enjoyed it as much as I did. I do have one regret, and that is that I had the older gentlemen steal a bit too much of the spotlight for this book, and I say that as someone who fancies dandy older gentlemen. I'll make the next installment of my slice-of-life story about the young girl it is supposed to be about.

I also, with the advice of my editor, decided to bring back some of my Carlo-style footnotes for this volume. If my fans take a liking to them, I may do this more in future volumes, so let me know what you thought of them.

Let me finish by saying thank you to everyone who should be thanked.

To the designers; the workers at the Tokyo Printing Service Center; my editors, Fujita and Tamai; and my illustrator, Shinotsuki. Thank you all again so much for your work to make this volume happen.

And to my readers. I appreciate you all from the bottom of my heart. I am so grateful when you send me words of encouragement and, even more, when you tell me you love my books. It's what gives me power when I need it most. I am truly sorry for keeping you all waiting for this for so long. I am truly thankful for your continued support.

Thank you, and until next time.

February 2020, *Carlo Zen*

HAVE YOU BEEN TURNED ON TO LIGHT NOVELS YET?

86—EIGHTY-SIX, VOL. 1–11

In truth, there is no such thing as a bloodless war. Beyond the fortified walls protecting the eighty-five Republic Sectors lies the "nonexistent" Eighty-Sixth Sector. The young men and women of this forsaken land are branded the Eighty-Six and, stripped of their humanity, pilot "unmanned" weapons into battle...

Manga adaptation available now!

WOLF & PARCHMENT, VOL. 1–6

The young man Col dreams of one day joining the holy clergy and departs on a journey from the bathhouse, Spice and Wolf. Winfiel Kingdom's prince has invited him to help correct the sins of the Church. But as his travels begin, Col discovers in his luggage a young girl with a wolf's ears and tail named Myuri, who stowed away for the ride!

Manga adaptation available now!

SOLO LEVELING, VOL. 1–8

E-rank hunter Jinwoo Sung has no money, no talent, and no prospects to speak of—and apparently, no luck, either! When he enters a hidden double dungeon one fateful day, he's abandoned by his party and left to die at the hands of some of the most horrific monsters he's ever encountered.

Comic adaptation available now!